The Family Business 6:

A Family Business Novel

The Family Business 6:

A Family Business Novel

Carl Weber

with

La Jill Hunt

www.urbanbooks.net

Urban Books, LLC
300 Farmingdale Road, NY-Route 109
Farmingdale, NY 11735

The Family Business 6: A Family Business Novel
Copyright © 2023 Carl Weber
Copyright © 2023 La Jill Hunt

The Family Business 2012 Trademark Urban Books, LLC

ISBN 13: 978-1-64556-148-4
ISBN 10: 1-64556-148-8

First Hardcover Printing February 2023
Printed in the United States of America

10 9 8 7 6 5 4 3 2 1

This is a work of fiction. Any references or similarities to actual events, real people, living or dead, or to real locales are intended to give the novel a sense of reality. Any similarity in other names, characters, places, and incidents is entirely coincidental.

Distributed by Kensington Publishing Corp.
Submit orders to:
Customer Service
400 Hahn Road
Westminster, MD 21157-4627
Phone: 1-800-733-3000
Fax: 1-800-659-2436

Prologue

It was almost six o'clock when the caravan of dark SUVs exited the Long Island Expressway and headed toward the affluent town of Great Neck, New York. The vehicles made their way past North Shore Hospital in Manhasset, across Northern Boulevard, and through the quaint upscale shopping area of Great Neck proper, then made their way down Main Street into the exclusive beach community of Kings Point. A mile or so in, they turned onto the private road marked Beach Lane, stopping at the guarded gate of the Duncan estate.

Inside the guard house, DJ Daniels, a former drug dealer and now a Duncan security officer, shut off the music video he was watching on his iPhone. He stared at the three SUVs as they pulled up to the gate. It was obvious from his expression that the occupants of the vehicles were not expected guests.

"Who the fuck is this?" DJ mumbled to himself, picking up the portable guard house phone. He dialed a memorized number, which was answered on the third ring by the Duncans' security chief, Daryl Graham.

"What's up, DJ?" Daryl was on his way to the dining room, where the Duncan family had gathered around their oversized table for Sunday dinner.

Daryl, a ruggedly handsome man in his early forties, was as close to being family to the Duncans without being blood as you could possibly be. He was the best friend of Vegas Duncan and super close to all the Duncan siblings, especially the oldest daughter, London. LC and Chippy had practically raised him. They considered Daryl a fifth son. They'd even paid for him to go to the exclusive European finishing school that most of their children had graduated from—the same school their grandson Nevada now attended.

"We've got three SUVs with tinted windows at the front gate," DJ replied.

Daryl stopped at the dining room entrance and listened intently. Like DJ, he knew that the Duncans hadn't been expecting anyone.

"Any idea who they are?" he asked.

"Nah, that's why I called. They're just sitting there like they're waiting for me to approach the car. They haven't even rolled down their windows." DJ, who wasn't easily scared, sounded wary. "I'll be honest, D, I don't like it."

"Yeah, neither do I," Daryl agreed, though he didn't want to overreact just yet. When it came to the Duncans, it could have been anybody sitting outside their gate, from the Mayor of New York City to a Colombian hit squad. You just wouldn't know until the shit hit the fan.

"So, what you want me to do?" DJ asked.

"Keep me on the line and let's see who the hell they are," Daryl replied. "And be ready for anything."

"You already know." DJ unsnapped the leather gun holster strapped to his chest, giving himself easy access to his weapon. He then opened the guard house door and cautiously approached the driver's side window of the lead SUV. A few steps from the vehicle, he confidently stood his ground as the window slowly rolled down. He was now face to face with a very attractive forty-year-old Latina woman.

"Can I help you?"

"Yes, you can. My name is Janel Martinez, and I'm a special agent with the FBI." Agent Martinez quickly flashed her badge at DJ. "I'm here to see LC Duncan."

"Mr. Duncan is unavailable at the moment. Can I ask what this is about?"

"No, you can't," Agent Martinez responded coldly with a hint of an accent that only came out when she was annoyed. "Now, why don't you tell whoever that is on the phone to let Mr. Duncan know that the FBI is at his gate, and we'd like to talk. If not, I'll come back with a fugitive warrant and break down the goddamn gate."

Irritated by her attempt to intimidate him, DJ lifted the phone to his ear, glaring at Agent Martinez. "Did you hear that, D?"

Still standing in the entrance to the dining room with his back to the family, Daryl felt his uneasiness rise. Although he could not see Agent Martinez's face, he could tell by her tone that she meant every threatening word she'd said.

"Yeah, I heard it. See if you can stall them for a minute or two while I inform the family, then send them up."

"Gotcha," DJ replied.

Daryl hung up the phone and exhaled. It was times like this that he wished he'd taken Vegas up on his offer to go to France to visit Nevada at the finishing school. But duty called, and there was no time to waste, so he headed into the dining room to inform LC of the situation. He casually walked to the head of the table, then leaned over and whispered into LC's ear in an effort not to disturb the family's dinner.

"What? Are you serious?" LC lifted his head and gazed into Daryl's eyes.

"Yes, sir, I am,"

LC noticed the concern etched in Daryl's expression, and he felt himself become a little unnerved.

"What do they want?"

"I wish I knew," Daryl replied. "All they said was that they were here to speak to you."

"What? What's going on?" Chippy asked when she noticed the looks on their faces. "Who wants to speak to you?"

"Yeah, what's going on, Pop?" Junior chimed in from the other side of the table.

LC sat up in his chair and exhaled loudly. "It appears the FBI are at the front gate and are headed up to the house."

The concerned reactions of everyone at the table was immediate. Despite owning one of the country's premiere high-end automobile dealerships and several other lucrative businesses, the Duncan family was also among the country's largest drug distributors. LC and his associates prided themselves on staying below the radar, avoiding the scrutiny of law enforcement. A visit from the FBI was the last thing they wanted or expected

"The FBI? What do they want?" Paris, the beautiful youngest daughter of the Duncan family, asked. She was one of the Duncan triplets. Her brothers Rio and Roman sat on either side of her.

"Apparently they want to talk to me," LC said as the doorbell rang and he eased out of his chair.

London automatically turned to Harris Grant, her wheelchair-bound husband, who also served as the family's attorney. Their relationship was tedious at best, and most people in the family knew she was only with him out of pity after he was shot in the back and lost the use of his legs.

"Do something. You're our lawyer," she commanded.

"Don't you think I know that, London?" Harris barked at his wife, unlocking his wheelchair and backing up. He rushed behind LC, who was already headed to the door with Chippy on his heels.

"Don't say a word, LC. Let me do the talking."

"This is not my first time talking to the police, Harris," LC replied with attitude.

It was apparent to Harris that LC's annoyance was interfering with his better judgment.

"No, but it's your first time talking to the FBI. Let me handle this. That is what you pay me for." Harris caught up to him and grabbed his arm before he could open the door.

"He's right, LC," Chippy agreed.

LC paused for a moment and considered the advice, then nodded in agreement as he looked back at his family, who were all standing around the dinner table, watching the scene unfold. "Everybody sit down and finish your dinner. Let's not make a show of this."

Most of them followed the instruction given by LC—except Paris, who defiantly strolled behind her parents with her arms folded. LC, who had always had a soft spot for his stubborn youngest daughter, didn't protest.

"Ready?" Chippy looked at LC and Harris. They nodded, then the three of them faced the front door and waited as Daryl opened it. Agent Martinez and an average-looking, balding white man in his late forties stood at the door, both wearing government-issue wind breakers.

"I'm LC Duncan. How can I help you?" LC quickly sized up the two agents. Neither one of them was holding any paperwork, which meant most likely they didn't have a warrant for anyone's arrest and weren't there to search the property. He felt a moment of relief, but then he looked over their shoulders and noticed the dozen armed men in flak jackets standing twenty feet behind them.

"Mr. Duncan, my name is Jonathan Fritz. I'm a special deputy with the United States Marshals Service," the man said, then turned to the woman. "And this is—"

"U.S. Marshals? I thought you was with the FBI." Paris cut him off before he could finish the proper introduction.

"I'm with FBI," Agent Martinez announced. "We'd like to talk. Can we come in?"

"That all depends. What do the U.S. Marshalls and the FBI want with my client?" Harris asked.

Martinez and Fritz shifted their gaze down toward Harris in his wheelchair, a little surprised that the family just happened to have a lawyer at the house when they showed up.

"I beg your pardon. Who are you?" Martinez replied.

"I'm their lawyer," Harris replied with confidence. Harris might have been a piece-of-shit husband, but he was one hell of a lawyer. "Now, state your business. Do you have a warrant?"

"Is that what you want? Because I can get one," Martinez's Latin accent once again slipped out, showing her annoyance. She hated when anyone challenged her or the Bureau's authority, especially slick-ass lawyers. "And tear this place apart."

"You do that, and I'll sue you into poverty," Harris retorted.

Fritz glanced over at Martinez, giving her a stern look. "Calm down, Martinez. We don't need all that. They're not the enemy." He looked pointedly at LC Duncan. "At least we don't think they are."

"Look, why exactly are you here?" LC asked, trying to pull the conversation back from the brink.

"Have you heard of FCI New London?" Agent Fritz asked.

LC remained poker faced, but Chippy, Paris, and Harris couldn't hide the fact that they knew it better than they'd have liked.

"Yes, it's a federal psychiatric prison and hospital in Connecticut. Why do you ask?" LC replied.

"Four prisoners escaped from the facility last night and killed a correctional officer," Deputy Fritz replied. "Mr. Duncan, one of those escapees was your brother, Larry Duncan."

"Larry escaped?" LC repeated.

"Yes, along with three other very disturbed and dangerous individuals," Fritz added. "They are considered armed and dangerous.

"And they had help," Martinez added, staring at LC.

"Is that an accusation?" Harris shot back. "Because it sure sounded like it to me."

LC shared a concerned glance with his wife, then said, "I honestly thought he was getting better."

"Evidently not," Agent Martinez said sarcastically.

Fritz rolled his eyes in Martinez's direction again before speaking. "Have you seen your brother, Mr. Duncan?"

"Not since we visited him last month."

Chippy took LC's hand. "We try to visit him at least once a month. The doctors said he was doing good. He was in a good place."

"Yeah, well, tell that to the family of the officer he killed," Martinez snapped.

"Mr. Duncan, we'd like to search your property. Confirm that you're not harboring a fugitive," Fritz said.

"Not without a warrant you won't," Harris snapped.

"Like I said, we can get one." Martinez stared him down.

"That won't be necessary. We don't have anything to hide. Just be respectful," LC said, speaking directly to Fritz. It was obvious he was the more rational of the two.

"We will. You have my word," Fritz replied.

LC stepped aside for them to enter, along with the dozen storm troopers behind them.

Larry

1

Fourteen hours earlier

I took hold of a tree to steady myself as I caught my breath. From the way I was huffing and puffing, you would have thought I'd run a marathon, but in fact, I couldn't have gone more than a mile because I could still see the halogen search lights of the facility in the not-so-far distance. The barking of the blood hounds echoed through the forest where I was hiding. They hadn't picked up our scent yet, but it was only a matter of time.

"Shit."

"What's wrong?" I glanced over at Holly, who was a few feet away, bent over with both hands on her knees. She was out of breath, but not even close to coughing up a lung like I was. Then again, she was almost half my age.

"Dogs. They've got the dogs after us," I replied.

"Then come on, Larry. We've gotta keep moving." She placed her hand on the small of my back and pushed me. "Let's go."

"Okay." I was still struggling to catch my breath. She surprisingly took the lead, heading east toward the moon like I'd taught her. "I'm coming,"

Holly was a beautiful, cocoa brown girl with long, naturally curly hair that hung around her shoulders. Her piercing hazel eyes and a body with curves in all the right places could have men reconsidering their marriage vows.

She was one of those people you either loved or you hated. There was no in between with her. I think that's why I liked her. For a young person, she wasn't about the bullshit. She was either a pussy cat or a sleeping lion, and Lord help you if you poked that fucking lion even a little bit.

"Come on, boss. We're almost there." She turned to encourage me. In truth, she was helping to motivate me, but it didn't stop the overwhelming need to stop and catch my breath. I was heaving so much it felt like my lungs were going to burst out of my chest.

"Come on, Larry. We can do this."

"Okay, okay, just give me a second to catch my breath." I was embarrassed, but I couldn't go another step without leaning against a tree again. I swore to myself that if I ever got through this, I would get myself back in shape by hook or crook.

"Okay, rest time is over. We gotta keep going," Holly pleaded. "We don't have that much further to go. I can hear the highway."

I thought maybe she was bullshitting me because I couldn't hear the damn highway. What I could hear was the distinct howling of those fucking dogs they'd sent after us.

"Shit, do you hear that? They've caught the scent."

Our eyes locked, and Holly nodded her understanding. The moonlight highlighted the fear in her hazel eyes.

"Come on! We gotta go! Get your ass off that tree!" she demanded.

I stood up straight and pulled in a deep breath. Call it will power, adrenaline, or just plain fear, but the sound of those dogs coming our way motivated the hell outta me, and I started to run like my life depended on it—which it did. A few minutes later, Holly was proven right when we burst out of the woods into a clearing and in front of us was the damn highway. Eighteen wheelers and cars zoomed past us at eighty miles an hour.

We'd made it! Or at least we'd made it to the highway and now the rest was up to—

"I thought you said your son was going to be here," Holly said, sounding concerned. "Those fucking dogs are getting closer."

"He's supposed to be here!" I snapped, searching from left to right as if he might magically appear. I was trying not to let Holly see me panic, but the sound of those hounds was unnerving, now that we were out in the open, we would be easy targets.

"Come on, Kenny. Don't let me down, son. Where the fuck are you?"

I could see the disappointment in Holly's eyes, and then out of nowhere, there was hope. "Boss, over there." She pointed, and I saw the flashing lights of a car parked about a hundred yards from us on the side of the highway.

"That's him!" I shouted.

Holly didn't waste time. She sprinted to the car like a track superstar, and I wasn't far behind her. We reached the car, and I jumped into the front seat. Holly dove into the back and slammed the door. I'll never forget the smile on my son's face when I slid into that seat, panting and sweating.

"Hey, Pop." He grinned nervously.

"Hey, son," I huffed. "It's good to see you."

"Good to see you too. I was starting to think you wasn't gonna make it."

"You and me both. Let's get outta here."

"Wait. What about Dennis?" Holly insisted. "We can't leave without Dennis."

Damn, in all the commotion with the dogs and trying to get the hell out of there, I'd completely forgotten about Dennis. He was an old friend from my days in the army. We were the only two members of our platoon to survive the Vietnam War, and we'd both come home with PTSD. Dennis snapped as soon as he came home. He killed twelve people, including his wife and kids. He had been at the facility for ten years before I showed up.

Dennis was a smart guy. He'd come up with our escape plan, which was flawless. It would have gone off without a hitch, except that Thaddeus, who was supposed to be leaving with us, went off on his own tangent and attacked a female guard. Dennis had stayed behind to try to save the woman's life. Escaping prison was one thing, but attacking a federal corrections officer was as good as signing your own death warrant. There was nothing we could do for her, so I'd kept running.

I turned to the woods.

"Shit. She's right. We gotta wait for Dennis," I told Kenny.

"Fuck, whoever the hell Dennis is, we need to get the hell outta here." Kenny turned to me, looking determined. He'd grown up a lot in the last five years. "I didn't come here for Dennis, Dad. I came here for you."

"I know that," I said, appreciating his dedication to me. Still, the idea of leaving Dennis behind didn't sit right with me.

I glanced back at Holly, whose eyes screamed what I was thinking. We'd never have escaped that place if it wasn't for Dennis.

"Son, I need you to give him another minute or two," I said.

"Why?"

"Loyalty. That's why. If it wasn't for him, I wouldn't be sitting in this car with you. Dennis has stuck by me from day one, so we're gonna give him a minute."

Kenny didn't speak, but he did roll his eyes, which I let slide. He'd risked a lot helping me, possibly even prison, so he got a pass this time.

I turned back to Holly. "If he doesn't get here soon, we are gonna have to leave him."

"What the fuck is that?" Kenny pointed at the large figure exiting the woods about a hundred feet in front of us.

"It's Dennis!" Holly shrieked, rolling down the window and calling his name. "Dennis! Dennis! Over here!"

Dennis's six foot four, 350-pound body was moving like a freight train through the tall brush towards us with three angry barking German shepherds on his heels.

"He ain't gonna make it. Those dogs are about to tear his ass up," Kenny mumbled.

"I can see that," I snapped. "Where's your fucking gun?"

"Glove compartment."

I flipped open the glove compartment, revealing two 9 mm Glocks. I took both guns, cocked them, and stepped out of the car. Dennis was about twenty feet from us. I watched as one of the dogs finally reached him and locked its jaws to the back of Dennis's legs.

"Aaaaggghhh!" Dennis hollered in pain and fell face first as the dog ripped through his pants leg.

I lifted my left hand and right hand, firing at the beast until he dropped, but not before a second dog was on Dennis. As Dennis wrestled with the second dog, I had another problem. The third dog was now heading for me. I watched him leap into the air with a running start, fangs bared. I almost felt sorry for him when I pulled the trigger of each gun and he fell to the ground at my feet.

"Larry!" Holly shouted. "They're coming!"

There were voices coming from the woods. I turned toward Dennis, surprise to see that he was on his feet, limping toward the car. The second dog lay dead behind him. That son of a bitch must have broken its neck. Dennis was strong as hell.

"Let's go!" I jumped into the front seat, Holly threw open the back door so Dennis could climb in, and we took off.

"Where to?" Kenny asked.

"Head west. They'll be looking for us down south." I turned to the back seat. "How's your leg, Dennis?"

"It's fine, Sergeant. Nothing in comparison to when I got shot up in Nam."

"Good. And what about the guard?"

He shook his head. "She didn't make it."

That was not what I wanted to hear. "Come on. Let's get the hell outta here. They're going to be after us for real now."

Harris

2

I turned over around midnight, blinking my eyes open when my fumbling hand realized that my wife wasn't in bed. I glanced over at the bathroom door, which was closed, but there was no light streaming from under the door. Something wasn't right, and I had a bad feeling about it.

Truth be told, things hadn't been right between London and me for quite a while, but never more than lately. London was a woman with high sexual appetite, and she wasn't above cheating to fulfill her needs if I was unable or unwilling. Not that I was a saint before the accident, but I handled my husbandly duties sufficiently. However, now that I was paralyzed from the waist down and impotent, London made me feel like she was only tolerating me out of pity because I was in a wheelchair.

"London?" I called her name, but she didn't answer, which quickly ramped up my anxiety and hyped up my paranoia. I tried to convince myself to stay calm, remembering what happened the last time I accused her of wrongdoing. She had stayed out of my bed for three months.

London had a bad habit of slipping out of bed and going to our old room upstairs in the main wing of the house to sleep because as she put it, "I couldn't take your snoring." I can't lie; I do snore, but my daughter Mariah sleeps in the bed with me all the time and doesn't complain, so I was skeptical.

"London!"

I'd known London over fifteen years, most of which we'd been married. Our relationship had more ups and downs than a carnival ride, but in spite of it all, I swear I loved my wife to death. She and my daughters meant the world to me.

I knew it couldn't be easy having a wheelchair-bound husband, and I appreciated her effort, but I wasn't stupid. As of late, my wife had been too polite, too kind, and way too accommodating—nothing like her usual stubborn-ass demeanor. Shit, she even sang in the shower, which oddly enough, raised my suspicions even more. London only sang in the shower after an especially good night in bed, but lately she was singing like it was the '70s and she'd just signed with Motown.

It took me almost five minutes to get into my wheelchair and out of my bedroom. I wanted to investigate and see what was really going on for myself. As I continued through the foyer, I looked out the window and saw London's BMW X7. It was parked at the edge of the property over by the entrance to the pool, instead of in her usual parking spot in front of the house. Something wasn't adding up.

I headed to the center of the foyer, looking up at the winding staircase, which, for a man in a wheelchair, was intimidating as shit. Intimidating or not, I knew that if I wanted to rid myself of the terrifying thoughts that my wife was stepping out on me, I was going to have to tackle them head on.

And with that, I eased my way out of my chair and crawled up the stairs one by one. It was hard as hell, but I didn't stop until I finally made it to the top of the staircase. I took a minute to catch my breath as I looked proudly down at my wheelchair. Shit, this was one hell of an accomplishment.

LC and Chippy weren't around because they had taken half the family down south to see what family down there might know about crazy-ass Larry's escape. The only people at the house were Junior and Sonya, who were always in bed by midnight, and Rio, who wouldn't be home until the sun came up. I couldn't decide if it was too bad no one had been around to witness it, or it was a good thing no one was around to see a grown man having to crawl up the stairs. I felt strong and pathetic at the same time.

From the top of the stairs, I made my way down the hall using my arms to slide along the hardwood floors on my belly like a seal. I reached the room London and I had shared before I was shot and we had to relocate to a room on the first floor. I hesitated, leaning against the wall before opening the door, because I knew London was gonna lose her shit if I woke her up on some bullshit.

I finally reached up and turned the knob, opening the door slowly. I scanned the room, and a queasiness took over my stomach as my fears were realized. My world was rapidly crumbling in front of me. The bed was made, and the room was empty. London was not there.

"Fuck."

It took me twice as long to get down the stairs and into my wheelchair as it had to go up. By the time I finally got settled in my seat, I was ready for blood.

Fuck! Fuck! Fuck!

Where the hell was she? The kids' rooms maybe? No, that didn't make any sense because the kids had gone with LC and Chippy to spend time with their cousins. Besides, I wasn't tackling those stairs again.

I stared out the window at London's car. The fact that it wasn't parked in the right place was still raising alarm bells for me. I headed outside, rolling through the compound until I reached her car. I imagined I might find her sitting in there, talking on the phone to some dude or something, but the car was empty. I still didn't understand why it was parked there. What were the chances she was going for a swim at this time of night? And that's when it hit me.

"Those dirty motherfuckers."

How the hell could I have been so naïve? The answer was literally staring me in the face the whole time. I knew exactly where my wife was and who she was with, but getting there took a lot more time and effort than I anticipated. Maneuvering the wheelchair through the grassy terrain was a bit scary, but I propelled my chair forward with venom running through my veins.

At first glance, the pool house, which was used to house security, looked dark and empty. Had my intuition not been screaming in the back of my head, I might have turned around and headed back to the main house. Some things you just don't want to know. But I had to be honest with myself: I had strong suspicions, and there was no way I was leaving without knowing for certain.

Unlike at the main residence, there was no wheelchair ramp, so the rear door was my only option. I went to the back door, punched in the code, and tried to steady my breathing before I turned the knob. The door opened, and I went inside as quietly as a guy in a wheelchair could. I entered the main room that contained a small kitchen and sitting area. On a desk in the corner, there were security monitors, a laptop, and a few of the handheld radios the security team used when they were spread out around the compound, but there were no people in the room.

Then I heard a sound that kicked my heartbeat into overdrive. It was the unquestionable sound of two people getting busy, and I suddenly felt like I might really throw up. There was no mistaking the fact that the high-pitched, whiny moans were coming from my wife.

"Son of a bitch," I groaned—perhaps a bit too loud, because the noise stopped.

"Did you hear something?" I heard London ask.

"No. You're just paranoid." Her bed partner laughed, and it was a voice I knew all too well.

"I'm telling you I heard something," London said. "I'll be back."

"Where are you going? London, wait!"

As crazy as it sounds, I suddenly had the urge to hide, but before I could even reach down to the wheels of my chair, my wife walked into the room. She was wearing a very revealing negligee, and her hair was all over the place. I took my hands off the wheels, wishing I could use them to wring her neck in that moment.

"Oh, shit! Harris, what the fuck?" The look of astonishment on London's face was priceless.

"That's exactly what I want to know. What the fuck?" I yelled back.

It wasn't often that my wife, with her sharp tongue, was speechless, but now she stood there staring at me, unable to speak or to move.

"You out here fucking somebody in our home?"

"That's not what I'm doing at all, Harris!" Those were her words, but her face screamed otherwise. She knew she was busted.

I stared at her tousled hair and silk teddy she wore and shook my head. "You gonna stand there in your damn drawers and lie to my face? At least have more respect for me than that. It's bad enough you got your side nigga in our house—"

"It's not the house, and he's not my side nigga. We was just talking!"

"Yeah, and as you were talking, he just accidently slipped his dick in you, right?" I looked over her shoulder toward the closed bedroom door. "Tell him to come out!"

"Harris, now isn't the time to talk about this. Just go back to the house and I'll be there soon. All right?" London exhaled.

"I ain't going nowhere. Now, who the fuck is back there? Or do you want me to guess?"

I went to roll past her, but she grabbed my arm. "Harris, stop! Stop it!"

"Get your damn hands off me!" I snatched back, shifting my wheelchair and nearly falling in the process. Instinctively, I reached out to steady myself, and I ended up grabbing her nightgown. It ripped, exposing one of her breasts.

"Get your fucking hands off her!"

London and I froze. Standing in his boxers in the entrance to the bedroom was my worst nightmare: Daryl Graham.

Curtis

3

I knew I should've said no when Pete from Ware County Bail Bonds offered me the job of picking up Danny Jackson for bail jumping. The pay wasn't that much, and based on our previous interactions, I knew that Danny was a runner. I hated runners. But business had been fairly slow, and I'd promised my momma I'd stay in the Waycross area until my brother Kenny returned home, so I had taken the job.

"Hey, I'll be right back," I said, turning toward my pain-in-the-ass, know-it-all little sister Lauryn. She was sitting in the passenger seat of my Jeep, chewing gum and blowing bubbles.

Despite everything I just said, Lauryn was the real deal: tall, slender, and real pretty, with greens eyes just like mine. She was so pretty that my brother Kenny use to have to fight dudes on the regular. But don't get it twisted. Lauryn could handle herself, especially after she came home from that fancy finishing school my momma paid a fortune for.

The problem was that now that she was home, she'd been pestering the shit outta me about teaching her the bounty hunting business. I knew she was capable, but my business was rough, and I didn't want any part of her having regrets. Somehow, she'd convinced my momma that it was a good idea, and well, I could never say no to my momma, especially since I had a good idea what Momma's real motives were. It wasn't that she wanted Lauryn to be a bounty hunter. She just didn't want my sister going up to New York to work for my uncle LC. My mother had always been afraid of what the fast lifestyle of my New York relatives would do to us, especially Lauryn, who seemed to be five steps ahead of us at all times. She was sort of a fish out of water in Waycross.

"You really think he's in there?" Lauryn asked, looking over at the small house across the street. It looked dark, except for the glow of what was possibly a TV in the front room.

"Yeah, he's in there."

She gave me a skeptical look. "You sure about that? How do you know?"

"Because I do!" I snapped. I was getting sick of her second guessing me with her fifty million questions. On top of that, she was making me question my own rationale for being there.

I glared angrily at her. "See, this is why—"

"This is why what?" Lauryn retorted. "I'm just asking a question, Curtis. You're supposed to be teaching me."

"I am teaching you." *Why the hell did I even agree to this?*

"No, you're not," she shot back. "You haven't even told me who we're after, or why you think he's in there. Whoever it is could have skipped town for all I know."

I held my breath then released it slowly. She was right. I was supposed to be teaching her, and I hadn't told her a thing. Somehow, I was going to have to get over the fact that my little sister was growing up.

"Okay. Danny Jackson is a small-town hood that's never left Waycross. Folks call him Stick on account of he's so skinny. Now, Stick's stupid, which is half the reason he got caught trying to rob the Walmart. He's also a creature of habit, and there's only five places he could be, and out of town isn't one of them. Okay?" I held my hands out, palms up, as if that was all I was going to offer.

"No." Lauryn looked frustrated.

"No?" I repeated, taken aback.

"No, that's not teaching me. That's placating me. I wanna know why you made this decision, Curtis. How did you come to this conclusion? I need you to teach me, like Daddy taught you!"

Wow, that was a gut punch to the groin.

"A'ight, a'ight, calm down. You can't learn shit if you're talking all the damn time."

She sat back in her seat, smug in the fact that she'd made her point.

"Like I was saying, I've brought Stick in twice before, and based on our previous interactions, the only places he can be is with one of his two baby mommas, at his house, his momma house, or Big Shirley's. Stick loves to look at big titties and—"

Lauryn interrupted. "That still doesn't tell me why we're here."

I glared at her angrily as she popped a huge bubble in her face. "You gonna talk, or do you wanna listen and learn something?"

"Okay, sorry. Damn." She pouted as she pulled the gum off her chin and popped it back in her mouth.

"I already called down to Big Shirley's before we left the house and asked Crystal the bartender if she'd seen him. She said he wasn't there. Said she'd call me if he showed up. So now I'm down to three possibilities, one of which we eliminated about thirty minutes ago."

"We did?" Her look of confusion was satisfying to me.

"Yeah, we did. When we stopped at the Circle K for gas and that Pepsi you needed so bad."

Lauryn gave me a perplexed look.

"Remember the girl working the counter?"

"Yeah, the one with big-ass breasts?"

I started to smile when I saw the look of recognition coming across my sister's face.

"She was one of his baby mommas, wasn't she?"

"Yep, her name is Shea, and she's his daughter's mother," I told her.

"So, you think he's at her house?"

"Doubtful," I said, shaking my head. "Shea's car was parked outside. If Stick and her were kicking it, Stick woulda had her car. And I know he's not at his place. Stick stupid, but he ain't that dumb, and Pete said the police been to his house three times."

"So, there's only two possibilities. His other baby momma or his momma."

"Right. And it can't be LaShonda, his other baby momma."

Lauryn raised an eyebrow. "Why not?"

"You know Tyrone Jenkins?"

"Yes, the big, light-skinned guy who went to jail for killing Barry Allen with his bare hands. I went to school with his sister Tanisha."

"Yeah, well, rumor has it that LaShonda, Slick's baby momma, is having Tyrone's baby. Trust me, Stick don't want no part of that crazy motherfucker. So, that leaves us only with his momma." I glanced across the street at the small brick house.

"And that's his momma's house. Now it makes sense." Lauryn popped another bubble as she reached for the door handle. "Come on. Let's go."

"Where you think you're going?" I said, reaching in the back seat for my shotgun.

"I'm going with you," she stated matter-of-factly.

I shook my head adamantly. "No, you're not. You're staying right here."

"The hell I am," Lauryn whined. "I didn't come with you to stay in the damn car. I wanna help."

"You can help by staying your ass right here. I don't need no distractions, Lauryn. Now, you wanted me to teach you like Daddy taught me? Well, in the beginning, he made me stay in the damn car. Chill out. This is not a game." I gave her a look that let her know how serious I was. All of us Duncan men knew how to use that look when we needed to.

"I know it's not a game, Curtis. Shit, I'm probably better at your job than you are. You keep forgetting where I went to school."

She was probably right. I mean after all, that finishing school is just another name for mercenary school. But that didn't mean I was just going to throw her to the wolves on the first night. Danny was known to carry a knife, and he was good with it.

"I know what school you went to, but this ain't no damn finishing school. People shoot real guns with real bullets. This is real life shit with real criminals," I said. "You are my baby sister, and if anything happened to you, I wouldn't be able to live with myself. So stay your ass right here until I get back. We gonna take this one day at a time."

I opened my door and hopped out before Lauryn could say another word. As I walked across the street toward Stick's momma's house, I caught a glimpse of the attitude on my sister's face. I knew she was capable, and I was going to have to loosen the reins soon, but was I wrong for not wanting anything to happen to her? Lauryn was eight years younger than me, and she hadn't seen much of what the real world had to offer.

It didn't take long to sneak around the house and make my way onto the back porch, which, thankfully, was dark and empty. Dogs were one of the biggest pains in the ass when it came to sneaking up on a fugitive. I took one last look around and carefully eased the raggedy screen door open, then I wrapped my fingers around the brass doorknob and turned. It always amazed me how many people in Waycross didn't lock their doors.

I tiptoed inside what turned out to be the kitchen, dimly lit by the clock on the stove.

"That's what the fuck I'm talking about!"

A man shouted from another room. I froze, startled by the yelling, and eased my shotgun to point straight ahead, waist high.

"Get his ass!"

I recognized Stick's voice, giving me confirmation that the motherfucker was definitely in the house. My only question now was who the fuck he was talking to, and were they going to be a problem?

"Shoot his ass! Shoot him!" Stick commanded.

What the hell had I gotten myself into? Eight hundred dollars was not worth dying over. The only thing that gave me solace was that I had left Lauryn in the car. I ducked down to the floor, holding my breath as I braced myself for the impact of bullets.

"Die, you bastards!" I could still hear Stick screaming, but there were no shots.

What the fuck was going on? I carefully lifted myself up from the floor and continued in the direction of Stick's voice. When I got to the entrance to the living room, I saw Stick's skinny ass on the sofa, playing a video game in front of a big screen television that he probably stole. The noise-canceling headphones he wore were probably stolen too.

I approached him from behind, and he was so engrossed in his game that he didn't even notice. I slipped my hand in my pocket and pulled out a pair of zip tie handcuffs as I crept closer. Just as I was about to grab him, something hit me in the back of my head so hard that I fell to my knees. I was actually seeing stars.

"Motherfucker! What the fuck you doin' in my house?" a woman shouted.

I turned to the voice, but it took a moment to get my bearings and understand exactly what was happening. When the haze from the blow to my head cleared, I could see an older woman dressed in a floral housecoat, clutching a cast iron skillet. She was standing over me, and when I didn't answer her right away, she began swinging that skillet like she was Willie Mays.

"I'm right behind you, man! Shoot him to the left! Shoot him!" Stick screamed at the television. Those must have been some hellafied headphones because I don't think he realized we were there.

"Danny! Get off that damn game and help me!" the woman yelped as she swung that frying pan. It landed on my arm, which I'd lifted to protect my head. "Can't you see we being robbed?"

"Momma, what the hell's going on?"

Stick must have finally noticed something and snatched the headphones off his head. I couldn't be sure because I was too busy fending off his crazy-ass momma and her black skillet as she tried to bash in my head.

"We getting robbed!" she screamed, swinging that frying pan like a mad woman. Thank God she was getting tired because a few more of those heavy-handed blows and she might have broken my arm, or quite possibly, my skull.

"I ain't no fucking robber!" I shouted, fighting off another blow. "I'm a bounty hunter. I'm here to take your son in. He jumped bail."

She paused mid-swing, huffing and puffing as she glared down at me. It gave me enough time to get on my feet.

"You a lie! I paid that damn bail bondsman myself." She swung the pan toward me again but missed, most likely because she was so spent from the exertion.

Unfortunately, while I was fending off his ma, Stick picked up my shotgun.

"You paid it, but his ass ain't go to his fucking court date. The judge issued another warrant, and it's my job to take him in."

"Boy, I know you didn't miss court with all that money I had to scrap up to get your narrow ass outta jail?"

My attention was now only half on her because Stick had the shotgun pointed at me.

"Don't do nothing stupid, Stick," I warned. "Tell your momma the truth. You ain't go to court."

"Shut up!" he yelled. "I ain't supposed to be in court until the fifteenth."

As if he had smacked the shit outta her, Slick's mother's eyes got huge, and she raised the frying pan, but this time, Stick was her intended target. "Boy, what kind of fool are you? Today is the twenty-first."

"It is?" Slick said with a stupid-ass look on his face.

"Boy, I oughta knock your ass out." She stepped toward Danny, who looked confused by everything that was happening.

His mother and I looked at him, waiting for him to say something, but he stayed silent. After a beat, he dropped the shotgun, and in true Stick fashion, he took off running toward the door. I bent down and scooped up my shotgun.

"Don't you shoot my son in the back!" his momma wailed. She started swinging that frying pan again, which gave Stick just enough time to run out the door.

It took a minute, but I finally managed to fend his momma off and run after him. When I got to the front of the house and looked around, Stick's ass was nowhere to be found. So much for easy money.

Frustrated, I turned back to the front door, where his momma was still holding that damn frying pan, looking smug.

"Curtis!"

I heard my sister calling my name, and my eyes followed the sound, which was coming from behind the house next door.

"Ain't that some shit," I mumbled to myself.

"Told you I could help." Lauryn beamed as she led Stick out from the shadows.

I looked back to his momma, whose smug look had disappeared. I was annoyed that Lauryn had disobeyed my instructions, but I couldn't help but be proud of how she had handled herself. My little sister had definitely proven she was a Duncan.

London

4

You ever wish you could crawl in a hole, shrivel up, and die? That's how I felt standing between my husband and my boy-friend. Like I wanted to fucking die. For a year and a half, Daryl and I had been creeping around unnoticed, having the time of our lives, and now the cat was outta the bag, and I honestly didn't know what to do. Did I run to Daryl and form a united front against Harris, or did I stand by the father of my children and hope Daryl would understand until we could figure it out? There were just so many unknown variables that I wanted to start running and never stop.

"I told LC you were a piece of shit, you fucking Neanderthal!" Harris screamed and lurched his wheelchair toward Daryl.

"Harris, stop!" I yelled, more concerned about him hurting himself than harming Daryl, who simply jumped out of the way.

"Harris, man, calm down," Daryl said.

"Fuck you! You want me to calm down and you're fucking my wife?" Harris roared as he continued trying to roll over to Daryl.

"Harris—" I tried to stop him, but it wasn't easy trying to keep my torn nighty up and hold him back. I finally jumped between the two of them and turned toward Harris. "Stop it!"

"Wait until LC hears this shit!" Harris seethed, glaring angrily at me. "You cheating-ass bitch! How could you? And with the fucking help." He scowled toward Daryl as if he wanted to kill him.

"Help? Who the fuck you calling the help?" Daryl yelled back.

"You. You the fucking security guard, ain't you? Deputy Dog ass," Harris muttered.

"I'ma let that one slide, Harris," Daryl said with a half-smile. "Because you seem to forget you work for the Duncans just like me. Plus, I get it. You're just mad because she's sleeping with me since we all know damn well she ain't sleeping with your impotent ass." He looked down at the wheelchair that had robbed Harris of his sense of masculinity.

I snapped my head back at Daryl, whose response was so unnecessary I wanted to slap him. I stared at him, praying that he would back down. He was not helping one bit; he was just throwing gasoline on the fire.

Harris looked mortified. Daryl's low blow had left him speechless. He reversed his wheelchair and sped out the door without saying another word. I went to go after him, but Daryl grabbed my hand and pulled me into his arms.

"Let him go, London. He's not gonna wanna hear anything you have to say anyway."

"You shouldn't have said that to him," I replied.

Daryl shrugged unapologetically. "He knows now. We don't have to be a secret anymore."

"You don't understand. We don't need him calling my father." I stared out the door after Harris. "My father's not going to see this the same way we do. You're talking about a man who has been with the same woman for almost fifty years. He believes in commitment and loyalty, and more than that, he likes Harris and feels sorry for him."

"He likes me too."

"Yeah, but I'm not married to you," I said, returning to his room for my robe. Without another word, I kissed him goodbye and walked out the door.

I decided to give Harris time to calm down, taking the long way around the house. I walked past the guard house, where I bummed a cigarette off DJ, who tried not to show how confused he was by my attire. I used the time it took to have my smoke to think of how I might convince Harris not to say anything about what he'd seen. Truthfully, I wasn't sorry for being with Daryl, but I did feel guilty about Harris finding us the way that he did. I decided that the right thing to do was to have a heartfelt conversation, if that was even possible. So, I made my way back to the main house.

"Harris." I calmly sauntered into our room.

Harris was sitting in his wheelchair, drinking from a bottle of Crown Royal. His eyes remained on the television in front of him. He wouldn't even look in my direction.

"Look, I know you're upset . . ."

"Actually, I'm not," he stated, taking another swig from the bottle.

"You are, and I understand why. I'm sorry you—"

"You already gave me that flimsy-ass apology, London. Please don't insult me by telling me again."

"But I really do apologize," I insisted. "I know you've been through a lot the past few years, but I have too. It hasn't been easy for me either."

"Oh, really? Forgive me, London. I wasn't aware that you were shot and in a wheelchair for the past three years," he retorted. "A wheelchair I would have never been in if I hadn't met you and your criminal family, so save me the bullshit."

"Harris, that's not—"

"You know . . ." He finally turned the chair around, wheeling closer as he stared at me. "I knew you were fucking around on me. I could sense it. I just didn't know that it was Daryl until I saw him the other day around you and the kids. He was too damn friendly with my kids. You been telling them that's their new daddy or something? That is so fucking foul, London."

"You're crazy. You're their father. I would never do that."

"You don't even realize it, but you've been subconsciously preparing my kids for my replacement. How many times have you had Mimi around him using the guise that he's head of security? How many times?"

From the way he looked at me, I knew he believed that shit, and now that he said it, maybe I believed it too. *Shit.* I was not used to feeling guilty. I had always been a person who did what I wanted, when I wanted, with no regard for anyone else—especially Harris, who'd been known to put his hands on me over the years we'd been married. No matter how I felt, though, my biggest concern was still convincing him to keep his mouth shut.

"Harris, you're blowing this all outta proportion. Now, I know you're upset, but I'd really like to keep this between us."

"Oh, so you want me to keep this bullshit a secret? What's wrong, London? You don't want your family to know that you're a whore?"

I bit my lip, but if he called me a whore again, I was going to forget I was the one at fault here.

"That's all you're worried about, how you're gonna look in the eyes of your precious family."

"I'm not a whore, and I . . . we didn't plan for this to happen, but we both know shit between you and me hasn't been right since long before you found out about Tony Dash," I said.

"Oh yeah, I almost forgot you fucked my cousin."

Our marriage had been in disarray long before Daryl and I rekindled our childhood romance. I had found evidence of lipstick and another woman's perfume on his clothes plenty of times, and he'd retaliated against my accusations by putting his hands on me. When I had finally had enough, I stepped out on my marriage with a gangster named Tony Dash. That turned out to be a shit show, because not only was he Harris's cousin, but he was also part of the Mob family that was out to get my father. When the dust settled from that fiasco, I found out I was pregnant with Mimi, so we had stayed together in spite of our hella dysfunctional relationship. I'd thought about leaving when Mimi got a little older, but when Harris was shot and paralyzed from the waist down, sympathy and obligation led to my decision to continue our relationship. It seemed like the right thing to do. Now that he'd caught me with Daryl, it was time for us to face some hard truths.

"Look, I'm a woman with needs. I fucked up. I'm sorry."

"What the fuck? Don't you think I have needs too?" Harris looked me up and down. "But I ain't out here fucking randoms."

I stopped myself from telling him that Daryl wasn't a random, but another set of words slipped out that he wasn't too pleased to hear. "Don't act like you haven't fucked more than your share before this happened, Harris."

"Whether I did or didn't, I was always discreet." Harris rolled a little closer, and his voice sounded vulnerable when he spoke again. "Let me ask you a question, London. Is he better than me? I mean not now, but when I was at my peak?"

"What?" I gasped. "I'm not gonna even justify that damn question with an answer."

"Why not?"

"Because that' not what this is about."

"Okay, let me ask you this. Are you gonna stop fucking him?"

I froze, becoming so lost in my own thoughts that I couldn't answer Harris's question even if I wanted to. The time I spent with Daryl was fulfilling in so many ways that I couldn't imagine stopping. Images of us in bed, exploring each others' bodies before Harris had interrupted, flashed in my mind. I could still smell the lingering scent of his cologne on my robe and feel the touch of his hands on my body. Hell no, I wasn't going to stop. I was going to stop fucking him in the pool house, but I was going to be with Daryl no matter what.

"Answer me, dammit!" he barked. "Are you going to stop fucking Daryl?"

I realized I'd zoned out and snapped back to reality. For a second, I thought I was seeing things. Harris was no longer sitting in the wheelchair. He was rising from the chair, standing directly in front of me.

"Oh, shit. You're standing?" I gasped. How the hell could I have not known this?

"Thanks for noticing," he said sarcastically. "I can take a few steps, but I'm still limited. The doctors said it'll take time, but I'll be able to walk eventually. The good thing is I'm no longer impotent. I was going to surprise you on our anniversary, but now you know."

"Wow. I mean, that's great."

"Now that you see I'm getting better, I can handle those needs you have." Harris raised an eyebrow. "So answer my question. Are you still going to fuck that Neanderthal?"

"Harris, I'm glad that you're better, but—"

Harris's hand gripped my neck, and he pulled me to him. I tried to get away, but he was stronger than I anticipated. Months of pushing and pulling that damn wheelchair and his physical therapy had given him more strength than I could have imagined.

"Let me go, Harris!" I pleaded through strangled breathing. I tore at his arms to try to release his grip.

"Answer me! Are you going to stop fucking him?" he growled, squeezing a little tighter.

When I realized I would never overpower his arms, I did the only thing I could. I let my training take over and kneed him in the crotch. He doubled over, and I kneed him in the chin, sending him slumped back into his wheelchair, groaning.

"Well, I guess you're right. You do have feeling down there again. Too bad you won't be able to put it to good use, you abusive motherfucker," I hissed before I rushed past him.

I should've known that reasoning with Harris was impossible. The man had proven time and time again that he was a selfish, narcissistic tyrant, and wheelchair or not, I was sick of it. Now that things were finally in the open, it was time for me to make a decision once and for all.

"Oh, and Harris, yes, I'm going to continue to fuck him. And I want a fucking divorce!"

Larry

5

After driving all night, we crossed the Indiana state line, and I informed Kenny that we were stopping in Gary. Escaping FCI New London was one thing, but enjoying and sustaining our freedom was going to require something we didn't have: money. Our first stop had to be somewhere that would provide the key element to make that happen.

"This raggedy place?" Kenny looked toward Value Food, the tiny, rundown grocery store sitting in front us. "I'm saying, this joint ain't even worth robbing. We probably would get two hundred dollars, if that."

"We could probably get some snacks, too," Holly volunteered from the back seat, looking just as unimpressed by the convenience store as Kenny.

I had to admit, the place had aged tremendously since the last time I'd been there, almost ten years ago, but I knew better than anyone that looks could be deceiving. There would be a hell of a lot more than two hundred dollars inside, and that was on a slow day.

"We ain't here to rob nothing," I told him as I opened the car door. "I'm here to visit one of my longtime associates. He owns the place."

We entered the store, if that's what it could still be considered. The shelves were almost empty, other than a few staples consisting of sugar, flour, and a couple of loaves of bread. A wire rack near the front counter held small bags of chips, candy, and cookies. The beverage rack, on the other hand, was full. There was plenty of beer, wine, and alcohol. In addition to the fully stocked cooler of spirits that spanned the back wall, a large barrel of ice had plenty to choose from near the register in case anyone forgot.

"Can I help you?" the young girl at the counter asked with an attitude. "What you looking for? We keep swishers, rollers, rubbers, and horny goat weed behind the counter if that's what you want."

"I don't want none of that," I told her. "I'm looking for Biggs. Where is he?"

"Who is that?" She frowned.

I stepped closer to the thick plastic shield that she stood behind. "You know who the fuck it is. And I know he's here. That fat motherfucker is here every day because he doesn't trust anybody to lock up his shit other than himself. Now, tell him Larry Duncan is here for a visit. Better yet, I'll tell him myself."

"I don't—" she stammered.

I looked directly into the state-of-the-art security camera pointed toward us and smiled. "Biggs, I know your lazy ass sees me. Either you come out, or I'm coming in."

A moment later, there was a buzzing sound and the door located on the side of the store opened. A hand poked out, beckoning me in.

I smirked at the girl. "See?"

Henry Biggs couldn't have asked for a more suitable name. At nearly four hundred pounds, he was certainly big. He'd been big when we met in the late eighties, and he was still big, only now his head was bald, his face weathered, and his sloth-like movement even slower.

"What the fuck are you doing here, Larry?" He wheezed as we made our way to his office.

"Came to see you, Biggs. It's been a long time, ain't it?" I hoped there was an oxygen tank somewhere nearby because he damn sure needed it. Just looking at him made me want to keep that promise I made to myself about getting in shape.

"Hell yeah. I heard you was locked up in a crazy house somewhere after that little visit you paid me a few years back." Biggs raised an eyebrow at me as he sat at his desk, which looked more like a table. The dim office was full of boxes and two large safes in the corner. "They let you out?"

"They gave me early release. I got some things to handle," I told him. "Time to get back to work."

Biggs frowned. "Work?"

"Yep. That's why I'm here, Biggs. To collect that fifty grand you owe me for that last package I gave you."

Biggs took a deep breath, wheezing as he exhaled. "I ain't gonna sit here and try to act like I don't owe you. But the fact is, I ain't got it."

I shook my head. "Sure you do."

"Honestly, I really don't."

"We both know better than that, Biggs. This little dinky-ass convenience store ain't just convenient for chips and malt liquor. It's convenient for a whole lotta other things too. Illegal things."

"Used to be, but not now, Larry. Them fucking snacks and beer is 'bout the only thing I'm selling these days. That's the only thing keeping the lights on. That and the little bit of weed I push to my regulars," Biggs sadly admitted. "Now that marijuana's legal in half the states, I barely sell that. These young boys is flying out to Cali, buying that legal shit at retail and doubling the price."

"You mean to tell me you ain't got shit in those safes?" I gestured to the two safes he had in the corner.

"Nothing," he replied as he rolled his chair, which was on wheels, to the safes. I watched him put in the combinations on both, then open them. The fat bastard wasn't lying. They were both empty.

"What the fuck happened? Those safes used to be filled with cash. You used to push more dope and pills than anybody in the Midwest."

"Shit, ask your brother. He's the one who helped push me outta business," Biggs explained. "Market changed thanks to the so called 'designer drugs' like HEAT that he started pushing. We was making a killing until he just stopped making it. Fucked my whole business up. Next thing I know, the streets was taken over by a young cat named Torrey that deals with the Mexican Cartels. He runs shit now, and he's pushing some new shit called FIRE. He's one bad-ass motherfucker. I'm lucky he lets me sell to my regulars."

"You let some youngster come in and take your spot, Biggs?" I asked. "You used to be the feared one. Would take out anybody that looked at you sideways. You telling me you 'round here scared of a motherfucker?"

"It ain't like that. Torrey got a payroll that I can't compete with, Larry. He pushing major weight right out of his place on Lake Michigan Beach to fifteen different stash houses. I'm talking major weight. Bringing in about three hundred thousand a week in that bitch. Everybody knows about it, too. Police, local government folks, they all on payroll. I ain't got money like that to pay folks off."

"Everybody knows about it?" I asked, more interested in the house than anything else.

"Yep. He's untouchable."

"Nobody is untouchable," I replied.

"With the Mexican cartels and his brother Tommy, who runs all of Chicago, behind him, this dude is."

"Look, Biggs, I need you to pay me something."

"Larry, the most I got is about three, maybe four grand. That's it," Biggs said with sincerity. "That's my entire intake for the month."

"I guess it'll have to do." I sighed. "I tell you what. You give me four grand and the address of that house, and if it pays off, we'll consider your debt forgiven."

Biggs turned around and looked at me. "That's a mighty generous offer, Larry. But listen, we known each other a long time. I know how you maneuver, but these younger dudes ain't regular gangsters like us. They don't scare easy, and they use assault rifles. And they damn sure won't care that your last name is Duncan."

"I appreciate the sentiment, Biggs, but unlike you, I fear no one. Torrey and his people ain't never met a crazy-ass motherfucker like me and my crew before." I smiled. "Truth be told, I'm the one that should be feared. Now, give me what you got so I can get going."

Biggs wheezed even louder as he opened his desk drawer, took out the small stacks of cash, and handed it to me. "This is it."

"And the address?"

Biggs told me where Torrey's cash house was located. Feeling sorry for him, I peeled off a couple of bills and tossed them onto the table. He needed them just as much as I did.

"Good luck, Larry."

I shrugged. "I don't need it."

Curtis

6

It took damn near the rest of the night for Pete to show up at his office and finally take Stick into custody. I could tell he was surprised as hell that we'd captured him so fast, and he had no problem paying me the $800 bounty in cash. I gave Lauryn $300, and we went to Waffle House for breakfast, my treat.

"Look, sis. I'm not gonna lie, you did good tonight, but you've still got some shit to learn—like how to follow my directions," I told her over a plate of country ham and eggs.

She put her fork down and stared at me for a few seconds, then a smile slowly spread across her face. "Of course I did good. You didn't ever really doubt me, did you? Matter of fact, I think you need to put me on payroll."

I chuckled at her cockiness. "You wanna get paid?"

"Uh, yeah. Who else you know works for free?"

"You wasn't working, Lauryn. I was training you, remember?"

"Yeah, and your man would've gotten away if I hadn't stopped him. Remember *that*?" she snapped back.

I hated to admit to myself that it was true. I sighed. "A'ight, I'll tell you what. I'll take you on, but you only get paid for the jobs you do, and the split is seventy-thirty."

"What!" She nearly spit out her coffee. "I work fifty-fifty or I'm out."

"A'ight, cool. Have it your way. Be out," I said, calling her bluff. "But you're gonna have to explain to Ma why you're not working with me."

Lauryn flopped back in her seat with a pout on her face. I knew bringing my momma into this would set her straight. "Fine," she said. "But I don't really see why it can't be fifty-fifty."

"It can't be fifty-fifty because these are my contacts that I've built up over the past ten years. Of course, you're welcome to strike out on your own and build your own client base if you think you're ready," I said.

She rolled her eyes. "Whatever, Curtis. Can you at least make it sixty-forty?"

I thought about it for a minute. She really had saved my ass that night, and even if she still needed to be tamed a little bit, her skills were strong. "Okay, sis. Sixty-forty. But only 'cause your family."

She let out a happy squeal. "Bro, you won't regret it. I promise."

By the time we got home, it was a little after nine, and I could hear my momma singing to herself as we approached the porch. I also could smell something that reminded me of a backed-up cesspool.

"Jesus, do you smell that?" Lauryn covered her nose as we approached the door.

"Yeah, smells like Momma making them doggone chitlins again."

The moment Lauryn and I walked through the door, the familiar stench filled my nose, causing my eyes to water.

Lauryn gagged. "I'm opening a window."

"I can hear y'all! You better not open those windows and let those flies in my damn house!" Momma's voice came from the kitchen.

"And we can smell them stanking thangs, Momma," Lauryn groaned. She began opening windows.

"They stink now, but they gonna smell good in a little while and taste even better once I add some more vinegar and hot sauce."

We walked into the kitchen. Momma, wearing her favorite apron, was wiping her hands on a dish towel. A large, bubbling pot sat on the stove. Momma walked over to hug my sister, but Lauryn stepped out of the way, her nose wrinkled in disgust.

"Not 'til you wash those hands," Lauryn said.

"Girl, whatever. My chitlins always taste good," Momma said as she kissed me on the cheek.

"I'ma have to take your word on that because I ain't eating them," Lauryn announced.

"I ain't gonna lie. I'm gonna eat 'em, but Momma, they sure do stink," I concurred, reaching under the kitchen sink for some Febreze.

"I know, but your sister's exaggerating. She used to love chitlins until she came back from that fancy school. Now she's acting all bougie, like her cousin Paris. You can put on all the makeup and fancy clothes you want, but you can't hide the fact you're country, girl." My mother smirked as she shifted her eyes at my sister.

"Momma, this is not about me," Lauryn replied. She'd snatched the Febreze out of my hand and started spraying down the room.

"So, how did it go? You two find who you were looking for?" Momma asked.

"We did." I took out the folded bills tucked in my back pocket and handed them to her.

Momma pushed my hand away. "Boy, stop it. You know I ain't taking that from you. I got plenty of money from that trust LC set up for Larry and me. Money is the least of my concerns. I'm just happy you took your sister with you. Looks like you two make a good team."

"I mean, I did help out, Ma, but I was just following Curtis's lead." Lauryn placed her hand on my shoulder. "But you're right, we do make a good team, right Curtis?"

"She's being modest, Momma," I chimed in. Lauryn always tried to tone it down in front of our mother. "But yeah, she did good. Real good."

"That makes me smile." Momma gave Lauryn a genuine look of approval. My mother was tough but loved to see her children shine. She stepped over, and this time, Lauryn accepted a hug.

"I'm glad. Now, I want you to use this and pay the light bill or something. I told you I just want to feel like I'm contributing. It's what a man should do." I slipped the money into my mother's apron before she could stop me, then turned toward the window when Spot, our yard dog, started barking. There was a sprinter van pulling into the driveway.

"You expecting somebody, Ma?"

"No." Momma moved closer, staring out the window as hard as I did.

As if we were thinking the same thing, Lauryn and I locked eyes. Neither of us was in the mood for taking chances. We weren't against visitors, but we lived rather far out in the country, so people usually called before they showed up unannounced.

"Who you think that is? Don't nobody drive black vans around here like that," Lauryn said.

"I don't know, but I'm 'bout to find out." I headed for the door.

"I'm going with you." Lauryn was right behind me. "Momma, stay in here."

"I'll be damned," my mother told her in no uncertain term, pushing her way past Lauryn to be at my side. "It's probably UPS or one of them Amazon deliveries. You know I love me some Amazon."

"Amazon trucks aren't black." I reached for the door handle, easing it open so we could get a better look through the screen door.

"Lawd, that look like LC getting out that van!" Momma grinned at the suited man and the woman who followed him.

Uncle LC and Aunt Chippy were standing with their backs against the van, keeping an eye on Spot, who had his fangs bared. He'd always been a good protector.

"Spot! Take your ass somewhere and lay down!" Momma pushed open the screen door, rushing onto the big wraparound porch. Spot ran away once she came busting out the door.

"Chippy!" Momma yelled.

"Nee Nee!" Aunt Chippy hollered back.

I swear the way they ran toward each other with their arms out, they looked like that scene at the end of *A Color Purple*. Momma and Aunt Chippy were jumping up and down, hugging each other and crying. Uncle LC just walked past them, shaking his head at their dramatics the same way Lauryn and I were doing on the porch.

The rear door of the van opened, and Paris, Rio, and a bunch of kids piled out.

"What in the world?" Lauryn asked. "Are we hosting a family reunion that I didn't know about?"

"It appears so. Come on. We might as well greet them."

We walked over and hugged our New York family members—Paris, who was stunningly beautiful, and her brother Rio, who looked a little less flamboyant now that he no longer had the rainbow-dyed hair I'd seen on him last time.

"What's good, cousins?" I said.

"Rio, I don't think I've ever seen you with dark hair," Lauryn commented.

"That's not Rio. That's Uncle Roman," Mariah informed us with a giggle. She was London's daughter who had grown up in the blink of an eye.

"Damn, my bad. I thought my momma was messin' with us when she told us that story about you. Y'all really are twins." I blinked at my newfound cousin, who looked just like his brother, only a little more cut and a lot more masculine. "Nice to meet you, cuz. I'm Curtis, and this is my sister Lauryn."

Roman dapped me up and gave me a side hug, then hugged Lauryn.

I turned to Paris, who was dressed in all black with a studded designer leather jacket and high heels. She'd always been the best dressed among all the cousins, and she had some stiff competition from London and our other cousin Sasha.

"What's up, Paris? How's motherhood treating you?"

"Ain't nothing changed, cuz. I'm still a bad ass, and so is my son." I had to give it to her, she said that shit with so much New York swagger that you had to believe her. I could also see the admiration in my sister's eyes.

"Well, everyone looks so good," my momma stated for all to hear.

"You do too, Nee," Aunt Chippy said. She came over and gave us hugs.

I have to admit I was kind of happy Uncle LC hung back by the porch. He had always intimidated me, and after some things that happened a few years earlier, I was a little scared of him.

"Okay, now that we've all hugged and kissed, y'all cut the crap. What in the world are y'all doing here?" Momma asked. It was the same thing I was wondering. "Y'all don't just do pop-up visits."

Uncle LC looked serious as he stepped over and said, "We need to talk to you, Nee Nee, and we wanted to do it face to face. Something's happened."

"What's this about, LC? What's happened now?" Momma looked nervous.

Sensing the tension, I walked over and stood next to her. "What's this about, Uncle LC?"

Uncle LC looked over at Chippy, who was now by his side.

"Tell them, LC," Chippy said.

"It's about your father, Curtis."

Momma gasped. "Lawd, is he dead? Is that why y'all came all this way? To tell me my husband is dead?" I placed my arm around her because she wobbled a little like her legs were about to give out under her.

"No, Nee Nee, he's not dead." Aunt Chippy took Momma's hand. "At least not yet."

"Then what about him, LC?" Lauryn snapped with very little respect. "Is he sick?"

"He escaped the facility. He's out, and the authorities are looking for him," Uncle LC said.

"When did all of this happen?" Momma asked.

"Yesterday. The feds showed up at our house last night," Aunt Chippy explained. "We figured it would be best if we told you face to face rather than use the phones. I'm sure they're tapped."

I took control because Momma was about to lose it. "Y'all come up on the porch so we can talk."

LC

7

It had been years since I was in my hometown of Waycross, and it felt good to be back in spite of the very serious business we had to attend to. Once this situation was handled, maybe I'd even stick around a few days to see some old friends and family.

I was glad that Roman had decided to come. I wanted to show him my hometown, which all of my other kids had visited many times over the years. Paris and Rio had never really liked it. They were New Yorkers through and through, and Waycross was too slow for their tastes. So, Rio had chosen to stay behind and work at his club, but Paris surprised me by volunteering to make this trip with us. Junior and Sonya wanted to come, but with Sonya two weeks away from her due date, we all decided it wasn't safe for them to travel. Bringing the grandkids was Chippy's idea. I loved those kids, but with everything going on with Larry and the feds, this wasn't exactly a casual visit. Chippy thought having the kids around would be a good distraction for her and Nee Nee, and like always when it came to my lovely wife, I gave in.

Thankfully, Nee Nee, Curtis, and Lauryn seemed to be taking things in stride, for now. I guess they were used to a certain amount of chaos after years of Larry and his issues with mental health. I expected it would be a different story, however, when the feds showed up and started searching the house. There was no doubt in my mind that they would show up. I was just glad they hadn't beaten us there because from my experience, Curtis was a known hothead who despised authority and had no problem pulling the trigger without thinking. Things could go from bad to worse in a hurry. And Lord help us if Larry decided to pay his family a visit at the wrong time.

"Aunt Nee Nee, can I have something to drink?" Jordan, my rambunctious grandson, asked as he ran around the yard, spinning like he was an airplane. I didn't know what Chippy was thinking about when she insisted that we bring these kids. That boy was a ball of energy.

"You sure can. Do you like lemonade?" Seeing the big grin on Nee Nee's face gave me a clue. Having the kids around was a good distraction from all the stress.

Jordan nodded his head eagerly.

"Good, and I have some homemade chocolate chip cookies. Would you like some of them as well?"

"Me too," Mimi, my youngest granddaughter, shouted before Jordan could reply. She ran to her great aunt's side.

"Why don't we all go in the house and get something to eat and drink?" Chippy suggested.

"I hope y'all like chitlins," Lauryn warned.

"What's that?" Mariah asked.

"You don't wanna know," Paris replied.

"Come on in and see for yourselves," Chippy told her. "I love your Aunt Nee Nee's chitlins. Put some hot sauce on them, and you got some good eating."

Lauryn looked at Chippy with a side-eye and I had to stop myself from laughing. Nee Nee's chitlins were definitely an acquired taste, and obviously her daughter hadn't acquired it.

As everyone went inside, I called out to Curtis, who was trailing behind the rest of the family. Since we'd arrived, he hadn't even come over to shake my hand, let alone say hello.

"Curtis, can I speak to you for a minute?"

I could see the hesitance in his face, but he stood on the porch and waited for me while everyone else went inside. I took a seat on the porch swing, while Curtis leaned against the wrap-around porch railing not too far away.

"Before you even go there, Uncle LC, I need you to know, I don't know where Daddy is," Curtis blurted out before I could speak. I believed his words were genuine because he looked like he was just as flabbergasted by the whole thing as I was. "And I ain't have no part in it."

"I believe you, Curtis."

"You didn't expect me to be here, did you, Uncle LC?" He studied my face.

"No, son, I didn't." I shook my head and looked down at the porch floor. "And I'm sorry for not believing in you."

He didn't reply right away, probably because he knew I had my reasons, and they were valid. Five years ago, Curtis, with the aid of his younger brother Kenny, had broken Larry out of a private psychiatric hospital my brother Lou and I had him admitted into. We'd tried for years to get him the help he needed, but Larry would have one nervous breakdown after another, and each time, some innocent person or persons would end up dead. We finally came to the conclusion that we couldn't cover up things for him anymore, and we talked Nee Nee into letting us admit him.

Once Kenny and Curtis freed him, Larry went completely off his meds, and with Lou dead, he became fixated on the idea that I stole his money. He somehow convinced his sons of the idea, and the three of them went on a killing rampage and vendetta that damn near destroyed my business. When it was all said and done, they'd taken the lives of sixty people, including Lou's ex-wife, Donna. It took everything we had, but the family finally took them down.

Larry had taken things too far, and he was admitted to a psychiatric prison for the criminally insane in Connecticut. Curtis and Kenny should have been thrown in prison as well, but after a whole lot of effort, Chippy and Nee Nee convinced me to give them a chance. They believed the boys weren't at fault because they were both young and under Larry's influence. I finally agreed to give them the second chance every young black man needs and paid over two million dollars in bribes and payoffs to have them set free.

"I did a lot of soul searching after what happened last time, when I helped Daddy escape," Curtis said. "A lot of innocent people lost their lives because of us, because of me, and I can never forgive myself. I haven't had a good night's sleep since. Those peoples' deaths haunt me. I don't know what I was thinking. He made me into some kind of monster."

I reached out and touched his shoulder. "You wanted your father home, and you would have done anything to make that happen. My boys, I want to think, would probably have done the same thing, and I know Paris would have."

We were both quiet for a second.

"What I'm trying to say is that what happened doesn't make you a monster, Curtis. It makes you a devoted son. Unfortunately, your father was not well enough to realize what he was doing to you boys at the time."

"You think Daddy's going on another killing spree, Uncle LC?"

"I hope not." I shook my head.

"Shit. I can't believe he's got the feds after him."

"Yes," I sighed. "He was at a federal facility, and he killed a guard."

"They're not gonna stop until they kill him." I could hear in his voice that no matter what Larry had put him through, Curtis still loved his father.

"That's why I'm here. I'm hoping to prevent that. But there is one thing I need to know, Curtis."

"What's that?"

"Where's your brother?"

Curtis exhaled, and there was a silence between us for more than a little while before he shrugged his shoulders and spoke. "I don't know where Kenny's at, but I'm figuring he's with my daddy."

At that moment, the dog started barking, and a couple of dark SUVs appeared in the distance across the field. They were driving down the private dirt road that led to the house.

"Speak of the devil," I said.

"Feds?"

"Mm-hmm. Try to remain calm."

The SUVs pulled into the yard and parked behind the sprinter van. Curtis and I waited and watched as Agent Martinez and Deputy Fritz stepped out, followed by the rest of the storm troopers. Both wore the same nylon jackets with the government insignia representing their agencies on the back and front. The storm troopers, like the night before, wore all black with flak jackets.

"What are you doing here, Mr. Duncan?" Agent Martinez had a frown on her face.

"Nice to see you again as well, Agent Martinez. You too Deputy Fritz," I said.

"What brings you to Waycross, Mr. Duncan?"

"With everything going on, my family and I decided to come down and support my sister-in-law and the rest of the family."

Fritz wasn't buying it. "Would that family happen to include your brother Larry?" he asked.

"Actually, no, we haven't seen my daddy since the last time we visited him in prison up in Connecticut, but I'll give you a call if he shows up. You got a card or something?" Curtis said.

Agent Martinez scowled at him. "You wouldn't mind letting us check inside and make sure, would you?"

"Hell no!" The door opened, and Nee Nee stepped out, followed by Chippy, Lauryn, and Paris. "You ain't stepping one foot in here without some kinda warrant and my lawyer here."

I jumped to her side. "It's fine, Nee Nee. We know Larry's not here. They came to my house and did a search too. It's the only way they are going to go away."

"That's your house, LC. This is mine, and they ain't coming in here." Nee Nee looked like she was about to cry. "And I'd appreciate it if you left the premises. My family and I would like to enjoy our time. We haven't seen each other in a long time."

The two agents didn't hide their dissatisfaction at Nee Nee's lack of cooperation. They wore the matching grimaces as they turned to leave the porch.

"We'll be back," Agent Martinez stated.

"Make sure you got a warrant when you do," Nee Nee retorted.

"Count on it," Agent Martinez snapped back.

"You know they're not going away, right?" I said as we watched Martinez and Fritz get into the SUVs along with the storm troopers.

Nee Nee sighed. "I know. Let's just hope Larry has enough sense to stay away from here."

"Now, you know that's wishful thinking." Chippy chimed in as we watched one of the vans stop just past the property line and park. The other SUV with Martinez and Fritz continued down the road. "You know your husband better than I do. If he don't go nowhere else, he's coming to see you."

Larry

8

I was surprised when we drove past the address Biggs had given me for Torrey's stash house. Most of Gary was beat to shit, but this place was in an upscale home near Lake Michigan. Was this motherfucker so bold he was really selling dope out of this house? I guess I'd find out in a minute.

"Park on the corner," I instructed Kenny.

"What's the plan, boss?" Dennis asked from the back seat.

"We go in and ask nicely," I told him, making sure I had the tech nine that was in the bag of "additional assistance" Biggs had given me after he wished me good luck. The contents inside the duffle bag would definitely come in handy. In addition to the tech nine, there were also two Glocks, a Ruger, and an old school Smith &Wesson, along with clips and ammunition. Hell, the only thing we needed were a couple of ski masks and we'd have been outfitted to knock off a couple of banks. From what Biggs told me, what this guy Torrey had in his house was probably more than any of the local financial institutions anyway.

"Ask nicely?" Kenny raised an eyebrow as he took the gun I was handing him.

"Yep, we ask nicely first, and if they don't give us what we want, we take it," I said calmly. "Let's go."

We stepped out of the car, and I checked out the area. Other than a classic Caddy and a minivan, there were no other cars in sight, and no one was standing watch from what I could see. I began to wonder if Biggs was mistaken because this damn sure didn't look like a dope spot.

My three companions walked close behind me. As we got to the front of the house, a tall, lanky guy walked out. He was so busy stuffing something into his pocket that he didn't see me until he nearly hit me with the gate.

"Oh, my bad, Unc." He apologized and rushed past.

"I don't know about this, Dad," Kenny said. "We don't know what's waiting behind that door."

"Nothing we can't handle," I told him. "Whoever this dude Torrey is, he's gotten comfortable, too comfortable. They ain't even got nobody standing watch at the gate. Rookie mistake. Holly, you go first."

"Sure thing." Holly stepped forward, adjusting her T-shirt to reveal a little more cleavage. She went to the front entrance, while Kenny, Dennis, and I stayed back a little, but close enough to make our move.

A young guy opened the front door and checked Holly out from head to toe. "What's good, sexy?"

"I'm looking for something good," Holly told him.

"Oh, really? What you got in mind?"

Holly giggled coyly, beckoning him closer with her finger. He stepped out of the doorway, and without warning, she shanked his ass repeatedly with such precision that even I was stunned as he fell to the ground. She waved to us, and she held the door open as we slipped inside.

"Yo, Vic, who the fuck was at the do—"

I blasted the guy standing in the front room before he could finish his sentence. Knowing the gunshot would cause a reaction, I scanned my surroundings in preparation for whoever would be heading our way.

"What the fuck was that?" Two more guys came running down the hallway, guns drawn. Before they could even pull the triggers, Dennis and Kenny unleashed a barrage of bullets, and they met the same fate as their two buddies moments before.

"Handle down here. I'm going up," I told the other three.

I eased up the shiny, wooden staircase, listening for voices. I'd been out of the game for a long time, but I still remembered a thing or two—one being that you never keep product and money in the same spot. The dope was always where it could be easily accessed, but the money was under lock and key. I was certain that what I was looking for would be upstairs.

"You don't wanna do this." A voice came from above.

I looked up and saw a guy who couldn't have been older than sixteen aiming a gun at me.

"No, you don't wanna do that."

"I don't know who you are, old man, but you fucked up," he said.

I continued up the steps, my gun by my side, finger on the trigger. "I can either be the man who kills you, or the one who lets you live. Your choice."

"You ain't gonna be neither, especially once you're dead," he told me. "It's over."

He pulled the trigger, and a shot rang out before he fell to the floor. I turned around to see Holly right behind me, holding the Ruger.

"Jarvis!" A woman screamed.

Holly and I turned around. She stared at us briefly before taking off down the hallway.

She started pounding on a door at the end of the hall. "Torrey, let me in! They got Jarvis!"

I took off after her just as the door opened and she rushed inside. It closed right behind her, and we heard the unmistakable sound of the lock clicking. Muffled voices revealed the panic happening on the other side of that door.

Holly raised her gun and shot the knob off the door. The woman was screaming and clinging to a tall, thin guy wearing a bulletproof vest when we busted into the room. It was a huge open space with several small tables holding bill counters. There was also a large desk sitting in front of a curtained wall. For some reason, I was amused. This guy was such an amateur that he didn't even have a gun on him.

"Sorry to disturb your afternoon, Torrey. I just need you to open that safe of yours and we'll be on your way." I smiled.

"Fuck you. What the fuck I look like doing that shit? You crazy, motherfucker."

"He doesn't like to be called that," Holly warned, stepping closer with her gun raised.

I touched her shoulder. "It's fine. He's right. I am a crazy motherfucker. And if you don't open that fucking safe, I'll show you just how crazy I am."

Torrey jutted out his chin. "I ain't afraid to die. I worked too hard for my shit to just let someone come and take it. You gonna have to kill me," he said, full of bravado that he'd soon regret.

"Torrey, are you crazy?" the woman shrieked.

"That's where you're wrong. I don't plan on killing you." I walked over to the desk and picked up a photo with two small children, a boy and a girl. "Beautiful kids. They go to Orchard Academy, right? Shouldn't they be getting ready for dismissal? I have an associate of mine that happens to be there right now."

"Oh my God, please don't hurt my kids," the woman started crying. She looked at Torrey. "Open the fucking safe."

"Nah, I ain't doing that."

"You got a lot of mouth for a brother who don't even have a weapon on him," I said. "You have a lot to learn, young blood." I stepped closer to them.

"They're our fucking kids, Torrey! Open the safe!" the woman screamed, tears streaming down her face.

"I said—"

Losing patience with his tough-guy act, I swung at him with the butt of my gun. It landed so hard on his skull that he dropped to the floor in a heap.

"Torrey!" his baby momma cried out, kneeling down beside him.

"Holly, call our friends and see if they've spotted the kids yet," I said.

The woman whipped her head around to look at me with terror in her eyes. "No! please don't hurt my kids. I'll open the safe."

She jumped up from the floor and headed for the desk. She pulled back the curtain behind it, revealing the door to the safe. With trembling hands, she punched a code into the keypad, then stepped out of the way.

I opened the door and let out a laugh. Biggs was right. The money stacked inside that safe had to be at least a half a million dollars.

"Looks like we might need a few more bags to carry this out of here," I told Holly.

We'd hit the jackpot. Now it was time to go home.

Paris

9

I really needed to have my head examined. What the hell was I thinking about when I volunteered to come to Waycross of all places? Yes, I was bored shitless sitting in the house on mommy duty, but what I should have done was take Sasha up on her invitation to fly down to Miami and party. Not that it would have been easy, because I could already hear my mother now, slapping me with a guilt trip about, "What kind of mother would miss her son's first T-ball game?" Me. That's who. I'm the type of mother who would do that. I loved my son, but what my mother failed to realize was that the worst part of being a mother was missing out on the fun shit, and dammit, I knew Sasha was having fun.

"Okay, where the fine men at around here?" I asked Lauryn as we pulled out of her driveway and onto the road. We'd been planning all day to go out and have drinks, so once Aunt Nee Nee and my parents agreed to keep the kids, I didn't waste any time changing clothes and pushing Lauryn out the door before they changed their minds. I have to admit, though, that it was a little weird going out for drinks with someone I use to baby sit.

"You ain't finding no fine men in Waycross. At least not single ones, that's for sure." Lauryn shook her head. "But there is a cool bar in Jacksonville called The Loft that's chill. The drinks are good, and they've got a pretty good DJ if you like dancing. It's usually filled with a decent amount of hot guys. We can go there if you want."

"How far is Jacksonville?"

"About an hour the way I drive. If you want to stay local, there's always Big Shirley's. It's a strip club, but for us, the drinks will be free."

"Nah, fuck that. Jacksonville here we come." I pointed toward the sign the said: JACKSONVILLE 76 MILES. "And it's a good thing you're driving, 'cause I do plan on getting my drink on. I ain't been out in a month, and it's time to get in some trouble."

Lauryn laughed. "I like the way you talk. Trouble is my middle name."

"Well, we about to find out." I took out my weed vape and took a hit.

Lauryn was eight years younger than me, but she seemed cool, and based on how much fun we were having laughing, singing, and smoking in the car, I knew we could have a great time if the club was the right vibe. Besides Miami, I'd never partied in Florida, so I really didn't know what to expect. I just hoped we wouldn't be pulling up to a barn with a bunch of 'bama-ass dudes.

With Lauryn's speed-racer skills, it didn't even take a full hour to get to Jacksonville. It didn't look like a huge city, but at least it had more to offer than Waycross, which felt like the kind of place where everyone's in bed by nine o'clock.

We pulled up to the nightclub and Lauryn started driving around the parking lot.

"I wanna find something in a well-lit area," she said.

"Wait, they don't have valet?" I asked.

She glanced over at me. "Girl, get over yourself. This is not New York City." She pulled into a spot. "The door isn't that far. You'll be okay."

"Damn. This gonna take some getting used to." I couldn't remember the last time I went to a club without valet service. "With no valet, the cover better not be over fifty."

"There isn't a cover." Lauryn smirked as we got out of the car.

"No cover?"

I carefully walked across the graveled parking lot in my thousand-dollar stilettos and black Versace dress. Meanwhile, Lauryn's all-black attire—jeans, tank, and heeled booties—was cute, casual, and understated, very much like her personality. I didn't understand why she didn't wear something a little more revealing. She definitely had the body for it.

There wasn't much of a line outside the club, and the few people who were standing around looked pretty basic, which made me a little worried about what we'd see inside. I swear I would be pissed it we'd driven all this way and the club turned out to be full of losers.

The security guy checked us out from head to toe, but at least he didn't try any lame-ass lines on us. Lauryn gave him a twenty, and he gave us VIP access bracelets and waved us through. Inside, the crowd was thick, but not too tight. A few guys tried to make eye contact as we brushed past them, and one grabbed my arm, but I was too high to really be bothered. I just swatted him away and kept it moving.

"What's up, ladies?" The waitress welcomed us as soon as we found a table and sat down in the VIP section. "Just wanna let you know that your first round of drinks have already been taken care of by the gentleman at the VIP bar."

"Damn, that was fast. Which one?" I asked, turning toward the bar to see the generous patron.

"In the light blue shirt."

"Hmmm, he's cute as hell." I smiled at the tall, exquisite chocolate man raising his glass toward us. "And I like the bald head. I may have to properly thank him. Who is he?"

"I'm not sure what his name is, but he used to be a navy fighter pilot. Now he's some big-time defense contractor."

"Hold on, cuz. What if *I* want to properly thank him? He bought me a drink as well," Lauryn teased after we ordered our drinks.

"Respect your elders." I gave Lauryn an affectionate smile as I stood, then made my way over to the bar.

"Thanks for the drink," I said as I approached our new friend.

"No doubt. Couldn't let a beautiful lady like you be thirsty. I'm Gavin." He spoke in a slow country drawl that usually would have turned me off, but with his deep baritone voice, it was pretty sexy.

"Nice to meet you, Gavin. I'm Paris." I found myself getting lost in his hazel eyes as the smell of his Invictus cologne drifted over to me. He had to be at least six foot three, with the build of an NFL running back, a bald head, and a full beard. To say this man was sexy would be an understatement.

"So, Gavin, you wanna dance?"

"I thought you'd never ask."

By the end of the night, it didn't take much convincing for me to agree to go back to his place. I'd already subtly checked out what he was working with as he danced up against me, and I knew he was packing just what I needed. The question was, did he know what to do with it? There was only one way to find out.

"We're gonna get out of here and go back to his place." I spoke into Lauryn's ear so she could hear me over the music. She'd been sitting with Darnell, Gavin's friend, kicking it and dancing most of the night. He wasn't as fine as Gavin, but he was cute. "You and old boy wanna come?"

"What? Why?" She frowned.

"Why do you think?" I replied, giving her a knowing look. She was younger, but there was no way she didn't know why I wanted to go. It was times like this that I missed Sasha, who was down for anything and damn near anyone. She was the perfect wing woman.

"I got a nice setup in my backyard: pool, surround sound, a bar, and a Jacuzzi. Don't worry. My boy is coming too. We just gonna vibe." Gavin nodded toward his homeboy.

"You cool with that?" Darnell asked. "I've got some real good bud."

"I mean, I guess." Lauryn shrugged. "Just remember we gotta drive all the way back to Waycross."

"It's just for a nightcap. And maybe a little more," I reassured her, winking at Gavin.

"A'ight, cool," Lauryn said, looking anything but excited.

Gavin and Darnell escorted us to the car. Before I got in, he kissed me, his tongue giving me a preview of his other talents. I was so horny I couldn't wait to get to his house.

Lauryn drove, following his silver Escalade for the fifteen-minute drive to the gated community where he lived. I have to admit

I was impressed. The houses weren't mansions, but the neighborhood was full of manicured lawns and large, well-maintained homes. Almost every driveway had a luxury car or two parked in it. Obviously, there was some money around here.

Gavin took us into his house. My heels clicked against the marble floors and echoed through the high-ceilinged rooms as he led us to the kitchen. I leaned against a granite counter as he opened a bottle of tequila and poured drinks for everyone.

"Let's go out back," he said, handing me a glass.

Gavin flipped a switch, and R&B music started playing in the back yard, where a huge pool surrounded by palm trees sparkled under the string of lights hanging above it. It looked kind of like a mini resort, and I was feeling it.

Lauryn sat down in a lounge chair, and Darnell sat next to her, rolling a joint, but I didn't join them. I put my drink on a table, slipped out of my dress and shoes, then dived into the pool wearing my lace bra and matching panties. Gavin stripped down to his boxers and dived in behind me.

The look on Lauryn's face was priceless.

"Y'all not coming in?" I yelled. "It feels amazing."

"Nah, I'm good," she said. Darnell handed her the blunt and she took a hit.

"Stop being boring and come in, Lauryn!" I giggled, tossing my arms around Gavin's neck. "Tell her, Darnell. Get your girl into this damn pool."

Lauryn shook her head again, looking a little annoyed. She got up and went in the house with Darnell following behind her.

"Fuck 'em," Gavin said, swimming up behind me and pressing his erection against me as he kissed my neck.

I let out a moan, encouraging him to go further. He unhooked my bra and tossed it out of the pool, then swam around in front of me. His hot mouth on my breasts sent a tingling sensation right between my thighs. I was ready for more.

I guided him over to the shallow end, where I leaned back against the steps to give him full access to whatever he wanted. His tongue flicked over my hard nipples as I eased his boxers down his hips and explored the length and width of one of the most perfect dicks I'd ever touched. I was going to have fun with this.

I lowered myself into the water and put it in my mouth, staying down there for as long as I could hold my breath. When I popped my head up, his eyes were literally rolled back in his head.

"Like that?" I laughed.

I did it again, but this time when I came up for air, Gavin lifted me onto the edge of the pool and buried his face between my thighs. His oral skills were pro-level. He devoured me as if I was the sweetest, most delectable thing he'd ever had his mouth on.

"Oh, shit," I said over and over again. That man gave me back-to-back orgasms, sending me into a fit of uncontrollable leg shaking. He had to carry me inside and up the stairs to his bedroom.

I tried to sit up, but he gently pushed me back down into the plush pillows of his massive bed. "Lay back. I got you," he insisted as he took out a gold foil-wrapped condom and slid it on his rock-hard erection.

When he entered, I was more than ready to receive. This man did not disappoint. He fucked me exactly like I needed to be fucked. He flipped me around in all kinds of positions, sometimes ramming it hard, and other times slow and sensual. And he turned me on even more by talking to me in that sexy, country-ass accent as he brought me to orgasm over and over again.

By the time he finally climaxed, I was exhausted and satisfied. It had been a long time since I'd felt that way, and I knew if we didn't get the hell outta there, I'd be asleep in a few minutes.

"Thank you," I said, sitting up and rubbing my fingers against his broad chest.

"You leaving? You ain't gotta go." He pulled my arm.

"Baby, the sun's coming up, and we got a long drive back to Waycross," I told him. "This was good, though. Really good."

He followed me down to the back yard and helped me get dressed.

"Maybe next time you're down south, you'll stop by," he said. "Or maybe we can hook up in NYC."

"Maybe. I gotta find my cousin so we can get outta here," I told him. I also wanted to hear how Lauryn's night with Darnell had gone. I hoped it was as satisfying as mine.

Curtis

10

"Well, well, well, if it isn't the sexiest man in Waycross," Opal shouted to me when I entered Big Shirley's with my cousin Roman. She was one of my favorite dancers at the strip club. She walked up and kissed me on the cheek, squeezing my ass for everyone to see. "Oh, tonight's gonna be a good night, ladies."

"Damn, cuz, you got it like that?" Roman whispered, checking out Opal's barely covered ass in her G-string as she walked away. "You the fucking man."

Roman wasn't far from the truth, because walking into Big Shirley's for me was like walking into the bar from the TV show *Cheers*. It was the one place in town where everybody knew my name. Hell, I'd practically grown up in the place, and our family still owned the building. Originally a brothel, Big Shirley's had been owned by my father and my uncles, and my aunt Shirley ran the place. Then, around the time that all the Duncans moved up to New York, the church folks started pressuring the city officials, who forced the new club managers to transition Big Shirley's to a strip club. Truth be told, you could still buy ass. It just wasn't advertised on the menu.

"She's just being extra," I told him. "Trying to get my attention so I ask for a lap dance."

"Shit, with a body like that, it shouldn't take much." He looked over at Opal, who was standing near the bar, waving. "She definitely got mine. She can give me a lap dance right now. She is fine as fuck."

"That she is, cuzzo." I laughed. "But you ain't seen nothing yet. Come on. Let's head over to the VIP section so we can chop it up."

As usual, Big Shirley's was packed, full of men who'd gotten off from their eight-hour shifts, looking to enjoy the watered-down drinks and naked women and willing to pay for both. The women who worked there were more than welcoming, ready to serve lap dances and more if you had enough money.

Roman followed me over to the VIP section. It was a good night, and the vibe was right. The house DJ was playing trap hits mixed with a little R&B. Guys that knew me by name stopped watching the naked woman floating at the top of the pole in the middle of the room long enough to dap me up or speak to me as we walked by. Inside Big Shirley's, I might as well have been the mayor of Waycross, and Roman was impressed.

"This is cool. Real cool," Roman said when we got to the booth. He started staring at this big-booty stripper named Bertha, who was twerking on the stage. "Damn. Look at the ass on her. Now that's the woman I wanna lap dance with. How much they charge?"

"You can probably get one for ten dollars. She'll suck your dick for fifty, but you gonna have to get a private VIP room for another ten."

Roman's eyes got large. "That's all?"

"Yeah, this ain't New York. Ain't nobody going to pay hundreds of dollars for some shit you can get for free."

I stared at him as he started digging in his pockets for cash. He looked up at me and frowned.

"What? You not judging me because I'm willing to buy some pussy, are you?"

I sat back in the booth and shook my head. "Nah, nah, I don't give a shit about that. It ain't like I never paid to get some."

"Then what's up? Why you staring?"

"I was staring because . . ." I paused for a minute, trying to figure out the best way to say this. I didn't want to offend him if he was one of those politically correct types. "Well, to be honest it's kinda strange hearing you talk about women's asses because you look so much like Rio."

"Yeah, I get that a lot." He chuckled, looking slightly uncomfortable.

"I'm sure. It must be a little weird having a twin brother that's gay."

"It's a little weird having a twin brother period. Two years ago, I was an only child. Now I got two sisters and four brothers."

"Yeah, that's a little crazy. Sorry if I hit a sore spot with that Rio shit."

"Nah, we good. It's not a sore spot. I love my family and my twin brother. It's just a lot to get used to."

"I can imagine." I looked toward the stage as a new girl stepped up to the pole. "Man, fuck that shit. We here to have a good time. Big Shirley's isn't the classiest spot like the Hellfire Club y'all got up north, but it's got all the titties and ass you can ask for. Just look around."

"It sure does. And fuck the Hellfire Club, that place is over-rated," he said. "I'm trying to see some ass clapping, not a bunch a fake titties that cost you a thousand dollars to touch." Roman shook his head, and I laughed. "That ain't me. I'm from the hood. I'm good right here."

"Damn, that's what I'm talking 'bout, cousin. When I found out about you, I was a little worried because the New York Duncans are good people but they bourgeois as shit. I can rock with you, Roman." I lifted my hand, and we fist bumped.

"Back at you, cuz."

"You gentlemen drinking tonight?" Crystal, the VIP hostess, sashayed over, smiling at me before briefly glancing over at Roman.

"Damn right. Why you think we in here?" I smirked, my eyes glued to her large, natural breasts popping out of the lace bustier top she wore.

"We both know the answer to that." She licked her lips seductively.

I elbowed Roman, who was staring just as hard as I was. "Pick your poison, cuzzo."

"Some kinda vodka," he replied.

"Bring us a bottle of Cîroc, girl, and a chaser," I told her.

"Oh, and can you let ol' girl in the red over there know I'd like to get a dance?" Roman pointed to the big-booty girl he'd been eyeing before. She'd just finished sliding down the pole. "I like her style."

"Bertha. Great choice. I'll let her know."

I high-fived Roman as Crystal walked off.

I was having a much better time with him than I had expected to. Since Uncle LC and the family would be staying a few days, my mother had said I needed to get to know my family better.

"Take your cousins out and show them a good time," she had said to me and Lauryn.

I'd hung out with my New York cousins before and to me, they were too self-centered and entitled. I had no interest in spending time with them. So, I was relieved when Lauryn said she was taking Paris out for a girls-only night.

"Yeah, Ma, I would, but I'm gonna go over to Big Shirley's, and I don't know if Roman would be down for that," I told her, thinking that the strip club was the best way to get out of the obligation.

But then Roman said, "Yeah, cuz, lemme go with you and see what these Georgia girls are working with," and now here we were, sharing toasts and rating all the tits and ass in front of us. He might have been a twin, but he was different from his spoiled, bougie siblings, and I was having a good time with him.

"So you really think the hellfire club is overrated?" I asked him.

"Look, don't get me wrong. My siblings are cool, and I kinda enjoy the family, especially my parents. But I'm not like them. That fancy shit is not me."

"I feel you on that. I can relate."

"No, you can't. I mean, you less bougie than them, but you can't really relate," Roman said. "Not to my struggle."

"What you trying to say, cuz?"

"I grew up in Marcy Projects in Brooklyn. The fucking hood." He swallowed the rest of his drink. "You grew up in one of the richest families in Waycross. I saw your house. That shit has like six bedrooms and sits on acres. Your struggle damn sure ain't like mine."

"Yeah, well, now that you put it like that, I guess there's some truth to that," I had to admit, but it was a bitter pill. I didn't like to think of myself as anything but a simple country guy. "It's not like a grew up a pauper, and I am a Duncan, but I'm still my own man. And it ain't like you ain't benefiting from being a Duncan now yourself."

"If you say so, but I'm still the kid from the projects." Roman shrugged. "That shit you saying sounds likes rich folk talk to me."

"Let me ask you something, Roman. I mean, since you down on your luck and your story is so tragic. What kinda car you rolling in these days?"

"Me? Right now?" Roman paused. "A Porsche 911."

"That's what's up. You bought that yourself?"

"Nah, Pops gave it to me." He leaned back in his seat.

"Makes sense. And if I had to guess, you probably got a trust fund with a couple hundred thousand sitting in it too, right?"

"It's a half million, but I can't touch it yet," Roman confirmed.

"You just proved my point," I said. "You're acting like I'm privileged or something, when your ass is out here enjoying all the benefits of being a Duncan. Admit that shit."

"I ain't say I wasn't enjoying it." Roman smirked. "I said I didn't grow up enjoying it. There's a difference."

Crystal came over to the table. "You fellas want another round?"

"We sure as hell do!" I yelled, then looked at Roman. "This one is on you, trust fund baby."

"That's cool." Roman stood and raised his glass toward me. "Matter of fact, I'll take care of the next two. And tell Opal to treat my cousin here to a lap dance."

"Oh, hell yeah. You're officially my favorite cousin." I roared with laughter. "I fucks with you, Roman Duncan."

Lauryn

11

"Lauryn, you ready?"

"Huh?" My eyes fluttered open, and I stared at Paris. She was standing in front of me, now fully dressed. Gavin was behind her, wearing a robe.

I sat up on the sofa where I'd fallen asleep in the great room of Gavin's house. Darnell had been nice enough to give me a blanket once it became obvious, based on the moaning coming from upstairs, that we wouldn't be leaving any time soon. I appreciated the fact that he had been a gentleman. He did try to get a little touchy feely while we were watching a movie, but I turned my head when he tried to kiss me, and he backed off without an argument. He even slept on the chair and ottoman instead of trying to squeeze in next to me on the sofa.

"You ready to go?" Paris asked me again as if I was the one holding her up, not the other way around.

"Yeah," I said, hopping to my feet. I turned to Darnell, who was now wide awake. "Nice meeting you."

"Same." He gave me a quick hug.

"Thanks again, Gavin," Paris said as she rushed me out the door.

"Guuurrrllll!" Paris exclaimed when we got into the car. "Guuurrrllll!"

"Is that a good *girl* or a bad one?" I asked, putting my home address into the GPS system and easing out of Gavin's circular driveway. I was still sleepy and couldn't wait to get home to get in my bed.

"It's a damn good one." Paris leaned her head back against the headrest. "I gotta come back and visit you more often. Daaammmnn! I ain't been slayed like that in a minute."

"I'm glad you enjoyed yourself."

"Oh, I did. I feel like I hit the fucking lottery. That man made me feel so good." She sighed.

"You definitely ran up on a unicorn, that's for sure." I laughed. "I've lived here my entire life, and I can tell you there ain't many Gavins around here."

"How was ol' boy? What was his name? Daniel?" Paris nudged me with her arm.

"Darnell, and he was a nice guy. We chatted for a while, watched a movie, then fell asleep." I gave her the highlights of my night, which were significantly less eventful than hers.

"Fell asleep? That's it?"

"Yeah, pretty much." I turned toward her and was shocked when I saw her staring at me with her jaw open.

"Was he a whack kisser? Wait, did he have a small dick? Sometimes the little-dick dudes have great stroke game, and they can get you where you're trying to go. I talk a lot of shit, but size doesn't always matter. It's all about how a guy works it."

I laughed. "I didn't kiss him, and I don't know what size his dick is."

"I'm so confused right now. He was a nice-looking guy, and he seemed sweet. Plus, he was looking at your ass the whole time while y'all were dancing, so I don't think he's gay. Being around Rio, my gaydar is real."

"Nah, I don't think he's gay," I concurred.

"So, what was the problem? You got a boyfriend?"

"I wish," I replied. "But I did give him my number, so we'll see."

Paris turned all the way around in her seat to face me. "Wait, are *you* gay? No judgment if you are. I mean, I'm here for you. I kept Rio's secret for five years before he came out."

"No, I'm not gay, Paris."

"Okay, that's good to know . . ." she said. "So are you bi or pansexual? What exactly are you?"

"I'm straight. I'm just not in a rush. I wanna make sure he's the right guy," I confessed.

Paris's face registered more shock than if I had told her I was gay. "Bitch, you're a virgin?"

"Yes, I am," I said, holding my head high. "And proud of it."

"Shut the front door! How old are you?"

"Twenty-two."

"Fuck. I didn't think there were any virgins left over the age of eighteen. What the fuck are you waiting for? A marriage proposal?"

"That'd be nice, but not necessary."

"Aren't you curious?"

It wasn't as if I'd planned to be a virgin this long, but the fact that the entire town where I grew up knew that I was Larry Duncan's daughter and Curtis and Kenny's little sister had not given me many options as far as dating was concerned. Guys were cool, but they definitely stayed a far enough distance away to let me know that they wanted no parts of my brothers. Even when I went to finishing school, the opportunity never seemed to present itself, at least not one I was going to be happy about for the rest of my life. Unlike a lot of my girlfriends and classmates, I wanted my first time to be with someone I loved. I'd been waiting for the right person. The one who made me feel butterflies when he looked at me because we were in love. I wanted more than sex. I wanted love, and yes, I want to be married.

"Of course I'm curious. It just hasn't happened yet, but it will," I said attempting to reassure myself more than Paris. "When I meet the right person."

"Wow, that's some real nineteen sixties shit. Wait 'til Sasha and Rio hear this." Paris shook her head in disbelief, embarrassing me a little.

"Paris," I said hesitantly. "Do you think we can keep this between you and me?"

She considered it for a minute and then gave me an affirmative nod. "Sure. But I gotta tell Rio. We don't have any secrets."

"Okay," I replied.

"Don't worry," she said. "You can trust him."

We drove in silence for a few minutes. I was thinking about how relieved I was that Paris hadn't made a bigger deal about my confession. I had always felt like my northern cousins were so chic and worldly compared to me. I usually felt like a country bumpkin around them. So, I was pleasantly surprised that Paris was not judging me for what she no doubt saw as a weird lifestyle choice.

"So, what else have you missed out on in life?" she asked.

I thought about all of the dangerous missions they'd done in glamorous places ever since they graduated from Chi's Finishing School, and I felt slighted in a way. I heard stories about yachts and tropical islands, along with super hot guys. To me, they were more like female versions of James Bond than just Duncan cousins. I'd followed the same path and attended the same school, gained the same skills, but unlike all of my cousins, I hadn't done much of anything other than tagging along with Curtis when he let me.

"Being part of the family business," I answered.

Sasha

12

I hadn't even realized how much I needed a fun-filled trip to Miami until after it was over. Shopping at the boutiques in the design district, a full day of treatments at the hotel spa, and of course, non-stop partying. My friends and I had VIP status at every club and bar we went to, thanks to Rio's friend Sebastian, who ran a handful of clubs down there. The food, the liquor, and of course, the sexual escapades with a player from the Miami HEAT who shall remain nameless, made for a great and memorable excursion that left me both satisfied and exhausted. By the time I arrived home, I was looking forward to a hot shower and an all-day nap.

"Thanks, DJ," I said to the security detail who'd picked me up from the airport and carried my bags inside the house.

"No problem, Sasha. You want me to take them upstairs for you?"

"Sure, I'd appreciate that," I replied. "You can put them right near my bedroom door."

"I gotcha." He picked up the two large Louis Vuitton suitcases along with the matching duflfle bag and headed up the stairs.

All of the cars were in the driveway, so I expected someone to be home, but the house was noticeably quiet. That was odd, because it was after eight a.m. and there was no sign of my baby cousins running around like they'd lost their minds. Paris's bad-ass five-year-old son, Jordan, was always the ringleader, and that boy never stopped moving.

I was about to head into the kitchen when Harris rolled his wheelchair into the foyer.

"Hey, Harris, where is everyone?" I asked.

"London's God knows where, Rio's probably 'sleep, and I don't know where Sonya and Junior are. The rest of them left about ten o'clock last night."

"Left for where?"

"They went to Waycross."

"Waycross? Jesus, who died?" I panicked. Other than Aunt Chippy, the family hardly ever went to the small Georgia town where the Duncan family had originated. I was confused because no one had called or told me anything.

"You haven't heard?"

"Heard what? I just got back."

"That crazy-ass motherfucker Larry escaped from the looney bin again yesterday." His tone and demeanor was just as sour as the look on his face.

I stared at him for a moment, hoping he would smile, confirming that it was some kind of sick joke or a prank that he was playing on me. Harris was enough of an asshole that it wasn't above him to do that.

"You're lying." My jaw clenched from the tension rising inside of me.

"Why the hell would I lie about something like that?" He frowned. "I'm very much telling the truth. Your uncle Larry is free as a bird. Somewhere out there running from the law. They had the U.S. Marshals and the FBI here and everything. So, LC and them packed up and went to Waycross to warn Nee Nee. Well, not London. She stayed behind to fuck her boyfriend."

I had no idea what his last statement meant, and I was too concerned with everything else he'd revealed to even care. Uncle Larry was out and on the run, and no one had bothered to tell me. The tension I'd felt was now replaced with anger.

"I'll get the truck and meet you out front," DJ yelled as he came rushing down the stairs. Harris and I both looked up to where he'd come from.

Junior was standing at the top of the staircase. "Ok, DJ. We're on our way down."

"Junior, is it true?" I asked him as I headed up there.

"Is what true?"

"Harris said Uncle Larry broke out of the hospital and they can't find him." I repeated what I'd been told moments before.

"That's what they say." Junior seemed distracted.

"Why the hell didn't anyone call me?" I shouted. "Don't y'all think I should've known this shit? The man that killed our"—I quickly corrected myself—"my mother is on the fucking loose."

He hadn't caught my slip. His eyes were full of sympathy as he touched my arm. "Look, Sasha. I'm sorry. I thought Pop called you, I swear. If I had known, I woulda called you myself. You know how I felt about Aunt Donna. I loved her. She was my godmother."

No, she was your mother, I thought. *Our mother!*

"Look, Junior, I need to talk to you. There is something you should know." It was time for him to know what I already knew.

"Sasha, I know you're hurting, and I do wanna talk to you, but I can't talk about this right now."

I was about to cuss him out for blowing me off until Sonya came out of the bedroom.

"Junior, it's another one!" she moaned.

Junior rushed to his wife's side. "Okay, baby, that means they're five minutes apart. I called the doctor, and DJ is already waiting outside with the truck. Let's go."

"Oh, shit! She's having the baby? You need me to help get her downstairs?" I offered. There was a lot going on, but Junior and Sonya having a baby took precedent.

"No, I got her." Junior put his arm around Sonya and guided her down the circular staircase. "Can you call Mom and Pop and let them know what's going on?"

"Sure," I told him. "Good luck, Sonya."

"Thanks," she whispered.

I watched them walk out the front door, then went into my bedroom. I took my phone from my back pocket to call my aunt and uncle, but I couldn't. Anger took over. Why the fuck was I expected to let them know something important was happening, but no one felt the need to tell me shit? The monster who'd taken the life of my mother was roaming the streets, but no one had taken the time to even send me a fucking text.

I went into the back of my closet and reached onto the top shelf, removing the keepsake box. I carried it to my bed and sat down before opening it. Inside were the few precious mementos I owned: photos of my parents' wedding and other holidays and happy times before they divorced, and copies of both their obituaries. I didn't bother to wipe the tears that fell. Both my parents were gone, taken away by violence, and all I had now was their memory and my brother who didn't even know he was my brother.

"Momma, that bastard may have escaped, but I promise, I'm going to find him and avenge your death. And I'm going to make sure your letter is delivered when the time is right. You and Daddy are gone, and I'm an orphan. No one else cares, but I do." I sobbed as I stared at the photo of my mother in my hand. Our relationship was one filled with ups and downs and plenty of fights, but I loved her, and she was still my mother. I'd been distraught and guilt-ridden over my mother's death, so I'd given into this psychiatric prison hospital bullshit once before, but family or not, Larry Duncan was going to pay for taking my mother from me.

Harris

13

The steps I took with the walker were slow but steady. I'd gained the strength to stand a few weeks prior, and my initial progress had been gradual. Now, I'd moved up from standing to taking a few assisted steps with a walker to using the walker on my own to cross the room. I didn't tell Carol, my physical therapist, the real reason for my enthusiasm, which was that I was taking steps to save my marriage. Finding London with that motherfucker Daryl was one thing, but her threat of divorce was entirely another. Divorce meant leaving my kids and the house I'd lived in for thirteen years in disgrace, not to mention the fact that I'd probably lose my job in the long run. I'd worked too hard to become an accepted part of the Duncan family, and to have it ripped away from me by some brain-dead Neanderthal like Daryl Graham was not going to happen.

"Great job, Harris. I've never seen you work so hard." Carol grinned as she watched me. "I can't believe how far you've come in the last few weeks. You're really motivated."

"I told you I've got a daddy-daughter dance coming up that I plan on attending. I want to surprise my daughter Mariah." I grunted with the effort to take another step. "The two of us are going to waltz the night away."

"Well, let's not get ahead of ourselves. We've got a long way to go before you dance."

"Yeah, I know, but I love my kid, and I don't plan on disappointing her."

Although the feeling had returned to my lower extremities, I hadn't mentioned it to anyone other than Carol because I had originally planned to utilize my wheelchair status to my advantage for as long as possible. Standing in front of London when things got heated had ended that opportunity, so I had to take things in a different direction. To start with, I was really going to have to play the victim with this divorce shit. I would place the blame squarely on London's shoulders, especially with the kids. I also knew that I would need a powerful ally in my corner. So, I set my sights on the one person London respected more than anyone: her father. Getting LC to side with me would take extreme measures, but I knew where all the bodies were buried—literally—so I had some sway. Now, I just had to keep up appearances and show what a good husband and father I truly was.

"You keep this up and you'll be ready for Father of the Year," Carol said. "Look, I have to run into the office and do a Zoom session. I'll be back in twenty. Think you can do five more laps?"

"I can do ten if you want."

"No, five is good for now."

Once she was gone, I focused on finishing the five laps, taking slow steps. Suddenly, the walker went flying forward, and my body crumped to the ground. Looking up, I understood why.

"What the fuck do you want?" I shouted at Daryl, who had obviously kicked my walker from behind.

"Damn, it's true. You really can walk." Daryl leered at me, both hands balled into fists. He was obviously there to intimidate me.

"What are you doing here?" I stared venomously at him, grabbing the walker to pull myself up from the ground.

"I came to give you fair warning," he replied.

"Leave me alone." I pulled myself to a standing position, leaning against the walker. "I mean it."

"I'm not going anywhere until I've said my piece."

Daryl looked determined, so I didn't bother to stop him. Better to let him get whatever off his chest as soon as possible so he could get the fuck away from me.

"I'm glad to see you on your feet, actually, Harris. It makes this an easier conversation to have. I don't have to look down at you when I tell you this."

"Tell me what? There ain't shit you need to tell me." I gripped the sides of the walker tightly. "Except you're going to leave my wife alone."

"Not gonna happen. But I'll tell you what is gonna happen if you ever put your hands on her again."

"And what's that?" I snapped back. "I'm not scared of you."

"You should be, you little bitch!" As soon as the words left his mouth, Daryl wrapped his hands around my neck the same way I'd gripped London's the night before. He yanked me six inches off the ground towards him. I might have said I wasn't scared of him, which I wasn't. I was terrified.

"Get the fuck off me, motherfucker!"

"Not until I have my say." With his free hand, Daryl took out a switchblade and held it against my throat. "Now, as London's friend, I'm warning your ass that if you ever touch her again, it won't just be your legs you can't feel. I will make sure your ass won't be able to use your body from the neck down."

My heart was beating so fast that I wondered if I was going into cardiac arrest. I gasped for air, both from fear and the pressure of the fingers crushing my larynx. Glancing around, I prayed that Carol or someone else would come into the damn room and save me from the man threatening me. I was unable to talk, scream, or do anything other than moan, so that was what I did.

"Shut the fuck up and listen," Daryl growled. "Now, you're going to leave London the fuck alone, and you're going to keep your mouth shut. Do you understand?"

I nodded as best I could.

"Good, because if you don't, I promise your wife will become a widow, and I'll be raising those beautiful girls of yours, you little bitch."

He released me, and I fell to the ground. As he put the knife away and slipped out of the room, I lay there, gasping for air. He'd left me with a painful new reality. As long as Daryl Graham was anywhere around, I didn't have a chance at keeping my family.

Roman

14

Curtis and I strolled down the driveway about eight o'clock in the morning, laughing and stumbling after one of the best nights of my entire life. There are a lot of ways a man can bond with another man, but having an orgy with five of the finest women in Waycross sure as hell had to be one of the best.

"Dude." I stopped about twenty feet from the porch. "I still can't believe we just did that. I mean, that was like some bucket list shit." I gave him a humbled smile. "Thank you."

"Ain't no need to thank me, cuzzo." Curtis wrapped his arm around my shoulder, chuckling as we continued to walk. "You the one who gave them two hundred a piece and came up with the idea."

"Yeah, but I didn't think they was gonna say yes." I was still in shock.

"Roman, this is Waycross, Georgia. Those girls wanted to fuck us to start with. Throw in a couple dollars, some liquor, and some weed, and you don't know what these girls gonna do. We in the middle of a recession down here."

"Bullshit. I got video proof of what they will do." I laughed, holding up my phone proudly.

"Yeah, well, you might wanna delete that shit. What happens in Waycross stays in Waycross. Remember I gotta live here."

"Shit, you ain't gotta worry. I might be moving down here myself," I replied as we walked in the door. I stopped talking about that shit right away, but not because I was afraid someone might overhear me. The smell of breakfast overwhelmed my nose.

"My God, that smells good."

"Momma cooked breakfast," Curtis replied, "and I'm starved."

"Me too."

We rushed into the dining room to see a smorgasbord of foods from eggs, bacon, sausage, home fries, grits, and fried apples, along with fluffy buttermilk biscuits. The whole family was sitting around the table, feeding their faces.

"You boys have a seat," Aunt Nee Nee said, and we complied right away, grabbing plates and gobbling up the food as if it were our last meal on earth. In addition to tasting good, the food was the perfect remedy for those of us suffering from a hangover. I didn't know where Paris and Lauryn had gone the night before, but it was obvious that they'd had a pretty good time themselves.

After breakfast, I went straight to bed and didn't wake up until late afternoon, around four, when I ventured outside to find my father sitting on the porch swing, sipping on a cup of coffee. I sat down next to him, and we both stared out at the field. As crazy as it sounds, and maybe it was because I'd never had a man in my life, but I cherished moments like this. He was slowly becoming the most important person in my life, and I'd do just about anything for him. Oddly enough, I also felt quite at home in my father's hometown. I wasn't sure if it was the fresh air, the good-ass food, or hanging with my newfound cousin and my new friends at Big Shirley's, but I was enjoying myself immensely. I'd been born and raised in the city and never imagined being a country boy. I wondered if possibly it was in my DNA.

The house that my father and his brothers grew up in was long gone, replaced by the one Uncle Larry had built in the eighties that Aunt Nee Nee, Curtis, and Lauryn still lived in. It wasn't as large as ours in New York, but it was nice as hell. Not to mention the yard was huge enough to build three other houses and still have land left over.

My father and I watched while the kids took turns riding on the tractor and playing in the open space.

"It's my turn, Jordan!" Mariah yelled.

"I just got on," Jordan told her.

"Actually, it's Mimi's turn," my dad shouted, then Curtis picked MiMi up and placed her in front of him on the tractor.

"You ready, baby girl?" Curtis asked.

"Yup." Mimi nodded.

"Curtis, you know if anything happens to London's baby, she's gonna kill you!" Lauryn yelled, causing all of us to laugh as Curtis pulled off.

"LC! LC!" My mother burst through the screen door onto the porch with Aunt Nee Nee behind her. "Oh my God, Sonya had the baby." She held up her cell phone.

"What? When?" Paris asked from the far side of the porch as we all gathered around and stared at the picture of my brother beaming, holding his newborn baby girl.

"An hour ago," Mom said. "I can't believe this."

"Well, I guess we need to get ready and head on home and see our new grandchild," Pop added.

"Yes, we do."

"I hate to see y'all leave, but I understand." Nee Nee sighed. "I wish y'all could stay a little longer."

"We'll definitely be back," Paris stated warmly. "Lauryn and I still have some unfinished business down in Jacksonville."

"No doubt. Cousin Curtis and the folks down at Big Shirley's made me feel real welcomed last night," I said. "Real welcomed."

"I bet they did." Mom playfully hit my arm. "You need to stay outta there!"

I smiled and looked at her, then said the words that I'd been thinking since I woke up. "I'm just saying, I think I wanna hang back and stay in Waycross for a little bit. That is if it's all right with Aunt Nee Nee, of course."

I glanced over at my aunt, ignoring the unhappy look on my mother's face.

"Baby, you can stay here as long as you want. I'd love to have you here." Nee Nee grinned.

"You sure about this, Roman?" My mother frowned. "I mean, you've only—"

"I wanna stay with Aunt Nee Nee, too." Mariah skipped over and told us, putting her arm around Nee Nee, who beamed with pride. "She's gonna teach me how to cook."

"I sure will," Nee Nee replied.

"Me too." Jordan joined them.

"Y'all can stay too," Nee Nee said, then added, "If it's all right with your grandparents. And your momma, Jordan."

"Oh, he can stay as long as he wants," Paris volunteered. Obviously, she was ready to get rid of Jordan's bad ass for a while. I loved my nephew, but he was a handful. "Just send me the bill for anything he breaks."

"Then it's settled. The kids are staying and spending the summer in Waycross," my father announced. I have to admit that surprised me, but if he felt the kids would be safe down there, I wasn't about to argue. However, from the look on my mother's face, I knew she had something to say.

Mom sighed. "LC, maybe we should talk to London first."

"You think she's gonna object?" He laughed. "She will probably welcome having a break with everything she's got going on."

"That's true." My mother looked over at Aunt Nee Nee. "I just don't want it to be too much on you, Nee."

"It won't be. This'll give me a chance to enjoy your grandchildren since it don't look like I'll be getting any of my own anytime soon." She glanced over at Curtis. "And don't you get any ideas, Lauryn."

"Yeah, don't. Trust me, girl," Paris chimed in.

"Besides, I'll be here to help," Curtis said.

"And Lauryn," Aunt Nee Nee volunteered.

"Um, not really." Lauryn spoke up.

"Whatchu mean, not really?" Aunt Nee Nee raised an eyebrow at her daughter.

"Uncle LC, I was gonna ask if I could go back to New York with y'all." Lauryn took a deep breath, turning to her mother, who did not look happy at all. "Just for a visit. Paris promised to take me shopping."

"Now, you know you're not used to that big city life, and—"

My dad interrupted Aunt Nee Nee and moved so that he and Lauryn were face to face. "Of course you can, Lauryn. I'm sure Paris and Sasha would love to show you around."

The apprehensive look on my aunt's face let us know that she wasn't with that idea at all.

My mother must've noticed as well because she quickly asked permission. "Is that all right with you, Nee?"

Aunt Nee Nee paused, staring at Lauryn for a minute before she answered. "She's a grown woman, so if that's what she wants to do, I can't stop her," she said, making it clear that she wished she could.

"Well, I guess you need to go and get packed then, little cousin," Paris told Lauryn.

"As a matter of fact, anyone that's heading back to New York needs to go ahead and pack now," Dad stated.

While everyone else went inside, my father and I remained on the porch.

"You sure about staying here, Roman? That's what you want to do?" he asked me.

"Yes, sir, I do. I'm really digging it here. You don't want me to stay?"

"No, I'm perfectly fine with it," he said. "I'm actually kind of glad. None of your other siblings enjoy it the way you have. Plus, it'll be some added protection and help around here just in case Larry shows up."

"So, real talk. Are you worried about Uncle Larry?"

"Not worried, per se, but I guess you could say I'm optimistically cautious. Let's hope for the best but remain aware because Larry can be rather . . . unpredictable." He reached into his jacket and took out a gun that he handed to me. "Take this. Again, it's just a precaution in case you need it. Like your aunt Nee Nee, children, for some reason, have a calming effect on Larry. He won't hurt them, but just in case . . ."

"I feel you, Dad." I took the gun and placed it into my waistband and covered it with my shirt. A large part of me was proud that he even trusted me enough to give it to me. I'd had my share of gun play out on the streets, but nothing like the rest of my siblings. "And don't worry. I got this. Ain't nothing going to happen to my nieces and nephew."

"I know you. I trust you, son. The more I get to know you, the more I see that you truly are a Duncan."

I nodded. "Through and through. I may be new to this, but I'm true to this."

"Good. And make sure you call me if anything happens or anyone shows up."

He hugged me and for a moment, I felt a lump in my throat. I'd really grown to love him in the short time he'd been in my life, and sometimes it choked me up to think of all that I'd missed by being taken from them so young. I'd never had a father figure before, so this bond I was developing with him felt like a gift I'd never expected to receive. I didn't know what my Uncle Larry was capable of, but I would protect my newfound family with everything I had.

Nee Nee

15

"You sure you okay with this, Nee? I know you're trying to be helpful, but those kids can be a handful. Believe me, I know," Chippy said as we drove down Oak Street toward McDonald's on our way home from Walmart. Chippy had insisted that before she left for New York, she would fill up the house with groceries and snacks for the kids.

"Girl, I'm positive. You see how much fun they've had over the past couple of days, and I could use the company. Especially now that Lauryn's leaving with y'all." My voice drifted off. I was still a bit unsettled about my only daughter visiting New York. Having her away for so long in school had been hard enough. In my heart, I knew this talk about a visit was just that. A bunch of talk. I knew my daughter, and once she got a whiff of the big city, she'd be gone for good. The same thing had happened to Sasha. She came to visit Chippy and LC for a month and never left, not that her Momma was too concerned. I, on the other hand, would love it if my kids lived with me forever. But I knew I couldn't keep her with me all her life. I had to let her go.

"I know how you feel," Chippy said as if she had been reading my thoughts. I glanced over and saw the sad expression on her face as she stared out the window.

"Do you? All your kids still live with you. Mine are going to be scattered to the wind. Kenny's gone God knows where. Lauryn's been gone for three years, and now she's goin' up there with you. And Curtis might as well be a nomad with all this bounty hunting shit he does."

It wasn't my intention to sound rude, but once I'd said it, I realized it may have come off that way. There was truth to my statement, though. Every single one of Chippy's children lived in that compound of theirs.

Chippy whipped her head around, and she frowned at me. "At least Lauryn's been with you since the day she was born. I just got my baby back a year ago, and now I'm leaving him here with you."

"Is that what this is all about? Roman?"

Seeing the tears in her eyes, I pressed the gas and sped down the street, barely slowing down as I turned into the parking lot. The building looked quite different than it had decades ago, but there was still a feeling of nostalgia and comfort as we sat in front of it. It once housed my first restaurant, Nee Nee's Chicken and Waffles, right across the street from Big Shirley's.

I reached for her hand, squeezing it. "Now, tell me how things have been with my newfound nephew, girl. I swear he looks so much like Rio that it's scary."

"He does. They're the mirror image of each other, minus the goatee and Rio's colored hair," she said.

"How has it been with him living at the house? I know it must have been a hard transition for you all." I reached into the back seat and grabbed the bag of snacks we'd picked up from Walmart earlier, then placed it between us. Snacking and chatting had always been our thing.

Chippy took a deep breath and stared at the chocolate bar that she'd taken out of the bag. "It's actually been nice. He gets along great with everyone so far. I think everyone's just happy he's there."

"And what about you and him? How y'all get along?"

"We're getting to know each other. But I've quickly learned that my baby boy is way more like Paris than he is Rio. And in saying that, he gravitates more to LC. He's a firecracker and a little rough around the edges, but he's kind and loving." Chippy looked me in the eye and smiled. "Sometimes, I get jealous of LC, I'm not gonna lie. Roman is always trying to prove himself to his father, and me, well, I'm just there, Nee."

"I understand, but you are not just there. Like you said, that's your baby."

"Which is why I'm scared to leave him, Nee Nee." Chippy became serious. "Roman lived a street life, and I don't want him to go back. I want to keep him close and know that he's safe and protected."

"I know you're worried, but from what I gather from talking to Roman, he's just as happy to have found y'all as y'all are to find him," I reassured her. "True, he may have had a rough upbringing and be from the streets, but like you said, he's smart. He ain't gonna risk losing what he's gained in becoming a Duncan. One thing we both know about them Duncan men, they may be strong willed, but they also have strong love, especially when it comes to family."

"You're right. At least he'll be here with you and Curtis," she said. "Just keep an eye on my babies. All of them."

"And you make sure you keep an eye on mine." Leaning over the bag of snacks, I gave my beloved sister-in-law a tight hug.

Sasha

16

I was sitting at the dining room table, cleaning my gun when I heard the front door open and the sound of voices. The family had returned. My emotions were still all over the place about their lack of contact, and I needed an explanation. Even more frustrating was that Rio, of all people, had tried his best to avoid the subject when he finally came downstairs. Usually he'd be the first one running his mouth about the latest gossip or drama that effected the family, but this time, he could barely make eye contact with me.

Just as I stood to go and seek answers, my aunt and uncle walked in.

"Sasha, honey, how are you? When did you get back from your trip?" Aunt Chippy greeted me with a hug.

"Yesterday," I answered, my eyes zoned in on Uncle LC.

"How was Miami?" he asked.

"It was fine. But I do need to talk to you, though, Uncle LC."

"Sure." He nodded. "Just give me a minute to change out of these clothes and check in with Junior. He's at the hospital."

"Yeah, okay."

"Is something wrong?" Aunt Chippy asked, sensing my mood.

You tell me. I mean, where do I start? Your psycho-ass brother-in-law escaped captivity, and no one seems concerned. Of course shit is wrong, I thought.

Instead of snapping, I decided to remain as calm as possible. "Well, I don't understand why nobody—"

Aunt Chippy's ringing cellphone interrupted me. She looked down at it. "It's Junior."

She rushed out of the dining room with Uncle LC on her heels. Once again, it was obvious that everything and everyone else took priority over me. I went back to my seat and resumed cleaning my gun.

"What's up, Sasha?" Paris sauntered into the dining room. "Look who we brought back from Waycross."

I glanced up and was shocked to see my younger cousin, Lauryn. The last time I'd seen her, she was a teenager. I had no idea how old she was now, but she had definitely grown up. She looked so much like her older brother Curtis: same complexion, green eyes, wavy hair, and dimpled smile, but softer and prettier.

"Hi, Sasha. It's so good to see you again."

I allowed Lauryn to hug me, but my reception damn sure wasn't warm or welcoming, something Paris easily picked up on.

"What's got you looking stank? Your Miami vacay wasn't fun?" Paris asked.

"It was fine," I answered, then looked at Lauryn. "What's up with you?"

"Well, Lauryn finally graduated top of her class from Chi's, and she's come to visit. Thought we might take her out and show her the town," Paris answered as if Lauryn needed a spokesperson. "Right, cuzzo?"

"That's right."

"Where's Curtis? Shouldn't you and him be dealing with this situation with your father?" I asked, salty.

"No," Paris said. "She wanted to come back to New York, and Daddy said it was okay. He's not too worried about Uncle Larry. I mean, he even let Jordan, Mariah, and Mimi stay with Aunt Nee Nee."

"What?" My head turned quickly toward Paris. "He shouldn't have don't that."

"Girl, please. I needed a break from Jordan. Daddy knows what he's doing. I love him, but my son is a little monster sometimes. I mean, Curtis and Roman are there with them. But isn't it cool that Lauryn is here?" Paris put her arm around Lauryn. "It's about time we showed them some girl power around here!"

"Not really." I cut my eyes, feeling the anger returning.

"What's your problem? Our baby cousin is all grown up and can now hang out with us," Paris bragged. "And I'm kid free for a while, too? We def gonna turn up!"

"Sorry, turning up is the last thing on my mind. I got more important shit to deal with right now, unlike y'all." I picked my gun up from the table and walked out.

Twenty minutes later, I was sitting in the gazebo in the back yard, trying to cool off, when Uncle LC joined me. He'd changed from his slacks and button-down shirt into a sweat suit and sneakers, perfect for the cool evening breeze.

"So, tell me, what's got you so wired up?" He sat beside me.

"A lot." I exhaled and turned toward him. "Why didn't anyone call and tell me about Larry?"

"Well, your aunt and I didn't want to bother you while you were on your trip," he explained.

"Bother me?" I balked. "You act like this wasn't a big deal."

"It wasn't."

"It was a big enough deal for the U.S. Marshalls to come knocking on our door. And it was a big enough deal for you to pack up the whole family and go to Waycross. I'm so confused by all of this." I shook my head.

"Looking back, we should've let you know. We certainly weren't trying to keep it from you. I hope you don't think that's what it was," Uncle LC said. "At that moment, we just felt that after everything you've dealt with, you needed some time away to enjoy, and we didn't want to disrupt that from happening. I'm sorry, Sasha. It was an error in judgment."

Hearing Uncle LC's reasoning and apology was enough for me to get past his lack of communication. The damage had been done, and nothing would change that, but his heart was in the right place. Besides, there were other more important things for us to deal with.

"You're back now, so what's the plan? How are we going to get him? I know Curtis and Roman aren't here, but are we gonna have a family meeting?"

To my surprise, a confused look came across his face. "A meeting? No."

"Why not? Aren't we going to go look for him?"

"Not yet, Sasha. Well, not right now. I don't think we need to do that." He shook his head.

"What? Uncle LC, this is Larry that we're talking about. I hope you don't think the Marshals or the FBI are gonna find him. They're not."

"You're probably right. But I don't think Larry's a threat to anyone right now."

"The man killed my mother! Or did you forget that? Doesn't that make him a threat?" I tensed. "I get it, no one really cared about my mother. But the fact of the matter is, I did. And I'm not gonna let him get away with it. You promised me that once he was locked away, he'd stay there."

Uncle LC sighed. "And I believed that he would. That facility was state of the art and had maximum security."

"Well, obviously it wasn't secure enough. We have to go after him." I stood, grabbing my gun from the bench beside me.

"Sasha, listen to me. I know my brother. He's on the run now, but eventually, he will show back up at home, and when he does, your Aunt Nee Nee will let us know, and we'll take care of it."

"How can you be so naive? That man has killed countless people."

"That man is my brother." He said it with so much conviction and a hint of devotion that made me want to scream.

"You know what? Don't even worry about it. I'll take care of it myself."

Uncle LC stood and faced me. "What do you mean?"

"I mean since my mother's killer isn't a priority to anyone else around here, I'll go find him myself. I'm more than capable." I clipped the magazine into the bottom of my firearm and shoved it into my holster as I stormed off.

"Sasha, wait!" Uncle LC called after me, but I continued walking. We'd done enough talking for the day.

Paris

17

Lauryn and I showed up to Rio's rooftop lounge right around the end of happy hour, and shit was popping. It wasn't unusual for the bar to have a decent crowd, but it was so packed we could barely make our way across the floor to the back of the club and into the VIP lounge, where we found Rio flirting with a very sexy Spanish guy. I mean, he was sexy enough for me to push my brother aside, and Lauryn looked like she was thinking the same thing. I'd seen my brother with some good-looking men, but this one took home the prize.

"Damn, what kind of drink specials y'all got going on in here tonight?" I interrupted him, plopping down on the very expensive soft gray leather sofa. "Folks so deep in here, you'd think you were giving away a PlayStation 10 or whatever number they're up to now."

Rio laughed as he gave me and Lauryn hugs. "Girl, it's been like this all night. It's crazy. I think folks have finally decided that the pandemic is over."

"So, who's your friend?" I asked, smiling over at the gorgeous man.

He turned to the guy. "Oh, this is Mario. Mario, this is my sister Paris and my cousin Lauryn."

"Nice to meet you." Mario smiled at us politely then looked back to my brother. "Rio, honey, thanks for the drink. I'll see you at my place later."

Mario leaned over and tongued my brother down like it was the last kiss he'd ever have in his life, then stood up and walked away. Both Lauryn and I stood there with our mouths gaped open as we watched him walk away.

"I see you, Rio." Lauryn grinned, then took one final glance at his friend making his way through the crowd. "You got the finest one in here, don't you?"

"Oh, lawwwd. First Paris, then Sasha, and now you, Lauryn. Why are y'all clocking my every move? I'm trying to keep my shit on the low."

"As fine as he is, you can't keep him on the low. That's some buy-a-ring-and-take-him-home-to-momma shit right there." I laughed so hard I started to have a coughing fit.

"Mmm-hmmm, he got a straight brother? Because he can get it. Anyone related to someone that fine can make a new woman out of me any time they want," Lauryn said boldly, surprising the hell out of me.

"Damn, looks like you got the stamp of approval, Rio. Should I buy a wedding dress?" I teased.

Rio ignored me and looked over at Lauryn. "And what are you doing rolling with her anyway? You really must enjoy living life on the wild side, Lauryn."

"I ain't saying all that. But how could I resist a few nights in the city with Paris?" Lauryn grinned.

"Uh, tell her no thanks?" Rio teasingly suggested. "I'm sure you've heard enough tragic stories to know that this girl is crazy."

"We had a blast when we hung out back home. She doesn't seem too crazy to me." Lauryn looked around. "Besides, it finally gave me a chance to check out Vertigo. This spot is dope."

"Thanks. I'm glad you like it." Rio looked at me. "And I'm glad y'all came through."

"Okay, where's this package you have for me?" I asked.

Rio had sent me a text earlier, telling me he had received a delivery that I needed to pick up at the lounge. I made a habit out of not letting people know where I lived. So, I figured it was some guy I'd messed with trying to get back in with an expensive gift.

"We have to go to the office," Rio said. "Come with me. I don't know how you gonna get this shit home."

"What the hell is it?" I asked.

"You gotta see this shit for yourself," he answered.

"Stop playing games, Rio. Tell me what it is. I don't know why you're being extra."

"Nope!"

Lauryn and I followed him out of the VIP and down the hallway to his office. Rio dramatically opened the door.

"Oh, shit." Lauryn gasped.

"Exactly." Rio nodded and folded his arms. "And she got the nerve to call me extra. This some extra shit."

It was obvious why Rio couldn't bring the package to me. And he was right to wonder how the hell I was going to get this shit home. I stared at what had to be at least twenty crystal vases throughout his office, all holding a dozen or more roses. While Rio and Lauryn were amazed by the quantity, I was stunned by something else. It wasn't the number of flowers that had been sent, but the type.

"That is a *lot* of flowers. And I've never seen roses this color before." Lauryn entered and picked up one of the bouquets and brought it out to me. "They're freaking gorgeous. I didn't even know roses came in navy blue."

"They're royal blue Ecuadorian roses," I murmured.

"Sheesh. I guess Rio's not the only one getting laid tonight." Lauryn inhaled the scent of one of the roses. "Who sent them?"

I stared at the flowers she was holding and slowly shook my head. "I'm not sure."

I thought about the only person who'd ever sent those distinct roses to me. It had been years since I'd gotten them, and never in a million years did I think I'd receive them again. But here they were.

"Well, maybe there's a name on the card." Rio shrugged.

I glanced over at him. "There's a card? Why didn't you say that?"

"I'm saying it now." Rio sighed. "It's in my desk."

"You could've given me that first."

"I could have, but first I wanted to show you the damn florist showroom that was delivered." He reached into the drawer and presented me with a small royal blue gift bag. Sticking out was a card with *Paris* written in perfect calligraphy. Again, I stared without saying a word.

"Are you going to open it?" Lauryn asked.

Instead of opening the card first, I reached my hand in the bag and took out a silver gift box. Nervously, I opened it and stared

at the contents inside: a charm in the shape of the Empire State
Building. I dropped it, my heart racing.

"What is it?" Rio asked, bending over to pick it up.

As he studied the charm, I opened the card and read the six
words written inside: *Can't wait to see you soon.*

"Fuck!" I exhaled, letting the card float to the desk.

"What's wrong? You look like you've seen a ghost," Lauryn
said.

"I have."

Rio scrambled to pick up the card. "Oh, shit. This isn't from
who I think it is, is it?" Rio's voice was damn near a whisper. I
could see that he was just as freaked out as I was.

"That's what somebody wants me to believe," I snapped.

"But who? Other than me, who else would know this? You
haven't even told Sasha about this," Rio insisted, holding up the
charm.

"The roses, the note, the charm. Someone is fucking with me,
Ree. They want me to believe he's alive and in New York."

"But he can't be alive. You . . . you . . ."

"Yeah, I know. That's why I said someone is fucking with me."

"I ain't trying to be nosy, but can someone kinda fill me in on
who and what y'all talking about?" Lauryn asked.

I'd gotten so caught up in trying to solve the mystery sitting
in front of me that I'd damn near forgotten that Lauryn was
standing beside me. I turned and looked at her. "Someone is
trying to make me think my baby daddy wants to see me. The
roses were always his calling card whenever he went out of
town and wanted me to meet him. The charm is a symbol of the
destination that we would meet at."

"Whoa, sounds like one fascinating and romantic man, this
baby daddy of yours." Lauryn sighed.

"He was in the same line of work as us, only he was more work
for hire, the best in the business. Charismatic, charming, and
the body of a Greek god, plus he was smart as hell, spoke five
languages, and flew airplanes. He had the power to make even
me, the most jaded of women, fall in love with him."

"Wow. How long has it been since you've seen him?"

"That's something I'll never forget because that was the day my
son was conceived," I replied, looking around the room at the

roses. I wasn't normally the sentimental type, but I felt my eyes mist over a bit as I recalled the last time he and I were together. I could still remember the taste of his spearmint gum and the smell of his cologne from our last kiss goodbye. He was the only man I'd ever loved. Too bad it couldn't last.

"That was also the day I killed Niles Monroe."

LC

18

I tossed and turned all night. Whenever I dozed off, I'd have nightmares about Larry killing people, and when I was awake, I'd replay the conversation with Sasha over and over in my mind. In a way, I commiserated with her. I felt guilty as hell for leaving Larry out on the streets, but my gut told me it would be a lot worse if we went after him. What Sasha didn't understand was that by going after Larry, our entire family would most likely end up in a civil war, with Larry and Nee Nee and their kids on one side, and me, Chippy, and our family on the other. As highly trained as we were on our side, Larry's family and the two people he'd escaped with were trained as well and probably more ruthless. Not to mention the fact that we had more visible, vulnerable, and obvious targets, a lesson I'd learned from our last encounter.

Not able to sleep, I decided to go downstairs and have a slice of the chocolate cake Nee Nee had baked for us before we left Waycross. I cut a slice so big it would have had my wife lecturing me about healthy eating, poured myself a tall glass of lactose free milk, and sat down to enjoy it.

As I was finishing the cake, I saw motion out of the corner of my eye. Something or someone was outside on the gazebo. I checked the clock on the microwave. It was 4:23 a.m. I guessed I wasn't the only one having trouble sleeping that night. I washed my plate to get rid of the evidence, put the glass in the dishwasher, then turned off the kitchen light and headed out to the gazebo.

It was dark outside, but as I got closer to the gazebo, I saw the silhouette of the wheelchair and realized it was Harris. He was by himself, just sitting there, facing the pool.

"Hey, Harris." He didn't turn around or react, so I wasn't sure he'd heard me. "Harris, you all right, man?"

He still didn't answer, and I was becoming concerned. It turned out I had good reason to be worried. Just as I stepped onto the gazebo, he lifted his arm and placed a handgun under his chin.

"Whoa. Hold on, Harris," I said as I slowly stepped closer. There were tears streaming down his face. Shit, this was the last thing I'd expected, but I was glad I was there.

"Harris, listen to me." I forced myself to remain calm and cautious. "Whatever it is you're thinking about doing, you don't have to. I'm sure there are other solutions. We can get you some help."

"Get out of here, LC. I don't need any help, and you don't want to see this."

"You're right. I don't wanna see it, because you don't want to do this." I took another step.

"Don't come any closer."

"You need to talk to me, Harris," I pleaded. "Think about your kids. Think about your wife."

"Ain't nothing to talk about. She's divorcing me." He swiped at the pile of papers that was on his lap. "She had me served with these today. I'm losing my family, LC. I love my wife and my kids. There's nothing for me to live for anymore."

"That's not true, Harris. You have a lot to live for." I carefully placed my hand on his shoulder. "Your girls love you, and no matter what happens between you and London, you'll still have them. You're important to them and us, and we'll always be family."

"Tell that to them," he barked back at me, glaring across the pool to the pool house. "Your daughter's in there fucking your son's best friend."

I'd heard what he'd said, but it didn't make sense. "What are you talking about?"

Harris looked at me. "Your daughter is in the pool house fucking Daryl Graham, and she's been doing it ever since he came back from the dead."

I didn't know how true that was, but the man had a gun in his hand and was positioned to kill himself, so I was willing to say whatever I needed in order to stop him. "But if you do this, it's like you're giving up. Is that what you want, Harris? A man just doesn't let go of his family. He fights! You say you love London and your daughters. You don't wanna at least fight for them?"

"Fight?" Harris repeated.

"Yes, Harris, fight. You think my wife and I have lasted this long without a fight? You gotta fight for love," I said, sounding like a Baptist preacher right before altar call. All that was missing was a Hammond organ in the background.

"London wants Daryl, not some cripple in a wheelchair. I'm not a perfect man, LC, but I try. Even in this chair, I'm trying to get better to be a husband and a father. She just doesn't see that."

I took a few steps closer thinking that if I had to, I might be able to snatch the gun away.

"You've been through too much to go out like this, man. Ain't your family worth fighting for?"

"It is." Harris nodded slowly.

"Good, then you don't need this." I put my hand on the gun. "I'll deal with London and Daryl. I promise, if what you're telling me is true, this will be the last night this happens under my roof."

Harris allowed me to take it from his hands, then hung his head and sobbed. I put a hand on his shoulder and waited for him to pull himself together.

"Thank you, LC," he said a few seconds later. "I'm sorry you had to see me like this."

"It's okay." I sighed. "I'm just glad you aren't giving up."

"Now that I know you have my back, I won't," Harris said with a level of confidence that made me uneasy. Harris had always been a shrewd, calculating guy, and for some reason, I wasn't sure if I'd just been played.

"I do," I told him, making sure I took the gun with me as we exited the gazabo.

Between Larry's escape, dealing with the feds, Sasha's emotional pain, and now Harris and London's marriage woes, I needed another piece of that cake and a couple shots of tequila.

Curtis

19

The street was dimly lit as I eased my Jeep down G Street past the row of ragged houses with my lights turned off. My hands gripped the steering wheel as I squinted at the battered mailbox sitting in front of the house I was approaching. Between the darkness and the rusty-ass numbers, it was damn near impossible to see. After blinking several times and confirming my exact location on the GPS screen, I felt confident enough that I was at the right place.

"Fifty-seventeen. This is it," I whispered as I turned off the engine.

"Are you asking or telling?" Roman turned and looked at me. "Because you ain't sounding real confident right now, creeping down this dark-ass street in the middle of the night."

"And you sounding real scared for somebody who swore they were from the streets and insisted on coming with me to do this," I reminded him.

"Correction, I told you I ran shit in the Brooklyn streets. And I did. This right here is more like a shantytown. And there's a difference in being scared and being aware of where the fuck you are."

"A'ight, aware." I reached into the back seat and handed him one of the black nylon jackets. "Here, put this shit on."

"What the hell is this?" He held the jacket up and read the lettering on the back. "Fugitive Recovery Agent. Is that even a real thing, or did you get this shit off Amazon?"

I shook my head. "No, I didn't. It's legit and the thing that will keep law enforcement from shooting us if they happen to roll up. So, like I said, put that shit on."

"Got me out here looking like the man." Roman sighed as he slipped the jacket on, then looked at me. "We looking like bootleg-ass Starsky and Hutch out here."

There was no point in trying to hold onto the laughter I'd been suppressing. One thing I'd learned about my newfound cousin was that he was funny as shit. We stayed laughing.

"Shut the fuck up, Roman. You got your piece?"

"Yup." He pushed the jacket back to reveal the nine in his waistband.

"Bet, let's roll." I reached for the Glock under my seat before I eased my door open and stepped out.

We crouched down and remained low as we made our way toward the house. As we reached the front, Roman motioned with his head before taking off along the side, while I continued to the front entrance. I slowly opened the screen door, then turned the knob. I wasn't surprised that it was locked. But like the rest of the house, it was cheap and raggedy, so it didn't take much force for me to pop it open. I looked around to make sure I was still clear before stepping inside.

Even in the darkness, I could make out the scattered beer bottles and trash on the coffee table in the living room. I paused to look around, and when I heard movement coming from the kitchen, I raised my gun and aimed toward the doorway. That's when I saw Roman emerge. His ass had beaten me inside.

He shook his head at me. "Man, put that shit down."

Just as I was about to lower my weapon, a noise came from the hallway. I led the way, attempting to be as quiet as possible with each step on the creaky-ass wood floor. I peeped inside the bedroom door that was slightly open. Laying in the middle of the bed was a fat man, moaning and smiling as a woman in a bad wig gave him a blowjob. He was so caught up in getting his dick sucked that he didn't even realize I was standing beside him.

"Get the fuck up. Slowly," I said as Roman flicked on the lights.

"What the fuck?" Gus McNeil, the portly Italian man in his sixties, looked startled and confused. The orgasm he was in the middle of having was interrupted by the sudden bright lights and the barrel of my gun pressed against his temple.

"You heard him, bitch. Get the fuck up!" Roman stepped past me and grabbed the woman kneeling between Gus's legs. As he pulled her to her feet, we got a better look and realized it wasn't a woman after all. It was a man—an ugly one.

Roman looked at me with an expression that said *what the fuck?*

"Get your fat ass up," I told Gus, making sure my eyes didn't go any lower than his fat-ass shoulders.

"You're making a mistake. A big one. I don't know who the fuck you are, but you don't wanna do this," Gus panted.

"You're right. And I really don't wanna see your crusty balls, but since you won't get up, I don't have a choice." I sighed, reaching into my back pocket with my free hand and removing the zip ties.

Roman's gun remained on Gus while he held tight to the he-woman dick sucker. I tucked my Glock into my waistband and forced Gus's arms behind his back.

"Ouch. Get these things off me," he whined as I tightened the zip ties around his wrists and bound them together before snatching him to his feet.

"What about her? Him? Uh, this person?" Roman asked, looking at the petrified, whimpering man.

"I ain't got no beef with him," I said as I pushed Gus toward the door.

Roman shrugged and let the poor man go, then followed behind me.

"Yo, grab that blanket," I told him. "I don't want his nasty ass on my seats."

Roman grabbed the crusty blanket off the bed, and we exited.

"Yo, that was fun as hell," Roman said, grinning as we pulled away from the house.

"That was work," I commented.

"This is some bullshit!" Gus yelled from the back seat.

"You shut the fuck up!" Roman turned around, his gun aimed at Gus. "Don't say nothing else, or we will put your corpse on the side of the road."

"You really are having fun with this, huh?" I raised an eyebrow at Roman when he turned back in his seat.

"Damn right."

Other than Lauryn, I'd never brought anyone along with me on a job, but we'd been at Big Shirley's when I got the tip about

Gus. When I told him I had to leave and offered to drop him off at the house, he insisted on going with me. It turned out not to be a bad thing. He showed no sign of fear and had proven to be a useful partner. The more time I spent with my cousin, the more impressed I was.

It was morning when we arrived at Fairway Bail Bonds. I parked in front of the rustic office building with a large, faded sign in the window that read: FAST, BONDED AND INSURED and FAMILY OWNED, along with the phone number. Those signs had been there for decades, but there was a newer one in the corner that caught my attention. I would have to ask Jimmy about it.

Gus was asleep, his flabby body slumped over in the back seat, hands still cuffed behind his back. I nudged him with my shoe until he finally sat up.

"Come on. Get your ass out."

He blinked for a few seconds to get his bearings.

"I said let's go."

He slid out slowly and stood there staring at the building. I grabbed his arm and pushed him to the front door. As we went inside, he stumbled and nearly fell.

Jimmy Fairway, the owner, was seated at a desk behind the counter.

"What the hell?" His eyes traveled from Gus to me.

"I got him."

"Jiminy Christmas, Curtis. I see that. Where the hell is his damn clothes?" Jimmy walked over and looked at Gus with disgust.

I shrugged. "He ain't wanna cooperate and put 'em on. I bring 'em like I find 'em, Jimmy. You better be glad I ain't bring who was wit' him."

Jimmy laughed as he took Gus by the arm. "I don't even wanna know. Spare me the details, please."

"Fuck you," Gus growled.

"Be careful, Jimmy." Roman spoke up. "I'm pretty sure he means that."

Jimmy ushered Gus through a door leading to the back. I looked around the office while Roman and I waited. He returned a few minutes later.

"Your pay." He handed me an envelope. "Three grand. You still gotta sign the paperwork."

I didn't even bother opening it. Jimmy never shorted me, and he always paid cash on the spot, which was why I liked working with him. I walked over to the counter and signed the forms Jimmy laid out, then pointed to the sign in the lower corner of the front window.

"You selling the place, Jimmy?"

"Yep. I'm getting too old for this shit. Time to let it go."

"How much you letting it go for?" I asked.

"For you, Curtis? Two million, but for you I'll do one point five mil."

I raised an eyebrow. "Shit, I ain't got that kinda money. You think you can let me put something on it and pay you in installments?"

He gave me a doubtful look. "I don't think that'll work. I mean, I like you and all, which is why I'm willing to cut a deal, but you gotta pay the whole amount."

"Damn, I wish I had—"

Roman pulled me to the side. "What's wrong with you?" he whispered. "This place is a gold mine. A million-five is a steal."

"I know that. Why you think I'm trying to negotiate a payment plan? You heard him. He won't take it."

"Fuck a payment plan. Just tell him you'll pay it," Roman said as if he didn't understand just how many dollars it took to be a million.

I looked at him like he was crazy. "What you forgetting is I ain't got a million five hundred thousand dollars laying around. Do you?"

"No, but my pops does," Roman replied.

I shook my head. "Nah, I don't wanna go to Uncle LC, not for this. I love him, but I wanna do this on my own. I know you don't get it, but I wanna be a self-made man, cuz."

"Hell, didn't you tell me the other night that the Duncans became the success that we are because your dad, Uncle Lou, LC, and Uncle Levi all helped each other? That's what family does, or at least that's what everyone keeps telling me."

I looked at the FOR SALE sign again, considering Roman's suggestion. I was proud of what my father and my uncles had built, coming from poverty in Waycross to unimaginable wealth. Still, I couldn't explain why, but something inside of me just wanted to believe that I could find success on my own terms.

"I mean, there is another way you might be able to get the money." Jimmy, who'd been ear hustling, walked from behind the counter and over to the wall covered with mug shots, wanted posters, and other important news headlines. He took down a photo and passed it to me. Roman looked over my shoulder.

"Dominique LaRue." I read the name on the photo.

"One of the most wanted women in America right now. Killed an entire family, execution style," Jimmy explained.

"Damn."

"Bounty is a cool two million. Dead or alive," Jimmy told me. "You find her, and you'll have the money to buy this place and then some. Plus, you'll be on the radar of every county in the U.S. needing someone to be found."

I stared at the photo of the woman I was now determined to find. "Guess I need to get started then. Jimmy, don't sell the place. I'll be back with your money."

Roman stepped up and corrected me. "*We'll* be back with it."

London

20

It was almost five thirty in the morning when I damn near floated into the house. After the confrontation with Harris, Daryl and I had taken off for a few days to my family's summer home in the Hamptons. We'd returned about midnight and gone straight to his pool house apartment for even more amazing sex. I was tempted to stay a little longer, but considering my family had just returned from Waycross, I wanted to make it into the house before anyone noticed I wasn't home. Well, everyone except Harris. I was sure he'd noticed.

In spite of the fact that I said I wouldn't end things with Daryl, Harris had been relatively calm. I think Daryl had scared him so much that he knew to keep his hands off me now. That was a welcome change after so many years of a turbulent marriage— but it wouldn't change my mind about divorcing him.

Now that they were back, I was going to have to tell my parents about the divorce. I wasn't sure how they would take the news, so I wanted to make sure they heard it from me before Harris got a hold of them and put his own spin on the story. I tiptoed into the kitchen, thinking that if I prepared Daddy's favorite breakfast for him, he might be in a better mood to receive my news. He was an early riser, so I wanted to have everything just so when he came down the stairs in about an hour.

"Good morning, London." My father's voice came from across the kitchen. His sudden appearance was so jarring I damn near dropped the carton of eggs I'd pulled out of the refrigerator.

I turned around to see him sitting at the kitchen table in his robe and slippers. The whole scene gave me a flashback to my teenaged years, when I broke curfew and he'd wait up all night to bust me.

"Jesus, Daddy, you scared the hell outta me."

"Kinda late for you to be sneaking in, isn't it?" He looked at his watch to check the time.

"No offense, Daddy, but I'm a grown-ass woman, I have my own kids to look after. I don't have a curfew anymore." I said it with a smile even though I was a little annoyed.

"You're right, you don't. I was just waiting for you to come home so we could talk."

"Talk about what?"

"About your marriage. From what I've been told, you've decided that it's over and you've filed for divorce."

Shit, he knew. I guess Harris's miserable ass decided to inform them. He probably couldn't wait until they walked in the damn door. Now, I was the one having to have an uncomfortable conversation with my father at o'dark thirty in the damn morning while his ass rested comfortably.

"I mean, I was gonna talk to you and Mom about it this morning, Daddy. I was just waiting for you to get back in town," I explained.

"Well, I'm here now."

"Now?" I asked.

"Seems like as good a time as any, don't you think?"

Feeling even more guilty than I already was, I told him, "Now is fine, I guess."

I sat down at the kitchen table across from him and waited for him to start, knowing it would be easier to listen than speak first, especially since I had no idea how much he knew.

"London, is this really what you want to do?" He sat beside me. "Harris has been through a horrible ordeal. He's still recovering. You think now is the right time to do this?"

"Daddy, I've been wanting to do this for a while now. Ask Ma. I just didn't say anything because I didn't want to rock the boat." I sighed, staring at the plaid pajama pants under his robe.

"The man is paralyzed, London." He shook his head.

"I know that, Daddy. And as sad as that is, there's nothing I can do about it. Staying married to him won't make him walk again."

"True, but screwing around with Daryl in the pool house isn't exactly helping either."

I lowered my head, stung by my father's words. Telling them about the divorce was one thing, but Harris' bitch ass mentioning me and Daryl was another. He had no right to do that. It made an already complicated situation worse than it needed to be.

I decided there was no point in trying to cover up anything or lying, especially since everything was pretty much out in the open anyway. I turned and faced him. "Daddy, I didn't plan for this to happen, and neither did Daryl. You have to understand that."

"Look, I'm sorry your marriage isn't working out. Lord knows I know it isn't easy. And I'm sure you were vulnerable, but Daryl knew better," he said.

"Daddy, this is not Daryl's fault. I've had feelings for him for a long time. A long, long time. But because he's Vegas's best friend, things got a little complicated."

"London, Daryl is practically family. You don't think things are complicated now?"

"They are, but this life with Harris ain't what I signed up for," I said. "I deserve happiness."

He frowned. "Yes, you did, London. When you took those vows, you said for better or for worse, in sickness and in health. This is what marriage is, baby. This is the worse."

Part of me couldn't blame my father for the position he was taking. In all the years that Harris and I had fought and all the times he had cheated on me, I hadn't revealed any of it to my parents. He was the father of my kids and also the family's lawyer, and I knew that things could get really messy if my brothers found out about what kind of a husband he was. So, I had hidden my bruises, focused on my babies, and endured it alone. Now I guess I was paying the price for keeping those secrets, because Harris looked like the victim, and I was the horrible person who was ruining our marriage. I felt myself growing frustrated by how unfair that was.

"I don't know what you want me to do, Daddy. I don't love Harris anymore." I looked him in the eye. "I know you mean well, but there is a difference between the marriage I desired and the one I am walking away from. Now, this is my life, and I'd appreciate it if you'd stay the fuck out of it."

My father sat back, eyes wide, looking like I'd just struck him. I had a smart mouth, but I'd never directed that kind of disrespect at my father.

"Daddy, I'm sorry. I—"

He put up his hand to stop me. "I apologize if I've overstepped my boundaries." He stood up from the table. "I was trying to help both you and Harris."

I felt terrible. "I know you were, Daddy, and there's nothing to apologize for." I jumped up. "I appreciate your concern and advice."

"Good." He nodded, kissing my forehead as he'd done since I was a baby. "I love you."

"I love you too, Daddy."

He turned to walk out of the kitchen, then stopped in the doorway.

"Just one more thing," he said.

"Yes?"

"I know you're certain about your decision, and I won't try to talk you out of it, but you need to understand that there is one thing I have to do."

"What's that?"

"Once I take a shower and have my breakfast, I'm going to fire Daryl and have him escorted off the property. He may not have done anything in your eyes, but in mine, he was disrespectful as hell and brought chaos where there should have been peace."

I grabbed the table to keep myself from falling over as Daddy walked out of the room.

Harris

21

The private car service I had hired arrived right on time. I'd made sure to schedule it at a time before anyone in the family came downstairs for coffee or to hit the gym. I was purposely trying to avoid LC after he'd walked up on me with the gun to my head. He'd inspired me to man up, but I was still embarrassed that he'd seen me so weak, and I did not want to be there after he spoke to London.

The only person I had to be concerned about running their big mouth about me slipping away was C-Note at the guardhouse gate, who seemed a bit confused when he called to let me know my ride had arrived.

"Uh, Harris, did you order a car service?"

"Yes, I did. Let him in," I answered, waiting at the front door.

"Sure thing, but why did you need a car service? Me or DJ can take you anywhere you need to go," he insisted, making a damn good point. There really wasn't a reason I needed a car service other than I didn't trust him or DJ, or any of the other Duncan staff for that matter, to keep my business discreet. I was sure they were all tight with Daryl. Shit, for all I knew, they already knew about him and London and were down with it. These were loyal guards, and if any of the Duncans asked where I was, they would report it without hesitation. Not to mention the fact that all Duncan vehicles had high-tech GPS trackers. If I wanted to be incognito, then a hired car was the only way.

"Listen, why am I even explaining myself to you?" I snapped at C-Note through the phone. "You work for us, not the other way around. Just send the damn car up."

There was a long pause, and for a moment, I thought he had hung up on me. If he was angry, that could be a problem for me. C-note was a big motherfucker and a former Navy SEAL. He'd forgotten more ways to kill a man than most people could think about in a lifetime.

I was afraid he might be on his way up until he finally said, "Understood. Your car is pulling up now."

The call ended with neither one of us saying goodbye. By the time the car arrived at the front entrance, I'd made it out the door and down the ramp. The driver assisted me into the back seat, and after he placed my wheelchair into the trunk, we headed out.

As we approached the gate, I saw C-Note glaring at me, and after we passed him, I turned around just in time to see him flipping me the bird. God, I hated these fucking rent-a-thugs.

"Asshole," I muttered, opening the CNN app on my phone to read the latest news headlines to pass the time.

Forty minutes later, the car arrived in Howard Beach, Queens and pulled into the driveway of a mini-mansion on the water. After being helped out of the car and back into my chair, I maneuvered my way to the front door, staring directly into the security camera as I rang the doorbell. A minute or so later, the door opened.

"Harris, what the hell are you doing here?" Antonio Dash, the newly appointed Italian godfather, answered the door wearing a Hugh Hefner robe and flanked by two beefy bodyguard types. There were no women in sight, but with his chiseled features and salt-and-pepper hair, Antonio was something of a ladies' man, and it was rare to see him without a few beautiful ladies by his side.

He was cut from the John Gotti style of gangster, always dressed impeccably and wearing expensive jewelry. However, unlike Gotti, Antonio hated the publicity and the press and kept a low profile when it came to business. He had mostly run the Caribbean rackets for the mob, until Don Federico fell ill a year ago, and he was brought in as muscle to keep thing in order. Within six months, he had taken over most of the family and was made underboss, and then subsequently boss, after Don Federico's untimely death six months ago.

"I hate to stop by unannounced, but I need to speak to you about something important," I explained. "I promise I won't take up too much of your time."

"Well, come inside. I'm not going to talk to you out here." He gestured for his men to help me with my wheelchair.

Inside, I took in the spacious open area that included the foyer, great room, and living room. Marble floors, large columns, and Venetian style furniture—it was opulent, totally befitting Antonio's personal style. Around the great room were the women I'd expected to see, his ever-present harem. There were a dozen or more women, some strutting around in bikinis, and each one was more beautiful than the next. There was one thing they all had in common, though. There was not one white woman in sight.

His men closed and locked the doors as Antonio led me into the living room.

"Nice place you've got here," I said. "I see our family's love for the sisters hasn't evaded you."

Not that he'd ever acknowledge it, but the truth was the truth—Antonio and I were related by blood. Antonio was my first cousin on my father's side. While his uncle, Sal Dash, hadn't raised me, he was my father, and he also had a thing for Black women. My mother was one in a long line, no doubt.

"I lived in Jamaica for twenty years," Antonio said. "A man develops, shall we say, certain preferences? Mine happens to be for dark meat. It has nothing to do with our family." He sat down on the sofa between two beauties. "What can I do for you, Harris? Have the Duncans developed a new product?"

"No, I'm here because I need a favor. A personal favor."

He sat back in his seat, looking surprised. "So, this has nothing to do with the Duncans?"

"No, this is me asking for a personal favor. One cousin to another."

He chuckled. "And you expect that to be enough?"

"That's all I got."

Antonio glanced at the girls beside him. "Okay, I'm not going to deny you're my cousin, because you are, but what makes you think that's deserving of a favor?"

"I would hope my reputation as a money man for the Duncans would be enough. Having me owe you a favor could be valuable."

It didn't take Antonio long to recognize the truth in that statement. "Okay, I'll bite. What's going on?"

"Well, a situation has come about, and I am in need of some special assistance. I'm hoping you can help me locate someone that can get the job done." I shifted in my seat.

"Special service of what kind?"

"I need to eliminate a problem. A major one." I said it in a way that he'd know exactly what I meant.

Antonio's brows furrowed, and he angrily snapped his finger for the girls to leave, which they quickly did. When they were gone, he stared at me until I was uncomfortable.

"Are you asking me to commit murder, Harris?"

"Not you, but maybe one of your people."

He leaned back and put his arms on the back of the sofa. "Why would you need to hire someone to take care of that for you? You have some of the best in the business living under the same roof with you. You think I don't know the firepower the Duncans possess?"

"All true, but none of those are an option. Not for me. This is a sensitive matter and has to be handled with the utmost discretion. No one in the family can be attached or know about what I'm asking, hence why I need to outsource it."

Antonio smiled, wagging a finger at me. "You're making an unsanctioned move, without LC's or Vegas's permission. This is personal."

"Very much so."

"I see." Antonio nodded. "I'm sorry, Harris. I can't have you using any of my people. If it ever got back to the Duncans, it could start a war that would be very bad for business. And trust me. I haven't forgotten that son of a bitch Orlando Duncan killed Vinny, and LC had something to do with Sal's death. My first interest is my family."

He might as well have punched me in the gut. I felt defeated.

"However, I can refer you to someone, elite and discreet, that has nothing to do with my family. But the price is hefty." The way he smiled as he said it, I could almost read his mind. He couldn't involve his family, but he'd do whatever he could to fuck over the Duncans.

"I would expect that." I shrugged. "Money is no object, especially if they are everything you say they are."

"Trust me, the Guild is worth every penny."

"The Guild, as in the Assassin's Guild?" I repeated the name, but I was impressed.

"I wasn't talking about the Actors Guild," he said sarcastically. "I'll put you in contact with my guy over there. They're in town for some big killers' shindig and can provide you with exactly what you need."

"I appreciate that." I nodded. "And like I said, this is an extremely private matter. Discretion is key, including this conversation."

"What conversation? You were never here," Antonio stated. "But invisible man or not, cousin, now you owe me."

Paris

22

It had been a day since who-the-fuck-knows sent me the flowers, and my nerves were a wreck. I wasn't easily spooked, and rarely did things ever take me by surprise, but the arrival of those damn roses and the charm had me shook. Niles Monroe was dead. Hell, I was the one who'd killed him, and it was the hardest thing I'd ever done. So whoever sent those gifts couldn't be Niles, but they had to be someone close enough to know the details of our relationship and his distinct calling card. But who the fuck could that be?

"So, what do you want to do?" Rio asked. We'd been talking about the flowers, which I had left in his office, as we sat on the gazebo eating tuna fish finger sandwiches and drinking ice tea.

"I honestly don't give a shit. Get rid of them. Throw them away, all of them."

Rio lifted his head, raising an eyebrow. "Like, in the trash?"

"Trash, dumpster, garbage can. Hell, you can throw them in the fucking Hudson River for all I care," I stated without remorse. "I don't want them."

"I mean, but do you have to throw them away?" Lauryn whined. "I'll take some. They're so pretty."

"Congratulations. They're yours." I glared at her. I knew that my aggression wasn't necessary, but at that moment, I didn't care. I wanted nothing to do with any of it. "And take this shit too." I tossed the gift bag with the charm in it at her.

"You sure?"

She glanced at Rio, who shrugged his approval. "She's sure. Take it,' he said.

Lauryn opened the gift box, smiling like she'd won the fucking lottery.

"Oh, and Paris, I'm not throwing those blue roses away. I'm giving them out to the female customers tonight at the lounge." Rio made sure I understood for clarity.

"I don't care," I snapped at him. "What I care about is who the fuck is trying to play mind games with me." I turned to my brother. "Seriously, Rio, you don't have anything to do with this, do you?"

"No!" Rio sounded annoyed. "How the fuck I look, spending thousands of dollars to piss you off when all I gotta do is go in the bathroom and leave your toilet seat up at night?" He was laughing, but his point was well made. He'd gotten me many a night when I got up hung over and drunk and landed in the damn toilet because he didn't put the seat down. There were much easier ways for him to piss me off. This stunt with the flowers was elaborate.

"Now, if you want to get to the bottom of this, I'll help you, but lashing out at me,"—Rio looked me directly in the eyes—"especially when I'm the one who always has your back? Not cool, sis."

"I got your back too." Lauryn sat on the edge of her seat. "Where do we start? I'm thinking the florist."

"That makes sense, only the delivery van didn't have a sign, and there was no card with the florist's name on it," Rio pointed out.

Lauryn and I turned to him.

"How do you know?"

"I checked the camera before I locked up last night. You didn't think I knew we were going to play Inspector Clousseau?" Rio smirked. "Anyway, the florist is bust. You know how many florists are in New York City?"

"Yeah, but like Paris said, these roses are rare. They ain't come from FTD or 1-800 Flowers," Lauryn pointed out.

"She's right," I said, thankful that Lauryn was putting her brain to good use because mine was all over the place.

Rio lifted his phone, clicked the keypad, and the search began.

A half hour later, we'd located five New York City florists who sold the Ecuadorian roses.

We spent half the day going from florist to florist, and the first four had been a bust. We'd just dropped Rio off at his lounge, and Lauryn and I were on our way to the fifth when Sasha called. I hit the answer button on the Bluetooth of my red Audio R8 convertible.

"Hey, Sasha."

"Paris, where are you? I need to talk to you about something. It's important."

"Uh, can it wait til later? I'm kinda out taking care of something right now."

Lauryn pointed to the GPS map on the screen. "Slow up. It's gotta be the one on the right. The one with the big floral sign."

"Yeah." I nodded, staring at the upcoming strip mall and praying that we'd hit pay dirt. The uncertainty was stressing me out, and the wild goose chase was becoming more frustrating by the minute.

"Paris!" Sasha yelled my name, reminding me she was on the other end of the phone.

"Huh? Oh, yeah, Sasha. I'm here. Sorry."

"Who is that? Who are you with?" Sasha asked.

"It's Lauryn. I told you we're taking care of something. Look, I gotta call you back when we're done."

I ended the call without saying goodbye as I pulled into the parking lot. We hopped out and entered the door with the words *Luxe Floral Design*. The elegant floral showroom was stunning. There were displays of roses, tulips, lilies, and a few exotic-looking flowers I'd never seen before. While Lauryn looked around, I headed to the counter.

"Hello, welcome to Luxe. Can I help you find something special today?" An older lady who looked Brazilian smiled at me.

"Yes, please," I told her, admiring her dark tan skin, full lips, and long, curly hair that flowed down her back. This wasn't a three thousand-dollar weave. It was real, and so were her curves. "I'm looking for Ecuadorian roses."

"Ah," she exclaimed and clapped. "Those seem to be in high demand these days. Excellent choice. Such a beautiful and unique selection."

"Do you have royal blue ones?" Lauryn rushed beside me and asked before I could.

"Oh, sorry, we don't have those." The woman gave me a disappointed look.

"Damn it." Lauryn exhaled.

"Unfortunately, we had a customer buy all that we had in stock yesterday."

My eyes widened. "That's actually why I'm here. The flowers were sent to me."

"Oh, you're Paris?" The woman seemed impressed.

"Yes, I'm Paris," I confirmed. "I need to know who sent them to me."

"Was something wrong?" she asked, sounding concerned. "Did you not like them?"

"No, they're gorgeous, but there was no name on the card."

"No card?" She frowned. "It was with the gift, no?"

"Yes, there was a card, but there was no name. I need to know who they're from. Who placed the order?" I tried not to sound agitated, especially since at this point, this was the only woman who could help me.

"Such an exquisite gift." She shook her head. "The woman who sent them was so detailed about what she wanted. And no name? You sure?"

"We're positive. No name," Lauryn told her. "We need the name of the customer."

The woman shook her head. "She gave me no name. Paid cash and told us where to deliver, that's it."

"Fuck." I tossed my hands up in disgust then turned to leave. "Thanks for nothing."

"Wait." Lauryn touched my arm, then pointed to the ceiling at the camera looking down at us. "You have security cameras. You said the woman was here yesterday. Can we see them?"

The woman stared at us as if to say "That's not happening." But I was LC Duncan's daughter, so I never took no for an answer, and I wasn't above bribery. I reached in my purse and pulled out five hundred-dollar bills and slapped them on the counter.

"Can we see it now?" I demanded.

She looked down at the cash. "Si, I'll have my husband get it right away." She turned toward the back room "Pascal, Pascal! Get the video, Pascal!"

An older gentleman strolled from the back of the store. "Si?"

"We need the security tape for yesterday so we can see who sent me the blue roses," I explained. When the man stared back at me with a blank look, his wife picked up the money and waved it at him.

"Si, señora. Right away." He disappeared into the back room. A few minutes later, he reappeared, carrying a laptop. He placed it on the counter and turned it toward us. There on the screen was the very place that we stood.

"Here it is, señora."

We all watched the empty store for a few seconds. Then, a tall female figure came into view. As I watched her approaching the counter, my heart began pounding.

"I can't see her face," I said.

Pascal clicked the keyboard, and the camera switched to another angle. There was a clear view of the woman's face. There she was, dressed in a crisp, light blue skirt suit, wearing a pair of designer sunglasses.

"Do you recognize her?" Lauryn asked.

"Yeah. Nadja's not the type you forget." I felt my anger begin to build. "She tried to kill me twice."

Nee Nee

23

It was a beautiful morning. The sun was high and the breeze was perfect as Mariah and I picked tomatoes and cucumbers in my garden. Jordan and Mimi rode bikes Curtis had bought them in the yard. Jordan constantly complained about not having a video game system to play, and Curtis had offered to let him use Kenny's, but I put my foot down. These kids needed to run around in the fresh air. They'd have plenty of time to play games when they went home to New York.

"Is this one good, Aunt Nee Nee?" Mariah asked, pointing to a half-ripened, pinkish-colored tomato on the vine.

"Nah, let's leave that one for a couple of days. But get the one next to it. It's nice and ripe."

"And it's huge." Mariah grinned. "You think I can plant a garden when I go back home? This is fun."

"Maybe. Y'all got plenty of space for you to make one." I was happy that she was finding comfort in the simple things. "I'm sure your Grandma Chippy can help. She used to love gardening."

"Really?" Mariah looked surprised.

"She did back in the day," I said. "And she would plant the most beautiful flowers."

"We have a flower garden, but the gardener plants them," Mariah told me.

Once again, I was reminded of how different my family had become when they moved to New York years ago. I prayed that Lauryn wouldn't succumb to the flashiness and lifestyle of my brother- and sister-in-law and that eventually, she would return to the basic comforts of her own home. And even more importantly, I hoped she'd call me. I'd barely spoken to her since she'd left a few days ago, and I missed my baby bad.

"Can we go inside now?" Jordan whined. "I wanna play my Nintendo Switch, and it's hot out here."

"It's not hot." Mimi looked at him sideways. "It's nice. I don't wanna go inside."

"Nobody's going inside. Not yet anyway." I told him. "We're all going to stay—"

My instructions were interrupted by Spot barking like crazy and what sounded like a caravan of trucks coming from the front of the house.

"They're back," I mumbled to myself. I went to see who it was, even though I instinctively already knew. Sure enough, when I turned the corner, I spotted several black sedans coming up the driveway.

"Who is that?" Mariah, who hadn't left my side, asked.

"Looks like the feds." Jordan answered for me with his know-it-all self.

"Y'all get on the porch and stay," I instructed the three of them. Mariah grabbed her sister's hand, and the two girls rushed onto the wraparound porch. Jordan continued to stare at the cars as they parked.

I tapped his shoulder. "Little boy, if you don't do what I told you to do, I'll take that game of yours and give it to Spot as a chew toy."

Jordan's eyes widened and he stared at me for a second. He looked over at Spot, then quickly ran to join his cousins.

I patiently waited for the woman who'd been the first to jump out of the lead SUV to stroll toward me, but she dared not move with Spot standing between us. I could see the slight fear in her eyes as she moved away from him, just in case.

"Control your dog or I'll have him shot," she shouted at me.

"He's just doing his job, protecting his family. He doesn't care for uninvited guests." I folded my arms. "Come here, Spot."

"Well, this isn't a social visit, Mrs. Duncan, but I'm sure you know that already." She sneered at me, waving the piece of paper she was carrying toward me. When I didn't reach for it immediately, she said, "This is a warrant to search your property for the fugitive Larry Duncan and any known associates."

I nodded toward the other agents who were wearing the same identical black nylon jacket that she wore. All of them were coming toward me. Curtis and Roman weren't home, and although they really couldn't have done anything, I wished they were there now.

Reluctantly, I took the document and unfolded the stapled sheets, carefully reading each and every word. After confirming that I truly had no choice but to allow them entry into my home, I took a deep breath to try to control my anger.

"Go ahead, but I'm telling you I ain't seen or heard from my husband. He ain't here."

"So you say. But we're gonna go in and make sure." Agent Martinez stared at me for a second, then turned to her partner, Fritz, who was now standing beside her.

"Let's get inside," she told him.

The large group of agents followed them inside, passing right by the children. The kids looked more confused than afraid, which was a good thing. The last thing I wanted was for them to be scared.

I walked over and put my arms around Mimi and Mariah, reassuring them. "It's gonna be all right. They're gonna leave soon."

"It's okay, Aunt Nee Nee," Mariah stated. "They came to our house too. We know."

"I don't like the feds," Mimi added.

"Me neither," Jordan added, folding his arms defiantly. I couldn't help but smile. He sure was his mother's son. One thing about Duncans—they weren't easily intimidated. It was in them to be fearless.

As soon as I took out my phone to dial Curtis's number and tell him to get back to the house, Agent Martinez came strolling outside.

"I told you he's not here," I said.

"We haven't finish searching yet. But whether he's here or not, I'm gonna find him. I can promise you that. Finding cops and law enforcement killers are my life's mission, and I don't plan on bringing them home alive."

"What do you mean, cop killer? He hasn't killed any cops."

"Yes, he fucking did," she replied without any regard for the children. "He killed a female corrections officer when he escaped. She had three kids probably about these kids' ages."

"Oh, Lord," I mumbled.

"Oh, Lord," she echoed me mockingly. "So, if you find him, hear from him, or just come up with a fucking epiphany about where he might be, give me a call. 'Cause if you don't and I find him, he's dead." She handed me a card just as Agent Fritz came storming out the door.

"Let's go! Let's go! Everyone in the vans," Fritz's voice boomed. He held the screen door open, and the cavalcade of storm troopers came rushing out even faster than they'd entered. "Let's go, Martinez!"

"What's going on? "Martinez asked the question I was thinking.

"They've been spotted in Knoxville. Positive identification. They are holed up in a motel. Local PD has the place locked down. We've gotta roll. It's an eight-hour drive."

"We've gotta get these bastards," I heard someone growl. "This is the tip we've been waiting for."

"See, I told you we'd get him. The only question is will we get him dead or alive?" She smiled wickedly, following Fritz off the porch.

Knoxville. Larry had friends in Knoxville. Shit. Until I felt the slight disappointment in that moment, I hadn't even realized that I'd been hoping LC was right and Larry would eventually come home. In spite of the danger, I wanted to see my husband.

For a split second, I considered heading to Knoxville myself. I knew better than to do that, though. Instead, I watched with relief as the federal employees drove off.

London

24

The balcony of my bedroom provided a full view of the front of our home, and standing on it had my heart in my mouth. I had hoped my father would change his mind about speaking to Daryl, but as I stood and watched him walk toward the security booth, I knew his mind was made up and he was about to fire Daryl.

Once Daddy had told me what he planned to do, I didn't hesitate. I made it my business to call Daryl. Despite my pleading attempt to forewarn him, Daryl disregarded my warning, assuring me that he had everything under control.

"Calm down, London. I've known your father since I was ten. He respects me. The two of us are just going to talk man to man, and it'll be fine," Daryl said through the phone.

"But you don't under—" I tried to explain, but he cut me off.

"Look, I'm down at the gate helping DJ with something. We'll talk later." He hung up before I could say anything else. It was clear that he didn't grasp the magnitude of what was about to take place. All I could do was watch and pray.

Daddy stood outside the booth for a while, and a few seconds later, Daryl joined him. The two of them walked toward the pool house. I couldn't hear what was being said, but I could see their expressions as they talked. The conversation seemed relaxed at first, but then became more intense. Daryl's back stiffened, and I could see the tension in his face. My father put his hand on Daryl's shoulder, but Daryl just shook his head. Finally, Daddy walked off, leaving Daryl standing alone. I wouldn't put money on it, but I think I saw Daryl wiping away tears.

My heart couldn't take any more. Daryl didn't deserve this. I had to do something. I fled the balcony, rushing out of my bedroom, down the staircase, and into the kitchen, where my mother was sitting and drinking coffee.

"Mom, please. You've gotta talk to Daddy."

"London, there's nothing for me to talk to him about," she told me. "I'm sorry. The two of you are grown, but you shouldn't have been sleeping with him in our house."

"This isn't fair. You know how much Daryl means to me. How much we mean to each other." I sobbed. "We can't let this happen."

"Honey, I know you're upset, but it's already happened. There's no way we can allow him to continue working for the family under these circumstances. The man broke our trust. You're married."

"Not for long I won't be," I reminded her. "I'm divorcing Harris. It's not like we're even physically together. We just happen to live at the same address."

"Your father feels like this is best for everyone involved," she said in that calm voice that usually would've helped me feel better, but it didn't.

"He's wrong. This isn't best for anybody."

"No, you're wrong, and it is what's best." My father's voice came over my shoulder. "Like it or not, he's been terminated."

I whipped around to face him. "You've ruined this man's life because of Harris."

"His life isn't ruined. But there was no way I could allow the two of you to continue carrying on and having a full-on affair in my house as if it's okay. For God's sake, your children live under this roof, London, not just Harris."

"The girls love Daryl," I stated. "He's family. Which is why I don't understand why you're doing this. He's Vegas's best friend."

"Honey, you're not making things any better for yourself." Momma walked over and put her arm around me.

"At this point, it can't get any worse." I stormed out.

As I walked through the foyer, I looked out the window and saw Daryl placing things in the trunk of his car. My heart melted, and I rushed out the door, running straight to him.

"Daryl!" I called his name before he slid into the driver's seat. I did not even try to hide the fact that I'd been crying. "Wait."

"It's okay, London."

"It's not okay, and it's not fair." I threw myself into his arms, and my tears stained his shirt. "You shouldn't have to leave."

"I don't really have a choice." His shoulders sagged with sadness. "To hear how disappointed your father was in me almost tore me apart. He trusted me, London. The man told me I broke his heart. I would take a bullet for that man. I owe everything to him."

"I know, but the heart wants what it wants. I can't help but love you."

"And I love you. That's not gonna change, but as long as Harris is here, I can't be. That's just how it is."

I turned and looked back at the house for a moment, hating the thought of having to stay there without Daryl. "So be it. Fuck 'em. I'm going with you."

"What do you mean?"

I gave him a brief kiss before running to the passenger side. "Unlock the door."

Daryl used his key fob and unlocked the doors of his Audi, and I hopped into the passenger seat.

"What are you doing?" he asked as he slid in the driver's seat.

"I'm going with you," I told him. "If you aren't staying here, then neither am I. Now, let's go."

"Are you sure about this?" The corners of his sexy lips curled, and he could no longer hide a smile.

It felt good to know he was happy about my last-minute decision. I was doing the right thing. "I've never been more certain about anything in my life, Daryl Graham. Now, turn this damn car on and let's get the fuck outa here."

Daryl leaned over and kissed me as he hit the start button. Seconds later, we zoomed out of the driveway, past the security gate, and away from my home. I didn't know where we were headed, and I was sure Daryl didn't either. The destination didn't matter to either one of us, as long as we were together.

Roman

25

Curtis and I had just returned from catching another bail jumper. I was pleasantly surprised at how much I enjoyed this bounty hunting shit Curtis was introducing me to. Real talk, it wasn't much different from anything I'd done as a stick-up kid robbing drug dealers, bodegas, and jewelry stores back in Brooklyn, except this was way more fun. To me, it seemed like both occupations called for simply doing what needed to be done to get the job finished. Sometimes, that meant fucking somebody up; other times, zip tying someone at gunpoint and hauling them off.

"Hey, cuz, this your cut." He tried handing me some money as we entered the house, but I pulled my hands back and shook my head.

"Nah, Curt, we good. You ain't gotta do that. I just like hanging with you, fam."

"I know I ain't got to, but I want to. You did your part. Far as I'm concerned, you earned it." He tried to shove the money at me again.

"Man, stop it. We both know you coulda handled that fat motherfucker by yourself," I told him. "Save your money for that bail bonds spot you want so bad."

I'd thought about the bail bondsman business Curtis wanted to buy as we drove back to Waycross from Brunswick. It seemed like a perfect opportunity for him, especially since he was already established as a bounty hunter. Although I respected his wanting to be his own man, it didn't make sense for him to not utilize his resources to make that shit happen. Had it been me, I would have wasted no time calling my wealthy uncle for a loan. It didn't seem any different than his brother Kenny taking over Big Shirley's, my twin brother Rio having his own nightclub, or my older brother Orlando running his own pharmaceutical company. Family business was family business; we all had to help each other. Then again, I was new to the Duncan family, and I'd learned that there were definitely levels to the family dynamics. The Duncans up north were different than the ones in the south, that was for sure.

"Damn, it smells good as hell," I said when we entered the house, where the aroma of Aunt Nee Nee's cooking filled the air. In the short time that I'd been with them, I'd had some of the best meals of my life.

"Sunday dinner." Curtis laughed. "I hope you're hungry."

"You already know," I told him.

"Uncle Roman!" My little nephew ran across the top of the sofa and jumped into my arms like a superhero. He was a wild little boy, but he sure loved me, and in turn, I loved him back.

As soon as we entered the kitchen, Aunt Nee Nee called out from behind the stove. "Y'all back?"

"Yeah, Ma."

"Good. Jordan, you go call the girls so we can eat," she instructed.

We washed up then went and sat at the dining room table. I was about to sit in the seat beside Curtis when Aunt Nee Nee stopped me. "No, Roman, you sit here in Lauryn's chair across the table. That seat is for Kenny."

I was about to say something, but when I looked over at Curtis, he gave me a look that let me know to just do what I was told.

"Is this everything?" she asked, placing a platter of fried chicken in the middle of the dining room table.

"Come on and sit down, Ma. It's everything," Curtis said.

Aunt Nee Nee paused for a second, then snapped her fingers and walked back to the kitchen. Moments later, she returned carrying a plate of hot, buttered biscuits. We had to make room for her to put them on the table. Finally, she took her seat, and we said grace. Aunt Nee Nee began fixing the kid's plates.

Mariah had a confused look on her face. "Aunt Nee Nee, can I ask a question?"

"Sure, baby. What would you like to ask?"

"Why do you have two empty place settings?" Mariah motioned toward the empty place at the head of the table, and the empty seat across from me. She'd asked exactly what I'd been wondering. Curtis lowered his head into his plate.

"Those seats are for your Uncle Larry and cousin Kenny," she said with conviction.

"But they're not here." Mariah still looked confused.

"They aren't here now," she replied. "However, your uncle and cousin could come home at any moment. Might be tonight, might be next year. Either way, this is their home, and they'll always have a plate and plenty to eat when they get here."

"What makes you think they coming back, Aunt Nee Nee? Didn't y'all say they're in the wind and long gone?" I asked.

From what I'd learned about Uncle Larry, he was a troubled man who loved his family. His severe PTSD as a result of the Vietnam War had progressed over the years and caused him to become maniacal and deadly. After he committed several murders, my father and his brother Lou pulled some strings and had him placed in a psychiatric facility instead of going to jail. Eventually, he was sent to the federal facility that he had recently escaped.

Aunt Nee Nee stared at the empty seats for a moment before answering. "Because home with his family is the only place your uncle wants to be. That's why."

"She's right about that," a voice announced.

We all turned around and I saw an older man with a strong resemblance to my father. He stood in the doorway. I was pretty sure I knew who he was, and that scared me. I nonchalantly lowered my hand to make sure I had the gun my father had given me.

"Who are you?" Jordan stared at the man.

"I'm your uncle Larry. Who are you?"

"I'm Jordan! And this is Mimi and Mariah."

"Nice to meet you, kids." He smiled pleasantly. "Mariah, you've gotten so big."

Finally, he turned to the other side of the table, where Aunt Nee Nee looked like she was about to burst with excitement.

"Hey, Nee," he said casually, as if he had just been away for a short trip, not a federal lockup.

Aunt Nee Nee jumped up and ran into his arms. They kissed as if they were the only two people in the room. Uncle Larry was smiling from ear to ear once they separated. He turned his attention to Curtis.

"Curtis." He sounded sad.

"Daddy," Curtis replied grimly without looking up from his plate. I didn't know what was going on between them, but there was clearly plenty of tension.

"You're just in time for dinner. Your place is already set." Aunt Nee Nee pointed to the chair at the opposite end of the table. "I figured you would be here for dinner."

"You figured right." Uncle Larry kissed her again before taking his seat.

He looked over at me and said, "How you doing, Rio? I ain't seen you in damn near twelve years."

"Uh, I'm not Rio. I'm Roman, Uncle Larry," I corrected him. "Rio's my twin brother."

He frowned. "Roman? I thought Rio had a twin sister."

"I'll explain later, baby," Aunt Nee Nee whispered, then asked, "Was Kenny with you?"

"He was. He had an errand to run, but I told him to get by the house to see you before we head outta town. He'll come to see you."

Aunt Nee Nee didn't waste time piling his plate with food while everyone else fixed their own. After a quick blessing, we began to eat.

For a while, it seemed like a normal family dinner. Aunt Nee Nee told him about the kids and I staying for a few weeks in Waycross and updated him on the rest of the family. The kids excused themselves and went in the den to watch TV. I could hear Mariah fussing with Jordan.

Then, Nee Nee stated the elephant in the room as if it was part of the regular conversation. "Larry, you know the federal marshals came here looking for you."

"I know they did." Uncle Larry chuckled as he shoveled another forkful into his mouth. "But they're in Knoxville now. Somebody gave them a tip that they saw me and my people there."

"I wonder who did that?" Curtis's voice was full of sarcasm.

"Don't know." Uncle Larry shrugged. "I'm sure they'll be back here, though, which is why I can't stay long. Only gonna be here long enough to take care of some business, including my wife."

"Larry, you need to stop." Aunt Nee Nee blushed.

"Why? These boys here grown. They know what husbands and wives do. Don't you, boys?" He looked over at us, and I smiled, but Curt exhaled loudly, purposely not trying to make eye contact with his old man.

"I think I'm done eating." Curtis put down his fork and stood. "I'm gonna go check on the animals."

"Yeah, think I'll go outside and get me some air as well," I said, following his lead.

We quickly exited the house, Curtis heading toward the barn, and me to the porch swing. I sat down and dialed my father's number.

My father answered. "Hey, Roman, how things going? Jordan behaving himself?"

"Yeah, yeah, Jordan and the girls are fine." I looked around to make sure no one was nearby to hear me. "But, uh, Pop, Uncle Larry is here."

There was an eerie silence, and I could imagine my father sitting back in his chair as he processed my news.

"I figured he'd show up eventually. He was gonna check on Nee Nee if nothing else." Pop sighed. "How is he acting?"

"I don't really know him, but he seems to be fine. Happy to be home, if you ask me."

"That's good. Nee Nee has that effect on him. Always has."

"So, what do you want me to do? Should me and the kids leave and come back home?" I asked.

"No, y'all will be fine. I don't think he'll be there very long. Larry may be crazy, but he's damn sure not stupid."

"Yeah, he said something about not staying long."

"That's good, but listen to me. Do not go anywhere with him. Even if he asks, don't go. Last thing we need is a harboring fugitive charge on you."

"Yes, sir," I replied. "I guess I'm confused because you were really concerned about Uncle Larry being out, and now it's like you don't care."

"That's where you're wrong, son. I care, otherwise I'd be on a plane right now headed there," he explained. "My not being anywhere near Larry is the best thing I can do. One day, I'll explain. Until then, I need you to be there. Keep an eye on things for me, Roman, but keep a distance."

"Okay, I will," I promised, appreciative to hear the vote of confidence he had in me.

"Oh, and Roman?"

"Yeah?"

"Larry is my brother, and I love him, but you are my son, and I love you more. Make sure you stay armed around him," he warned. "And if you have to, don't hesitate to pull that trigger."

Sasha

26

I couldn't believe what I'd just overheard. After Paris's rude ass hung up on me, I decided to try to talk to Uncle LC once more to get him to see my side of things. Just as I was about to walk into his office, I overheard him on the phone with Roman. My eavesdropping confirmed what I'd already suspected. Making his brother pay for what he'd done to my mother wasn't a concern for my uncle.

It took everything in me not to storm in his office and go off on my uncle, but I maintained my cool. I would take out my frustration on the Duncan who really deserved it, especially since my ear hustling let me know something even more important: the exact location of Larry Duncan.

I quickly turned around and headed upstairs to the left wing of the house, searching for the one person who'd promised to have my back.

"Junior." I tapped on the door of the bedroom he shared with his wife.

A few moments later, Junior eased it open. "What's up, Sasha?"

"I got the information we were waiting on," I told him with a look so he'd know exactly what I was referring to.

"You did?" He looked surprised.

"I need you to go with me."

"Junior? Can you please take her. You promised to take night duty." Sonya's voice came over his shoulder. "Who is that?"

"When you trying to leave?" Junior asked in a whisper, opening the door wider so I could see inside.

"Now," I said with a quiet urgency.

Sonya was sitting on the side of the bed, looking exhausted. She waved at me. "Hey, Sasha."

"Hey, Sonya." I waved back. "How you feeling?"

"Tired, but happy she's here." She looked down at the baby in her arms.

"Baby, I need to holla at Sasha right quick. I'll be right back," Junior told her.

"Okay, but don't think you're getting out of night duty."

"It'll only take a minute," Junior promised, then stepped outside, closing the door behind him. He motioned for me to follow him down the hallway and waited until we were a few feet away before he said anything else.

"What's going on?"

"I know where—"

"Shhhh." Junior stopped me.

I lowered my voice, then continued. "I know where Larry is. I found him. He's in Waycross at Aunt Nee Nee's. We have to go get his ass."

"What? How do you know that?" Junior's voice was barely above a whisper.

"Because Roman called and told Uncle LC, that's how. His crazy ass showed up at the house, and he's still there."

"Damn, I can't believe he'd be that bold." Junior shook his head. "He's gotta know they're after him. You'd think his house would be the last place he'd go."

"We're talking about somebody who ain't working with a full deck, Junior," I reminded him. "And I don't give a damn why he's there. I just know we need to get there fast."

Junior took a deep breath and ran his hand through his hair. "Look, Sasha, why don't we leave in the morning? I'll get the jet fueled, and we'll head down there. I just can't do it now—"

"Junior, you promised." My voice rose an octave. "You're the only one I can depend on right now."

"I get that, Sasha, and you can depend on me," Junior said. "But you know I got my own situation going on right now with Sonya and the baby. She was pissed the other night because we got back late. Plus, you heard her. I promised to do night duty."

"Then let me explain it to her. She'll listen to me." I was becoming more frustrated by the second, especially when I tried to push past him and he stopped me.

"No, I can't let you do that. She just had a baby. I'm not going to abandoned her. She feels weird enough as it is with no family other than me." He stood firm.

"We just gotta get to Waycross, do what needs to be done, and be out. Sonya will barely notice you're gone."

"I tell you what. How about we make a call to—"

"Who the hell we gonna call, Junior? Aunt Nee Nee? Curtis? We damn sure can't call Lauryn because even she's made herself at home right here instead of being concerned about her murderous-ass daddy." I glared at him. "It's cool. I knew everyone else in this family didn't give a damn, but I really thought I could count on you. I was wrong."

"I do care," he protested. "And I promise we'll figure this out, Sasha. You gotta respect the fact that I got a baby and a wife that's a bundle of nerves right now that I'm taking care of. Those two in there are my priority right now."

I looked Junior in the eye. My desperation had me damn near on the verge of telling him the secret I'd been holding onto, hoping it would intensify his loyalty to me. But it wasn't the time. I didn't want to use the truth as a weapon.

"It's cool. Go be with Sonya." I swallowed the lump that was forming in my throat.

"Sasha." Junior reached for me.

"Nah, like I said, it's cool." I pulled away and walked past before the tears that I'd been holding back started to flow. I had hoped that this wasn't something that I would have to do alone, but now I understood that I had no choice. Every person in my life that I thought I could depend on had let me down. This was going to be a solo mission.

I went directly to my room and grabbed my suitcases that were already packed and sitting in the back of my closet. I carried them out of the house, walked directly past the black Maserati that I usually drove, and continued into the garage where my mother's white Mercedes was kept. I put the bags in the trunk and then went back upstairs to my closet. This time, I took out a long, black case and my cherished keepsake box. I took one final glance around my room, then turned off the light and went back to the car that now held my belongings.

I opened the trunk once again, then carefully placed the black case inside along with my keepsake box. I climbed into the driver's seat and entered the destination of Waycross, GA into the navigation system.

"Seventeen hours and thirty-six minutes." I sped past DJ standing outside the security booth and flipped him the bird, screaming, "Fuck all of y'all!"

Orlando

27

It was a beautiful, warm Caribbean day, and all I could see for miles and miles were blue skies and ocean. I'd come up to the top deck of the super yacht from my lab, followed by Aries, my personal bodyguard/babysitter/assistant to see what the chef had prepared for lunch. We both stepped up to the buffet line, piling shrimp and broccoli along with flavored brown rice on our plates, and sat down to eat. I have to admit, for the two and a half months that Ruby, Li'l Man, and I had spent on the private yacht, I couldn't name one time that the food was less than fantastic. Not only was it tasty, but it was always healthy.

Speaking of Li'l Man, I could hear him laughing and playing. I glanced over the rail to a lower deck, where he was splashing around with his mom in the pool, having a good time. That boy was just like me. He really loved the water, and he was quickly becoming a swimmer. I stared at them briefly, unable to describe the unconditional love I had for both of them. It was so touching, I could almost feel tears welling up in my eyes—until I saw Aries's face staring at me.

"Hi, Daddy!"

I was snapped out of my nostalgic moment by my son's yelling.

"Hey, Li'l Man." I waved back.

I was going to have to stop referring to him by that nickname soon. Truth is, I just couldn't stomach calling him Vincent or Vinny or any other name associated with that son of a bitch Vinnie Dash, who had married Ruby while she was pregnant with my son. Even in death, that bastard haunted me. Ruby and I had spent the past year together, healing our relationship and getting to know each other on a deeper level, and I tried to avoid thinking about or speaking about him because of all the bad memories it brought up.

"Mr. Duncan, you have a call on ship to shore. I think it's your father." Tyrrell, one of the twenty or so ships African security guards, said in his thick accent.

"Okay." I was halfway through my meal. I put down my fork and wiped my mouth with a napkin.

He handed the phone to Aries, who placed it on the table and hit the speaker button.

It had been almost two weeks since I'd spoken to Pop. He and I were close, but our relationship was one that didn't require daily conversation. He wasn't big on trivial small talk, and neither was I. We spoke when we needed to speak, but I was always glad when we did.

"What's up, Pop?" I answered.

"Hey, son. Just checking on you. How are Ruby and that grandson of mine?" I could almost hear him smile as he said those words. Pop loved his grandchildren.

"They're good. Li'l Man seems to be getting bigger every day." I glanced over the rail at the pool. "Ruby is teaching him Patois. She thinks it'll make him bilingual. I don't agree, but I know not to argue."

"Smart man. I see you're learning the secret to a great marriage already." He laughed, and it made me realize how much I missed him. I had seen my siblings who came down for some fun in the sun, but it had been more than a year since I'd seen either one of my parents. "Pick your battles and know when to retreat. That's the way to a successful marriage."

"I've learned from the best," I teased. "How are things back home?"

"Things are complicated."

I sat up in my chair, my senses on alert. My family was always complicated—this was nothing new—but until I knew what level of complication we were talking about, I was uneasy.

"What's going on?"

"Well, you'll be pleased to know that you're an uncle again. Sonya had the baby, and your beautiful niece, Bettie Jean Duncan, is healthy and beautiful."

"Wow, that's great to hear. I bet you she's got Junior wrapped around her finger." I imagined my big, burly brother holding his tiny bundle of joy. "He was probably a crying mess in the delivery room."

"Sonya said he did great. And as far as spoiling her, I don't know who's worse around here, him or your mother."

I laughed. "I'm sure they are running neck and neck. But that doesn't sound too complicated. What else is going on, Pop?"

He hesitated for a moment. "London and Harris are getting a divorce."

"I'll be honest. That doesn't surprise me, Pop," I said. "Their marriage hasn't been in great shape for a while."

"Well, it surprised the hell outta me, and Daryl's involvement surprised me even more. Did you know about that?"

"Know about what?"

"Your sister's having an affair with Daryl Graham."

"London and Daryl?" My voice rose an octave. I'd been a little out of touch being so far away, but I usually had at least some idea of what was going on with my siblings.

"Yup. Things got so bad I had to terminate him."

"You fired Daryl?"

"Yes, son, I did, but I'm having some seller's remorse. I've been thinking about rehiring him and sending him down to Jamaica with you."

I looked up at Aries, who was frowning, and I knew why. He wanted me all to himself, for selfish reasons. Having Daryl or anyone else from back home come down was not what he signed up for.

"Damn, things really are complicated. That's a lot."

"It is, but nothing your mother and I can't handle. I'll definitely keep you posted as things move along. But London's situation is only the tip of the iceberg."

"There's more?" I asked.

I could hear him exhale wearily before he spoke. "There's a situation with your uncle Larry."

"What about him? He's not dead, is he?" We didn't talk about my uncle much ever since he was locked up in that federal institution, but I knew my pop still felt a lot of guilt about that whole situation. He was always trying to make things right between them.

"No, he's not dead."

"Good," I said.

"He's escaped from prison and is on the run again."

"Whoa, are you serious?" I said. "That's not good. He can't be on the street, Pop. I don't have to remind you what happened last time."

"No, you don't. I'm working on it. But for right now, he's on his meds as far as I know, and he isn't a real threat to anyone."

"I mean, do I need to come—" I couldn't even believe those words were coming out of my mouth, and I was glad he cut me off.

"No! You don't need to do anything except what you're doing now, son. Continue your research. Right now, that's more important to the family. I'll call you if you're needed."

"Okay, Pop. If you need me, I'm there."

"I know you are, son. And I appreciate it," he said. "We just have to prioritize these situations as they arise, but everything will work out in the end."

"I hope so," I said, staring down at my family swimming in the pool. "Love and miss you, Pop."

"I love you too, son. Kiss Ruby and the baby for me."

"I will. Tell Junior I said congrats, and hopefully, we'll be home soon to see everyone. Kiss Mom for me," I said, suddenly feeling homesick as he ended the call.

"You got a good father," Aries said, interrupting my thoughts. "I like the man even though I've never met him. But you shouldn't push your luck. We are on the threshold of something big. Bigger than your father, mother and your whole family. Please do not jeopardize it."

I glanced down at Ruby and Li'l Man getting out of the pool. "I'm not. I give you my word."

Nee Nee

28

"Ohhhhh, gawwwwdd, Nee!" Larry groaned, and I smiled to myself.

The lovemaking session we'd had was brief but satisfying. Hell, being able to have sex at all at our age was pretty damn impressive as far as I was concerned. For me, the best part was when he released himself inside me, his body twitched and jerked uncontrollably. It gave me a sense of power that I could not describe. Sure, I loved it when he brought me to orgasm, but knowing he was satisfied was when I felt most like a woman and knew deep down that I'd done my part.

Being a breast cancer survivor, one of my biggest concerns had been if my husband would still find me attractive. I'd been blessed not to have to undergo a full mastectomy, but I'd had several surgeries that left scars on my once perfect breasts. Larry didn't notice at all, or at least if he did, he didn't say anything about it. He made love to me the same way he had for the forty-plus years that we'd been married, and I thanked God for that.

When his convulsions finally subsided, Larry and I lay there in silence for a while with him on top of me. I rubbed his back, and he kissed my neck and ear, and I think we could both say we were happier than we'd been in years.

"I love you, Nee," he said with sincerity, breaking our silence.

"Love you too, Larry Duncan." I kissed him square on the lips.

He lifted his body off me then rolled over onto his back. I snuggled up against him, and we both stared up at the ceiling as if we were lying on a blanket outside, staring up at a million stars.

"I got something for you, Nee." He rolled over and picked up his pants from the floor, reached into his pocket, and handed me an envelope.

"What is it?"

"Open it and see."

I opened it with caution and gasped when I saw the thick wad of cash held together with a rubber band. "Larry Duncan, where did you get all this money from?"

He raised his eyebrows playfully. "We both know I got my ways, woman."

"And we both know this money ain't legal either."

My statement didn't seem to bother him at all. He just lay back and said simply, "Don't matter if it is or not as long as my family is taken care of. And I always take care of my family."

"Yes, you do. And we are grateful for that, baby, but Larry,"—I leaned up on my elbow to look into his eyes—"I'm scared."

"Scared of what?"

"The feds. They've got the FBI and the U.S. Marshals looking for you!"

"Baby, calm down. I've dealt with police before."

"I will not!" I shouted. "This isn't the Ware County Sheriff, or the Georgia State Police that's after you. This is the federal government. You killed a federal corrections officer, Larry. They are not going to let this go. They are going to hunt you down like a dog."

"They've already had the dogs after me, and I won." He laughed, trying to be lighthearted.

I slapped his arm hard. "This isn't funny! This is some serious shit! And that FBI bitch isn't playin'."

Larry pulled back from the sting of my slap. "I didn't kill that guard, Nee. Me and my people tried to save her."

"Well then, they have got you guilty by association, and they are going to give you the chair because of it. And I'm not trying to be no widow," I said sternly.

"I can fix this." Larry looked troubled, but I could see he was formulating a plan. "You said there was an FBI agent involved?"

"Yes." I turned over and reached in my night table to retrieve the card she had given me. "Her name is Agent Janel Martinez." I handed him the card, and he studied it, flicking the card with his thumb.

"I think I know how to get her off our backs for a while."

"How?" Larry was always smart, but sometimes he was too smart for his own good.

"You let me worry about that," he said.

Whenever he said that, I knew it meant he was done answering questions, but there was something else we needed to talk about.

"Where's Kenny? You got my baby mixed up in this?" I asked.

Larry sighed. "Yeah, a little. He should be on his way back from Knoxville to pick me up any minute."

"Larry Duncan, you gonna get my son killed messing around with you," I snapped at him.

"He'll be all right once I get everything straight with the feds. And I will get everything straight. I promise."

I heard a chirp, and he reached back over to his pants, pulling out his phone. He studied the screen then sent a text.

"That's Kenny. I gotta go. He's waiting for me over by the creek. You damn sure know how to welcome a man home. Lord knows I missed this." He squeezed my inner thigh and went to kiss me, but I turned my head.

"Is that why you came here?"

"Of course not. I missed that fried chicken of yours too," he said with a laugh.

"I hate you sometimes." I playfully hit him, then laid my head on his chest.

Larry looked down at me as if he could read my thoughts. "You know I can't stay, Nee, especially with all these children around. If I could, I would."

"I know, but they ain't always gonna be around. And you and Curtis need to talk."

"That boy ain't got nothing for me right now. He's still mad about the past. Thinks I'm crazy and evil and I tried to turn him into the same."

"I know, but you're going to have to fix that too. He needs you, Larry, more than ever. Maybe you can talk some sense into him."

He raised a concerned eyebrow. "About what?"

"He called me this afternoon about an opportunity." I knew Curtis would be a little upset if he found out I was talking to his daddy about his plans, but I felt Larry needed to know. "He wants to buy Jimmy Fairway's business."

"The bond company? That's not an opportunity. That's a damn godsend." Larry's face brightened into a huge smile. "I'm so proud of that boy. If he can do that, he'll set this family up for life. Him, Lauryn, and Kenny can work side by side."

"Yeah, that's exactly what I told him." I sighed. "Only Fairway wants one point five million dollars for it."

"Curtis got that kinda money?"

I shook my head. "Hell no. Which is why I told him to go talk to LC."

Larry sat up so fast that I almost fell. "No. My son doesn't need to go see LC for no money. We don't need no handouts. I'm not in jail anymore."

"Now, Larry, you know it ain't no handout. LC is family, and he loves Curtis. It would be an investment. A good one. We just have to talk his stubborn ass into going to see LC."

"I said no!" he yelled.

Most people feared Larry when he was angry. I was never afraid—well, not for myself—and I had no problem speaking my mind. I replied in a voice that was just as loud as the one he used. "I know what you said. And you ain't gotta yell, because Curtis said the same thing. He's gonna get the money himself."

Larry calmed down a little and looked at me. "How?"

"There's some fugitive out there with a bounty that's over a million dollars. Curtis says he's gonna find her and use the money to buy the business."

"Who is it they're looking for?" Larry seemed both impressed and curious about the task our son was undertaking.

"Some woman," I answered.

Larry's face tensed slightly, but he didn't say anything. I knew something crossed his mind, so I asked, "What are you thinking?"

He looked deep in thought, then locked eyes with mine. "Don't tell Curtis I know about this. It may take some time, but he'll get his money. He don't need LC. He's got me."

I'd seen that look of determination before, and it made me uneasy. The last thing Larry needed to be doing was getting caught up in some nonsense. He was already on the run from the feds as it was. From what Curtis had told me, this woman was one of the most dangerous people in the United States, so I could only imagine how dangerous she was. My husband was not one to back down, though, so putting him in the path toward another fugitive was bound to create a firestorm.

I thought telling him about Curtis's dilemma would help somehow, but I was afraid I'd done the opposite.

Paris

29

The shrill ringing of my phone woke me out of a deep sleep. I woke up feeling confused and hungover. I looked around the room, shaking my head to try to dislodge the remnants of the nightmare I'd been having. It was a sexual dream about my ex-boyfriend, Niles Monroe, and Nadja, his right-hand woman and sometimes lover. Niles and I were making love. I mean, we were really getting it in, when I looked up and saw Nadja on a platform above us, pulling strings like she was our puppet master. I'd had some crazy sexual dreams before, but this was truly disturbing.

Ring! Ring! Ring!

I patted around the bed, searching for my phone, only for my hand to land on hairy flesh just as the phone stopped ringing. Shit! That's when I realized I was not in that bed alone, though I had no recollection of being with anyone other than Lauryn and Rio last night. I blinked open my eyes and saw that one thing was for sure. This was not my room, and I was not alone. I reached out again to make sure my mind wasn't playing tricks on me.

"What the fuck are you doing, Paris? That shit hurt!"

I swear I was never so happy to have Rio yell at me in my entire life. "Making sure this is not part of my dream. I think I had way too much tequila last night."

"You're going to have a knot on your head if you keep pinching me like that," he snapped at me, burying his head in the pillow.

"Where the fuck are we anyway?"

"My room."

I turned to my left where the voice had come from, and there was Lauryn, lying on the floor, snuggled up in a comforter like a cocoon.

"At least it's my room while I'm here. My bed too," she said.

"Uh-oh, did I detect a little bit of an attitude from Ms. Southern Belle?"

"I'm just sayin', how am I on the floor when y'all both have beds down the hall?"

Rio pointed at the two empty bottles of Don Julio on the dresser. "Blame it on the alcohol!" he groaned.

"Facts. I have the worst hangover." I reached over for my purse and some Advil.

"Couldn't have been too bad. You kept moaning Niles' name half the night," Rio cracked, lifting his head from the pillow.

"I wasn't moaning, I was having a nightmare, and he was part of it. Him and that bitch Nadja."

After leaving the florist the day before, I was still trying to process what I had suspected. Somebody was fucking with me, and it appeared to be Nadja. But why, after all these years? It had been six years since I'd killed Niles, and longer since I'd seen Nadja. Now she was playing games with me. I had no idea why, but I was certain she hadn't gone to all these lengths unless she wanted to kill me, which was why I had to find her first.

"We've got to find Nadja," I said, sitting up and finally planting my feet on the ground.

"I'm down. Where do we start?" Lauryn asked. She was folding the comforter she had been sleeping on.

"Easier said than done. Nadja is a contract broker who places clients with assassins. A major part of her job is to be invisible. People only see her when she wants to be seen, and only if it's in her best interests."

"Then why did she get caught on camera in the florist shop?" Lauryn asked. It was a damn good question.

"I wouldn't be surprised if she wanted me to know she was in town, just to fuck with me. The question is, where is she now?"

"Well, someone has to know where she is," Lauryn replied. "Does she have any family or friends that you know of?"

"Why the hell would I know her family or friends?" I snapped at her.

"Because she used to fuck your baby daddy, that's why," Rio snapped back, defending Lauryn, "Now, I know your nerves are on edge, but we are trying to help, so you need to check your tone."

He was right. My anxiety was on overload. "I'm sorry, Rio. Is that better?"

"There is another person in the room," he stated, and I turned to Lauryn. "Sorry, Lauryn."

"It's okay. I really do just want to help."

"See now, Paris, think. I know you know more about this woman than you want to admit. You probably even had a plan to kill her," Rio said.

"All I know is that her name in Nadja Bajaur. She's a contract broker, and her family belongs to the Assassins Guild. Other than that, I know a couple of her aliases, and that's it," I said flatly.

"Well, that's something. Brother Minister is a member of the Guild. Maybe we can ask—"

There was a light tapping at the door.

"That's probably Sasha. She's been in her feelings the past couple of days." Rio stood to open the door.

"About what?" Lauryn asked.

"She's pissed about your dad's escape," Rio answered. "I told her to come down here and drink with us last night so we could all talk it out, but she never came."

"I guess now's the time," Lauryn said with trepidation.

"She'll be all right, and so will you," I said. "Let her in. We could use her help."

Rio opened the door, and my mouth dropped. It wasn't Sasha standing in the doorway. It was my nephew, Nevada.

"Hey, Uncle Rio." Nevada smiled excitedly.

"Nevada!" I squealed, jumping up and running to him before Rio could even attempt a hug. I threw my arms around his neck and hugged him tight. I loved all my nieces and nephews, but there was something special about Nevada. "Look at you. When did you get here?"

"About an hour ago. I came to see the new baby and enjoy a couple weeks with the family before me and my friends go down to the house in Jamaica for summer break," Nevada told me.

He'd only been gone a few months, but Nevada looked older. Not only was he more filled out, but his voice was deeper, and he was sporting a goatee. My nephew was a grown-ass man, and a cute one like his father.

"Come on in. Where's your dad?"

"He stayed in Paris with Marie. She's been through a lot, and they need some alone time," Nevada said as he walked into my bedroom. "He should be home in a few days."

"Hey, Nevada." Lauryn, who was now sitting on the bed, stood up and hugged him.

"Hey." Nevada looked a little hesitant, but he hugged her back.

"You remember our cousin Lauryn? Aunt Nee Nee's daughter from Waycross. She graduated from Chi's too." I introduced our cousin.

"Oh, Lauryn! Yeah, I do. Brother Elijah speaks highly of you." Nevada grinned, now realizing who Lauryn was.

"He was tough but a good teacher." Lauryn nudged him. "I heard you're doing your thing. Proud of you, cousin."

Nevada laughed. "I'm just trying to keep the Duncan legacy intact, that's all."

"Well, you're doing a damn good job," I told him. "I heard about you breaking my marksmanship record."

"And acing Brother Minister's ironman challenge," Lauryn added. "How the heck did you do that?"

"I had a good teacher." He wrapped his arm around my neck and kissed my cheek.

It came as no surprise that Nevada did exceptionally well at school. After all, he spoke five languages, had a genius IQ, could shoot firearms almost as well as I could, not to mention he held a couple of black belts in various martial arts and had an expertise in computers.

"Oh, shit! That's it!" I exclaimed, causing both him and Lauryn to jump. It had just hit me that Nevada was just the person we needed, and his arrival was right on time. "Nevada, I need your help."

"Help with what?"

"I'm looking for someone. Someone who doesn't want to be found. Can you work your magic for me, please?" I gave him the puppy dog look I gave my father when I really wanted something only he could provide.

He shrugged. "Sure, Aunt Paris. Lemme just grab my laptop. I'll be right back."

"You really think he can find her?" Lauryn asked when Nevada walked out of the room.

"If anyone can, he can," I told her. "The boy is a hacker. He used to hack into the Pentagon and fly their drones, then divert the signal to the local library, just to fuck with them. Daddy had to make him promise not to use his skills unless it was absolutely necessary, which this situation is."

Nevada returned to Lauryn's room, laptop in hand. He sat on the bed beside me and opened it. "What's the name?"

"Her name is Nadja Bajaur. She's an Iranian national, but her family lives in Dubai. She's mid-thirties and mainly travels internationally, but she may be here in New York," I said.

"Okay, I'm searching. One sec." Nevada's fingers clicked as he quickly typed on the keyboard.

"She's gone ghost. She's totally off the grid."

"What does that mean?" Rio asked.

"I'm not finding anybody using that name in the past three years. She was real active up until then. She's probably using an alias or is dead," Nevada told me.

"She's not dead," I whispered. "Try Nadja Muhammed and Marie Hernandez. She was known to pass for Spanish, the slick-ass bitch."

He entered the names, then shook his head. "Nope. That's not working either. Got anything else?"

I shook my head. "Fuck."

"Try Nadja Monroe," Rio blurted out, and I turned my head to glare at him.

"Not funny, Rio," I spat.

"I'm not trying to be funny," he retorted. "Maybe she's trying to honor his legacy by using his last name. It's not like you don't have an ID that says Paris Monroe."

Nevada smirked at that comment as he typed the name in. "No good, but give me a second to try something else. I've been checking FBI files. I'm gonna cross check right quick with Interpol records." He worked for a few more minutes, then announced, "Bingo! I think I got something."

"You do? What do you have?" I said, feeling anxious.

"Nadja Bajaur was arrested on arms charges six years ago in Tel Aviv. She remained off the grid for three years and is suspected of resurfacing as Nadja Monroe in 2019. Most recent ties are suspected to be with the Mexican cartels. Her date of birth would put her in her mid-thirties. And look at this." He turned the computer toward me. "Is that her?"

On the screen was a Canadian passport for Nadja Monroe. I leaned in closer to see the photo. "That's her! The bitch died her hair, but that's her."

"Now we're getting somewhere. Let me search her passport number and see what we come up with," he said and went back to typing. "You're right. She's in New York. Flew in through Toronto via Barcelona. Landed at JFK three days ago. Here's the TSA footage." Nevada pointed at the video of Nadja moving through the airport.

"You are the best, Nevada. Can you find out where she's staying?" I asked, looking at the video.

"I'm checking credit card records," he said. "Looks like she checked into a hotel in Tribeca, The Greenwich."

"I know exactly where that is," Rio said. "Very discreet. Good place to have discreet meetings."

"Room six thirty-seven," Nevada added. "Ordered bagels and coffee for breakfast this morning along with a bottle of very expensive merlot. She also asked for a late checkout today, so you might want to get down there."

"We're on it, Nevada." I reassured him. "Thanks. I appreciate you for this. I'm so glad you're home."

"Love you too, Aunt Paris. Glad to be home." He turned to Lauryn. "And I'm glad you're here too. But where's Sasha?"

I realized that I still hadn't spoken with my cousin. "She's around. I'm sure you'll see her later."

"Cool. Well, I gotta go unpack." Nevada gave us another hug then left.

"Wow, Paris." Lauryn looked at me. "Damn, he really is good."

"He's the best," I agreed. "Gonna run this family one day. And my son Jordan is gonna be right there beside him."

"So, now what? Are we going to the hotel to find Nadja?"

I smiled. "I wouldn't have it any other way."

Larry

30

I checked my watch as I got up from my chair and went to the refrigerator, trying to decide between the orange juice and a can of Diet Sprite. What I really wanted was one of those Pepsis I'd seen my son Kenny walking around with earlier, but he must have gotten the last one. I opted for the juice, removing the half gallon container along with a glass from the cupboard. I poured myself a full glass and returned to my chair in the living room, reaching inside the pocket of my tweed blazer and removing my medication. I took the last pill, chasing it down with half the glass of juice.

I hated the sluggish way the medicine made me feel, but I couldn't deny the fact that it kept away most of my demons. Those demons were what prevented me from being with my family because when they were around, they made me into a homicidal maniac. I didn't want to be that person anymore, so I had sent Dennis, Holly, and Kenny to break into a CVS in the next county over to refill my prescription.

I sat in the darkness, waiting patiently for my crew to return. I had no idea how long it would take, and I really didn't care. We'd been staying in the East Orange, New Jersey home since we'd left Waycross two days ago. With my crew gone, I was bored, so I reached in my pocket and removed the card from the FBI agent that Nee Nee had given me. I took out my burner phone and dialed.

"Martinez here."

"Agent Martinez, this is Larry Duncan." I could almost envision her stopping dead in her tracks when she realized who was on the phone. It made me laugh. "I understand you're looking for me. Do you have a minute to chat?"

"Uh, ah, yes, we are looking for you," she stuttered. "I have a fugitive warrant for your arrest. We have a lot of manpower and resources dedicated to your capture."

"So I've been told. Seems like a little overkill, don't you think?"

"We don't take people killing federal officers lightly. Officer Williams was a mother of three." She sounded like she was taking it personally.

"I didn't kill that officer, and neither did Holly or Dennis. Thaddeus Jefferson did. Look at the tape. That place has cameras everywhere. We tried to save her," I replied sincerely. I needed her to understand. She wasn't lying when she said the feds didn't take kindly to people killing one of their ranks. "I may be crazy, but I'm not stupid enough to kill a fed. At least not an honest one."

"Then turn yourself in, Larry. It's the only way I can guarantee your safety."

"I appreciate your concern, Agent Martinez, but I'm kind of enjoying my newfound freedom. You're going to have to kill me to take me in," I said in no uncertain terms.

"Well, that can be arranged. Where are you?" she asked.

"That's not important at this time. However, I do have a proposal we should discuss."

"A proposal? Interesting. How about you tell me where you are?" she suggested. "I'll come over and we'll talk now."

I heard the sound of a car engine, and the beam of headlights streamed through the front windows.

"I'm not sure how smart that would be. Besides, I'm about to have company. I promise you we'll chat soon. Real soon." I hung up and retrieved my gun from the coffee table, pointing it at the door.

Sure enough, a few seconds later, I heard the jingling of keys and the door opened. I watched in the shadows as a female figure entered, then closed the door and locked it. A gun was laid on the table near the entryway, and she ran without hesitation the fifteen feet to the half bathroom. She had to pee so bad she didn't even close the door. I could hear her sigh along with the dribbling sound as she relieved herself. Not long after that, I heard the bathroom sink come on, and a minute or two later, the lights to the townhouse clicked on.

"Hijo de puta!" Agent Martinez shouted when she saw me causally sitting in her overstuffed chair, pointing a gun at her.

"Did you just call me a son of a bitch? I sometimes get my Spanish curses mixed up." I rose from my seat, stepping over to the entry table to retrieve her gun, which I tucked away in my waistband. "Told you I was close."

"How did you know where I live? And how the hell did you get in here?"

"I used to own the only KDP alarm system franchise in Waycross." I chuckled. "I'll be honest with you. Despite their reputation, they're really not dependable. A snip here and snip there and the whole system is disarmed. Horrible."

"That doesn't explain how you knew where I live."

"No, it doesn't, but did you know for thirty-nine ninety-five you can get a service on the internet that will give you the address of anyone who has a utility or phone bill in their name? These fucking utilities will sell anything, even the address of an FBI agent."

I had decided I needed to talk to her face to face after my conversation with Nee Nee. My brothers and I had dealt with law enforcement most of our lives. I found that deep down, most of them were dirty. There wasn't anything special about them. They were human beings with bills and problems just like the rest of us, only they had a gun and a badge. To get to them, you just had to find out what their price was. For some, it was cold hard cash. For others, it was information that would help them climb the political ladder in their department. But they all had a price. I was prepared to offer Agent Martinez $150,000, almost half of what we'd taken from the robbery in Gary, if she and her task force would lay off Nee Nee and the kids. However, what I found in her home was something that could benefit us both, and I'd be able to hold onto my cash.

The agent's face was a mixture of fear, shock, and anger. I could see the wheels turning in her head and knew she was processing the fact that I was standing in her living room while at the same time trying to figure out what to do next.

"It's not there," I told her as she inched closer to a small desk. I was already ten steps ahead of her.

She spun to the left and rushed toward the closet door, opening it and reaching for the top shelf.

"Neither are the shotgun you had in there or the Glock you had in your bedroom." I slid a bullet in the chamber, and that finally stopped her from moving around.

"You know you're making a huge mistake, right?" she growled, her Spanish accent more prevalent now.

"Please call me Larry, Janel." I nodded. "It is Janel, right?"

"Yes, Larry, it is."

"Good. Now, like I told you, I have a proposition for you," I said. "Let's sit down and chat."

"I'd rather stand." She folded her arms.

"Suit yourself, but please don't try anything stupid. At this point, I have very little to lose." I took a seat in the chair. "Now then, I believe you and I can help one another."

"The only help I'm gonna get from you is the satisfaction of bringing your ass in."

"That doesn't serve either one of us, Janel. All that gets you is a pat on the back from your ungrateful supervisors. That's all. What I'm proposing will get you much more. What if I offered to be your confidential informant? Help you with a few cases. I may have been locked away a few years, but I have a shitload of contacts in the underworld. Could be useful."

"What the fuck are you talking about? You're a fucking nutcase!" She laughed at me, hard and long, until her dark olive complexion had a red hue. "Have you forgotten that you're a cop-killing fugitive? I don't have the authority to agree to anything like that and wouldn't give it to you if I had. Best I can do is speak to the U.S. Attorney and let them know that you were cooperative—after I bring you in, of course."

I took a moment to get my thoughts together.

"You just don't get it, do you? I'm trying to help." I sighed with a shrug. "It would seem to me that having me as an ally would be the way to go, especially since no one at the bureau seems to give a shit about the death of your fiancé, Jack Smith."

Janel's eyes widened. "Keep his name out of your mouth. You don't know anything about Jack."

"Oh, but I do." I lifted the thick binder from the coffee table. "I've been waiting for you for a few days. I've read your dossier. It's a great read. Quite thorough, I might add."

"That's private." She seemed hurt, like I'd read her diary.

"It shouldn't be. Seems like a travesty of justice if you ask me." I lowered my head slightly. "An FBI agent goes undercover for three years with one of the biggest arms contractors in the world, and his cover is blown because of a bureau fuckup, so he has to be pulled. No matter, though, because he comes home a hero and takes down half the organization with his testimony almost singlehandedly. But these people are arms dealers who never forget, and he's shot dead on his wedding day. Talk about fucked up."

For a moment, she softened up, and I could see that the memory still pained her. "Very fucked up."

"It all makes sense now. That's why you're on the fugitive task force. You don't give a shit about guys like me. You're a fucking analyst. You're after his killer. You, Agent Martinez, are looking for revenge."

"Wouldn't you be if someone killed the only person you ever loved?" She was starting to get emotional, and I wasn't sure if that was going to work in my favor.

"Absolutely, and nobody would be able to hold me back either," I told her. "I noticed there seems to be a particular person you're interested in capturing. The man whose photos are posted in the room you're using as an office. You think he killed your fiancé, don't you?"

"He might not have pulled the trigger, but he was just as responsible for it as the bastards that did," she said, caught up in her own reply. "So, what does this have to do with you? Why do you care?"

"I don't know. I'm kind of sentimental like that. I was thinking I might help you prove he's responsible, for a little leniency."

My answer caused her shoulders to straighten. "What is that, a joke? No! Hell no!" she said, shaking her head vehemently. "You killed a federal officer, Larry. That's a capital offense. There's no fucking way I can allow you to roam the streets a free man." I think she was trying to convince herself more than she was trying to convince me.

"And I'm sure if you watch the security tapes like I said, you'll see that we tried to save her." I frowned. "I could've easily killed you, but I haven't. I'm not the problem or the threat."

"That doesn't mean you won't be."

"If I wanted you dead, you would have been dead the moment you walked through the door." I sighed as a text came through, letting me know that my crew was waiting outside. "I came here to make a deal and prove that I'm sincere. I guess you need a little more convincing."

"I don't need shit from you, and the only thing I'm convinced of is that it is going to be a pleasure locking your ass up. Now get the fuck out of my house."

"I don't expect you to trust me, so I'm going to give you something in good faith. Something substantial. Get the monkey off my back, so to speak."

"Like what?"

"You'll see." I smiled. Reaching in my waistband, I handed her back her gun. "Give me twenty-four hours to complete the task, and you'll be anxious to hear from me. You have my word."

"You seem quite confident." She carefully took her gun and pointed it at me. "What makes you think I won't take you in right now?"

"Because I'm the best chance of bringing in the people who killed your fiancé, and your desire to seek revenge on them is greater than turning me in," I answered. "Oh, and the fact that there are no bullets in that gun doesn't hurt either." I laughed as I dropped the clip on the floor and headed for the door. "I'll be in touch."

Harris

31

"Mr. Grant, thank you for coming." The thin, graying man in his late seventies introduced only as the Employer, sat across from me and smiled pleasantly. He reminded me of someone's grandpa, and he damn sure didn't look like he was associated with any killers for hire. Then again, I damn sure didn't look like a lawyer who had worked for a crime family for the past fifteen years, so who was I to talk?

"Thank you for meeting with me." I picked up the glass of brandy the waiter had placed in front of me and took a sip. "Antonio spoke highly of you."

"He spoke the same about you." He nodded toward me. "So, how can I be of service?"

"I'm not sure how much Antonio told you, but I have a job that needs to be taken care of." I got straight to the point in an effort to show him that I was serious and there was no need for small talk. I was ready to get down to business. No regrets.

"He didn't share any specifics, which is customary. Our business is our business. I will not discuss it with Antonio or anyone else," he said.

"That's very comforting." I reached into my breast pocket and removed an envelope, placing it in front of him. "I'm aware that there is a substantial cost, and I'm prepared to take care of that now."

The Employer's eyes went to my hand. He shook his head. "Mr. Grant, I think you misunderstand."

"Did I do something wrong?" Why the hell was this man refusing the cold hard cash I'd brought? I looked around. Had Antonio sold me out to LC?

"I don't handle these types of things anymore. I've recently retired."

"I'm sorry. I didn't know." I exhaled, now frustrated and disappointed. I was back to square one. At this point, I was almost tempted to kill Daryl's ass my damn self. "I guess I came all this way for nothing."

"No, that's not totally true," he replied. "Yes, I am no longer the employer for the guild. However, I still may be able to provide you with some assistance."

"How's that?"

"My job has been split up between many operatives. I can introduce you to one of them, who can provide you with the service you desire if you'd like." He reached down and picked up the envelope, sliding it into his jacket. "For a finder's fee, of course."

"Of course." I gave him a half smile. "How soon can you set up a meeting?"

"Is now a good time? They happen to be sitting at the bar." I glanced over to where three huge, scary-looking men sat talking to an attractive woman who looked very out of place. She could be either a hooker or some undersexed Upper East Side housewife looking to get laid before she picked up the kids from soccer practice.

"Excuse me a moment. I'll be right back." He stood up and walked over to the bar.

I watched as he spoke to the group for a minute, then he picked up a few peanuts from a bowl on the bar before walking back alone. Anyone who observed this interaction would have no idea that it was more than a casual conversation between strangers at a bar.

"She said she'd be right over. She just wanted to finish her drink," he explained as he took his seat.

"She?"

"Yes, she." He turned his head to smile at her. "Ah, here she is now."

I watched the tall, slender, impeccably dressed woman glide over to our table. She had an aura of confidence about her.

"Mr. Grant, this is Nadja." The employer gave the introduction. "Nadja, Mr. Grant comes highly recommended and is interested in using your services."

"Nice to meet you." I shook her extended hand, which was soft and inviting.

"Mr. Grant." Nadja sat in one of the empty seats at the table.

"Now that I've made the introduction, I'm going to leave you to see if this is a good fit." The Employer stood and shook my hand. "Good luck, Mr. Grant."

"Thank you for your assistance, sir."

I watched him walk off and then turned to Nadja.

She didn't mince words. "Tell me what it is exactly you're seeking."

I reached into my inside pocket and handed her a photo of Daryl, then vaguely explained the situation at hand. "His name is Daryl Graham. He's the former head of security for my employer." I took a breath and sighed. "He's also screwing my wife."

She glanced at the picture. "He's handsome. You said he's the former head of security for your employer?"

"Yes. We both worked for my wife's father, a man by the name of LC Duncan."

"LC Duncan?" She sat back in her chair, staring at me in silence.

Did she know LC, or perhaps even Daryl? This might have been a big mistake.

"Everything okay?"

"Yes, however, I must admit I did not expect to hear LC Duncan's name mentioned."

"Do you know him?"

"Only by reputation. He's a very powerful man. Killing his security chief . . ."

"*Former* security chief."

"Okay, killing his former security chief will not be an easy job. Not easy at all," she said, looking uneasy.

"I understand your reluctance. Thank you for your time." I went to rise from my seat, but she grabbed my arm.

"I said not easy, but nothing is impossible."

"I like the sound of that." I returned to my seat. "But I need this done discreetly and with no blowback to me. If that man dies, I'm going to be the prime suspect."

Nadja stared at the photo for a moment before she answered. "A job of this magnitude will cost two hundred thousand dollars, half up front. You can wire it to this account."

She handed me a piece of paper. I unfolded it and stared at the number.

"That's more than I expected."

"You're asking for a lot. This isn't a simple shoot-someone-in-the-head killing, Mr. Grant. You're asking me to take out the security chief of one of the most respected crime bosses in America. It can be done, but not for cheap." She sighed liked she was bored with me. "Now, you either want the job done or you don't."

"Yes, I want it done. I was just having a little sticker shock. I'll wire the money today." I suppressed the smile of relief threatening to spread across my face.

"There are two things you need to understand before the contract is accepted."

"What's that?" I asked.

"There are no refunds. Once the deposit is paid, you don't get it back." Nadja looked me in the eye.

"And the second thing?"

"Should you change your mind after the deposit is paid, the balance is still owed." She said it with such intensity that I understood that changing my mind shouldn't be an option.

"Believe me, my mind won't change. I want this bastard gone forever. The sooner the better."

"Then once the wire is received, it will be handled in a timely manner."

"So, will you handle this yourself?"

"No. I have operatives for that. I am strictly a broker." Nadja stood and shook my hand. "Oh, and Mr. Grant, do you happen to be married to Paris Duncan?"

"No, her sister London. Paris is too much of a pain in the ass." I wondered how she knew Paris. Maybe they had gone to the same finishing school.

"Yes, so I've heard." She laughed. "I'll await your wire."

And just like that, I'd placed a hit on the biggest threat to my marriage and family. Knowing that he'd be dead soon made me feel good. Not only would Daryl be dead, but certainly London would be devastated. I would make sure I was there to comfort her during her time of need to help her pick up the pieces.

Lauryn

32

The Greenwich was located a few steps away from Wall Street. I stood outside for a moment, wondering if I was at the right building. From the outside, it looked like an apartment building. The simple sign hanging over the entrance didn't even mention anything about it being a hotel.

Paris had dropped me off at the front door and decided not to come in so that she wouldn't be recognized. My job was to do reconnaissance, find Nadja, and figure out a way to get her out of the building to somewhere we could snatch her up and interrogate her.

Walking in, I realized that it was indeed a chic, modern boutique hotel. The small lobby was impeccably decorated with muted colors and chrome accents. A gorgeous floral arrangement dominated the table beside the reception desk.

"Paris?" I spoke into the AirPods connected to my phone.

"What do you see?" she asked.

"Nothing yet. I'm about to go upstairs and check out her floor." I scanned the room for a moment, then headed toward the elevators, which were just past the reception area.

"Welcome to the Greenwich." The red-haired concierge stopped me with a smile. "Are you checking in?"

"Uh, no. I'm actually just visiting a guest."

He looked down at my empty hands. I had no luggage and held no key card. "Unfortunately, only guests and their accompanied visitors can go beyond this point. I can call upstairs and let them know you're here if you'd like."

"Actually, I can just call him myself," I answered. "I'll wait over here in the lobby."

"Or we have a nice bar you can enjoy as well. It's right through those doors." He pointed to his left.

"Thanks." I strolled away, then tucked behind a tall column. I needed to regroup and decide my next move.

"Paris, did you hear that?"

"Yeah, but I have an idea."

"I hope it's a good one."

"Let's just check in and request a room on her floor. I'll be right in. Let me find a place to park," she said.

"Sounds good to me."

"Oh, shit!"

I could hear the panic in her voice.

"What is it? Do you see her?"

"No, I see something worse. Harris just rolled out the side entrance of the hotel, and the last thing we need is for him to bring up at dinner that he saw me here. My mom has this eerie way of knowing when I'm lying, and I am not about to tell them about Niles."

"I get it. My momma has that same sixth sense. It's creepy as fuck. Has he seen you yet?"

"Not yet, but I won't be hard to spot in this Maserati with Duncan plates. I'm pulling around the block. Keep your eyes open for Nadja." Paris hung up.

Not wanting to lurk around the lobby under the gaze of the reception clerk, I headed toward the bar, which was fairly crowded. As I stood there looking for a place to sit, I heard a voice from behind me.

"Lauryn Duncan, is that you?"

I turned around. "Minister Farah?"

"It is you!" he said cheerfully. "How are you? It's so good to see you." He gave me a brief hug.

"It's great to see you too, Minister Farah."

Minister Farah was the acting headmaster at Chi's Academy, the finishing school that many of us Duncans had attended. He was a martial arts guru and one of the best mercenary teachers in the world, though you'd never know it by looking at his slight build and the unassuming black suit and bowtie he always wore. It was a little jarring to see him in this context, but nevertheless I was pleased. I'd always liked him.

"How are you? Are you living in New York now?" he asked.

"No, I'm just here visiting my family for a little while."

"That's good to hear. I'm sure LC and Chippy are happy to have you here along with your cousins. I hope they're all doing well."

"They are."

"Your cousin Nevada is one of our prize students, much like you were. Are you working with your family's business?"

"Well, not yet anyways. For now, I am jobless. I may go home and do some bounty hunting." I looked at the bodyguard standing close behind him. "And you? I heard you'd been reinstated as headmaster. What are you doing in New York?"

"The school is on summer recess, and New York is always home, so I came home for a conference I host every year. In fact, I'm headed to Montauk now." Minister Farah reached into his pocket and handed me a small card. "You should come out to the welcome reception for the school's graduates that I'm hosting tomorrow night. It's sort of like a job fair for old and new students. I think you'll enjoy it. Who knows? You might just find that job you're looking for." His wink told me this event would be well attended by potential employers from the underworld.

I stared at the card. There were no names or formal details, only a date, time, and address. "Okay, thanks, Minister Farah. I'll keep it in mind."

"I'll put you on the guest list." He hugged me again. "It was good seeing you, Lauryn, and I hope you'll join us this weekend."

"Good seeing you too," I told him. "I'll definitely think about it."

I watched Minister Farah through the large windows at the front of the bar as he exited and waited at the valet station. Then, a woman and a man approached him, and my jaw dropped. It was Nadja. I took out my cell phone and dialed Paris's number.

"Paris, where the fuck are you? You need to get back here now," I hissed.

"I'm still trying to find a parking garage that's not full, and this traffic is moving so damn slow." She finally took a breath. "Why, is she there? You see her?"

"I'm standing right here looking at her, but not for long. She's waiting at the valet with a suitcase. If you don't hurry your ass up, we're gonna lose them."

"Them? Who is them?"

"She's with Minister Farah and another guy," I said.

"What? Minister Farah?"

"Just forget about parking. Get back here now."

"On my way," she said, and I ended the call so I could open the camera on my phone.

Easing as close to the window as I could without being noticed, I took photos of Minister Farah, Nadja, and the man that was with her. I watched as a sleek, black Mercedes pulled up, and the valet handed the keys to the man, who got in the driver's seat. Minister Farah and Nadja climbed in the back, and Minister Farah's bodyguard sat in the front. The car pulled off and disappeared into traffic.

"Where are they?" Paris asked a few minutes later when she finally arrived and I hopped in her car.

"They're gone. You're like two minutes too late," I said, putting on my seatbelt.

"Fuck." Paris exhaled. "Are you sure it was her?"

I pulled up the photos and passed her my phone. "I'm positive."

"What the hell is she doing with Minister Farah?" Paris flipped through the pictures I'd taken. "And where the hell did they go?"

"I don't know, but he mentioned heading to Montauk for the weekend, and she was in the car," I said. "Good chance she'll be there. He gave me an invitation."

"Then I guess you're going to Montauk."

Larry

33

"Turn the lights off, Kenny. I don't want him to see us coming," I said, and my son quickly obeyed. It was just past sunset and getting dark quickly as we traveled down the dirt road deep into the Buford, South Carolina woods.

"So, let me get this straight, Sarge. Are we really doing what I think we're doing?" Dennis asked. Other than me, he was the only one who had a clue of where the fuck we were going, and it wasn't because I'd told him. It was because he'd heard the same creepy stories about this place.

"Yes, we are," I replied. I could feel his uncomfortable gaze from the back seat, and if I knew Dennis, he wanted to take his catcher's-mitt-size hands and squeeze my neck until my head popped off or until I showed some type of sense. "Trust me, it's a part of the plan."

"What plan?" Holly asked. She was seated next to Dennis, flipping her signature butterfly knife back and forth.

"The plan to keep our asses out of jail," I explained. "But we have to find Thaddeus first."

"Thaddeus! I knew his ass had something to do with this the minute we entered Bufford." Dennis's voice boomed through the car. "I'll follow you to the depths of hell and back, Sarge, but I don't want any part of Thaddeus's sick ass."

"Dennis, I'm going to need you to trust me!" I hollered.

Dennis and I went way back to the Vietnam War, where I was his sergeant. We both came home pretty fucked up, only I had my family—my momma, my brothers, and Nee Nee—to help keep my head together, at least for a while. Dennis had a cheating ass wife that was screwing his brother. They'd stolen all his money and had him sleeping in his car. One day, he woke up and decided to use all the training Uncle Sam had given him in the war. On that day, he killed his wife, his brother, and all the rest of his siblings, along with their children. He'd been locked up at FCI New London for twenty years before I got there and was a virtual loner that nobody fucked with. But the minute he saw me five years ago, it was like life had changed, and he reverted back to the private in my platoon, taking my orders and having my back like we were still in the military.

"I do trust you, Sarge. It's Thaddeus I don't trust," Dennis grumbled. "You know I can't stand him."

"And neither can I. He's creepy," Holly said. There weren't many people who put fear in Holly's heart, but Thaddeus was one of them. "You can drop me off right here!"

Their voices were demanding, and that sent me over the edge.

"Look, goddammit! You'll need to trust me!" I growled, out of control. My voice forced Holly to sit back in her seat like a child and Dennis to be more docile. Thaddeus wasn't the only person who knew how to put fear in people's hearts. He may have been a sick fuck, but they all knew what I was capable of. "Like I said, it's all part of the plan."

"But I thought the plan was that Thaddeus helps us escape and then we go our separate ways." Dennis was still pressing for answers, but without the urgency in his tone.

Kenny inched the car up to the cabin, where Satanic rock music was blaring from inside.

I glanced at them as I opened the passenger side door, knowing that their questions wouldn't stop until I gave some sort of insight into what was happening. "That was the plan, but the plan has changed. We need Thaddeus."

"Need him how?" Dennis asked, stepping out of the car.

"We're going to assist the feds."

"What? Are you crazy?" Dennis snapped, turning his head toward me with bulging eyes. "You mean the federal agents that are looking for us? Have you taken your fucking meds today?"

"Actually, I have, and my mind has never been clearer." I gestured for Kenny to open the trunk. "My plan is fool proof."

"No offense, Dad, but do you mind sharing the plan with us?" Kenny looked confused.

"Isn't it obvious?" Dennis replied. "We're snitches!"

"Damn, what's the irony in that?" Holly sounded distraught, shaking her head as she removed a *Dirty Harry* type .44 magnum. "Seven years in federal prison, and now I'm a snitch! Ain't this a bitch."

"I don't like it, Dad. I didn't sign on to be no snitch," Kenny said.

"We ain't snitching. This is different. I'm trying to work a deal for us to assist the government in capturing Thaddeus for killing the guard. That way, the murder is not on us, and hopefully some of this heat will die down. 'Cause right now, shit is hot!"

Dennis was the first one to soften. "Well, I'll be honest with you. If anyone needs to be locked up, it's Thaddeus. That bastard's a weirdo of a different kind. Did you know that he raped just as many men in prison as he did women on the outside?" Dennis cocked his gun and sighed. "His ass needs to be put under the jail."

"I don't know," Holly replied, still a little skeptical. "Why don't we just kill him?"

"Because bringing him in alive will show the feds we're cooperating, at least to a certain extent. But I promise, when it's all said and done, Thaddeus will get his, and you'll be a big part of it."

"You promise?" Holly smiled.

"I pinky promise. You know I've never lied to you." I winked at her, putting up my pinky so she could hook it with hers.

I looked at my crew, armed to the teeth. "Now, y'all ready?"

"Yup," they replied in unison.

"Kenny, you go around back and cover the back door and windows." It was best that he wasn't in the cabin. I didn't want his fingerprints or DNA found if things got out of hand.

"This shit looks creepy as hell, just like Thaddeus," Holly said as we approached the tiny cabin in the middle of nowhere. It did look like something out of a horror film. Ragged, with shutters hanging, and a leaning front porch. It was just like Thaddeus described when he would brag about raping and killing men and women in the rec room. "And listen to that crazy-ass music."

"Makes that goth shit you listen to sound like R & B." Dennis laughed.

"Fuck you, Dennis," Holly commented. She considered herself some kind of witch. She wore gothic clothes and loaded on dark lipstick and eyeliner. It wasn't exactly my taste, but she still had a sexiness to her.

"It looks empty. I don't think anybody's in there, Larry," Holly said.

"The music says different." I opened the door and stepped in. Dennis and Holly stayed close behind.

Just as we entered the front room, a loud scream came from behind a bedroom door, and it burst open.

"Oh, God, please help me! Somebody please!"

For a second, none of us moved. We were too surprised by the bloodied and bruised naked woman running out of the bedroom with her ankles shackled. She'd only gotten about five feet before she tripped and fell to the ground.

"Come back here, you bitch! I haven't finished the J!" Thaddeus came chasing after her, holding a red-hot cordless iron. He stopped dead in his tracks when he saw the three of us standing at the entrance to his cabin.

"Larry! Dennis! What the fuck are you doing here?" Thaddeus stood in front of us wearing nothing but his tattoos, which covered most of his skinny-ass body.

"You bragged so much about this place in prison, we thought we'd pay you a visit. It's exactly just how you described," I replied rather calmly considering everything in front of us.

"You remembered all that?"

"How could we not? It was all you would talk about, other than escaping," Dennis said.

"Yeah, well, nothing like pussy and freedom."

I stared at him briefly, then looked at the girl, who was sobbing on the floor. "So, what's going on in here, Thaddeus?"

"Just having some fun." He laughed. "Ain't that right, bitch?"

"Please, he's trying to kill me," the woman cried hysterically, struggling to crawl to me. "He's trying to kill me!"

That's when I saw the iron burns on her back. I had seen so many horrors in the war that nothing much phased me, but this was disturbing.

"He's not gonna do that," I told her, stepping between Thaddeus and the girl.

"You need to get the fuck away from her, Larry." Thaddeus's voice sounded manic. "She's mine! This ain't got shit to do with you."

"We ain't going nowhere. But you sure as hell are," I said to him.

"I ain't going nowhere. Except back in this room with her."

"Yes, you are. You're going right back inside." I looked over at Holly. "Take her to the car."

"Don't take that bitch anywhere," Thaddeus spat, raising the iron, "or you'll be next, cunt. I been wanting to put my brand on you for a long time. I bet you got a nice tight asshole!"

Holly calmly pointed her gun at him. "Just give me the word, boss. Please give me the word and I'll spray paint this motherfucker's brains all over this wall."

"As tempting as that is, I'll handle him myself. Just take her to the car."

"Don't forget your promise," Holly reminded me.

"I won't."

Holly lowered her gun, then helped the trembling woman as she hobbled beside her out the door. Thaddeus went to object, looking like he was about to throw the iron at Holly, but I shot him in the leg, and he fell to the ground.

"You bastard! You shot me! You fuck!"

Dennis grabbed him by the throat and forced him into the air.

"Get off me, you oversized, wobbly motherfucker!" Thaddeus strained to get away, but Dennis was too strong. It was useless.

"Sit his ass in that chair," I commanded.

Dennis slammed Thaddeus into a folding chair sitting in the middle of the floor, then stood behind him, holding him in a chokehold. I pulled up another chair and sat across from him.

"What the fuck do you want, Larry?" Thaddeus gasped. "I ain't got no fucking money. That's why that bitch is pissed off. I got out here, and I told her I wasn't about to pay for no pussy."

"You lying motherfucker. You raped her." Dennis let go of his chokehold and smacked Thaddeus across the face. Blood oozed from his nose, but that didn't stop him from struggling. "You're a sadist and a sick-ass individual."

"Fuck you, Dennis. As many motherfuckers as you killed, from your own family no less, ain't shit you can say to me." Thaddeus then looked at me. "You're both just as psycho as I am."

"Perhaps, but the difference between you and us is that you're going back," I told him. "Minus one little thing."

"Fuck you! I ain't going nowhere," he yelled just as Holly returned.

"Kenny's watching the girl. She's pretty fucked up, but she'll live," Holly said.

"Good. You got your knife?"

"Always." She pulled out her butterfly knife, spinning it around.

"Excellent, then as promised, you can do the honors and teach Thaddeus a lesson. Hold him, Dennis."

Dennis grabbed Thaddeus's upper body, and I grabbed his legs. Sensing what was about to happen, Thaddeus struggled to get free.

"What the fuck are you doing?" he screamed.

Dennis laughed, tightening his grip. "We're going to cut your dick off, you pervert!"

"Larry, please! Please! I helped you escape!"

"Yeah, you did, but that didn't mean I liked you, Thaddeus," I retorted, holding his legs tight. "You violated someone very special to me. You remember Melvin?"

"The fucking cook?"

"Yeah, the fucking cook. I liked Melvin. He used to make me the best jail house lasagna I ever had. At least he did until you raped him and fucked up his head so bad he couldn't make it anymore. So, fuck you. We're cutting off your dick."

"What the fuck? No!" Thaddeus panicked.

"Hold still. This should only take a second." Holly joined in Dennis's laughter as she reached for Thaddeus.

"Ohhhhh, nooo! No, Larry! Please, fuck no! Don't! Nooooooo!"

Curtis

34

Riding around Waycross wasn't that exciting, but Roman seemed to enjoy it. He never let me slip out of the driveway without being in the passenger seat. I wasn't sure if it was because he needed to get out of the house after dealing with the kids yelling and screaming all day, or because he really wanted to learn about the town where our fathers grew up.

"Hey, cuz, you wanna roll out for a little while?" he'd ask every evening after dinner.

"Sounds like a plan." I'd smile, grab my keys, and we'd jump into my car. I'd become his personal tour guide and historian, sharing family history until we wound up back home, half drunk.

"Curtis." Momma stopped us just as we were about to get in the Jeep to embark on one of our night rides. "Y'all wait for a minute."

"Yes, ma'am?" I turned around, expecting her to give me instructions to pick something up from the store while we were out. Instead, she handed me a piece of paper.

"Y'all need to go here right away. It's business."

"Business?" I raised an eyebrow, staring at the address on the paper. "Who is in South Carolina, and why am I going?"

"Your daddy called and told me to tell you to go there now," she said. "He said it's important business and be prepared for anything."

I hesitated, unsure of what to do. There was no telling what my father had going on, and the last thing I wanted to do was get involved with his shit. "Ma, I don't think—"

"Ain't nobody ask you to think, Curtis. I said go!" She exhaled. "You gotta trust me."

"Why? Because you trust Daddy?"

"Yes," she said simply.

"Ma, I get it. You trust Daddy and will pretty much do anything he tells you to." I remained calm as I spoke my truth that I'd been holding onto. "But I don't. Not anymore. And I can't risk getting caught up in his madness. This man has the U.S. Marshals looking for him. If I get caught somewhere with him, they gonna take my license and everything I've built up over the past five years."

My mother stepped closer and looked me directly in the eye. "Boy, don't you think I know that? Do you think I would ever send you into harm's way if it wasn't important? I love your father, but I will not sacrifice my son or sons for him because you came out of me. Now go. He's trying to help you. That much I know for a fact."

"Help me with what?" I asked, confused.

"I guess you'll have to go there and see, Curtis. Now, you and Roman need to get going before it's too late." She pushed me toward the car. "I love both of you, and I'll see y'all when you get back here. Be safe on the road."

Roman and I got in the car, and I stared at the address.

"What you wanna do, cuz?" Roman asked.

"Man, I don't even know," I whispered, thinking about the chaos I'd gotten caught up in the last time my father was a free man.

"I mean, it wouldn't hurt to at least go and see what's up, right?" Roman's shrug let me know that if nothing else, his ass was curious. One thing I'd learned about him was that he was just as adventurous, if not more than I was. "We really ain't got shit else to do. How far is it?"

"About three hours."

"Fuck it. We hurry and we might get back for last call at Big Shirley's."

Knowing that my mother really hadn't given me a choice, I started the car, and we headed out. A little less than three hours later, we were creeping along a dirt road in the backwoods of South Carolina, looking for God knows what. Finally, we got to a tiny cabin in the middle of nowhere. There was no signs of my father or anyone else, and I wondered if this was some kind of a setup.

"This shit looks abandoned," Roman said.

"This was a waste of time and gas," I said, angry that we may have just squandered three hours of our lives getting there and were about to do the same going back home. "I tried to tell Momma."

"Yeah, maybe. But we here now. Might as well check inside before we go."

"You're right." I'd driven all this way, so I might as well find out what the hell my daddy had sent me out here for. I stepped out of the car. "Let's get suited up. I'm not trying to go in nobody's house without at least looking official."

We went to the trunk for our jackets and firearms before heading toward the house. Roman turned on the flashlight I'd given him and aimed it toward the cabin as we crept up.

"Looks like there's a note on the door," he said.

"Probably a no trespassing sign."

Boy, was I wrong. There was a piece of paper tacked to the front door, but it wasn't a no trespassing sign. It was a flyer featuring the face of my daddy and the three fugitives he'd escaped with. One of the pictures was circled in red, a man by the name of Thaddeus Jefferson.

"Damn, they got twenty-five grand on your old man's head."

"I see that," I replied.

"Hold up. You hear that?" Roman whispered.

"Yeah, I think somebody's inside."

We raised our weapons before I opened the unlocked door and entered. We were immediately greeted by the smell of overcooked meat.

"Damn, it smells like somebody burnt they dinner," I said.

Roman pointed his flashlight inside, and my eyes focused in on a naked body slumped over, tied to a chair in the middle of the room.

"Oh, shit. I think he's dead."

"Are you sure?" Roman pointed the flashlight directly on the man's bruised and swollen face.

My stomach tightened up, and for a brief moment, I couldn't fucking breathe. He'd done it to me again. Once again, my father had pulled me into his bullshit, and I couldn't see any way out but to run. "We need to get the fuck outta here!"

"You just want to leave him here?" Roman asked.

"We ain't got no choice. Two Black men from Georgia and New York with a dead white guy in Buford, South Carolina. Shiiiiit! We might as well both plan on doing hard time."

"Aren't we covered as bounty hunters?"

"Bro, a Black man is never covered when a white man comes up dead in the south. Remember that."

"Help me." The voice was weak, but it was coming from the man in the chair. It scared the shit out of me.

"Fuck! He's alive!" Roman shouted.

"Help me," the man groaned again.

I ran over and flicked on the light. It took a moment for our eyes to adjust, and when they did, I could see the horrified look on Roman's face. The sight before us was disgusting.

There was blood on the floor around the chair, and the man had a tourniquet of some kind wrapped around his leg, but that wasn't the worst part. Between the man's leg where his dick should have been, there was a black, charred mess. I felt vomit rise up into my throat as I understood where the burned meat odor was coming from.

"Help me!" he cried out, a little stronger now. I could see that dude was in some serious pain.

"What happened to you?" Roman asked as he took a few tentative steps toward the guy. He obviously needed help, but neither one of us really wanted to get too close to that horror show.

"Oh, shit, Curtis. Look at his face and these neck tattoos," Roman said.

His face was swollen, but I saw what he was talking about. I studied the paper in my hand. It confirmed what I was pretty sure Roman was thinking. The man in the chair was Thaddeus Jefferson, the same person circled in red on the flyer. Roman and I didn't move.

I was confused about what we were looking at. I had so many questions, the first one being where the hell was my father, and why had he wanted me here?

"Who did this to you?" Roman asked.

"Larry," Thaddeus whispered.

Roman turned to me. "Sounds like your Pops left us a twenty-five-thousand-dollar gift," he said, giving me the explanation, I'd been trying to figure out.

I had no doubt he was right. My old man had sent for us to retrieve the bounty for capturing Thaddeus. The fact that he'd mutilated the man first told me my father was still not okay, but Momma had been right. In his own crazy way, he was trying to help me.

"Help me," Thaddeus said.

"Keep an eye on him," I said to Roman. "I'm gonna check out the rest of the place."

"I got him," Roman replied.

It appeared that we were the only people in the house, but I needed to make sure. The single bathroom and kitchen were a mess but empty. The bedroom was also empty, but the place was torn up like some kind of fight had taken place in there. There were ropes tied to the bed, and I wondered who had been tied up there.

I returned to the other room just as a pair of flashlights came beaming through the windows.

"Who the fuck is that?" I asked Roman as if he knew.

"It's gotta be cops."

"Yeah, you right," I replied, and within moments I could see bodies heading toward the open front door through the dirty windows. "Let me do the talking," I said, bracing myself for the entrance of some racist-ass cops who might want to shoot first and ask questions later.

A man in a flak jacket yelled, "FBI! Drop the guns and put your hands in the air."

I eased my weapon down and raised my hands. "I'm a fugitive recovery agent. My badge and credentials are in my car. I've taken the fugitive Thaddeus Jefferson into custody."

They didn't give a shit about what I had to say, and within seconds, Roman and I were on the floor in handcuffs.

"Curtis Duncan?" The voice sounded familiar.

I looked up from the ground to see a woman standing over me. I recognized her as the agent who had come to our house after my dad escaped. She was standing there with the U.S. marshal by her side. No way in hell this was a coincidence. These guys had been tipped off just like we had.

Agent Fritz stared at Thaddeus's bloody, cauterized crotch. "What the fuck did you do to him?"

"He was like that when we found him. We tracked him to this location." I turned to Thaddeus and said, "Tell him."

"He's telling the truth. It was Larry, Dennis, and that bitch Holly." Thaddeus moaned.

"Jesus, get this man some help." Agent Martinez instructed two more agents that had entered the cabin. "We need a bus."

They helped Thaddeus to his feet and out the door. Once they were gone, Fritz gestured for two more agents to help us to our feet. We remained handcuffed.

"Where the fuck's your father?" Agent Martinez asked, standing next to her partner. She was about a foot from my face, and she looked like she was ready to explode with anger.

"I haven't seen him."

"Bullshit! You just happen to run up on one of his fellow escapees after they mutilate him by fucking accident? What do we look, stupid?" Her spit flew in my face as she yelled at me.

"Your words, not mine. I'm here because I got a tip that Thaddeus Jefferson was here and he was worth twenty-five thousand dollars," I said, gesturing to the flyer that was now on the floor. "Now, who do I talk to about my money?"

The two agents looked at each other, and deputy Fritz finally smirked. "Sounds like he may have gotten the same tip as you, Martinez."

"Fuck you, Fritz." She walked out of the cabin while Fritz watched. He didn't trust her for some reason. That was obvious.

"Cut them loose," Fritz said and watched as two agents began uncuffing us. "The twenty-five-thousand-dollar check for your reward will be waiting at the U.S. Marshals field office in Charlotte in seventy-two hours. See Deputy Trenton behind you to fill out the paperwork and write a statement, then you can go ahead and leave."

An hour later, we'd filled out the paperwork and given our statements and were headed back to Waycross. I still couldn't believe they were actually going to give us the money. I guess my old man finally did something right. Maybe he was trying to make amends.

London

35

It took a few days for me to realize that I might have been a little too hasty in my decision to jump into the car with Daryl. In that moment, the only thing I cared about was getting the hell away from everyone and everything and being with the man that I loved. It didn't dawn on me that there were some items I needed and didn't have, such as my purse or a change of clothing—the purse being more of a priority than the clothes.

Daryl and I spent most of our time in the hotel room that we had checked into. We didn't have a planned destination, so we ended up at Baron's Cove in Sag Harbor, on the East End of Long Island. Being with him, uninterrupted, for an extended period of time was glorious. I was in Heaven, though it didn't take long for reality to set in. As much as I enjoyed it, I had no choice but to return home and pack a few things I needed.

After a quick call to Duncan Motors to confirm that my father was in his office, I calculated my window of time. While Daryl went out fishing on a charter boat, I took his car and ventured back to the house.

DJ waved as if it were perfectly normal for me to be driving his former boss's car through the gate. I parked, then went inside, going straight up the staircase and into my bedroom. Not wanting to be there any longer than necessary, I began packing quickly. I was in the middle of tossing what I considered would be essentials into a suitcase when my mother strolled in.

"London." She sighed, standing in the doorway.

"Yeah, Ma," I said, barely glancing up because I didn't want to see the scowl on her face. "Whatever lecture you're about to give me, please save it."

"I'm not going to lecture you. You're a grown woman."

"I can't tell the way you and Daddy are treating me around here. You're being unreasonable," I told her.

"And you think running away makes you look like Mother Teresa?" She folded her arms as she leaned against my dresser.

"Well, what can I say?" I shrugged. "Y'all are treating me like a teenager, so I may as well act like one."

"London, please. This has gone on long enough. Where the hell are you going, and how long do you plan on being there? You have children to consider."

"I'm going to be with Daryl."

"And what about your children?"

"My kids are fine. I talk to them every day. They won't be home from Georgia for at least a few more weeks. I have time to figure it out."

"Figure what out? The only thing you need to figure out is this situation with your husband."

"I've already figured that out. I don't want to be married to him anymore. That problem was solved the moment I gave him those divorce papers," I reminded her. "The crazy thing is, even after I told you and Daddy that I was leaving Harris, you made Daryl leave, but Harris still gets to stay. Where's the fairness in that?"

"I'm sorry, London." Momma reached out and touched my face. "I know this is a lot to deal with. No one expected things to get this complicated, including me."

"Well, too late now," I said bitterly. "The damage is done. I'll call you in a couple of days."

I zipped my suitcase closed and placed it on the floor, then grabbed my purse off the bed. My mother and I hugged briefly, then she walked me to the top of the staircase.

"Are you at least going to speak to Harris before leaving?" she asked.

I looked at her as if she had lost her damn mind. "You can't be serious. Speak to him about what? He's your problem now, not mine."

She didn't say anything, only shook her head as I picked up my suitcase and hurried down the stairs.

When I got downstairs, I sent Daryl a text letting him know I was on the way back. My hand was on the door handle, and I was about to pull it open to leave when I heard Harris behind me.

"So, you're fucking leaving again?"

A chill went down my spine. I took a deep breath. "I just came back for some clothes."

"I can't believe you, London," he said. "I never knew you to be a bitch ass."

I turned around and narrowed my eyes at him. "I've never been a bitch ass, Harris. Can you say the same?"

He rolled closer, looking at the suitcase on the floor next to me. "I'm not letting you do this to me, London. You're not going to destroy our family. I won't let you." He grabbed my purse. "You're not going anywhere. Not if I can help it."

He turned around and rolled away.

"Harris, give me my shit." I shook my head in disbelief. Clearly, he had lost what little sense he had left after his injury. I took off after him, jumping in front of him., snatching my purse back. "Have you lost your mind?"

"No, you have." He scowled. "You better pray I don't sue your ass for abandonment. Keep playing with me."

"You don't scare me, Harris. This shit is over and done with," I told him. "When I get back, I want you out my family's house."

"I ain't going nowhere," he said defiantly.

"We'll see." I smirked. "I've hired Bradley Hudson. He'll get you out."

I could see his bravado being deflated.

"Fine, London, go ahead and leave," he said with a sinister smile. "You think this shit is a game, but you're gonna see that I'm going to win it all."

Our eyes locked, and I fought the urge to slap the shit out of him. The last thing I needed was to give him something else to report back to my father. Instead, I put my purse on my shoulder, grabbed the handle of my suitcase, and walked out of the house.

Lauryn

36

The address on the card that Minister Farah had given me led to Gurney's Inn, a resort hotel located in Montauk Point, out at the end of Long Island. I was hesitant as I entered the waterfront property, not knowing exactly what to expect.

There was a sign in the lobby stating that the Chi's reception was being held on one of the patios overlooking the Atlantic Ocean, so that's where I went. Paris had given me an earpiece to wear so that she could listen, but it would be impossible for me to keep it in. Brother Minister's people had taken security to the next level. Before entering, each person was required to turn in all their electronic devices, which were to be placed in lockers then scanned. She was going to have to get the details later when I filled her and Rio in, if there was something to tell.

After turning in my cell phone, earpiece, and watch, I was issued a name tag and given permission to enter the huge deck area. Inside, there was a mixture of guests elegantly dressed for a black-tie affair and other who looked like circus freaks who needed to be under the big top. The network of highly trained assassins and thieves attracted all kinds of people, but that was a good thing, because you never knew where you would need an assassin to blend in. My short, black dress and heels were not as glamorous as some of the dresses other ladies had on, but I definitely didn't look like the weirdos.

"Champagne?" one of the tuxedo clad servers offered.

"Oh, thank you." I took one of the flutes from the tray. I definitely could've used something a little stronger to calm my nerves, but this was a good start.

I sipped as I scanned the room. A three-piece quartet played in the corner while servers passed out seafood hors d'oeuvres. I took in the faces of everyone in the room in search of Nadja, but she was nowhere in sight.

The familiar, deep baritone laughter caught my attention. I looked over my shoulder and spotted Minister Farah speaking with a small group across the way.

"Ah, Lauryn, you made it." He beamed when he saw me approaching.

"I did." I smiled politely at the people who were leaving as I walked up.

"I'm so glad you could make it." Minister Farah greeted me. Like the elegant half of the guests, he wore a formal tuxedo, along with a solid black Kufi cap.

"Me too, Minister Farah. But exactly what is this reception for?" I asked.

"Well, this is somewhat of a job fair for graduates of the school. People here this weekend are either looking for qualified candidates to hire, or qualified candidates such as yourself looking for work," he explained, looking around the room. "Those invited are the best of the best in their field of expertise."

"Oh, really?"

"Yes. For example, that gentleman over there is an expert in explosives." He raised his glass at the man dressed in a simple blue suit with thick glasses looking more like a banker than a bomb specialist. "Everything from a simple car bomb to weapons of mass destruction that can take out a city block, he can make happen. He's very popular in the Middle East."

"And the red- and purple-haired woman?" I asked, looking at an extremely thin woman whose dress was just as colorful as her hairstyle.

"Ah, that is the mastermind behind some of the world's biggest art heists. She can plan escapes like no one else."

"Minister Farah." A man who had to be seven feet tall and two hundred eighty pounds walked over. "It's been a long time."

"It has, Maurice. How have you been?" Minister Farah asked.

"I've been well. I was in Australia for the past year, but now I'm back." Maurice grinned. "The exotic animal trade market has slowed down a bit, so I decided to come back to the States."

"I see." Minister Farah turned to me. "This is Lauryn."

"Nice to meet you." Maurice extended what seemed more like a bear claw than a hand. I prayed he wouldn't crush mine as we shook. "Minister Farah, I do need to speak to you in private later, if possible."

"Of course, Maurice," Minister Farah said. "Let's catch up in a few. I have someone I'd like Lauryn to meet.'

"Great. Nice to meet you again, Lauryn." Maurice nodded.

"Exotic animals?" I asked once he was gone.

"I'm sure you noticed the size of his stature and hands. The man can capture any animal desired in the world with his bare hands, and he delivers them himself. You'd be surprised how much white lions and Tibetan Mastiffs are worth." Minister Farah laughed. "Come. There's someone I'd like to introduce you to."

We strolled across the patio, and my eyes lit up when I saw the woman sitting alone at a table wearing a simple black dress, her hair pulled into a tight chignon at the top of her head. When Nadja stood and nodded toward us, I could barely contain my excitement. I'd hit paydirt.

"Lauryn, this is Nadja." Minister Farah introduced us. "Nadja, this is the young lady I was speaking about earlier."

"Nice to meet you, Lauryn," she said politely. She was pretty, and her face was pleasant, but I could tell she was sizing me up.

"Nice to meet you too."

"Lauryn is a recent graduate of our school," Minister Farah bragged. "She is also one of only two graduates in recent years to specialize in poison controls. After our conversation last night, I thought you two might want to speak."

"Yes, thank you, Minister." Nadja motioned toward an empty chair. "Please, have a seat, Lauryn."

"Thank you," I said, taking the seat across from her.

"Enjoy your chat. I have other guests to attend to." The Minister gave me a reassuring smile then walked away.

"I'm sure you know that Minister Farah doesn't give compliments or recommendations very often," she said with something of a smirk on her face. "So, you must be something special."

"He is a hard man to impress. However, I'd like to think—"

"Lauryn?" I was interrupted by Saul, one of my former class-mates. He was cute, smart, and funny, and believe it or not, destined to be a James Bond type for the Israeli Mossad.

"Saul?"

"I can't believe you're here." Saul grinned, then looked over at Nadja as if they were also old friends. "Hello, Nadja."

"Hello, Saul. I didn't think you'd make it."

"Yes, well, people keep underestimating me. Everyone but Lauryn." Saul smiled at me.

"Yes, you have proven resilient," she replied. "I take it you two know one another?"

"Lauryn and I went to school together. She's the one who got me through Poisoning 301. I was in jeopardy of failing and not graduating." He touched my shoulder. "This beautiful lady helped me pass."

"Interesting." Nadja actually looked impressed.

"Well, I'll leave you two to talk. Lauryn, we should have a drink later and catch up," Saul said.

"Love to."

"I'll find you," he said then walked away.

Nadja turned back at me, once again staring at me as if she were sizing me up.

"You have a habit of impressing men that aren't easily im-pressed. Sounds like you really know your stuff."

"I pride myself on being the best I can possibly be."

"I hear you're seeking employment."

I nodded. "More freelance than anything. I'm just looking to get my feet wet. Nothing permanent. I plan on going into the family business."

"That's good to know. I have an exclusive client, but my background and passion is brokering deals. I love putting the right people together. I may have something that could use your expertise if you're interested."

Hearing this, I knew I'd found the opportunity I'd been waiting for. "Sure. I'm interested. What do you have in mind?"

"I just received a deposit for a contract I'm brokering. It's a small one, and I can't go into detail here, but it would give us both a chance to see if you're a good fit. It pays sixty thousand."

Sixty K! I almost jumped out of my seat and kissed her, but that's when I realized that the hit could be on Paris. I needed to get more information.

"I don't have a problem starting off small," I said.

"Good. How about you come by my hotel room in the morning and we can discuss the details? I'm in Bungalow four thirty-six." Nadja stood. "Let's say ten a.m.?"

"I'll be there," I told her. "Thank you."

She strolled off into the crowd, and I stood and watched her. The night had not only been intriguing but exceeded my expectations, and I couldn't wait to tell Paris and Rio.

Larry

37

Camellia Gardens Residential Home for Adults over 55 was reminiscent of an upscale garden apartment complex with its huge pool, recreation center, and surrounding golf course. Had it not been for the number of frail senior citizens everywhere I looked, I wouldn't have known it was also a nursing facility. It wasn't hard to enter the building unnoticed, despite it being advertised as one of the most secure facilities in Newark, New Jersey. Perhaps it was my salt-and-pepper hair, but we were pretty much invited in.

"Thank you so much." I nodded at the gray-haired woman holding onto a four-toed cane, who let me in the side door near the elevators. I wasn't sure whether it was because Dennis and I looked like residents or if the old lady was enamored with us, but she was quite friendly.

"You're so welcome." She smiled flirtatiously, looking me up and down. That's when I knew for sure why she was so friendly. She was smitten. "I haven't seen you around. You headed to the Bingo tournament in the activity room?"

"I sure am," I lied. "Just need to grab my lucky dauber."

"Well then, I'll see you there." She winked and continued down the hall.

Dennis and I continued to the elevator and rode it up to the third floor. We found room 308 and went inside to visit with Isabella, a spry old lady, 83 years young. She was sitting in a chair by the window, gazing outside at a rather depressing view of the parking lot.

"Hello, ma'am. How are you today?" I asked as we strolled into the room.

She turned to face us, looking a little startled. "Who are you?" she asked.

"Oh, I'm sorry. I thought your daughter told you we were coming. We're friends of hers, and she told us about this place. Said you might be able to give us the inside scoop. My friend and I aren't getting any younger, you know"—Dennis frowned slightly but didn't open his mouth—"and we're thinking about moving into someplace where we can get some assistance."

She studied us for a minute. "My daughter sent you? Huh. Maybe she forgot to tell me about it. She's very busy, you know. Very important job. But then again," she said with a sigh, "maybe she did tell me and I forgot. My memory is not what it used to be, you know?"

"Oh, I sure do," I said, making myself comfortable in the chair beside hers.

That small connection was enough to get her talking, and Dennis and I spent the next fifteen minutes making small talk about the facilities with this lonely old lady, until the person we'd really come to see stepped in the room.

"Ah, there she is!" Isabella said happily. "Hey, baby. Your friends beat you here."

Agent Martinez froze. Her eyes went from her mother sitting in the chair near the window, to me sitting beside her grinning, and finally to Dennis, standing directly behind Isabella, discreetly holding a gun.

"Good to see you, Janel." I smiled at her, although my voice was very pointed. "I tried to call you the other night. Nonetheless, I see from the morning news you got my text." Thaddeus's capture had been all over the papers.

Agent Martinez finally regained her composure and spoke. "Yes, I got it, but as you know, I was a little busy during that time."

She walked over to her mother and kissed her on the cheek. "Hey, Mama." She looked over at me and whispered between gritted teeth, "Is this really what we're doing now? You are poking the bear."

"I had to get the bear's attention," I whispered back. "It wasn't like I could just show up at your office."

"Did you bring me anything good today, Janel?" Isabella asked.

"I did, Ma." Martinez smiled and opened the large brown bag she was carrying. "Sudoku books, magazines, and your favorite peanut butter filled pretzels."

Isabella turned to me and bragged. "She's such a good daughter. Brings me goodies every Wednesday."

"I know." I chuckled as I looked up at Janel. "She posts picture of you two up on Facebook after every visit. I love the one you took last week in front of the Camellia Gardens sign."

"Fucking Facebook," Agent Martinez muttered, her face turning red because of her own stupidity.

"Dennis, why don't you escort Ms. Isabella down to the activity room for the Bingo tournament like we discussed? Janel and I will be right down. We have a few things to catch up on."

I could see the excitement on Isabella's face.

"No, Ma, you want to stay here with me, don't you? We can have our weekly chat and I can fill you in on who I'm after. Right, Ma?" Agent Martinez gave her mother a pleading look, but to no avail. The excitement of Bingo with Dennis was more appealing than spending time with her daughter.

Isabella shook her head. "We always sit in here talking. It'll be nice to get out of this room, and Dennis promised to help me play four cards. I'll see you later," she replied sassily.

"But, Ma." Agent Martinez looked panicked for a moment as Dennis helped her mother stand.

"Janel, I don't get many visitors, and I like your friends, especially this one." Isabella took Dennis by the arm, and they headed toward the door. "Come on, Dennis. I wanna get a seat up front so all those old biddies can see me with a real man."

Dennis smirked as he turned around to make sure Martinez saw that he still had the gun tucked away in his waistband.

"Don't worry, Janel. Dennis is harmless, unless I tell him not to be," I assured her after they left the room. "Your mother will be fine."

"Bullshit. I've read his rap sheet. The man is a killer. He killed his whole family." Martinez glared at me.

"Correction, reformed killer. We're not out to harm people anymore. We're here to help."

"Tell that to your ex-partner in crime." She shuddered. "That was quite a scene. Did you really have to cut his dick off?"

"Yes! Have you read his sheet? The man's a sadistic serial rapist, and he doesn't discriminate between boys and girls. He raped more people in prison than he did outside those walls." I could see the look of disgust on Martinez's face. "When we got to that cabin, that son of a bitch was using an iron to brand his initials onto a woman. By the way, you might wanna check up on her. We dropped her at Charleston Medical Center. She was in pretty bad shape."

Martinez nodded, making a mental note. "Okay, so now what? Why the fuck are you here, Larry? I'm sure it's not to play Bingo."

"First things first. I told you I'd have something significant to offer. I assume my tip on Thaddeus was significant enough? Your superiors were pleased with his capture?"

"Yeah, sure, other than the mutilation, the bosses are happy. However, they made it clear they'll be even happier when we bring you and your other two cronies in."

"Did you show them the tapes? Clearly, they could see that we didn't kill that woman. We tried to stop him."

"Yeah, they saw them, but they don't care. The crime was committed during a prison break. You're all being lumped into the same pot as Thaddeus. If there was no escape, that guard wouldn't be dead."

"So, then what are you saying, Janel? That we should have just left Thaddeus to rape and pillage? We did the right thing here."

"I don't know what I'm saying. I just know that the U.S. Attorney wants the three of you captured so they can put all four of you on trial for murdering a federal officer."

Her words hit me kind of hard. I'd promised Dennis and Holly the heat would die down, and Janel's revelation was quite the opposite, but I still had a few cards to play.

"That sucks," I said. "But what about you?"

"What about me?"

"Do you still want to take down the people who killed your fiancé?"

I could almost see the wheels spinning in her head. From spending time in her apartment and seeing the hundreds of pictures and newspaper articles, along with reading her notes and dossier, I knew there was nothing Janel Martinez wanted more than to take down the people who'd killed FBI agent Jack

Smith. The only real question was, did she want it enough to take my help?

"My team and I wanna get you the revenge you seek."

She laughed. "We are not talking about some street thug. The man who had Jack killed and his people have tentacles everywhere, including the United States government. Why do you think they keep shutting me down? He's not hiding out in the back woods of South Carolina like Thaddeus. This man meets with senators and congressmen regularly. He's hiding in plain sight." Her voice was turning angry, which I liked. "You don't have any idea who Alexander Cora is or what he's capable of. The man's a monster."

"Oh, I know exactly who Alexander Cora is. Sure, he runs around acting like a big shot billionaire now, but to a guy who has been there before, Alexander Cora is just another nigga in an expensive suit. You see, being rich and black is a very small and exclusive club. My brothers and I used to run in the same circles with him back in the day. Hell, my brother Lou taught him how to play golf." I was lying through my teeth. "I'm a little surprised you never uncovered that detail. But then again, I guess a crazy man behind bars kind of falls off the radar, huh?"

What I wasn't about to tell her was that I'd never met Alexander Cora personally. My brothers and I had gotten wind of him when he'd just gotten started back in the late 70s, selling large amounts of heroin out of Afghanistan to Sal Dash and the Italians. He was undercutting the shit out of us and severely fucking up our business, so LC came up with a plan to stop it. He discreetly let his buddy Juan Rodriguez know about Alexander's infringement on his U.S. operation. Juan, in turn, told Alejandro Zuniga, and somehow, they handled Alexander. They didn't shut him down, but their tariffs did stop his expansion into the United States, which we discreetly controlled half of. Alejandro controlled the other half, which was why he had a vested interest in stopping Cora. When his operation took a hit, Alexander was never the wiser that we were involved in it.

"So, you knew him back in the day? What does all that have to do with taking him down? So far, I'm not impressed."

I smiled. "The only way to take a man like Alexander down is from the inside, as you know. With the help of some of my friends from the past, I plan on becoming one of his biggest customers. You have to be a criminal to take down a criminal. I can take him down and hand him over to you for prosecution, along with everyone involved with Jack's death, if you agree to my terms."

I could tell that I'd struck a nerve. The fact that she was listening let me know she was at least considering it. I would even go so far as to say that she was a bit intrigued, which was exactly what I hoped that she would be.

"You can't do this without me, Janel. I have the contacts, the manpower, and the wherewithal to do it. Who would ever suspect a recent fugitive is working with the feds? I just need your say so, and me and my people will get to work."

"I'm not saying I'll agree to anything, but what exactly are your terms?"

"You and your partner Deputy Fritz run the East Coast fugitive task force, correct?"

She nodded.

"Well, number one, I'm gonna need you and your partner to look the other way when it comes to Dennis, Holly, and myself. Also, any fugitive we find or lead you to, the reward goes to my family, through my son as a bounty hunter."

"Is that it?" She looked like she'd expected more.

"That's it. What do you say? My people can do things yours can't, so I guarantee results."

She hesitated, and I could see her resolve was faltering. "I can't even believe I'm considering this."

I motioned for her to take the seat her mother had left empty. Instead, she placed the paper bag down beside her and sat on her mother's bed, leaving a few feet between us. "If we do this, I have a few non-negotiable rules of my own."

"Okay, let's hear them."

"My mother and any of my family members are off limits, got it? You come near them, the deal's off, and I hunt you down like a dog."

"Yeah, but I gotta tell you, I love your mom. She's a sweet old lady."

"Off fucking limits!" she growled.

"Okay, okay, off limits. Damn, that Latin heat is something."

"And no killing. I don't care if you bust a few heads or cut off a few dicks to get some answers, but I don't want a trail of bodies across the United States. One innocent person gets killed and our deal is off. It's going to be hard enough to convince my team to look the other way."

"That's fair, but if motherfuckers shoot at us, we are shooting back," I said in no uncertain terms.

"Deal, but only if they shoot first," she conceded. "So, where are you going to start?"

"I don't know. I have to make a few calls, but I'll be in touch. Just make sure you answer the damn phone."

Paris

38

It was a little after six o'clock, and Lauryn still hadn't showed back up at our house in the Hamptons, where Rio and I were waiting. I was livid—and scared. I'd given her specific instructions to keep that fucking earpiece in so I could listen and tell her exactly what to do, but she'd gone silent. She may have completed finishing school, but she was a rookie, and Nadja was an experienced killer with plenty of dead bodies to brag about. There was no way I could risk anything happening to my little cousin. Her parents and mine would kill me.

"Where the fuck is she?" I tried calling her for the hundredth time, but her phone went straight to voicemail.

"Calm down. She's fine. She's at a cocktail party, not a bank robbery," Rio said calmly from the lounge chair where he was sprawled out with a cocktail in his hand. "And it's not like Minister Farah is going to let something happen to her. Her battery probably died."

While he enjoyed sipping a drink by the pool, I paced back and forth. "Then she should've used the portable fucking charger I gave her."

"You're being really aggravating and killing my vibe." Rio sighed. "I didn't come out here to be stressed. I came to relax."

"Technically, you came to be nosy."

"That too." He adjusted his Versace shades over his eyes.

"Hey, y'all." Lauryn strolled onto the back patio as if she hadn't been missing for hours.

"What the hell? Where is your phone?" I yelled, relieved to see her but still angry.

"Oh, they took it, and I forgot to turn it back on when I left." Lauryn pointed to the tiny clutch hanging on her shoulder.

"Get it back from where?" I asked.

"They took our phones, purses, everything, and locked them up." Lauryn sat on the lounge chair beside Rio. "It was like no electronics allowed whatsoever. They had that joint on lock."

"I guess that makes sense," I said, feeling some of my anger dissipate.

"So, what happened? Did you see her? Was she there?" Rio questioned, not interested in how secure the event was.

"I did. I sat down with her and had an interesting chat."

Rio sat up. "Oh, shit. You talked to her?"

"I didn't just talk to her. She offered me a job." Lauryn smirked.

"Get the fuck outta here. She wanted to hire you to kill me?" I asked, halfway expecting her to say yes.

"I don't know yet. I have a meeting about a job assignment tomorrow morning in her hotel room."

"That's perfect." I smiled. "You did good, little cousin. Tomorrow morning, we can go and slice that bitch up, down, left, and right."

Lauryn stared at me. "Paris, we can't do that."

"What? Why can't we? You know exactly what room she's in, right?"

"Because we don't have a reason to kill her," Lauryn said as if her answer made sense.

"You do know why she's here, right? Not to mention what she did already. We saw her on the damn security footage," I reminded her.

"I don't know, Paris. We really don't know why she's here or what she wants," Lauryn told me.

"She has a point," Rio agreed. "All the woman did was send you flowers. Nice ones, too, I might add. We need to confirm she's out to get you before we start trying to kill international assassins."

I stared at my brother and cousin in disbelief, wondering whose side they were on. "She's here to kill me in retaliation for what I did to Niles. That's why. What kind of proof do you need?"

"A hell of a lot more than we have. It's been like ten years." Rio took off his sunglasses. "You can't just go and kill this woman based off an assumption, Paris. That shit is not happening again."

"Again? What's that supposed mean?" I snapped.

"Well, let's look at your track record." He held up a hand and started to count on his fingers. "There was the son of the cartel leader that you killed, and the senator's son, and let's not forget—"

"Fuck you, Rio. Fine. If you're too scared to help, I'll do it myself," I told them. "As you've pointed out, I've done it before. Doing it again ain't a big deal."

"Ain't nobody scared, Paris." Lauryn stood. "All I'm saying is you can't fucking kill this woman on a hunch."

"Why not?" I screamed.

While Lauryn looked taken aback by my tone, Rio stood firm and remained calm. "Because there are ramifications behind the shit that you do, dammit! You kill this woman without provocation, you might start another damn war, and this time with the Assassin's Guild. If we do this, the consequences could be deadly, not just for us, but for the entire family."

"You're both scared," I said.

"Damn right I am." Rio walked over to me. "And you should be too. Maybe we should just talk to Pop about this."

"No!" I grabbed his arm as he reached for his phone. "We aren't telling Dad or any fucking body else about this. This is my problem, and I'll solve it."

There was no way I could go to my father and tell him about Niles being Jordan's father. Explaining this situation with Niles would only complicate matters even more, especially since my father and my brother Orlando knew why I'd killed Niles. They just didn't know how much I loved him. You see, the day I killed Niles was not only the day I conceived Jordan but the day I found out that the love of my life had accepted a contract to kill my father. He was on his way to do just that when I blew up the plane he was flying.

"Then we've gotta be smart about this and let it play out." Lauryn gave me a look meant to calm me down.

Having no other choice, I relented. "Whatever. Okay, you two win for now. I'll let you see what's really up with that bitch. But don't be surprised if the job she's hiring you to do is to kill me."

Lauryn smiled. "And if that's really the case, don't worry, cousin. I will personally fuck her up, then call you to finish her off. I swear."

"And I'll be right there to help," Rio added.

The three of us stood in a circle, a united front. I hoped Lauryn and Rio were right in saying I was being paranoid, but I had a feeling that I couldn't shake. I felt as if I had a target on my back, and I was the only one who could see it. Nadja wanted me dead.

Sasha

39

I sighed thankfully as I passed a sign that said: WELCOME TO WARE COUNTY. I wasn't sure whether I was running off the amount of caffeine I'd consumed over the last six hours, or pure adrenaline. Either way, I wasn't just tired; I was exhausted and mad as hell at myself for not getting to Waycross sooner. I'd been beating myself up all day over stopping in Maryland to get food, but I couldn't help myself. I could never resist passing by Timbuktu without stopping to get a couple of crab cakes and french fries. I ended up getting them to go and eating them as I continued my drive south toward Waycross. By the time I reached Richmond, Virginia, I was dozing off at the wheel, so I pulled over at a rest area to catch a cat nap. Well, that cap nap ended up being damn near eight and a half hours. It also resulted in me getting caught up in rush hour traffic along with a three-hour backup from a wreck in North Carolina. All in all, a fourteen-hour trip had taken me almost thirty-five hours, and I was ready to fall out. I needed another nap, only I couldn't afford to sleep because I might have already blown my chance to kill Uncle Larry.

I headed past the property for the second time. I would have passed right by it if it weren't for the sign hanging on the mailbox with the Duncan name painted on it. My dad had taken me to the Duncan homestead at least a couple dozen times, and although it had been almost eight years, I thought I would recognize the house right away. The house I remembered was almost a hundred years old, small and unassuming, but the house that stood on the property now was much larger and looked to be pretty recently built. I was confused. Was I in the wrong place?

I pulled over about a hundred feet past the entrance to the property and ran back to the mailbox, opening it to see if there was any mail. There was an Allstate car insurance bill with my cousin Curtis's name on it. This was the right place. I ran back to my car, no longer feeling tired, but energized.

I found a place to park about a half mile down the road, then retrieved a few things from the trunk before heading into a wooded area and making my way back to the house.

Instinctively, I trekked my way toward a small grouping of trees on a hill overlooking the house, carrying my weapon of choice: a sniper rifle that I'd removed from the slender case in the trunk. Thirty minutes later, the trees thinned, and the large farmhouse came into view. I now had the high ground and a visual advantage.

They must have torn down the old house and put up a new one, I thought as I sat down on the ground, leaning my back against a pine tree. I'd positioned myself where I would have a clear view of all the doors except for the back. Now all I had to do was wait for that motherfucker Larry to come out, and his ass was mine. I had no idea how long I was going to have to wait and didn't care.

I was in place less than twenty minutes when suddenly, there was the sound of barking.

"Shit, a fucking dog," I hissed, sitting up and watching the farm dog standing at the rear of the yard, facing my direction.

"Spot! Shut up!" a female voice yelled.

I lifted the scope of my rifle and saw that it was Aunt Nee Nee. As if he could sense me staring, Spot kept barking. Aunt Nee Nee looked toward the trees, and I scooted back slightly so that I wouldn't be in view. She grabbed the dog by the collar and pulled him toward the house.

"Stop all that damn barking. It's just a fucking squirrel, stupid-ass dog. You gonna wake up the kids, and I'm gonna whoop you."

Sure enough, a squirrel ran across the yard into the woods on the other side. Aunt Nee Nee and Spot disappeared into the house. I hoped that the disturbance would be enough to cause Uncle Larry to come outside, but everything became quiet, and the house lights went out.

I leaned against the trunk of the large tree beside me and continued to wait. Next thing I knew, I was in Miami getting slayed by that cute basketball player.

"How about one more for the road?" I whispered after we'd finished and he was reaching for his clothes.

Click. Click.

I'd been trained well enough that the sound of a bullet entering a chamber would wake me from the best of dreams. Someone was behind me, and they were armed. Slowly, I turned around, my finger positioned to fire once I got my eye on whoever it was.

"Sasha?"

I locked eyes with my cousin Curtis with Roman. They were standing behind me, holding Glocks.

Shit. This certainly complicated my plans.

"What the fuck are you doing here?" Curtis demanded, the gun still pointing in my direction. Roman had lowered his weapon.

"Looking for your daddy."

"Why?" His eyes went to the rifle in my hands.

"Because he killed my mother," I yelled at him. "And you're just as responsible."

For a brief second, I could see the confusion and hurt in his eyes. We stood face to face, both forgetting that we were cousins and shared the same bloodline. In that moment, we were enemies and had a decision to make. Or at least that's the way I felt.

Roman

40

I was just as confused as Curtis to see Sasha in Waycross, let alone crouched down in the woods with a sniper rifle aimed toward the house. I thought she was in Miami on vacation. I'd only known her for a short while, but everyone treated her more like a sister than cousin, and she was always happy. This Sasha seemed like a totally different person.

"Get off me, Curtis." Sasha scowled.

I'd never seen the look of anger in her eyes that she had now as Curtis held her by the arm and we walked down the hill. I held onto the rifle he'd taken from her.

"Calm the fuck down, Sasha," Curtis warned. "I don't know what the fuck is wrong with you, sneaking around here with a fucking gun, dressed in all black like a ninja."

"You and your daddy. That's what the fuck is wrong with me," Sasha retorted, then glanced over at me. "What the fuck are you even doing here, Roman? Hanging out with the enemy?"

"Don't worry about all that," Curtis told her. "He family. He's welcome here."

"Family? What the hell do you know about family? That's a fucking joke, especially coming from you," Sasha snapped at him.

Curtis shook his head. "You need to chill out, for real."

"He's right, Sasha. You really tripping," I agreed as we entered the house.

"I'm tripping? Do you know what him and his family did to me?" Sasha looked at Curtis as if he were a monster.

"Sasha, it's cool. Pop said that Uncle Larry isn't really a threat to anyone." I tried to touch her arm, but she snatched away from me.

"Don't tell me you're falling for this bullshit too, Roman. I know you're new to this family, but even you've gotta realize how crazy that sounds, especially after what they did to my mother."

My eyes went to Curtis, who suddenly looked down, then back to Sasha, who was now staring at me. I was clueless.

"You don't know, do you?" she said quietly. "No one's told you."

"Told me what?" I asked.

"Sasha, don't—"

"Shut the fuck up," Sasha snapped at him, then turned her attention back to me. "Our dear cousin here, along with his brother and father, killed my mother. Larry, the one no one is worried about except me, strangled her, and your boy Curtis was with him. Isn't that right, Curtis?"

"You're lying," I responded.

"Why would I lie about something like this. I was the one who found her lifeless body," Sasha growled. "Ask him."

I looked at Curtis. "Is that true?"

Curtis pulled her into the living room. It was still late, so luckily, the kids were asleep. This conversation was getting pretty deep, and as disturbing as I found it, the kids didn't need to be a part of it. Aunt Nee Nee, however, was up. I hadn't noticed her standing on the steps, listening, until Curtis glanced in her direction.

"Answer him!" Sasha demanded.

He looked back to me and answered my question. "I mean, yes, but no . . . we . . ." Curtis was clearly struggling.

"Look, don't do this. I'm used to y'all doing this to me, but please don't insult Roman by lying to his face. He deserves the truth," Sasha commanded.

"Look, the truth is yeah, my Pops and I went to Donna's house." Curtis stared me in the eye. "But when I left out of the house, she was alive. I didn't touch her. I swear."

"So, Uncle Larry was in there with her?" I frowned, wondering why this was the first time anyone had shared this with me. I knew Uncle Larry was unstable and somewhat treacherous, but now I understood why Sasha was so furious and the reason for the sniper rifle. And in a way, I didn't blame her.

"You left my mother in with him alone and never came back in?" Sasha asked. It looked like the first time she was hearing this.

"Yeah, but—"

"But what? She was dead when I found her. And she didn't kill herself."

"I don't think Daddy killed her, Sasha. He wouldn't. He couldn't."

She laughed bitterly. "Are you delusional? He killed everybody else, didn't he? Why not her?"

"Everybody else wasn't family. Aunt Donna was," Curtis said.

"Who you trying to convince, me or yourself? 'Cause I know what happened. Y'all killed my mother."

Just as Curtis was about to answer, my phone rang. I looked at my watch and saw my father's number. "Hold on. It's my dad."

Sasha rolled her eyes. "How convenient."

"Hey, Pop," I answered.

"Hey, Roman. How are things going down there?"

I looked at both my cousins, and my aunt, who still hadn't said a word. "Uh, they're going."

"I'm calling to see if you've heard from Sasha. She's a little upset, and well, I'm afraid she might be headed your way."

"Actually, I'm looking right at her. She's standing right in front of me," I told him.

Sasha stared at me with the same level of anger that she had for Curtis. I knew it was because I'd told my father where she was, but I didn't regret it. I'd quickly discovered that this family was full of secrets that were detrimental. I may have been a member, but I didn't want to participate.

Orlando

41

"That was some brilliant shit you came up with today." Aries commended me as we walked across the deck to the staircase that led to my state room. "You really are a fuckin' genius. It would have taken me and my team years to break down those chemical components the way you did. I've never seen anything like it. You should be proud."

Under normal circumstances, he would have been right, and I would have been over the moon. But unfortunately, his praising fell on deaf ears because after almost sixteen hours in the lab, I was beyond tired.

"Let's see how you feel about it when we test the rats in the morning. We've only cracked the problem from a logistical standpoint. The true test is in the actual physical trials."

"I'm not worried about that right now. That's just a formality. By eliminating the carobine-opioid and substituting it with methadone, you've eliminated the cancer derivative by ninety percent, which is more than acceptable. But the even larger caveat is the fact that you may have increased the drug's addictive nature by seventy-eight percent. That's a win by anyone's standards. I can't wait to share the results with the old man."

"Yes, but it must be tested. We don't know if any of these new combinations are toxic. I've made this mistake once before with HEAT." Four years ago, I'd invented a drug call HEAT. For almost a year and a half, it was the hottest designer drug on the market, rivaling cocaine and heroin as the most desired drug in the country. My family and I were set to become bigger than Pablo Escobar and all the Colombian cartels combined— only HEAT turned out to cause cancer. After much debate within the family, we'd decided to remove the drug from the market. My family had no problem killing people to protect ourselves and what was ours, but we weren't mass-murderers. Unfortunately, when we stopped production, it created a vacuum in the market, and plenty of other underworld figures were eager to step into our place. It was part of the reason I was on the yacht now.

"You are being way too modest, and an even bigger worrywart. We are in the process of perfecting HEAT into FIRE, and this new drug FIRE is only months away from being street ready, perhaps even sooner," he replied happily, although I disagreed. He always had such a happy-go-lucky nature. Sometimes I just wanted him to shut the fuck up. "We are going to be rich beyond our wildest dreams," he said, dramatically gesturing toward the deck bar, which was crowded with about twenty members of the crew. "Come. Let's have a drink to celebrate before bed. Tomorrow is going to be a big day."

It was tempting, but I wasn't one to socialize with the crew because most of them were phony, patronizing me and my wife because they saw me as their meal ticket to wealth and fame.

"Nah, man, I just want to spend some time with my family and get some sleep. You can go over there and knock yourself out." I headed down the stairs toward my room, hoping he'd stay with the crew, but he was a step behind me the whole way. He nodded his head at the armed security guard who patrolled our floor.

As Aries reached for the door, I rubbed my eyes and shook off the feeling of exhaustion in preparation of what was waiting on the other side. The door barely opened before I was tackled.

"Daddyyyyyyyyy." Li'l Man ran toward me and hurled himself into my arms.

"Hey there, buddy!" I lifted him up as if he were weightless and planted a kiss on his cheek. Seeing the excitement in his eyes was enough to eliminate my fatigue. With my son still in my arms, I leaned over and kissed my wife. Her lips were soft and sweet and filled my head with images of what could possibly happen later that night when Li'l Man was asleep.

"Hey, beautiful."

"Hey yourself, handsome." She smiled. "Vincent, get down. Your father has been working all day and is too tired to be carrying you. You're too big."

"He's strong, aren't you, Daddy? You're the strongest one in the world. Tell Mommy."

"I'm always gonna be strong enough for you, son." I pressed my forehead against his then placed him back down on the floor.

"Do you all need anything?" Aries asked, reminding us that he was still in the room.

"No, we're fine," I told him. "I'll see you in the morning."

He gave a brief nod of his head, then exited the large, suite-style stateroom where my little family resided. Truth be told, it was the size of a hotel penthouse and had plenty of space, but it wasn't home, and we weren't exactly guests.

"Enjoy the rest of your evening," Aries said. Seconds later, the door closed, and there were several loud clicks reminding us that we were prisoners.

"Daddy, why do they lock the door when you're in here with us?" Li'l Man asked. "They don't want us out?"

I kneeled down and looked at him with a sad smile. "No, buddy, they wanna make sure we're safe and no bad people get in."

His eyes widened. "Is that why those men always carry guns? 'Cause bad people wanna come get us?"

The last thing I wanted was for my son to be afraid, so I reassured him. "Son, didn't we just say I'm the strongest man in the world? But no matter where you are, you should always make sure the door is locked: car doors, home doors. I mean, Mommy locks the bathroom door all the time."

"Yes, she says it's for pri . . . pri . . ."

"Privacy," Ruby said and rolled her eyes at me with a half-smile.

"Exactly," I said, grabbing her hand and pulling her to me.

"Vincent, be good and go play your game quietly," Ruby said to him.

"Yeah, Mama." Vincent's Jamaican accent mimicked hers. He ran off to the bedroom to play.

When he was gone, Ruby led me to the sofa, and we sat down to talk.

"How was your day? Any progress?" she asked, rubbing her finger along my arm.

"Yeah, unfortunately there was. I tried to hide it, but Aries was standing over me. The man watches my every move like a hawk."

"Orlando, I need not tell you what they will do to us if you supply them with this drug, do I?"

"No, baby, you don't, but I have to show them some progress or they will kill you and Li'l Man anyway. You know what they're capable of. Look what they did to my assistant." The people who had captured us six months ago had killed my assistant, Brandi. They had approached us as we were walking on a secluded beach, and at first, I thought it was just a random robbery or kidnapping. These things happen from time to time to rich people on the islands. You just have to stay calm and have your people pay the ransom. But I quickly realized this wasn't a random kidnapping. This was way too organized, and they had way too much manpower and weaponry. Hell, they even had motorized skiffs to make their escape.

They had taken us to this boat that was sitting offshore and whisked us away, locking us in this cabin. Eventually, I was brought before their leader and given a choice: help Aries develop a new drug without the side effect of cancer, or else watch my family die. I chose my family, but I was well aware that their safety was not guaranteed. My captors would not hesitate to use my family as leverage at any point.

The grim look Ruby gave me said it all. We were in a desperate situation. The Duncan family had been in plenty of precarious situations before, and my parents and siblings would have moved heaven and earth to get us out of here if they were aware of the truth. Of course, they knew none of it, and that was by design. I was allowed to talk to them on the ship to shore phone, but only so that no one got suspicious and came looking for us. They thought we were on an extended leisure cruise around the Caribbean. Aries was always within earshot when I spoke to anyone, so there was no chance for me to alert them. If Ruby and I were going to get out of captivity, we would have to do it on our own.

I leaned my head against her shoulder. Being beside her brought comfort that I had never experienced with anyone else and confirmed that finding and marrying her was the best decision I'd ever made. She was my place of peace.

"I'm trying, baby."

"I know you are, Orlando. I have faith in you and what you're doing."

"What about you? Have you overheard anything?"

Ruby's head turned slightly toward the far corner of the room, and her eyes looked over at the circular window. She leaned over and kissed me, then lowered her voice, speaking directly into my ear. "We must be getting close to the United States. I overheard two workers talking. One mentioned being excited about finally getting a slice."

"A slice? Like pizza?" I murmured between kisses, glancing at the same spot on the ceiling that she had.

"Mm-hmm."

"That's makes sense. We are going to have to refuel soon."

"Daddy, look." Vincent walked over carrying a plate of cupcakes. "Look what they made for me today."

"Wow, those look good," I told him.

"They're chocolate, my favorite. I saved some for you."

"Vincent, go put them back on the table. We'll eat them after dinner," Ruby instructed, and he obeyed. She looked back at me and said, "At least they do try and make sure he's happy. I'm grateful for that."

"Me too," I told her, allowing my thoughts to travel to a simpler place for a brief moment. "But that doesn't change things. Once we are off this boat, I'm going to kill every one of them."

Nee Nee

42

The conversation last night between my son, niece, and nephew had gotten intense, and I was still concerned. As I listened from the kitchen doorway, I debated whether to interrupt. On one hand, all three were adults, and it was certainly a conversation that needed to be had. But I also had maternal instincts that made me want to jump in and mediate in order to protect and defend not just my son, but all of them, before things got out of hand. Sasha may have been a woman, but she was a very dangerous woman, capable of taking Curtis and Roman out with her training if she so desired. Seeing how she had turned out after finishing school was half the reason I'd scraped together the money to send Lauryn to that school. I wanted my baby to be strong and formidable, just like Sasha, London, and Paris.

As I thought about the events from the previous night, my phone started ringing from a blocked number. Normally I wouldn't answer, but it was too early for telemarketers, and there was only one person would dare call this early morning.

"Good morning, Larry," I said.

"Morning, sunshine. How are things there?"

I took a deep breath. "Well, Sasha showed up, and things got a little intense last night."

"That's not good. What happened?"

"Curtis and Roman found her in the woods with a sniper rifle. She was waiting on you to show up so she could kill you."

"Ah, jeez, does that girl still think I killed her momma?"

"Mm-hmm, Curtis too. But I think he's changed her mind about that."

Now, I'll be honest. I never asked Larry if he killed Donna, and I never would, because I knew he'd tell me the truth and I might not want to know the answer. It was time to change the subject.

"What are you up to?"

"I'm looking to hook up with a big shot by the name of Alexander Cora. See if you can discreetly talk to Chippy about him and ask if his name rings a bell. It's a small world, and it's possible LC and his boys could be doing business with him, or at least know who he does business with."

"I'll see what I can find out."

"Thanks, baby. I'll talk to you soon. Love you."

"Love you too." As I hung up, I wondered about why he needed the information. Bringing LC's name into it made me a little nervous, considering LC had been Larry's target at one point. Years of medication and mental health treatment had helped him understand LC was not his enemy. Now, I truly hoped he wasn't headed to that dark place again. Our family had suffered enough because of Larry's delusions. I knew the damage my husband's actions had caused the family wasn't intentional, but the collateral damage was real. It was a lot to deal with, and I hoped there would be some resolution that kept every member of our extended family safe and alive.

I was staring out the window into the back yard when Curtis walked in.

"Morning, Momma."

"Well, that was a lot last night." I turned around, leaning against the sink with my arms folded.

"It was." Curtis came and hugged me, then stood beside me. "But I can't say that I blame her. She has every right to feel the way that she does and to ask questions. Her mother was killed, and me and Daddy were two of the last people to see her alive. Initially, I thought maybe Daddy had done it myself, but he swore he didn't. And real talk, after all the other people he killed, there wasn't a reason for him to lie. If he'd done it, he would admit it."

"So, whoever killed Donna is still out there too?" I asked.

"Yeah, I think they are." Curtis nodded. "You think maybe what Daddy is out there doing has something to do with that too?"

"Curtis, I don't know what your father is doing other than trying to stay free and help you," I said. "I take it you didn't see him when you got to the address?"

"Naw, no sign of him at all." Curtis shook his head. "Just the man on the Wanted poster. And before you ask, yeah, he was alive."

"No idea where your father could be headed?"

"No clue at all, Ma." Curtis glanced over at me. "What is he saying when he calls?"

"Nothing really other than he's staying out of trouble. The calls are always really short."

"What about this morning?" he asked.

I was busted. "Oh, you heard that, huh?" Curtis had always been a nosy child, but I guess his observational skills were part of what made him a good bounty hunter now.

"Of course I did," he said. "So what did he say?"

"He wants information on some man named Alexander Cora. Maybe it's another bounty he wants to collect for you?"

"Alexander Cora, the billionaire?" Roman asked as he and Sasha came into the room.

"Why would Daddy be looking for Alexander Cora?" Curtis asked.

"I don't know, but he's looking for him."

Sasha joined the conversation. "He will never be able to find him. Alexander Cora is a recluse. He spends most of his time on yachts and private islands."

"You don't know my father," Curtis told her. "If anybody can sniff him out, it's Larry Duncan. He taught me how to be a bounty hunter."

"You can't hunt down a man who has no trail," Sasha said.

Roman looked at Sasha curiously. "You act like you know him personally."

"I know enough," Sasha snapped back at him. Considering how fast my niece was, I was starting to think she may have slept with him.

"Hold up, Sasha. Do you know Alexander Cora?" Curtis asked.

"We've met, but I know his son Aries very well," she said, and I had no doubt she had slept with that one.

"Do you have a number or know how to contact him?" I asked.

"Why? So you can tell Uncle Larry and he can kill him? No thank you, Aunt Nee Nee." Sasha walked over and gave me a tight hug. That girl saw right through me. "Thank you for your hospitality. It was nice seeing you, but I gotta go."

You can't leave yet, Sasha," I said. "You just got here. We haven't even had breakfast yet."

"I'm not hungry, and I should get back on the road." She held up her keys.

"Where you going?" I asked the question, but I already knew the answer. She was going to find my husband and kill him.

Larry

43

It was a little after seven when we spotted the sign on the corner for Hong Kong Delight 24-hour all-you-can-eat buffet. There was something about a good, savory meal that got my mind going. Food always helped me think, which was why I decided our next stop after driving down to Virginia and back to pick up Holly and Kenny would be to get something to eat. Agent Martinez had given me a lot to think about, and I needed to formulate a plan.

"Pull over there," I told Kenny as I pointed to the sign. "Let's get something to eat."

"Chinese? Really? For breakfast?" he whined.

"Yeah, what's wrong with Chinese?"

I couldn't remember the last time I'd had Asian food, which was one of my favorites. I could already taste the savory sauces, and my mouth watered. I wasn't concerned about the disgusted look on my son's face. We were eating Chinese for breakfast whether he liked it or not.

"It's a buffet," Holly quipped from the backseat. "I love buffets."

"Me too," Dennis agreed.

"You're outnumbered, son," I said jovially.

Kenny parked the car, grumbling to himself the whole time. While Dennis, Holly, and I swiftly headed inside, Kenny took his time. By the time he got to the table with his plate, we were already thinking about second plates.

"This is really good," Dennis said with his mouth full of moo shu pork.

"And we can get more." Holly dipped her egg roll into the plastic cup of duck sauce beside her plate. Sometimes it was comical how excited she would get about the smallest things.

"So, where are we headed next?" Kenny asked as he sat across from me and picked at his plate.

"I'm thinking about it now," I said, twirling a forkful of lo mein noodles. "We need to start by finding out more about this fucking Alexander Cora. We need to find out how he operates. I can't do anything until we know that."

"What about the dossier you were reading? Isn't that all the information you need?" Dennis asked.

"Not really. Just some typical bullshit information about his corporation and business dealings, along with a whole bunch of speculation on his arms trafficking, and that's about it. That shit ain't helpful. At least not right now it ain't. What we need is some inside personal shit. You can't take a man down on newspaper clippings and shit his publicist put out."

"When we were trying to take Uncle LC down a few years ago, didn't you go after his business?" Kenny asked. "We blew up one of his dealerships."

"True, but that was just to get his attention," I explained. "We don't need this man to know we're coming for him."

"Sneak attack," Holly commented. "I like that."

"Well, seems to me that we can't attack him until we know where he is," Kenny said.

"No, sometimes it's better when you don't go straight for the head," I told him. "Instead, you dismantle his body, limb by limb. That's where we need to start. We gotta find the other parts of him, like where he lays his head, who are his mistresses, what school his kids go to, shit like that."

Kenny put his fork down and took out his phone.

"Who are you calling?" I asked.

"Nobody." He tapped on the screen. "I'm googling this guy to see what I can find."

"I can tell you right now it's gonna be as useful as that folder sitting in the car."

"Can't hurt to try."

"I guess not." I shrugged.

"What does it say?" Holly looked over his shoulder.

"He's hella rich, owns Cora International, has plenty of awards and accolades, that's it." Kenny continued scrolling on his phone. "No wife, no kids, no family."

"And that's bullshit," I said. "He has family somewhere."

"I'm telling you I'm looking everywhere. It's not mentioned," Kenny replied.

"The internet only tells you what people want you to know. That ain't real life." I shook my head. "A man that age and that successful got a woman and some kids somewhere. Maybe a couple of women. The only way he don't is if he was one of the gays."

Kenny looked up at me. "You can't say that, Pop. It's disrespectful."

"How? If you don't like the opposite sex, ain't that what gay means?" I asked.

"Yeah, but . . . it's not . . . you can't call them 'gays' like they're a gang."

"I don't give a shit, and that ain't my point." I picked up my napkin and wiped my mouth. "Alexander Cora ain't one of them."

"I think your dad's right." Holly pointed at the phone. "He definitely doesn't look gay to me."

"So, how are we gonna find his family?" Kenny put his phone away.

"We gotta find a resource who can help us." I took a deep breath, accepting the fact that I'd hit a snag and gotten to the point where I had to reach out for some assistance. I had no choice other than to call my Achilles Heel, the only person I knew who could point me in the right direction.

It took out my phone, dialed the number, and prayed he would answer.

"Hello?"

I hesitated, not sure I'd done the right thing, but shit—now I was stuck.

"Hello?"

"Hey, LC," I said. Not only did the phone fall silent, but the eyes of everyone sitting at the table bugged out. "How you doing little brother?"

There was an extended silence, and I thought he'd hung up until finally, he said, "Larry?"

"Yeah. It's me. How you doing?"

"Fine, I guess. Larry you shouldn't be calling me."

"Yeah, I know, but listen. I need a favor. I swear to you I'm try-ing to set things right, but I've hit a bit of a brick wall. I wouldn't be calling you otherwise."

"A favor?" he asked, and I was relieved that rather than dis-missing me, he sounded intrigued.

"If you were looking to find out some information on someone in our world, where would you go?" I asked. "Private informa-tion about their family and associates."

"Information," LC repeated.

"Yeah. I need it, and I'm hoping you can point me in the right direction. Who would have that kind of capability? You got any-body like that?" I asked. "It's probably better I don't tell you who it is, but the information I need is on a very powerful man with plenty of secrets that he wouldn't want the world to know."

"Well, I do, but it's my grandson Nevada, but I'm not bringing him into this shit or anywhere near you," LC said. "But if this man is as powerful as you say he is, I'd start with where most of the power players are known to gather."

"And where's that?"

"Hellfire Club."

"The Hellfire Club? That overpriced brothel on Riverside Drive. It's still open?" I almost laughed.

"It ain't Big Shirley's. And the new owner is notorious for how she runs the place. Taught her girls how to extract information from their clients, and you can get that information for the right price."

"Who the hell owns it? One of your kids?" I recalled Nee Nee mentioning that one of LC's kids owned a nice nightclub.

"No, my grandson's mother, Consuela Zuniga."

"Alejandro's wife?"

"Alejandro's widow," LC corrected me. "Look, Larry, I don't know what you're up to or what you got going on, but you need to stay out of trouble. The feds are after you, and they—"

"Don't worry about me," I told him. "I ain't making no trouble, and I ain't worried about the feds."

"If you say so, but be careful."

"I ain't locked up, but I promise, I'm still taking my medicine. My head is clear."

There was another moment of silence. "All right, Larry. But please, like I said, be careful."

"I will." I hung up, put my phone into my jacket pocket and took out the small pill bottle. I popped one of the tiny tablets and swallowed it down with the glass of sweet tea in front of me. "All right, finish eating. We got somewhere to be."

"Where's that?" Holly asked.

"New York City."

Orlando

44

"Just dump it! Toss it over, mon!"

I woke to the sound of Tyrell, one of the security guards, yelling, followed by a loud splash. I sat up, checked to make sure my wife was okay, then glanced toward the porthole window on my side of our bed. The sun was barely up, and the shouting continued as I eased up to my feet. I pressed my head against the circular glass window to get a better look at what was happening outside the boat. I was expecting to see another boat or skiff tied to us or coming alongside us, but because of the limited range of the small window, I couldn't see anything other than the water directly below our deck. Then there was a huge splash in front of me.

"What the fuck?" I whispered. The thing that they had thrown over was sinking quickly, and unless my eyes were deceiving me, it looked like a body.

I heard a third splash and quickly leaned forward, pressing my face against the window to try to get a better view.

"Fuck!" I said out loud as I saw another body in the waves nearby.

"What's wrong?" Ruby asked as she rose from the bed and came to stand next to me.

I turned to my wife and placed a finger over my lips.

Up above, Tyrell was laughing. "This fucker is heavy, mon!"

"Yeah, well, he shoulda said no to drugs," replied another man. A few seconds later, there was another splash. "That's the last one. Thank God they only tested that shit on five."

"This can't be happening," I whispered to myself. The word *tested* rang in my head. "They've lost their minds."

"Who, Orlando?" Ruby frowned.

"The drug I'm working on. I think they're testing it on people when I told them not to. They just threw five dead bodies in the water," I hissed.

Ruby covered her mouth to suppress her shock.

"Are you sure? Maybe they aren't bodies. Maybe they were something else," Ruby suggested weakly. She knew I wasn't wrong.

"Nah, I've seen enough dead bodies before." I could feel myself shaking inside. "Those men are dead because of me."

Ruby wrapped her arms around me as if she could sense the guilt I was beginning to feel. "This isn't your fault."

"Then whose fault is it?"

I walked out of our bedroom and into the living room area of our suite. I picked up the in-house phone that went directly to Aries.

"Hello?" He sounded tired, probably up all night making plans to undermine me.

"You motherfucker! Are you that fucking greedy? I told you we had to test it first! Why the fuck did you give those people FIRE?" I screamed.

"How do you know that?" he asked groggily, not even attempting to lie.

"Because your stupid-ass people are throwing bodies overboard. That's why, you stupid ass!"

"Orlando, I know you're upset, but I must ask you refrain from using that type of language with me. We are both civilized men—"

He never finished his sentence before I started cursing again.

"Fuck you! You're not civilized!" I screamed into the phone. "I'm done with this shit. I need a face-to-face meeting, ASAP. Otherwise, you can put a bullet in my head, 'cause I ain't doing shit!"

"I'll deliver your request, sir. I'll be down in twenty minutes. Please be dressed," Aries replied calmly.

Anger and frustration were growing within me by the minute. By the time Aries arrived, I'd showered and gotten dressed. I'd also forced myself to calm down for my family's sake. I heard the click of the latch.

"Kiss Vincent for me and tell him we'll play chess later tonight." Somehow, my yelling hadn't woken my sleeping son.

"Orlando," Ruby said as I headed out the door.

"Yeah?" I asked.

She pulled her robe tight before stepping out of the room to where I now stood, briefly looking over at Aries before whispering into my ear. "We've made it this far. Just keep working. This will be over soon."

"I know. I'm sorry. I just lost it. Those people unnecessarily lost their lives." I kissed her forehead. "I love you."

"Love you too."

I followed Aries out of the room and down the corridor to the staircase. My mood was stern, and I was deep in thought, so I remained quiet.

"I think you are blowing this whole situation out of proportion," Aries commented. "However, I apologize if it upset Ruby and Vincent."

I glanced over at Aries as if he'd lost his fucking mind. We'd only known one another a few months, but I was certain he at least knew me well enough not to patronize me. I don't know, maybe I had some form of Stockholm Syndrome or something, but I'd made the mistake of thinking Aries and I had a bond through science. Now I saw how wrong that was.

"I'd appreciate it if you don't discuss my wife and son. As a matter of fact, how about we don't discuss anything, okay? The only person I want to talk to at this point is the one you answer to."

From the way Aries reacted, I could see that he was taken aback by my response. Usually, I was polite, or at least cordial. All of the niceties were now gone after what I'd witnessed. I had no pleasantries for him or anybody else. My patience was wearing thin.

"He's already waiting for you on the upper deck," Aries said.

Lauryn

45

I arrived at Room 426 exactly at ten o'clock as instructed, despite having arrived at the hotel thirty minutes early. Not wanting to look too anxious, I'd gone to the hotel restaurant and had a cup of coffee until our designated meeting time. A few of the people I had met at the reception were still there, including the bomb expert and the colorful-haired chick, who nodded and waved at me.

When I got to Nadja's room, I tapped lightly and waited.

"Come in, come in." Nadja welcomed me inside with a phone to her ear. She pointed at a chair, and I took a seat, watching her as she paced.

"Why don't you meet me there?" she said in voice that women use when they're trying to talk a man into something he doesn't want to do. "We can spend a few days lounging on the ship, working out your next move. They have a terrific chef, and I can promise you some of the best nights of your life."

I took note of her simple ivory linen dress belted by a link of gold chains at the waist. Her hair was loose, hanging well past her shoulders. Nadja wasn't wearing any makeup, and I couldn't help but notice how naturally beautiful she was. Seeing her in the sunlight flowing through the windows allowed me to have a totally different view. Paris was my cousin, and she was definitely a baddie, but Nadja was also. I was starting to understand why they had a rivalry.

"Think about it," she replied into the phone, this time with a hint of desperation, before she hung up.

She exhaled, then looked over at me, taking a seat on the love seat across from me. "Men. Can't live with them, can't fuck without them." She laughed. "Well, I guess you could, but what fun would that be?"

Instead of glancing around the room, my eyes remained on Nadja. I shrugged, letting out a fake laugh. I wanted her to see that she had my undivided attention.

"Boyfriend?" I asked.

"More like a drug I've been addicted to the last eight years. He's the best thing that ever happened to me and the worst thing all at the same time. I just can't give him up," she said so sentimentally I was almost confused. I could have sworn Paris said she'd been involved with Niles, so who the hell was this other guy?

"Anyway, enough about me. Are you ready to get to work?" she asked.

"I am," I said with a satisfied grin, without even knowing what the contract entailed. It didn't matter if she told me I had to get rid of Denzel Washington. I was ready, willing, and able—as long as it had nothing to do with my cousin, who was still hell bent on believing she was the target. "When do I start?"

"Right now." She stood and walked over to a table near the door, where she picked up a folder. She returned to her seat and handed the folder to me. "Here is your target."

I hesitated before looking down at the photo I was now holding, knowing that there was a slim chance that it may be Paris's face that I saw. Finally, I looked down and was relieved to see a handsome, brown-skinned guy with wavy hair and a dimpled smile. I didn't know who he was or what he'd done to seal his inevitable fate, but it was a damn shame that someone wanted this fine man dead. He must have really pissed someone off.

That wasn't my business, though. I couldn't wait to get back to the house to let Paris know that she was wrong, and Rio and I were right. At least, thus far.

"This is a simple assignment. His name is Daryl Graham. Your job is to take him out quickly without a trace, and preferably make it look like he died of natural causes. Heart attack, strong aneurism, something of that nature."

"Okay, I can do that." I nodded. "I'm going to need a couple days to do some reconnaissance, figure out his routine. Do you know where I can—"

"That won't be necessary," Nadja interrupted. "We have all the information needed for you to complete the assignment. I just got a location notification from the client. He was smart enough to slip a geo-tag in the purse of the woman the target is with. They're actually staying at a hotel not too far from here. Do you have an account you'd like us to wire the down payment to?"

"Yes," I said, pleasantly surprised that this seemed easier than I'd expected. "They provided us all with Swiss bank accounts when we graduated."

"Good. As of right now, you're officially off the grid and on the clock. I'm sure you know the drill. Like you said, you're aware of the nature of what we do and how it's done. Poisoning is your specialty, right?"

"It is."

"Perfect. Like I said, this is a simple assignment."

I stood up, ready to leave. "Just give me some time to gather my materials. I'm not trying to be funny, but I don't ride around with arsenic in my purse," I told her. "I don't even have a gun."

Nadja reached over onto the coffee table nearby and picked up the notepad with the hotel logo and a pen, then handed them both to me. "Write down everything you need. All the materials."

"Okay." I blinked, wondering why she was rushing this.

"Oh, and I need your phone and any other electronics you have," she said, glancing down at my smart watch.

"My phone?" I said softly.

"Yes, don't worry. I have a burner for you that can only be used to contact me while you're working." Nadja held her hand out. "You can turn it off for a couple of days. You should be done by then."

There was no way I could go two days without contacting Paris. She'd lose her ever-loving mind, and she and Rio would come to find me, which was the last thing I needed them to do. I wanted this job, and I hoped it would lead to more of them. I just had to give Paris a heads up about what was happening, so she'd leave me alone for a few days. I quickly thought of a reason to make a call before giving it to her.

"I just need to make sure my dog is cared for."

"Okay." Nadja sighed. "Go ahead and do what you need to do."

"I'll call my roommate."

I stepped out onto the small balcony overlooking the water. I dialed Paris's number.

"Hey, Patricia. It's Lauryn."

"Huh? Oh, hey, how you doing?" Paris caught on fast.

"I'm just calling to see if you can feed and walk Chester for a couple of days while I'm working. I'd appreciate it a lot." I wasn't sure if Nadja was listening, but I had to assume she was.

"Oh, shit. A couple of days? Really?" Paris asked.

"Yeah, two or three days tops. That's it. But listen, I know you worry about getting bit, but I promise Chester isn't a threat to you," I told her, hoping she'd understand what I meant.

"It's not me?" she asked, sounding surprised.

"No. I probably won't have cell service either. Just in case my parents call you."

"No cell service either?"

"Thanks so much, Patricia. Speak soon." I ended the call, then went back inside.

"Everything good?" Nadja asked.

"Yep, everything's fine," I told her, turning off the phone and handing it to her.

"Great. I'm going to need that list." She passed me a sleek, black Ruger and a simple cell phone. "These are for you."

I looked at both items. It was official. I had my first job, and within seventy-two hours, whoever he was, Daryl Graham would be dead.

Orlando

46

Aries and I remained silent as we approached the upper deck of the boat, where he opened the door and allowed me to step outside first. I took in the warm sea air and enjoyed the feeling of the sun on my face for a moment, until he gestured for me to follow him. The man I desired to see was sitting in a chair, dressed in all white, waiting for me with a bloody Mary in his hand.

He took off his white fedora with his free hand and placed it on the table in front him. "Mr. Duncan, how are you this morning?"

I stared at Alexander Cora, the man who had kidnapped me and my family and forced me to transform the formula for HEAT into a new drug he wanted to call FIRE. He was tall and thin, and I could see where women would have found him attractive when he was young. He had to be in his early seventies, or thereabout. His company, Cora International, was the biggest Black-owned defense contractor in the world, and he was worth at least three billion dollars if you paid attention to Forbes. Other than Pop and Uncle Lou, Cora had been one of my idols at one time, a self-made Black man to be respected. It was all bullshit, which I found out the day we were kidnapped. The man was an arrogant asshole, no more than a poacher and a bully, and I'd promised myself that one day, he'd feel the Duncan wrath.

"I'm not in the best of moods, Mr. Cora," I told him.

"And why's that? Is there something unsuitable with your living quarters?" He pointed at an open seat, but I opted to stand. "We can move you to another room if you'd like, although don't think it will be as comfortable."

"That's not what this is about, and you know it," I snapped. "You took the samples of FIRE from the lab and gave them to people."

Alexander glanced over at Aries, then back to me. After a moment, he said, "Yes, we did give a few men the opportunity to try the new product. We did."

"Why? I've been telling Aries that it wasn't ready for human consumption yet. We hadn't even tested it on rats." My voice trembled with anger. "When I agreed to this farce, you told me nobody would die. You killed those people."

"Yes, that was unfortunate. He did tell me that." Alexander put on a fake expression of concern. "However, look on the bright side, Orlando. Your theory was correct. Currently, it's not safe for human consumption. It's been tested and proven."

He smiled as if we were talking about lab rats instead of actual human beings. I was starting to see just what a sick bastard he was.

"Jesus Christ, you're a fucking nutcase!" I tossed my hands in the air in disgust.

"Calm down, Orlando. This was an unfortunate incident, so to speak. But you'll be pleased to know that the test subjects were all in a state of euphoria that they'd never experienced before they died. At least we know that you're on the right track. Hopefully, the next round of testing—"

"No, there won't be a next round of testing unless I have some reassurances."

"Reassurances?" Alexander set his glass down on the table and laughed. "Aries, you can escort Mr. Duncan back down to the lab so he can continue his work."

"I'm not done here," I told him.

"I am. And it would be in your best interest not to push me."

I glared at him, refusing to back down.

He sighed. "Fine. You want a reason to see things my way?" He pointed to an upper deck. "Look up there."

I turned toward the upper deck and screamed, "No!" when I saw a strikingly pretty woman holding my son in the air as if she was about to throw him over the rail and off the ship. Li'l Man was laughing as if they were playing, but I could tell from her body language this was no game.

"She has no regard for human life. She will throw him over." Alexander smiled wickedly.

"You son of a—" I lurched toward him, but Aries grabbed me from behind. He had a gun to my head so fast that I didn't even get close to making contact.

"Orlando," Aries said in a low voice, "remember your son."

"Okay, okay, just let him go." I closed my eyes and took a deep breath. One day I would kill this man, but for now, my son needed me to be calm. "I'll do what you ask. Just don't hurt my son."

"Now, that's a reasonable way of looking at things." He waved to the woman, who kissed my son like a grandmother and placed him down, then took his hand and led him away. "I'd like to do another test this weekend, Mr. Duncan, so please, keep up the good work."

Lauryn

47

After spending the better part of a day and a half in a hotel room at Barons Cove Resort in Sag Harbor, I was feeling like a recluse. Nadja had put me in a room at the resort next door to her driver, Jonah, because this was where my target was staying. Unfortunately, I hadn't spotted Daryl Graham once, and I could barely make a move to contact Paris with Jonah watching my ass. I thought I was going to die of boredom watching Housewives shows until the phone she had given me finally rang. I scooped it up and answered it on the third ring.

"Hello."

"Mr. Graham has made a six o'clock dinner reservation at The Beacon restaurant across the street from you. You might want to be there to greet him," Nadja said in this methodical, no-nonsense tone.

"I'm going to need my supplies," I replied, holding my breath. I still couldn't believe this was real. Yes, I'd been trained to do this, to kill people, but now I actually had to do it, and it wasn't in self-defense. God, what a sobering moment.

"Everything you need is right outside your door."

I turned to the door.

"Time to see if you're as good as advertised, Lauryn. Call me when the job is done. We'll be watching."

The phone went dead. I strolled across the room and opened the door. A box lay on the floor outside my room. I looked around, but the hallway was empty. No sign of who had left the package there. I picked up the box and headed straight to the bathroom, where I inspected the contents.: glass beakers, stirrers, hot plates, precision scales, test kits, pH meters, a pair of

Nitrile gloves, a double-filtered gas mask, and the apron I had requested. In addition, there were bottles of acephate, sulfur, boric acid and other chemicals I needed to create the organophosphate compound that I'd perfected in school. In other words, my target would be poisoned by an untraceable pesticide and would most likely die in his sleep. His cause of death would be a stroke or perhaps a heart attack. The formula was fucking genius if I said so myself.

"Get over yourself, Lauryn," I mumbled to myself, checking my watch. It was two o'clock in the afternoon, plenty of time to do what I had to do, and head over to The Beacon. "Time to get to work."

By five-thirty, I'd completed the task of making a suitable poison and was headed to fulfill the contract. Nadja was right. The restaurant was literally across the street from the hotel, and it only took me five minutes to cross the street and climb the stairs to the upper dining room, which overlooked the infamous Sag Harbor bridge and the scenic harbor.

I sashayed myself into the bar area to wait for Daryl but was surprised to see him already sitting alone at the far end of the bar.

Damn, could this shit get any easier?

I walked over and nonchalantly eased up next to him. He was a little old for me, but the man's picture did him no justice. He was easy as hell on the eyes.

"Excuse me. Is this seat taken?"

He looked up from his phone and glanced over at me, then down at the empty barstool in front of me. "Nah, not that one. The one on this side is taken, though."

"Thanks." I slid onto the barstool, and he went back to looking at his phone until the bartender slid a glass of brown liquid in front of him. If he wasn't going to make small talk, I guessed it was up to me. "Whiskey?"

"Nah, I'm a Cognac guy," he said, looking up from his phone again and taking a swallow.

"Cognac? That's an old man drink, isn't it? You don't look that old." I smiled flirtatiously.

"Old man drink? Nah, Cognac is an established man's drink. Has nothing to do with age."

"I'll have to take your word for it. I can't do dark liquor. Makes me angry." I motioned to the bartender. "I'll have a tequila sunrise, please."

"You a local or weekend warrior?" I asked, trying to keep him from looking back down at his phone.

He half-smiled. I'm sure he thought I was coming on to him, especially since I chose to sit next to him, and we were the only people of color in the bar area. He shut that down quickly, though.

"Me and my girl are just out here for a few days for some fun in the sun. Nice place to get away. And you?"

"Same," I replied as the bartender gave me my drink.

In spite of mentioning his girl, he left his phone on the bar and engaged me in a little small talk. The Yankees game was on the large screen TV behind the bar, so we chatted about that, even though I didn't know shit about baseball. He was polite, but after a few minutes, he went back to checking his phone. He seemed somewhat troubled, and I almost felt bad about what I was about to do. He actually seemed like a nice guy. However, this was business, and when the moment presented itself and he finally placed his cell phone back on the bar, I "accidentally on purpose" knocked it on the floor.

"Oh, dammit. I didn't break it, did I?" I asked.

"Nah, I don't think so," he told me, standing and looking around to see where it had landed.

While he searched, I discreetly poured a generous amount of liquid into his glass from the vial that I'd slipped out of my pocket moments before. By the time he'd retrieved his phone, the vial was tucked back away, and I was sitting there looking stupid and remorseful.

His phone rang, and he answered it.

"Hey, babe. I'm at the bar," he said into the phone.

"Nice meeting you." I hopped up and strolled toward the door. I wasn't trying to be identified by a jealous girlfriend, so I needed to make my exit.

"You too." He was still talking on the phone as he waved goodbye.

As I headed down the stairs, I pulled out the phone Nadja had given me and hit the call button. "It's done. He should be dead by the morning."

"Excellent. Our client will be pleased," Nadja responded. "Return to your room and destroy any evidence. Jonah will pick you up in the morning. We are going on a little trip, you and me."

Paris

48

"Can you please stop that?" Rio glared at me as he poured champagne into his orange juice. We were on the back patio overlooking the bay, having an early morning breakfast—and I was pulling my hair out worrying about Lauryn.

I paced across the floor, checking my phone for the eighth time in the past fifteen minutes. I was anxious for a call or text from my cousin, and Rio acting like we were on a mini vacation was annoying as hell. Unlike me, he didn't seem worried that it had been more than a day and a half since we'd heard from her.

"I can't help it. Where the fuck is she? Her phone keeps going to voicemail, and her location isn't on."

"Bitch, you're getting all riled up and being extra. You are the one who insisted we couldn't go to Pop and sent her on this crazy-ass mission." He sighed, handing me the drink in his hand. "Here. Didn't she tell you she'd be busy for a couple of days and the target wasn't you? You should be glad about that."

"Yeah, but I thought that meant that she wouldn't be back, not that she wouldn't be reachable," I told him. "I don't like this, Rio."

"Drink," he insisted. "I'm sure she's fine."

I gulped down the mimosa so fast that it burned my chest as it went down. "But what if she isn't? I'm not going to be blamed for this. We need to go find her ass."

"We can always call Pop," he said.

"No the fuck we can't. I'm gonna handle this myself."

"The main reason for sending Lauryn instead of you was so you wouldn't be seen." He shook his head. "You can't just show up in Montauk."

"Why can't I? I don't give a fuck who sees me at this point. We need to know what the fuck is going on."

I turned to head upstairs and get ready. My twin brother knew damn well that I was a woman of action. Sitting around and waiting wasn't something I usually did. I damn sure wasn't going to do it anymore. I had to go and see for myself what was going on, and if that meant coming face to face with Nadja, then that's what I would have to do.

"Paris, wait!" Rio called after me.

"What?" I turned around.

"If you go, I go."

"Then hurry the fuck up, bro." I smiled, relieved that my twin had my back. Usually, it was Sasha who was by my side, but I hadn't spoken to her in days, which meant she was still in her feelings, and I didn't have time to deal with that. Rio was a capable partner, and I was confident in his abilities to do whatever needed to be done. We quickly got dressed, locked and loaded, then headed to Montauk to locate my baby cousin.

We walked into Gurney's Inn in Montauk, and the sign in the lobby that read WELCOME FUTURE STUDENTS let us know we were in the right place. The hotel was beachy but nice, which came as no surprise. Minister Farah and my alma mater never spared any expense when it came to impressing its students and the mega rich families they came from.

I tried calling Lauryn's phone once more, even though I knew it was pointless.

"She ain't gonna answer." Rio side-eyed me.

"Mind your business," I told him as I looked around the place. Lauryn was nowhere in sight, and neither was Nadja. From what I could see, it was all younger people hoping to be accepted as students at the esteemed academy.

There was a small group gathered on the patio, so I ventured outside through the large glass doors. Still, there was no sign of either woman, but I did see Minister Farah. My initial reaction was to avoid him, but he was the only option I had. I waited until the people he was speaking to walked away before pointing him out to Rio, whose attention was focused on the handsome concierge.

Rio leaned toward me. "Damn, he's fine. You think he's a little too young for me, though?"

"What I think is you need to focus on our reason for being here," I said and pulled him in the direction of Minister Farah.

"Hello, Minister Farah." I greeted my former teacher.

"Paris Duncan, this a welcomed surprise." He smiled and hugged me tight. "No one told me you were coming. How lovely to see you."

"It's nice to see you too," I said. "You remember my twin brother, Rio?"

"I do. How are you, Rio?"

"I'm well, sir," Rio answered.

"I wasn't expecting you. Are you a surprise guest on one of our panels?" Minister Farah asked me.

"Actually, I'm not here for the events," I told him. "I'm looking for my cousin, Lauryn. She is here somewhere. Have you seen her?"

"Ah, yes. She attended the welcome reception I hosted the other night, and I did see her this morning. It's my understanding that she met with a potential employer and things went quite well." Minister Farah explained everything I already knew.

"Yes, we're aware. We were hoping to surprise her. Any idea where we might find her?"

"She's on that helicopter, I believe." Minister Farah pointed toward the beautiful water and a helicopter headed over the sea. "You just missed them by five minutes."

"Shit," Rio cursed.

"Where are they going?" I asked.

"To that yacht." He pointed again, and the same *Oh, shit!* look came across my face and Rio's. There, in the horizon, was the largest yacht I'd ever seen.

"What? Where the hell are they going?"

"I'm not certain, but from what I heard, they may be headed to Europe." Minister Farah's words seemed to echo in my head as I felt my panic rising.

The good news was that being on a boat headed to Europe meant that she was still alive and they hadn't figured out she was a Duncan. The flip side of that coin was that we had no idea why or how to reach her. It was then that I realized shit had gone from bad to worse.

Rio must've been thinking the same thing because as he stared at the yacht traveling farther away, he asked, "So, now do you think we need to call Pop?"

Larry

49

LC was right. The Hellfire Club was nothing like Big Shirley's. It was definitely a more high-end establishment, offering a five-star experience, whereas Big Shirley's was just a hole-in-the-wall whorehouse. One thing both had in common, though, was a bar that extended the length of the room, and a plethora of scantily dressed women being extra nice to the male patrons. I must admit the Hellfire women were of a higher scale: Brazilian, Asian, Haitian, Dominican, all beautiful, exotic, and ready to make a man's wet dream come true for the right price.

"Damn, I'd always heard of this place, but to actually be here is something else," Kenny announced. "Dad, can I get some money?"

I could see him salivating at the possibilities and choices of women surrounding us. Dennis was too. I'm sure it had been a long time for the big fella.

"Boy, stop acting like you ain't never seen pussy before. You been going to Big Shirley's since you was fifteen years old."

"I know, but that's fifty-dollar pussy. This is thousand-dollar pussy," Kenny said, looking around like a kid in a candy shop. "I just want to see what the difference is."

"I can tell you what the difference is," I snapped back at him. "Nine hundred and fifty dollars. Besides, I told you we don't have no money to be wasted. We're here on business, not a damn booty call."

"Mr. Duncan, she'll see you now," said a young lady named Natalia, who'd approached us when we first entered the club and now came back over to us. "Follow me."

She led us through the club and down a hallway until we got to a secured area. The big, brawny dude standing guard looked straight at us, then back to Natalia, who gestured for him to move so we could get past. We eventually arrived at a large mahogany door and went inside, where we were greeted by Consuela Zuniga, the proprietor of the establishment.

"Hello, Consuela. It's been a long time." I smiled. "You're looking good."

"I wish I could say the same for you, Larry." She stared at me from behind a large, marble desk, still looking as beautiful as the last time I'd seen her nearly twenty years ago. "You look like shit."

"Yeah, well, being on the run will do that to you."

She got tired of the niceties in a hurry. "What do you want, Larry? You're wasting my time, and time is money."

"Relax, Consuela. It's just me. Don't act like we aren't old friends," I told her. "I'm not here to hurt you."

"You aren't my friend," she replied. "You were a friend of my ex-husband. Deceased ex-husband, I might add. The only reason I agreed to see you is because LC asked me to. Now, again, what the fuck do you want?"

"I need some information, and LC suggested I come to see you. Of course, I promised to be on my best behavior. So as long as you play nice, I will." I sat in one of the large wingback chairs in front of her desk. Natalia walked over and stood near Consuela, while Dennis and Kenny stood behind me.

"What kind of information are you looking for?" she asked.

"Secret information about a man named Alexander Cora."

Consuela leaned back in her chair and tilted her head to the side, giving me a look that was a cross between amused and puzzled. "What makes you think I'd have information on him?"

"Because you are the expert on powerful men, Consuela. I'm sure you know things that others don't. It's part of your line of work." I shifted forward. "Isn't that right?"

"It is." She nodded.

"Good, so are you able to assist me?"

"Possibly," she said tentatively. "Alexander Cora is a very powerful man. The information you're looking for is quite valuable. It's not going to come cheap."

"What do you consider not cheap?"

"I'm able to provide what I have for, let's say, one hundred and fifty thousand dollars."

"What the fuck did you just say?" I stood up, leaning angrily over her desk. "What makes you think I'd pay you that kind of money, even if I had it to pay?"

"Because like you've stated, Larry, I'm an expert at what I do, and whatever information I have will be priceless. I must be paid my worth."

She didn't budge, flinch, or anything I would have expected. Her little bitch standing behind her didn't even pull out a gun. Shit, Consuela had become a fucking real-life gangster.

"Now, sit down or this meeting is over," she said calmly.

"Clearly, you've lost what sense God gave you. I'm not paying you a hundred fifty K."

"Then it was a pleasure seeing you again. Good day. Natalia will show you out." She gestured toward the door dismissively.

I was too flabbergasted to even move.

She looked up at me, still standing before her. "You used to be a savvy businessman, Larry. I know you've been gone a long time, but I know you haven't forgotten how business works. Surely you didn't expect me to give you something for free."

I shifted a bit, easing my hand into my jacket to remove my gun. Then, I thought about the promise I'd made to my brother and Agent Martinez. I couldn't cause any undue harm. I was going to have to figure out another way. "I understand business, Consuela. But to be honest, I don't have that amount of free cash on hand. Is there a possibility that we can negotiate that number?"

"What are you offering?" Consuela asked.

"I can give you a hundred thousand dollars cash right now." I looked over at Kenny. "Go get that bag out of the trunk."

"I thought you said you didn't have—"

"Do what I told you," I growled.

He left, and I focused back on the business at hand. "Now, where were we?"

"I hope you were about to explain where the other fifty thousand dollars was going to come from," Consuela said.

"Well, like I said, I don't have it, but I may have something that would be even more valuable."

"What's that?" She leaned forward, clearly interested.

"A favor," I said. "I'll owe you a big one."

"A favor? That's it?" She laughed.

I remained serious. "Yes. Consider who I am, Consuela. I may not be Alexander Cora, but I've got some powers of my own, and you never know when they'll come in handy. And that is price-less."

Consuela laughed again, but then to my surprise, she said, "Fine. I can accept that. For old times' sake." She smirked. "After all, you were a friend of my ex-husband."

"One other thing."

"And what's that?"

"My son and my large friend would like to have a couple hours with a few of your ladies. Can that be part of the deal? Poor Dennis has been backed up for over twenty years."

Kenny returned with the bag in hand. I took it from him and handed it to Consuela. "Here you go."

Consuela opened it, looked inside, then passed it to Natalia. "It's going to take a while to compile all the information. By the time your son and his friend finish with the girls, we should have everything on a jump drive."

"Thank you. I'm sure they will enjoy that. I'll be at the bar."

"Oh, and just so you know, most of the information about him other than arms dealing and drug smuggling is already public knowledge. If you really want to know about Alexander Cora, all you need to know is Dominique LaRue."

"What? Who the fuck is she?" I frowned, thinking I'd just been scammed.

"His woman," Consuela answered. "But even I don't have very much on her."

Harris

50

The sound of the front door slamming was loud and unexpected, but it was nothing compared to the loud wail that followed. We'd just sat down for lunch, and Chippy, LC, Junior, Nevada, and I rushed to the foyer when we heard it.

Chippy arrived first, and London collapsed into her arms, crying uncontrollably.

"Maaaaaaaaaaaaa!" she screamed.

"London, baby, what's wrong? What happened? Are you hurt?" Chippy held onto her as LC and the rest of the family hovered nearby.

London delivered the shocking news. "He's dead! Oh God, Ma. He's dead." London sobbed into her mother's arms.

"Who? Who's dead?" LC jumped to his wife's side to help as Junior and Nevada stood nearby, watching the scene with confusion on their faces. I remained behind them in my wheelchair, my mind racing because I knew the answer before London even gave it.

"Daryyyyllll," London moaned. "Daryl's dead."

"What?" Junior yelled in disbelief.

"Baby, what do you mean?" Chippy sounded frantic. "Look at me. You've gotta calm down and tell us what happened."

London finally lifted her head. "He . . . we . . . we were in the hotel room watching a movie, and he said he didn't feel good, that he had a headache. I told him I had some Tylenol in my purse, and when he went to stand up from the bed to get it, he fell on the floor and started making all these weird noises. He was unconscious by the time I got to him."

Chippy gasped and looked up at LC.

Hearing the details about Daryl's death overshadowed the fact that he and London had been laid up in bed in a hotel room somewhere. I know this is going to sound a little morbid, but it actually made the news a little sweeter because of it. Despite being caught red handed in the pool house, they had continued to disrespect me and my marriage. As far as I was concerned, Daryl Graham got exactly what he fucking deserved.

"I called 9-1-1, but when they got there, there was nothing they could do. He died of a stroke." London began crying again.

"Sweetheart, I'm so sorry." LC went to reach for her, but London pushed him away. She stood, wiping away tears and glaring at me.

"Happy now?" she said as if she knew exactly what I'd done.

Our eyes locked in a good long pause before I spoke. "I never wanted anything like this to happen."

"You're a fucking liar."

"Baby, come on. Let's get you into the living room so you can sit." Chippy put her arm around London. She looked at Nevada. "Nevada, get your aunt some water."

Nevada took off for the kitchen.

"I'm gonna go call Vegas. He should hear this from me," Junior said.

"No, he should hear it from us," LC told him. "I'll go make the call with you."

"Daddy, I need to talk to you." London looked at me out of the corner of her eye. I felt a little nervous about what she might reveal, but then she said, "I need to talk to you about the arrangements. It's important."

I felt the tension leave my body. I had hired the best, and I was confident that there was no way any of this could be traced back to me.

LC glanced at me as well then turned to his daughter. "Yeah, we'll talk about that in a while. Let me make my call to your brother."

I'm sure LC was trying to be as politically correct as possible, but I didn't give a shit if he paid for the man's funeral. London was mad now, but I'd been with her long enough and through enough ups and downs to know my time would come. I was just going to have to be patient and eat a little crow. I knew it was just the grief talking because her side piece had met his demise. I would give her time to get over him, then make my way back into her heart and into our bed. My family would be back together in no time.

As Chippy and London passed, I reached out and touched London's hand. "Look, I really am sorry about Daryl. If there is anything I can do, just let me know. We had our differences, but Daryl didn't deserve to die."

London's head spun around, and she looked at me with hatred in her eyes. "You're probably glad this happened to him, you motherfucker."

"That's not true, London," I lied, even going so far as to act offended by her statement. "I admit I didn't like him, especially considering the circumstances, but I didn't want the man to die. What kind of monster do you think I am?"

"Do you really want to know?"

When they were gone, I exhaled loudly, releasing the breath that I'd been holding. Fuck! I'd really done it. Daryl Graham's ass was gone for good, and nobody was the wiser. It took all I had not to burst out in joyful laughter.

I looked up at the ceiling and said a little prayer. I wasn't a religious man, but I knew when things were purposely working in my favor. He was really fucking dead.

I pulled out my phone to make an important call.

Lauryn

51

It was my first time on a private helicopter, and I was having the time of my life. I'd always loved fast-moving vehicles, but flying twenty feet over the ocean was exhilarating. I glanced over at Nadja, who had her phone to her ear once again. She'd barely spoken a word to me since her man Jonah dropped me back off at her hotel and escorted us to the helicopter. I wondered if this latest call was from old boy who had her nose wide open, but I quickly realized it was business when I saw the confident smile on her face. Old boy had a tendency to stress her out.

"Yes, that's great to hear. Glad we could be of service. I'll await your wire," Nadja said to whomever was on the other end of the call. It wasn't my intention to eavesdrop, but she was speaking so loud to be heard over the helicopter's engine that I couldn't help it. "Thank you. Good doing business with you as well. Ciao."

Once she ended the call, Nadja turned to me looking satisfied. "That was the client. He just confirmed the target died a few hours ago. Well done, Lauryn."

"Thank you." I smiled. "It's been fun."

"Fun? I've never heard that before." She seemed amused as she glanced down at her phone, typing something in as we spoke. "The balance of your money has been wired to your account."

I was anxious to get in contact with Paris and Rio to update them on all the night's activities. I was sure they had to be losing their minds by now. "And my phone?"

"I'm going to need you to remain off the grid a while longer," Nadja explained as we circled what could only be described as a super yacht. "You said you'd be available for forty-eight hours. I still have twelve left."

I was taken aback. "I'm a little confused. I was under the impression that my obligation to you was done upon the completion of the contract. Isn't that typically how it works?"

"Yes, but I thought we might spend a little time together and talk about the future. I'm highly impressed by your work ethic and professionalism, not to mention the fact you come highly recommended. I've passed that information on to my full-time employer," Nadja explained as we began to descend. "She's having a small dinner party on board tonight and would like to meet you."

"What does that have to do with my phone?"

"This is a very private dinner party. You are new. My employer doesn't trust anybody."

"I see. Well, unfortunately, I'm not dressed for a dinner party." I looked down at my casual outfit.

"No worries. We'll find you something to wear. It's small and casual. There is no dress code," she said. "Consider it an extended interview for your next assignment."

"My next assignment?" I raised an eyebrow.

"Maybe. I think my boss would like to offer you another contract with a lot more zeros if you're open to it. It's a very special assignment and requires a certain touch. You may be just the woman we are looking for."

"Oh, I am." I was excited about the chance of working again and putting my skills to use.

"Like I said, we'll see."

The helicopter landed on the deck of the yacht, and the engines shut off. The sudden silence was a relief to my ears.

"Let me show you to your room," Nadja stated. "We set sail in ten minutes."

I tried my best, but there was no way I could hide the fact that I was somewhat mesmerized as Nadja gave me a tour of the yacht, which could only be described as a floating mansion. It had everything one would want in a dream home: swimming pool, Jacuzzi, state of the art kitchen, game room, and even bedrooms that resembled hotel rooms. The only drawback was that you couldn't come and go as you pleased. There were armed guards everywhere.

"This is incredible," I said, looking around the grand vessel.

"It's one of the finer mega yachts, but there are a few that are even bigger," Nadja told me. "I'm certain you'll enjoy it, though."

"Exactly how long do you think we'll be on here?" I was still concerned that Paris and Rio were expecting my return. There was still no way for me to call them, and even if I could, I had no way of letting them know where the hell I was. "I told my friend she'd only have to feed my puppy for a day or so."

"Not long," Nadja said as she opened the door.

I followed her inside and nearly lost my shit. It was a gorgeous en suite room with a small living space, bedroom area, and marble bathroom with a waterfall shower. I damn near told her that it didn't matter how long because I wouldn't mind staying there forever.

"Whoa," was all I could manage to say.

"As far as clothing and personal items, the closet has plenty of wardrobe selections for you to choose from." Nadja walked over to the paneled wall and slid what I now saw was a door, revealing a rack of clothes and shelves of shoes. "You're a size six?"

"Four," I corrected her.

"There are plenty of choices here for you. Also, there are additional things in the drawers." She closed the closet and opened the dresser beside it to show me the contents. "Everything is brand new, including the bathing suits."

"I can go to the pool?" I asked.

"You can enjoy anywhere you'd like. There are some areas that are off limits, but you'll know those because they are secured by personnel," Nadja explained. "There are personal items in the bathroom, but if you need anything specific, just let me or the porter know. For now, relax, enjoy, and change. Dinner is promptly at six."

I waited for her to leave before I began my exploration of the living quarters I'd been given. I ran toward the closet, running my hands through the designer fabrics and reading the tags still hanging on sleeves and inside necklines of dresses. The shoes were brand new, same as the clothes. I felt like Cinderella taking it all in, But I wasn't crazy or naive. This was all too good to be true, and I knew something had to be up.

Larry

52

Agent Martinez was so focused on her cell phone that she didn't even see me walk right past her in the diner. I took advantage of her distraction and slipped into the booth behind her, and we sat back to back. I even ordered a cup of coffee and a pastrami sandwich before letting my presence be known.

"Good morning, Agent Martinez," I said loud enough so she could hear. Despite not seeing her, I could feel her turn around and look behind me. "You on Facebook again?"

"What the hell are you doing here?"

"Well, I was working on locating Alexander Cora when, to my surprise, I discovered you and your partner were in the city as well." I chuckled, then my voice became serious and intense. "You wouldn't happen to be here on the hunt for me, would you?"

"No, I'm not," she murmured. "I didn't even know you were here, Larry. I'm sure you are aware that there is a fugitive task force office here in Manhattan."

"I do, and that's good to know. My man Dennis is in a really good mood and was just about to go see your mom. I just needed to be sure."

"I thought we agreed that you'd stay away from my family." I could hear that fiery Latin accent slipping through, so I was sure I had her attention.

"We did, and I am staying away from your family," I replied with deepest sincerity. "Dennis hasn't stepped foot on the grounds yet, but I needed a little reassurance that this chat was going to go right. You understand, don't you?"

The waitress brought my coffee and sandwich, placing them in front of me. As I stirred in two packs of sugar and a drop of cream, I continued the subtle conversation with my newfound co-conspirator.

"Yeah, I guess. How the hell did you find me anyway?"

"Facebook."

"Bullshit. I haven't posted anything about going to New York. In fact, after our little chat, I closed my account."

"I didn't say it was your account. I just said Facebook." I could almost hear the silent confusion going on in her head as I took a bite of my sandwich. "You partner posted last night about how he couldn't wait to get to NYC and have a pastrami sandwich from Klein's Diner. They are pretty good, but I'm a Katz deli kinda guy."

"What a fucking idiot." She sounded pissed off.

"Yeah, that is pretty stupid for a guy who chases people down for a living," I said then took a bite of my sandwich. "Since I've got you here, I do have a couple of questions to ask you."

"What? And you'd better ask quickly because I'm expecting Fritz any minute," she hissed.

"I wouldn't worry about him for a little while," I said, sipping my coffee. "Does the name Dominique LaRue sound familiar?"

There was a brief pause, then finally Agent Martinez answered. "No, I don't know anyone by that name."

"Interesting."

"What does she have to do with Alexander Cora?"

"From what I've been told, the two of them have been fucking for years. They may even have a kid or two together. I need you to find out whatever you can on her. I think she's the key to—"

"Fritz! You're here," Agent Martinez said a little too loudly. It was a definite warning, which made me feel good about our arrangement.

"Well, you're kinda excited to see me." Agent Fritz laughed. "Yeah, sorry I'm late, but you're not going to believe this. Somebody slashed all four of my tires. I had to take an Uber."

"Oh," Martinez said. "I believe it."

I had to hold back a laugh. I had given Holly instructions to slash one of his tires, but it would appear that crazy girl slashed all four.

"Did you order yet?" he asked her.

"No, I was waiting on you."

"Good. So, what's going on with you? You looked kinda stressed when I walked in," Fritz said to her.

"I'm fine. Just in my feelings," Martinez told him. "I was sitting here thinking about Jack."

Fritz gave her a very drab "oh," as if to say, "Are we back on that shit again?"

"Let me ask you something," Martinez said to him.

"Shoot."

"Have you heard of a woman named Dominique LaRue?"

I leaned back so that I could eavesdrop a little better.

"Well, yeah, of course I have," Fritz answered.

"You have?" Martinez sounded surprised.

"Yeah, I mean, you've only been with the unit for six months, but at one point, we spent the better part of 2021 trying to track her down. She's one of our most wanted fugitives. The woman is deadly with a knife. You remember the Harrison murders?"

"Yeah, wasn't he the owner of some big tech company? He and his entire family were all murdered on a skiing trip. Chopped to pieces."

"Yup. Well, it wasn't announced, but Dominique LaRue was the prime suspect. She was having an affair with him under the name Diane Simmons. She disappeared after the murders. And he wasn't the first rich man she killed. Her nickname with Interpol is the Black Widow."

"So, is she connected? Cartel, Mafia, or something?" Martinez asked.

"No, definitely freelance, but she has to have some pretty wealthy sponsors the way she seems to slip in and out of the country. Take a look at this." He must have passed her his phone.

"Oh my God. She's suspected of twenty-four murders?"

"Yup."

"Did you see this? Cora International took over Harrison's company after he and his family were killed? Alexander Cora now owns his company," she said.

"Who gives a shit? Why do you care?" Fritz replied.

"No reason really. I was just curious, that's all. You know my fascination with Cora," Martinez said.

Fritz had had enough. "Let it go, Martinez. You're grasping at straws again."

No you're not, Martinez, I thought. *It's plain as paint on the wall. Dominique La Rue killed Harrison so that Alexander Cora could take over his company.*

"Look, I'm gonna go clear out the old pipes for this pastrami," Fritz announced. "Tell the waitress I want extra mustard and extra sauerkraut and a cherry Coke."

"TMI, Fritz. You could have just told me what to order."

"What's the fun in that?" He laughed.

I could hear him get up, and I lowered my head, pulling down my baseball cap as he passed me and disappeared into the restroom. I got up from my seat and stood over Martinez.

"You need to find out everything you can about this Dominique La Rue. She's the key to this. I'll be in touch," I said.

My cell phone began to ring. Seeing the name on the screen, I placed a ten-dollar bill on the table, placed my hat on my head, then slipped out of the diner. It was time to go to work.

Lauryn

53

After a quick shower, I threw on one of the bathing suits, grabbed a fluffy white towel, and ventured up three flights of stairs until I reached the top deck and found the large swimming pool. I was pleasantly surprised to see a beautiful, brown-skinned woman in a bright yellow bikini and a little boy who was as cute as a button, playing in the water. She was gorgeous and could've easily been a model. Her skin was the color of chocolate and just as smooth, and her deep brown eyes with thick lashes sat atop perfectly chiseled cheekbones.

"Hi." The little boy spoke first.

"How are you?" I said, waving at them both.

The woman gave me a suspicious look but was polite. "Hello."

"Mommy, watch me go under. Count for me!" the little boy yelled, then tucked his head under the surface.

"One . . . two . . . three." The woman began counting. By the time she got to thirty, his tiny head popped back up, sputtering and coughing. She reached for him and patted him on the back.

"Is he okay?" I asked, beginning to panic.

"Yes, he's fine."

"Did I do it? Mommy, did I reach thirty? I heard you say thirty." The little boy asked excitedly once he caught his breath.

"Yes, you did," she told him then turned to me. "It's just a game we play."

"Oh, how adorable." I smiled, noticing her Jamaican accent.

"At first I could only make it to ten," he bragged as she held onto him.

"That's so good," I told him. "Next you can make it to fifty, I'm sure."

"And then a hundred!" he yelped. "Like my daddy! He's stronger than everybody!"

"Calm down, honey. Let's let this nice lady relax and swim," she told him. "Why don't you go grab your star float?"

The little boy paddled over to the opposite side of the pool and grabbed a huge inflatable star, then climbed into it.

"He's cute," I said.

"Thank you. He's a handful, for sure. Every day is an adventure." She stared at him. "But I'm grateful for him."

"I bet." I thought about Jordan and Mariah's constant bickering. "I love that he's having fun outside. Most little kids only think about being on their iPads or playing video games."

"Oh, he enjoys his tablet too. I limit his screen time," she told me.

"Speaking of screen time," I said, "I left my cell phone inside. You wouldn't happen to have one, would you?"

For some reason, her eyes widened, and she spoke almost in a whisper. "No, sorry, I don't."

Then, out of nowhere, a tall, extremely handsome guy walked over and said to her, "You two ready?"

"Yes." She nodded quickly, reaching for the hand he extended to her. "Come on, baby. Time to go inside."

The little boy looked disappointed at first, then seeing the man, he quickly maneuvered to the side of the pool, where his mother now stood waiting with a towel. The man leaned over to help him out, and I noticed the cell phone on his waistband. There was something weird going on, but I didn't have enough information to figure it out.

"Is that your Daddy?" I asked. "He is strong."

"No, he's not my daddy. He's Aries," the little boy answered.

Well, hello Aries, I thought. He may have had a little attitude, but the man was fine.

The woman wrapped the towel around her son, and the three departed without saying goodbye. I had no idea who this Aries was or why our interaction had become odd when he walked up, but it didn't stop me from deciding that I would do whatever I had to in order to get his phone.

54

The news of Daryl's death shocked me to the core. It was a lot to take in, especially since the last conversation we'd shared wasn't a very pleasant one. I knew that his death wasn't my fault, but I did feel guilty, even more so after my conversation with Vegas, who was devastated by the news. Vegas and Daryl had been the best of friends since they were boys. Daryl's loss would be felt deeply by my whole family.

I'd been avoiding it, but it was time to talk to London, who had withdrawn into the pool house with Chippy. Harris had retreated to his suite, and Junior went to share the horrible news with Sonya. I poured myself a drink and tried to think of how best to handle all of this. I was on my second glass of Crown Royal in my study when I heard the front door slam. A few seconds later, I turned to see my youngest two children walking in.

"Hey, Daddy." Paris came in with a worried look on her face.

"What's up, Pop." Rio stood by her side with the same look. "We need to talk to you."

"I need to talk to you too." I put down my drink. "You two have a seat."

Paris sat in one of the chairs in front of my desk, while Rio stood to the side.

"What's wrong? Is it Uncle Larry?" Rio asked.

"No, it's not him," I said, "although I did find out that Sasha is in Waycross."

"What? Why?" Paris leaned to the edge of her seat.

"Apparently, she was planning on killing Larry, but Curtis and Roman are with her now, and she's calmed down. She's in good hands."

"Curtis and Roman? Good hands?" Paris gave me a doubtful look.

"Well, at least we know where *she* is," Rio muttered.

Paris glared at him, telling me I was right to be alerted by the way he emphasized the word *she*.

"Oh my God, Rio. That's unnecessary," Paris said.

"Listen. I don't know what you two have going on, but we've got bigger problems." I interrupted whatever back and forth was about to ensue. "Daryl is dead."

They both fell silent for a moment, processing the shock. Paris finally composed her thoughts to ask, "When? How? Fuck!"

"Jesus Christ." Rio put a hand on the back of Paris's chair to steady himself.

"London came home earlier and told us. We really don't have any details other than the fact that he got sick. He had a stroke," I told them.

"My God. Is London okay?" Paris asked.

"I'm right here, and I'm hot as fish grease." London and Chippy walked in and closed and locked the door behind them. London was no longer crying. She actually looked angry.

Rio rushed over and hugged her. "London, I'm so sorry."

"There is no need for all that," London told him, then asked, "Where's Lauryn?"

Neither Paris nor Rio spoke for a moment. Their silence spoke volumes, and I knew something was seriously wrong.

"Well, where is she?" I asked.

Paris shrugged pitifully. "We don't know."

"What the hell do you mean you don't know?" London barked. "When I saw her last night, she said she was going to meet up with her handlers then head back to the house to meet up with you."

"You saw her last night?" Paris asked.

"Yeah," London said. "She was in Sag Harbor, and I bumped into her on my way into the restaurant when I was going to meet up with Daryl."

Paris whipped her head around to look at Rio, and they locked eyes.

"Meet up with her handlers?" I asked. Clearly, I was missing large parts of this story. I glanced over at Chippy, who shrugged. "What the hell is going on?"

"Oh, shit." Rio reacted. "Please tell me this isn't happening."

"Fuck, it's happening, bro," Paris exclaimed, then turned to me. "Daddy, I think Lauryn killed Daryl Graham."

London

55

"No, Paris, Lauryn didn't kill Daryl," I declared. "Daryl is very much alive, but no one can know that except us. Especially not Harris."

"London, have you lost your damn mind? Why the hell would you tell us some shit like that if —"

"Calm down, LC. Hear her out." My mother cut my father off. Walking around his desk, she placed her hand on his back, rubbing his shoulder blades in an attempt to soothe him.

I had hoped that once my father heard Daryl was alive, he'd be so relieved that he wouldn't be angry about my lie. I wanted him to understand why the lie was a necessary evil. However, from the way that he was looking at me, I wasn't so sure. His eyes were a mixture of confusion and disbelief, and for a brief moment, hurt.

"Daddy, I know I lied, and I'm sorry." I apologized immediately. "But it was the only thing I could do at the time."

"Dammit. What the hell is going on? And I want the truth this time." My father sat back down in his chair and drained the liquor from his glass in one gulp.

"I can explain." I walked behind the desk and stood by his other side.

"I hope your explanation is a damn good one. Do you realize how much you've upset this family?" He turned toward me and shook his head "Was this some kind of stunt to get us to support you and Daryl's relationship?"

"No, this was an assassination attempt on Daryl, and it would have worked if I hadn't bumped into Lauryn walking out of the restaurant."

I began telling them the details of what had transpired the night before.

"Excuse me. Sorry. I wasn't paying atten—" I looked up, and there was Lauryn, finishing up a phone call.

"Lauryn?"

"London." She nearly dropped her phone. "What are you doing here?"

"Don't play with me, little girl. Did my parents send you here to spy on me? I can't believe this shit." I was pissed and wanted answers, but she just stared at me, keeping her mouth shut until I flipped out.

"Lauryn, god dammit, answer me," I snapped at my younger cousin. "Did my parents send your ass to get me?"

"Uh, no." Lauryn finally answered. "I just met a friend for drinks before I head back to meet up with Paris and Rio. I didn't even know you were in town. What are you doing here anyway?"

"Not that it's anybody's business, but I'm here with my man," I told her.

"Harris is here?" She looked around.

"No, he's not here," I said. "Harris isn't my man. He's my soon-to-be ex-husband. Daryl is my man. I'm supposed to meet him at the bar."

Lauryn's jaw dropped. "Fuck. Daryl Graham is your man?"

"Yeah, why? Don't tell me he tried to holla at you or something." I was joking, but Lauryn had already turned and was rushing toward the bar. She was running so fast that I knew something had to be wrong, and I took off behind her. "Lauryn, what the fuck?"

"Don't drink that shit!" she yelled at Daryl, who was about to take a sip of his drink.

Confused by our erratic behavior, Daryl put the glass down as his eyes went from Lauryn to me. "What's wrong? What's going on?"

"I don't know," I said, looking to Lauryn from some kind of explanation.

Lauryn pushed the glass away from where it was sitting on the bar.

"There's poison in your drink," she said.

"How the fuck do you know that?" I demanded, stepping in front of Daryl.

"Because I put it in there," she told me, then looked at Daryl. "You drink that, you'll be dead by the morning."

"This is too much." Paris stood and began pacing, something she had the tendency to do when she was processing or thinking really hard. "So, Daryl was the person Nadja had the contract on? That's who she hired Lauryn to kill. Not me."

"You thought someone had taken a contract out on you and didn't tell me?" My father growled at Paris as he reached for the decanter and poured himself another drink.

"Daddy, it's a long story that turned out to be nothing . . . but then again something." She turned to me. "So, why would anyone wanna take out Daryl? Who would want him dead?"

"Who the hell do you think?" I frowned.

"Harris." Everyone in the room except my father spoke in unison.

"We don't know that, London, and we don't want to make any assumptions," he said then took a long swig of his drink. I could tell that he didn't want to admit it, but he had his suspicions.

"Daddy, I know you're team Harris right now, but let's be real."

"First of all, I'm not team anyone," he replied. "And I know that he's having a hard time dealing with the divorce right now, but there's no way I'm going to accuse that man of murder. Not without proof."

"Which is exactly why I put on that Academy Award–winning performance."

Proof was exactly what I had been hoping to get, which was why Daryl and I had decided that we had to fake his death. We figured Harris, thinking that Daryl was dead, would either slip and say something to incriminate himself, or we would find something that led back to him. I knew Harris was behind this, and I was going to prove it. It was taking everything within me not to do to my husband what he attempted to do to Daryl.

Vengeance was coming, though, and when it did, it was not going to be pretty, that was for sure.

"I get it. If we retaliate on Harris because you think he is behind this and he isn't, then we are dead wrong," Rio suggested. "Just like the other day, when Paris thought the contract was out on her, and it turns out it was on Daryl."

My mom and dad cut their eyes so hard at Paris I could feel it.

"Why would someone put a contract out on you?" my father asked.

"That's a good damn question," my mother added.

"Look, that's not really important right now. The question we need to be asking is where the hell is Lauryn?" Paris deflected, looking at me.

I gave the only answer I had. "I don't know. Like I told you, the plan was for her to go see her handler and meet up with you all."

"Who is this handler?" Daddy asked.

"Her name is Nadja. She's a contract broker. She hires assassins," Paris explained.

"Then we need to go and find this Nadja."

"We tried," Paris continued. "She's gone, and Lauryn is with her. They left on a yacht headed to Europe a couple of hours ago. Her cell isn't on, and we can't reach her."

"Like hell we can't," Daddy said, taking out his cell phone and dialing a number. "Nevada, I need you in the study right now. Bring your laptop."

The situation with Harris and Daryl was still at the top of my to-do list and at the forefront of my mind, but it was going to have to wait until after we found my cousin.

Lauryn

56

I lounged by the pool area for a little while longer, then went back to my room and got dressed for dinner. I chose a cute, simple Chanel cocktail dress and strappy stiletto sandals. I rarely dressed up because I'd always felt more comfortable in casual gear, and there never seemed to be an occasion to do otherwise. Even when I went out to a bar or nightclub, my jeans, jacket, and boots sufficed as far as I was concerned. But there was no way I was going to have a closet full of designer clothes and not take advantage of it.

One of the areas that Nadja had showed me during our tour was a bar area. It was empty when we passed by originally, but she mentioned that it was where most of the guests and crew would gather before dinner, so I headed to the bar. There weren't a lot of people at the bar, which made it easier for me to look around and hopefully locate someone with a cell phone.

"What can I get you?" the bartender asked.

"Uh, glass of chardonnay, please," I answered.

Soft jazz came through speakers hanging in the corner of the bar. Noticing the attire worn by the other attendees, I was glad that I'd opted for my dress and heels. Everyone was dressed in chic attire, but there was not a cell phone or even a handbag in sight, not to mention a plethora of armed security. I turned back around and watched the young man opening the bottle of wine and pouring it into a crystal glass. My eyes wandered to the shelves behind him, where I was hoping to see a phone, but they held high-end liquor bottles and nothing else.

"Here you go." The guy placed the drink in my hand instead of sliding it across the bar, which I appreciated. It seemed a bit more personable. It also made me think of Daryl Graham and London. By now, the family had probably convened and was looking for me. I just needed to somehow get a message to them that I was okay and to keep Daryl out of sight.

"Thank you." I smiled. "I don't have any cash, otherwise I'd leave a tip."

He laughed. "No tips are allowed. Thanks for the thought, though."

Just as I was about to ask him about a phone, Aries appeared. He spoke to a couple of other people before making his way to the bar, sitting on the far end away from me. I stayed put, observing rather than approaching.

"Your usual?" the bartender asked him.

"You know it." Aries nodded.

It took a few seconds, but he finally looked over at me. I turned my body away slightly, pretending not to notice him, but I kept my ears open for their conversation as the bartender placed his drink in front of him.

"I'm surprised to see you guys. Normally you don't ever come up for air," the bartender commented.

"It's been a long day, and I convinced this guy here to relax and have a drink. We both need one."

I glanced over and saw that another man had arrived at the bar and sat down in the stool next to Aries.

"What the fuck?" I whispered to myself. I did a double take and blinked several times as our eyes met. He didn't say anything, but I could see that he realized who I was. Just as I was about to say something, he subtly shook his head and glanced over at Aries, who was still chatting with the bartender.

A faint chime sounded, and Aries stopped talking to the bartender. *Bingo*, I thought. He looked down, and I zoned in on him as he took out a cell phone. He looked at the screen, then casually placed it down.

"Hey, you know what they say. You gotta pay the cost to be the boss," Orlando told him.

"Yeah, we'll that ain't me," Aries replied. "That's my father."

"Same difference."

I motioned for the bartender and gently called out, "Can I get another?"

"Sure thing."

Aries nodded toward me, and I smiled, raising my glass. I looked past him to Orlando's eyes that went from mine to the cell phone on the bar, then back to me.

"Get help," Orlando mouthed silently, confirming what I had begun to suspect. He was in trouble—which meant I was in trouble. We both needed that damn cell phone.

I decided that it was time to make my move. Picking up my wine glass, I stood and began walking toward them. Orlando saw me coming, and he made his move.

"Look, about earlier, no hard feelings?" Orlando muttered and gulped down the rest of his drink.

"None. I'm glad we cleared that up." Aries extended his hand, and Orlando took it.

"Thanks for having a drink with me, but I have a wife and kid. I can't be hanging out like you young people," he joked.

Hearing that they were about to leave, I quickly thought of a plan of action. I made it within a few feet of Aries, threw caution to the wind, and purposefully tripped. My wine glass shattered as it fell to the floor, and just as I was about to hit the ground, a pair of strong hands caught me.

"Oh my God!" I yelped, pretending to be embarrassed. "I'm so sorry."

"It's cool." Aries's hands remained on my waist. "Are you okay?"

"Yes, these heels." I extended my muscular calf out so he could see the sexy shoes I had on, and I pulled the bottom of my already short skirt a little higher, revealing my thigh. "I'm not really used to wearing them."

"Well, you look good in them," he said, enjoying the peep show I was giving him.

"Thanks for saving me." I gave an innocent shrug and batted my lashes flirtatiously. "I appreciate it. I need another glass of wine. Would you like to join me?"

"I'd love to," he said. "I gotta go do something right quick, but I'll be back later."

"If not, perhaps I'll see you at dinner," I said, watching Orlando in my peripheral vision.

Aries finally released me, but his hand lingered on my arm a bit. "I guess we'll see. I'll be back in fifteen," he told me, then motioned for Orlando. "You ready?"

"Ready when you are." Orlando nodded, then waited for Aries to be a few feet away before our hands made the exchange.

When they were gone, I moved away from the bar and headed to an outside deck so I could have some privacy. I shut off the phone Orlando had slipped to me and stashed it in the cushion of a lounge chair. I didn't need the battery to go dead or for someone to hear it ringing. Now was not the time to make a call, but I'd be back for it. I still had no idea why we were even on the damn yacht. This wasn't supposed to be a prison, it was supposed to be a job, the specifics of which I had yet to be given. After seeing Orlando, I was even more anxious to get the hell off the boat and get the help he obviously needed.

Nee Nee

57

Jordan walked into the living room where I was watching television.

"Aunt Nee Nee, can we go outside?" he asked.

I sat up in the recliner. Why the little rascal thought I wouldn't realize he was up to something was beyond me. He hated going outside, and I had to force him every day. Now, here he was, begging to go outside.

"Boy, it's dark out there. No, you can't go outside."

"But—"

"But nothing. Get yourself in there and play that game of yours."

Jordan shook his head and mumbled something as he turned to leave.

"What did you just say?" I called after him.

"Nothing."

"What's wrong with that boy?" I asked, glancing over at Mariah and Mimi, who were lounging on the sofa.

"He wanna play wit' his crackers," Mimi answered.

"His what?"

"His crackers. Uncle Roman and Cousin Curtis shot them off yesterday and gave me and him some, but they said we can only use them when they're around." Mimi's expression matched the excitement in her voice.

"You mean firecrackers?" Mariah asked.

Mimi nodded.

Lawd, what was Curtis and Roman thinking about giving that boy some firecrackers? The fool child might try and blow his hand off, I thought. I knew that he was up to something, and

Curtis and Roman were going to get an earful when they got back from following Sasha to who knows where.

Just as I was about to get up to see what he had up his sleeve and confirm Mimi's story, my cell phone rang. I looked over at the number on the screen, which read UNKNOWN.

"I'm so sick of these damn scammers calling my phone." I sighed and dismissed the call.

"Mommy always answers and cusses them out, then they stop calling for a while." Mariah laughed. "They get scared of her."

The phone began ringing again from the same caller.

"That's a good idea. I think yo' mama is on to something," I said. "Run and check on Jordan while I take this call."

"Yes, ma'am." Mariah hopped up and reached for her younger sister. "Come on, Mimi."

They headed out the door, and I answered the call with a full-blown attitude ready to light up the ears of whomever was on the other end. "What do you want?"

There was a brief silence, and I thought Mariah's advice had worked, until I heard the familiar voice. It was low and sounded far away.

"Mama?"

"Lauryn? Is that you?" I turned up the volume on my phone and pressed it to my ear.

"Yeah, Ma. It's me."

"Speak up. I can barely hear you. Where are you?"

"Ma, listen to me. I need you to call and get a hold of Uncle LC right away. I'm on a boat off Montauk, or at least we were last night. It's a yacht," she murmured.

"What? Whose yacht you on?"

"I don't know, Ma. Please just call Paris now. And Ma, let them know Orlando is on here, but they're holding him captive."

"What? Who is?" My voice raised in panic.

"Ma, please. I need you to send help. Call Uncle LC!"

The call ended. I could feel my heart racing as I stood up. Although the call had come in from an unknown number, I tried to reach Lauryn on her cell. I called it three times, but it went straight to voicemail each time.

I had to do something. My baby was in trouble and needed help. Don't get me wrong, I was going to call LC, but first I decided to call the one person who I knew would go to the ends of the earth to find her.

"Put Larry on the phone," I said as soon as Kenny answered his cell.

I heard some fumbling around, and then Larry came on the line. I probably should have been a little more careful because the feds could be tapping the line, but this was my baby we were talking about, and I'd have to deal with the consequences later.

"Something's happened to Lauryn," I said without even giving him a chance to say hello.

"What the hell you mean something's happened to her?" he barked into the phone. "I thought you said she's with LC."

"She is—I mean, she was. I don't know, Larry. She just called and told me she's on some yacht off Montauk." My fear gave way to tears. "You gotta do something. I ain't never heard her sound like that before."

"It's okay, Nee. Don't you worry 'bout nothing. Hold tight, and if she calls back, let her know I'm on my way. I'll handle it," he said before he hung up.

I knew he meant every word.

Lauryn

58

I discreetly slipped the phone back under the cushion of the closest lounge chair then went to the bar. I was hoping to see Orlando again like the night before and let him know I'd managed to make a phone call to my mom, but Aries showed up to the bar alone.

"Just the woman I was looking for," he said. "Nadja wants to see you upstairs in the lounge," Aries told me.

I followed him up the stairs, hoping a chat with Nadja would bring more light to the situation. The more information I could feed to the folks back home, the better, and time was of the essence. If the battery on that phone died, we'd be cut off from communication once again.

Nadja greeted us when we arrived on the upper deck a few minutes later. "Thank you, Aries," she said. "Can you let your mother know where we are?"

"Will do," Aries told her, then glanced at me. "Be careful in those shoes."

"I will," I said with private relief. He was still flirting, so I could be pretty sure he hadn't yet made a connection between my little fall and his missing phone.

"Come. Let's sit over here," Nadja said when he was gone. I followed her to the cushioned sofa. "I take it you're enjoying your stay."

"It's nice, but I'm hoping we leave at some point sooner rather than later."

Nadja looked surprised. "Already? Most people would love to enjoy this type of luxury for as long as possible. Five-star accommodations, perfect weather, plenty of free time to relax."

"Don't get me wrong," I said. "It's amazing, and as much as I'm enjoying it, I have a life. People are going to be concerned because they haven't heard from me in a couple of days. We don't want them to start asking questions, right?"

She dismissed my concern. "I'm sure they'll be fine." Leaning back, she studied my face for a minute. "But I can understand your concern."

"Thank you. You said that you needed me to come because there was a special assignment I was being hired for. I still have no idea what it is."

"Actually, that's why I wanted to meet. The client was delayed, but now she is ready to meet you."

I was intrigued by the mention of a woman. "She?"

Nadja laughed. "Yes, we don't discriminate in this line of work. We welcome all paying clients." She turned around when we heard footsteps approaching. "Ah, there she is."

I looked over my shoulder to see a statuesque older woman strolling toward us. Slender and graceful, with shoulder-length hair and rich brown skin, there was something regal about her. She moved with intention, and I instantly knew she had the ability to draw attention without even trying.

"Hello, ladies," she said in a voice that was deep and throaty.

"Hello." Nadja and I spoke at the same time.

The woman gave Nadja a brief hug and an air kiss, then turned and extended her hand to me. "You must be Lauryn."

"Yes." I shook her hand.

"Lauryn, this is Dominique LaRue." Nadja introduced the woman as she took her seat.

"Nice to meet you," I said.

"Nadja has been singing your praises over the past few days. My intention was to be here when you arrived, but prior business kept me from returning until late last night," Dominique explained. "I'm looking forward to you joining the team."

"I'm sorry, Ms. LaRue. Exactly what team is that?" I asked.

"I thought it best that you give Lauryn the details yourself," Nadja explained. "Hence why she's a bit anxious. She hasn't been briefed on anything."

"Oh, I see." Dominique smiled patiently. "Well, let me go ahead and fill you in then."

"I'd appreciate that."

"For the past few months, we have been putting a plan in place to take over a corrupt powerhouse," she began. "This man controls most of the drug traffic in the U.S. He has to be taken down, which is where you come in."

"Okay . . .?" I said, hoping she would still reveal more.

"Nadja and I have decided to bring you in as part of the strike team to dispose of him." Dominique looked over at Nadja. "Did you bring the file?"

"I did." Nadja reached down into the Balenciaga bag in the chair beside her and handed me a manila envelope. "Here's the target."

I opened the envelope and nearly fell out of my chair. I almost wished the photo inside was one of my cousin Paris. This was even worse.

What the fuck? It was becoming clear that whatever was going on with Orlando was connected to this, but there were still too many holes. I needed to know more.

"Are you familiar with LC Duncan?" Dominique asked.

"I've heard of him." I nodded slowly as I continued to stare at the headshot of my uncle, smiling in his pinstriped suit. "His children went to the academy."

"So, you understand why we have to be very cautious in our planning and execution. No pun intended," Nadja said with a smile.

"I do." My brain raced as I tried to figure out my next moves. "I hope you understand that doing this will put a target on my head for the rest of my life."

"Only if you're caught, which I'm sure you won't be." Dominique looked at me with determination that let me know she wasn't interested in hearing me say anything but yes. "But that's also why we're willing to pay you a million dollars."

"Shit," I mumbled before I could stop myself.

"Exactly." Nadja laughed. "That amount of money should be enough for you to disappear for a while, just in case. Is it not?"

A million dollars. Someone wanted my uncle dead and was willing to pay a million dollars. I wouldn't do it for all the money in the world, but I damn sure couldn't let anyone else do it either. I had to find Orlando and let him know what was going on so that we could stop these motherfuckers. There was no time to wait on my mother to send help. We were going to have to help ourselves.

My heart was beating so loud that I was surprised they didn't hear it. I sat motionless as I tried to process their request. I didn't even realize that I'd zoned out until I heard my name being called.

"Lauryn?"

I looked over at Dominique, who was staring at me. "Huh? Oh, I'm sorry."

"Are you ready?" she asked.

"Ready for what?" I frowned.

"To go. The helicopter is already waiting."

"Now?" My voice was barely above a whisper.

"Yes, right now." Dominique stood to her feet. "Let's go."

"Are you coming with us?" I looked over at Nadja.

"No. There's a boat waiting to take me back to shore. I will be in touch soon, though," Nadja answered. "Your payment and phone will be returned to you upon completion of this assignment."

I had no other choice but to stand and go with Dominique. Not only was it my only way off that fucking boat, but I had to make sure that whatever plan they had in place to kill Uncle LC never came to fruition. If I refused right now, they would hire someone else to do the job, and judging from the intensity of these two women, they might just kill me first. I followed Dominique off the deck and up another set of steps to the top deck of the yacht, where a large black helicopter was waiting to take us away.

Larry

59

I didn't waste any time getting to my brother's house. The sound of Nee Nee's voice was enough to light a fire under my ass. My wife wasn't one to worry unless it was serious. The woman had dealt with my crazy ass for almost fifty years, and if that wasn't enough, she'd battled breast cancer, and not once did she ever show any signs of fear. But when it came to our children, especially our youngest, we did not play at all.

"Where are we going?" Kenny asked as I got into the car. Dennis and Holly were already in the back seat.

"Long Island."

He looked surprised. "Um, you do remember who lives in Long Island, right?"

"Of course I remember, and that's exactly why we're going!" I replied angrily. "Your goddamned uncle done let something happen to your sister."

"What?" Kenny looked stunned. "What happened to Lauryn?"

"I don't know yet. That's why we gotta get to his house."

You wouldn't know it by seeing them interact, but Kenny and his sister were close. The way he hit the gas and swerved in and out of traffic, I knew he was just as anxious as I was. "Slow down, boy," I warned him. "I know you're worried, but the last thing we need is to get pulled over. Did you forget you got three fugitives in the car?"

"To be honest with you, yeah." He eased up on the gas. "For a second there, I did."

***

Traffic wasn't too heavy, so the drive from Manhattan to LC's estate took us less than an hour. The closer we got, the angrier I became. LC was supposed to protect my baby, and now she was in trouble. Hell, he hadn't even called Nee Nee to let her know that something had happened, and neither had Chippy. The level of disrespect was infuriating. Had it been one of their children, they would've made sure the world stopped until they were safe.

"Holy shit," Holly commented as we approached the big-ass mansion that housed my brother, his children, and grandchildren, and probably could've easily fit two other families, mine included, and had plenty of space left.

"It's a security guard," Kenny said as we turned into the driveway. "He might be armed."

"I don't give a fuck if he's carrying a grenade in each hand. Ain't nobody stopping me."

Kenny pulled up to the gate, where a man wearing all black and sunglasses stepped up to the car.

"Can I help you?"

He leaned into the car, and he was so busy looking at me that he didn't even notice the gun Kenny pointed directly at him until it was too late.

"Oh, shit."

"Dennis, get the gate," I said, keeping my eyes on the guard.

Dennis hopped out of the car and went into the small building. Seconds later, the gate lifted, and Dennis walked out carrying a pistol. He walked over to the guard and removed his shoulder-holstered gun.

"You won't be needing this," he said.

"You can let my brother know Larry's here," I yelled as Kenny pulled through the gate.

Before he could even put the car in park, I was out and headed to the front door, which was already opening. LC stepped out with Chippy by his side. Paris and Junior came out behind them, and then London's husband rolled out and parked his wheelchair next to them. My people immediately pulled guns on them.

"Larry, what are you doing here?" LC asked.

I grabbed him by the collar. "Why the fuck do you think I'm here, LC?"

I had to give him credit. LC was pretty cool under pressure. That some-bitch didn't even flinch.

"I don't know, Larry, but to be honest, I'm glad you and your people are here. We could use the help. Lauryn and Orlando are in trouble."

I was momentarily confused by the mention of Orlando. Nee Nee hadn't said his name when she called me.

"She's my daughter, LC. Why the fuck didn't you call us? Why did I have to hear about it from my wife, who's scared to death down in Waycross?"

LC looked over my shoulder, where the security guard from the gate and a few other black-clad guards had gathered behind my crew.

"I just found out," LC said. "She's working for a woman who is associated with the Assassins Guild."

"Assassins Guild? What's she doing with them?" When I had been locked up, Lauryn was just a kid. Sure, I knew she had been to finishing school since then, but she was still my baby girl, and it was hard to envision her working with that crew of killers.

"I don't know, Larry, but this isn't going to get you any answers. You've always been one of the best strategists I've ever known. We need to put our heads together and figure this out. I can't do it alone."

Chippy took a step forward and said calmly, "Like we used to do in the old days."

I had a quick flashback to our younger years. We Duncan brothers had really been a formidable team at one time, before life took us on the path that led us here. I wasn't completely sure I could trust LC, but I felt like I had to take that chance if I wanted my daughter back. LC had resources and a team that I didn't.

"This better not be a trick," I said warily, then turned to my people and ordered, "Stand down."

Dennis and Holly did what I asked immediately. It was Kenny who hesitated.

"I ain't doing shit until they lower their guns," he said. The stubborn little bastard was just like me.

"It's okay, Larry. You boys stand down too," LC said to his people, and they did as he ordered.

Kenny finally complied.

"Come on in, Larry. Let's see if we can figure this out."

Just as I was about to answer, Sasha appeared from the side of the house and placed a gun to my head. I heard Chippy gasp, and everyone's weapons were back up instantly.

"Sasha, put the gun down!" LC yelled.

"You motherfucker." Sasha pressed the gun against my temple. "You thought you got away with killing my mother?"

"Sasha, put the gun down," Chippy pleaded.

"No. He's going to die for what he did." Sasha's voice was trembling.

"I need to die for a lot of things, but killing your momma isn't one of them, niece," I told her. "Killing Donna would be like Lou killing my Nee Nee. Your daddy loved Donna, and I loved him. I'd never do that to him."

"My daddy was already gone," she said.

"I would never dishonor his memory that way, Sasha. I did not kill your momma."

She was still doubtful. "Then who killed her?"

"I don't know. I just know it wasn't me."

She pulled the hammer back on the gun.

"Sasha," Junior spoke up. "Put the gun down. This is not what Aunt Donna would want you to do. Please."

Junior's voice distracted her just long enough for me to raise my weapon. When she looked back at me, the barrel of my gun was aimed at her chest.

"Step back," I said.

LC whispered, "Larry, don't do anything you'll regret."

"You need to be telling her that."

Suddenly, tires screeched to a halt behind us in the driveway, and the doors slammed shut.

"What the fuck is going on here?" It was my oldest son's voice.

I turned my head to see Curtis and Roman standing in front of a car with Georgia plates. They held their guns but looked around like they weren't quite sure which way to aim. There were so many weapons around that it looked like a standoff in an old Western.

"Everyone needs to calm down," LC said cautiously. "All these fucking guns need to be put away. *All* of them."

"Junior, I'm only doing this because of you. I love you," Sasha said as she lowered her gun and took off.

Junior ran after her. Everyone else relaxed their shooting stances and stood around looking at each other, too stunned to speak.

LC

60

"What the hell are we gonna do, LC?"

I sat at my desk and watched Larry as he paced back and forth in my office. We'd barely gotten away without a shot being fired thanks to Junior, but I wasn't sure how much longer I could keep things together, and if or when Sasha would return to reignite the situation.

"I don't know yet, Larry," I said. "Give me a minute to get my thoughts together."

"We ain't got a minute, goddammit!" He exploded, loud enough for the entire house to hear. He was on the verge of having a breakdown, which I knew from past experience would not be good for me or my family.

Larry looked like he was about to jump over the desk. "My baby girl is sailing to God knows where with God knows who on that boat, and she's in danger. We need to do something! Now!"

"Larry, you're going to have to calm down." The sound of Nee Nee's voice took us both by surprise.

Larry stopped pacing and looked across the room, where Chippy had gotten up from the couch. She had her phone in her outstretched arm, holding it out to him.

"Talk to her. She's on speaker," she said to Larry.

He took the phone from her. "How am I supposed to calm down, Nee? Lauryn's gone, probably dead, and it's all his fault." Larry glared at me.

"We don't know that for sure." Nee Nee's voice was soothing. She'd always been good at lowering the heat when Larry started to lose control.

"Why the hell else would she tell you to send help?" Larry barked into the phone. "She wouldn't have called if she wasn't in trouble, and she wouldn't be in trouble if she woulda stayed her ass in Waycross."

I had to acknowledge to myself that he did have a point. I'd taken full responsibility for my niece and promised Nee Nee that she would be safe, and now she wasn't. My brother had every right to be angry, and the guilt I was feeling proved it. Now, I had to find not only her, but my son Orlando too.

I was surprised when Nee Nee's voice took on a different, harsher tone.

"What were we supposed to do, keep her prisoner? She's a grown woman. We sent her to that school to be trained, Larry. You and me, nobody else. Did you expect her not to want to do this crazy shit our family does?" Nee Nee said sternly. "So, if you want somebody to blame, look in the mirror, 'cause this is not on LC and his family. It's on us. We didn't send her to some fancy boarding school to learn how to walk with teacups on her head. We sent her to mercenary school."

Larry's expression crumbled, and he walked over to a chair in the corner of the room ad slumped into it. "I just wanted her to be safe, Nee. To be able to protect herself like London, Paris, and Sasha."

She asked bitterly, "How's that working out for your brother?"

It felt like a punch in the gut. My kids had all been highly trained. We told ourselves we were doing it to keep them safe as well, but given our current circumstances, I had to acknowledge that maybe that safety was something of an illusion. Our family business exposed us all to a great deal of danger all the time that even the best training couldn't prevent.

"So what you want me to do, Nee?" he asked.

"I want you to take your medicine and help LC find my daughter and my nephew."

"Okay," he said humbly, reaching in his coat pocket. He removed a small bottle of pills, took one out, and popped it into his mouth. His Adam's apple bobbed as he swallowed it. "I love you, Nee Nee Duncan."

"I love you too," she replied, then hung up the phone.

The Family Business 6: A Family Business Novel 277

Larry looked over at me, the energy drained from his body. "I'm gonna need you to come up with a plan to find them kids."

"Listen to me, Larry." I stood up and walked over to my brother, placing my hand on his shoulder. "I'm going to make this right. I promise you."

Chippy eased over to us. "Honey, do you really think Orlando and Lauryn are together?"

"I don't know. There's only one way to find out," I said, heading back to my desk and picking up the phone. I dialed the numbers written on the notepad beside it.

It wasn't the greatest connection, but after a few rings, someone answered. My plan was to talk in code, and hopefully Orlando would be able to pick up on it.

"This is LC Duncan. I'd like to speak to my son, Orlando Duncan, please."

"One moment, please." The man placed me on hold, then returned a moment later. "Unfortunately, Mr. Duncan is unable to be disturbed right now. I can have him call you back at another time."

This wasn't the first time that I'd been told he was busy, but this time it alarmed me. "This is an emergency. His mother is ill, and I need to speak to him now," I said.

"I'm sorry, sir. He is off ship. I'll leave him a message." The man ended the call without waiting for my reply.

I slammed the receiver down. "Damn it."

"LC?" Chippy frowned.

"They wouldn't let me speak with him. He's unavailable. Something's not right."

"We already knew that shit," Larry growled. "How we gonna fix it?"

"We need to find out who Orlando has been developing this product for. He never mentioned a name?" Chippy asked.

"No, no name. Only that he was working on some new pharmaceutical formula that he'd been hired to help develop. Sounded like medical research of some sort." I sighed, realizing now that I should have gotten more information when I did speak to my son.

"Oh my God, LC. Ruby and Vincent are with him. This means they're in danger too." Chippy placed her hand over her mouth.

"I think I found it." Nevada came rushing into the office, laptop in hand. "I found the yacht."

"Are you sure, Nevada?" I asked, though I didn't need to. He wouldn't have brought the information without making certain that it was valid. Nevada was as thorough as any top-secret government organization and just as accurate.

"Yeah, I am." He placed the laptop on the edge of the desk so that we could see the screen. "I tracked the number you've been calling Uncle Orlando on. There wasn't a ping from a cell tower, but I did get a marine satellite signal. From there, I was able to track where the ship went, and from the looks of it, there were only five ships that took that route. Only one of them is in U.S. waters now, and that's a yacht named Sagittarius. I was able to confirm that through the Coast Guard tracking system."

"God damn, you weren't joking, LC. That boy is a damn genius." Larry stared at Nevada in amazement.

"Yeah, he's smart all right," I replied. "Any idea who owns that boat, son?"

"Well, from what I can see, the yacht is registered to a Ukrainian dummy corporation. It refueled in Saint Thomas a week ago. But get this—I dug a little deeper and found out that the account used to pay for the fuel belongs to a shell company of Cora International."

Larry's eyes locked on mine. "LC, do you know who owns Cora International?"

"I sure do." I sat back in my chair. "It would appear that Alexander Cora is finally making a play at revenge."

"No, not after all these years? You really think that's what this is about?" Chippy asked.

"He's not the type to forget a grudge, not even a forty-year-old one."

The pieces were coming together in my mind. Everything happening with my son and niece was most likely one part of a revenge plot that was decades in the making. Alexander Cora was out to destroy me and my brothers, which meant that anybody connected to us was in danger of being destroyed.

"Nevada, do you know where that boat is now?"

"It's heading west along the coast of Long Island."

Harris

61

I was more of a drinker than a smoker, but that crazy mother-fucker Larry Duncan showing up on our doorstep had my nerves frazzled. I hated the way he looked at me with those creepy-ass eyes. It was going to take some herbal assistance to get myself together and go back in the house with him and his freakshow friends. Luckily, my doctor had prescribed medicinal marijuana, and I had some in hand. While everyone else dealt with the chaos of Lauryn and Orlando being missing, I eased out of the house and ventured toward the gazebo, where I could smoke in peace. I was halfway through a joint when I heard shouting.

"Yoooooo, man! I can't believe this shit!"

I maneuvered my wheelchair to turn around and looked over at the security gate, where DJ was speaking excitedly to whom-ever had just arrived. The gate slid open, and the car continued to the front of the house and parked. Curiosity got the best of me. I continued watching as the passenger got out. I recognized London right away, but it was the driver stepping out that sent my heart racing.

"No fucking way. It can't be," I whispered. For a minute, I thought maybe the weed had me hallucinating, but I saw them enter the house through the front door and knew it was real.

I was shocked and confused. My worst nightmare had just come true. My wife's lover was alive, which meant I was pretty much a dead man. No amount of marijuana was going to help me escape this reality. I hurried my ass to the gazebo and took out my phone, dialing with trembling hands.

"Mr. Grant, how are you?" Nadja answered as if we were old friends. "I don't have much time. I'm about to catch a plane to Atlanta."

"You can give me a fucking refund, you thieving bitch."

"Excuse me?" she snapped back.

"The man I paid you to kill just walked through the fucking front door of my house."

"That's impossible. You confirmed his death yourself, Mr. Grant," she responded confidently. "You must be mistaken."

"Trust me, there is no mistake, and what I confirmed was from a third party. I just saw him now with my own two eyes."

"I was assured that the job was complete. It was confirmed with the County Medical Examiner's office."

"I don't know what they confirmed, how or why," I said. "The man I wanted dead is so damn connected that I wouldn't be surprised if the damn coroner was in on it. Whoever you had handle this fucked up."

Nadja was quiet for a few seconds, then she said, "Hold on for a second. I'm making a three-way call. Don't say shit."

The phone went silent, and then there was the sound of a call being connected. I nervously hit my mute button so the person she was calling wouldn't hear the sound of my panicked breathing.

"Hello, Nadja. I'm glad you called. I wanted to thank you for your attendance this past weekend." I recognized the voice as Minister Farah's.

"I'm well, Minister, and there is no need to thank me," Nadja said. "I do need a few moments of your time, though. I need to confirm some information."

"Of course. What can I do for you?"

"The young lady I recently hired that you referred. You said she went to the school, correct? And she was a prize student?" Nadja asked.

"Most definitely," he replied. "Like I said, I felt that she was an excellent candidate. Lauryn is one of the most talented students I've ever encountered, and she comes from good stock. Many other members of her family graduated top of their classes as well."

I gulped. My luck could not be that bad, and the world could not be that small. It had to be some sort of crazy coincidence that he was talking about someone named Lauryn, who came from a family that sent all of its kids to Chi's.

"Minister Farah, I know we don't typically use last names as protocol for discretion, but I really need to make an exception," Nadja requested. "I need to know her surname before we move forward. I have received some concerning news that makes me need to look into her a little deeper."

"I'm sorry to hear that, but I understand." Minister Farah said. "We've done business for a long time, and I want you to be able to trust my recommendations in the future, just as I trust your reason for needing this information. However, I do hope your information confirms my faith in Lauryn's abilities."

"I'm sure it will," she said.

"Her last name is Duncan. I'm sure you've heard of her. Her uncle is LC Duncan."

"Fuck. Fuck. Fuck!" I reacted, grateful that I was muted. Not that it would've mattered if they heard me. Shit damn sure couldn't get any worse.

"Thank you, Minister Farah. We'll speak soon," Nadja said.

The line went silent, then she returned.

"This is—"

"Fucked up." I completed her sentence the only way I knew how. "Of all the fucking assassins in the world, you hired a fucking Duncan. Well, at least we know why Daryl Graham is still alive. Do you know the position you've put me in?"

"I do, and I will make sure you're refunded."

"You think I'm worried about a fucking refund?" I asked through my teeth. "That's not what this is about!"

I ended the call. There was nothing more I had to say. What I needed to do was get the hell away from the damn house and get far, far away as fast as possible. I pulled up my Uber app and requested a car.

For a split second, I remembered the fact that Lauryn was still missing and Nadja was the last person she was with. My conscience even urged me to call Nadja back, but my desire to save my own ass took over, and I decided to leave well enough alone and get the hell out of dodge.

Lauryn

62

I smiled politely at the older, very distinctive gentleman wearing white slacks, a pink shirt, and a white fedora, who was already seated in the helicopter when we came aboard. I had no idea who he was, but the fact that he and Dominique were quite affectionate did not go unnoticed. Dominique sat in the chair beside him, and I sat across from them and watched them interact. The man kissed Dominique like they were teenagers. Whatever they had going on reminded me of my parents. Why did love seem so simple for older people?

Less than a half hour later, the sun was going down, and we were landing.

"Teterboro Airport," the pilot announced.

"I'm going to take care of something for Aries while you and your friend take LC Duncan out of his misery. I'll meet you back at the yacht in the morning. We should be refueled and ready to head back to Barcelona by noon," the man announced, adjusting his hat in anticipation of the propeller's wind. "A car will be waiting for you in Farmingdale when you arrive."

"I like the sound of that. America is great for shopping, but it's a horrible place to live."

"I had hoped that the formula would have been done by now," the man said. "It's taking longer than expected."

"Aries says that it'll be any day now," Dominique responded. "Once it's complete, we can get rid of Orlando the same way we're getting rid of his father."

My chest tightened, but I forced myself not to react to anything being said. I couldn't risk either one of them suspecting that I was anything other than a newly hired member of the assassination team hired to kill my uncle and possibly my cousin.

Dominique leaned close, and he slipped his arm around her, giving her one last kiss before he stepped off the helicopter. I watched him walk to an SUV waiting on the tarmac. The doors to the helicopter shut, and within seconds of the SUV pulling off, we rose into the sky again.

Dominique hadn't spoken to me since before we boarded the helicopter. I needed to get her talking again.

"So, you've told me the target. How exactly are we going to take LC Duncan down?"

She smiled at me. "It's simple actually. We are not going to take him down. He's going to take himself down."

Talk about confusing.

"How's that?"

"LC Duncan has been on our radar a long time. We thought about bringing him down through other means, because a murder of someone this high comes with its own risks. We considered ways to break apart his family, as his devotion to them seems to be a weak spot. However, he's not a womanizer like most men, so setting him up that way would have been impossible. He's also a smart man. Over the years, he's cultivated very important connections with powerful politicians and judges on his payroll, so the likelihood of seeing him land in jail without a fight was slim."

I couldn't help but feel a little swell of pride. I'd always known my uncle was a brilliant man.

"So, that brings us to our current plan," she continued. "My husband has been patient for a long time, but he has had enough, and he's ready to see the end of LC Duncan."

"I see," I replied. "And I ask again—where do my services come in?"

"Mr. Duncan is a cognac enthusiast. He especially enjoys King Richard the Tenth. Nadja tells us you've already proven your worth when it comes to undetectable poisons."

"I am," I said hesitantly. "But spiking a drink at the bar is one thing. This doesn't sound like the type of man who would be easy to get close to."

She smirked. "You're right. But as I said, we've been studying and preparing for this for quite some time—long enough to have purchased the company that distributes his preferred brand of cognac. Our sales team tells us he's expected to place an order for another case very soon."

It was chilling to think about how long these people had been studying Uncle LC. This wasn't just a business decision; this was personal for them.

"Well," I said, "your research certainly has been thorough. I'm a bit surprised you even need my help."

"Call it fate," she said. "You came into our orbit just as my husband decided it was time to make this move. You're young, and Nadja tells us you're ambitious. If you finish this job, there is no limit to how high you can rise within our organization. So, are you ready to get to work? You'll need to prepare the chemicals so we can get them to the distribution warehouse."

"Of course," I said, already plotting ways to alert Uncle LC to the tainted liquor before the case arrived at his house.

"Splendid," Dominique said as her phone began to buzz in her purse. She pulled it out and checked the caller ID. "It's Nadja."

"Tell her I said hello."

She spoke into the phone. "Hello, Nadja."

I watched her face as she listened to Nadja, and the smile fell off her face.

"Yes? Oh, really?"

She glanced up at me.

"Hmmm, that's very disappointing. And you're sure? You've confirmed this?"

Her eyebrows came together. Something had her concerned.

"Well, this an unfortunate turn of events, but you know me. I always make lemons into lemonade. Thank you so much for that information." Dominique put her phone away, then leaned forward in the cockpit to speak with pilot. "How long will it take us to get back to the ship?"

"About an hour. I'm gonna have to land and refuel," the pilot shouted back.

"Do it, but don't waste any time. We really need to get back."

"Yes, ma'am!"

"Everything okay?" I asked.

"No, not exactly. We have to go back to the ship."

"Why? What happened?" I asked, trying to sound disappointed.

"There is something we forgot." Dominique's demeanor had become frosty.

"What's that?" I asked, sensing something was wrong.

"We forgot to say goodbye to your cousin Orlando."

When her words registered, my stomach did a flip. She reached into her purse and took out a gun, which she aimed at me.

"I'm sure he's eager to see you again."

Orlando

63

I walked into our room after another hard day and was immediately overwhelmed with concern when I saw Ruby's face. She could hide it from Aries by giving him that innocent smile, but I knew something was wrong, and I would be getting to the bottom of it when he left.

"Well, if you folks don't need anything else, I'm going to retire for the night." Aries placed his hands together, bowing respectfully to Ruby, then to me. Oh, how I wanted to wipe the floor up with his ass and that piece of shit Alexander.

"That was great work you did today, Orlando."

"Another step closer to the finish line. I'll see you in the morning," I replied, trying my best to continue the charade.

He stepped out of the room, and I waited to hear the locks clicking before I spoke to Ruby. "What's wrong?"

"Your cousin is gone," she said, her face flushed with panic.

"What do you mean she's gone?"

"She left the boat on a helicopter with the crazy lady who was going to throw Vincent off the boat," Ruby ranted.

"You sure about that?" I had been wondering all day if Lauryn had ever gotten a chance to use that phone.

"I saw her with my own eyes," Ruby insisted.

"Okay, okay. That's not necessarily a bad thing." I was certain that if nothing else, she would let the family know where I was. Then again, she didn't have a cell phone, so for all I knew, she was a captive just like us. I tried to have faith that help was on the way and would get there before we refueled and set sail, because they'd never find us on the open sea.

I turned to my wife. "Babe, I think it's time."

"Orlando, we're in the middle of the ocean."

"No, we're right outside of New York City. I could see the Verrazano Bridge in the distance when Aries and I walked across the deck. This might be our last chance. We can't wait for Lauryn anymore. Our opportunity to get the fuck off this boat is tonight."

"All right then, let's do it." Ruby looked me in the eye. The fear that was usually there when we discussed the plan was now gone.

"What about Li'l Man? Is he ready?" I asked.

"Yes, he's ready." She said it with such conviction that it erased any doubt that I'd had. In that moment, I knew my family and I were ready to flee.

"Good, then let's get to work."

For the past two weeks, I'd been smuggling tools from the lab and putting them to good use. Each night, after Vincent went to bed, I'd meticulously worked on the porthole located next to our bed, away from the camera in such a way that it wouldn't be noticed by the housekeeping staff or anyone else who happened to come into our room. Sometime around 9 p.m., I'd successfully removed the thick glass-and-metal window and poked my head out. The waves were perfect: gentle enough so that the chances of us being pulled under were slim, but loud enough to mask the sound of us landing in the water.

"Are we going swimming in the ocean, Daddy?" Vincent ran up and hugged my legs.

"Yes, we are, Li'l Man." I picked him up into my arms, holding him close. I glanced over at Ruby, watching both of us, her eyes filled with love. "You okay?"

"One hundred percent." She kissed me.

"You coming too, Daddy? You don't have on a swimsuit like me and Mommy." He frowned. Sure enough, I looked down and realized I was still wearing my lab clothes.

I laughed. "I'm going to get changed right now."

"Okay." Vincent nodded.

I went into the bathroom and changed into a pair of trunks and a tank top, similar to what my wife and son wore.

This is it. It's now or never. God, please watch over us and keep us safe the same way you've done thus far. Protect me as I protect my family.

"All ready." I stepped into the main cabin. I motioned for Li'l Man and Ruby to come to the open hole, then picked him up so he could see. "Okay, let me tell you what we're about to do. Mommy is going to dive in first."

"All the way down there?" His eyes widened as he pointed. "It's so far."

"It's not that far," I assured him. "Then Daddy is going to help you dive in next, and she's going to catch you."

"You remember how to hold your breath like we've been practicing, Vincent? Close your eyes and hold as long as you can?" Ruby rubbed his back.

"Yes, Mommy." Vincent looked at me. "I can hold until fifty now, Daddy."

"That's perfect." I pressed my forehead against his. "And by the time you get to fifty, Daddy will have jumped in, and we'll all go for a swim. Okay?"

"Okay." He clapped.

Seeing the fear that Vincent had earlier now replaced with excitement made me feel a little better, but the tears in Ruby's eyes nearly broke my heart. I had to hold back my own. I hugged her tight and kissed the top of her head. The three of us clung to one another for as long as we could as if we all wanted to hang on forever.

"I love you," I whispered into her ear.

"I love you too." Ruby exhaled. "Who's ready for a swim?"

"Me!" Vincent and I both said.

"Then, let's have at it." She moved to the opening and looked back at me once more, mouthing the words, "I love you."

I put Vincent down and helped her ease her thin body through the hole. She was halfway out and paused. I gently spoke. "Just dive, baby. Headfirst. You got this."

Ruby nodded, closed her eyes, took a deep breath, then using my chest as a springboard, pushed off and jumped. I quickly leaned out and watched as she went into the dark water, barely making a splash. Then, I waited for what seemed like eternity for her to reappear.

Dear God, please let her come up. As if He heard my pleas, Ruby's head appeared directly below, and she gave me a thumbs up.

I picked up my son and held him so he could see. "See Mommy? She's right there."

"I see her."

"Okay, so I need you to hold your breath and jump to Mommy. She's gonna catch you."

"And then you're coming with us?" Vincent asked.

"Yep, I'm coming right after Mommy catches you. I promise. Now, you ready?"

Vincent nodded.

I eased him through the hole, making sure he and his mother could see each other. After kissing him one final time, I began counting. "One, two . . ."

Before I could even get to three, my son hopped out. I gasped, watching him go down. He held his arms tight against his tiny body as it hit the water several feet away from his mother. Ruby rushed to the area where he landed, going under to find him. Her head came up, and I could see the terror on her face.

"Oh, shit. She can't find him." I could barely breathe. As I prepared to jump in myself, she dove under a second time. A few seconds later, both of their heads re-emerged. Vincent clung to his mother's neck, and she waved at me. My heart started beating again.

I poked my head out then, trying to maneuver and squeeze the rest of my body through, until I realized the painful truth. That was as far as I was going to get. The upper half of my torso would not fit into the tiny opening. I quickly made my way back out and tried going feet first, but it was no use. My athletic build was too fucking big.

"Fuck!" I climbed back out and looked down to the water. We were wasting time, and I knew that if there was any chance of Ruby and Vincent escaping without being noticed, they'd have to start swimming now.

"Orlando," Ruby called.

"Baby, swim! I'm too big." I yelled, pointing toward the coastline. "Swim now! And get help."

She hesitated for a moment, looking toward the land and then back at me, and then she finally turned and began swimming with Vincent holding on to her back.

I grabbed the tools and began tearing at the hole to make it big enough for me to squeeze through, sweating with determination. I worked as fast as I could, but it was no use. The boat was made of fiberglass, and there was no give.

64

I exhaled heavily when Rio pulled the specially outfitted black Sprinter van alongside one of our Black SUVs and stopped, making his way to the back. He got into the seat next to Nevada, and they both slipped on gaming headphones. They looked toward me, sitting in a captain's chair between Chippy and Larry, for instructions.

"Is everybody ready?" I said into the mouthpiece of my wireless headset.

"Black team, ready," London replied in my ear.

"Green team ready, Daddy," Paris chimed in.

"Blue team is a go, Uncle LC," Curtis replied.

"Brown team in place, but we're gonna need a few minutes," Roman finally replied.

I looked at Nevada and Rio. "Okay, boys. Deploy the drones."

Nevada flipped a switch by his chair, and we could hear what sounded like a sunroof opening, then a beep. He looked over at Rio, and they started to maneuver the drone transmitters. A buzzing sound flooded our ears and then began to fade away. Four of the five 4K TVs came on, giving Chippy, Larry, and me a full view of the cameras attached to the two drones. Chippy lifted the remote near her chair and turned on the local news with the volume down. Everyone's nerves were on edge, but we all remained calm and focused with one mission in mind: rescuing Lauryn, Orlando, Ruby, and the baby.

"Drones deployed," Nevada said.

"Do we have eyes on everyone?" I asked.

"The trailer has been offloaded, and everyone's in sight, Pop," Rio answered, maneuvering the controller in his hand. "Black and green teams should be on their way in the next two or three minutes."

I stared at the monitor of the overhead view of the van we were in, parked next to two SUVs with boat trailers attached to them. About forty feet away, members of the Duncan security team were deploying an electric pontoon motorboat into the water, while Paris and London loaded weapons onto a second boat already in the water. They were all dressed in black frogman gear.

"Rio, let's check on Roman. Nevada let's take a look at that boat, but don't get too close. I don't want them to know we're here."

Both drones sped away from where they were hovering above London's and Paris's teams. Nevada's went high along the Belt Parkway and then shot out toward the water when it hit Coney Island, and Rio's headed straight out toward Sheepshead Bay Marina.

"Wow, that yacht is huge." It was obvious Nevada was impressed.

"Yeah, it is," Chippy declared, staring at the huge yacht anchored just off Jamaica Bay. "It looks more like a cruise ship."

"LC, you see that?" Larry stood up and stepped toward the screen. "Those some-bitches is armed to the teeth, and they gotta have fifty men on the deck."

"Thermal recognition says forty-three, but we have no idea how many are inside," Nevada corrected him. "However, we do have a formidable plan and the element of surprise, along with forces that should be significantly better trained."

Larry studied Nevada, then turned back to me, chuckling. "Where the fuck you get this kid from, a goddamn encyclopedia?"

I didn't respond. I had other things to think about. "Curtis, how far are you and Junior out?"

"About five minutes. We can see the ship, and they should be hearing us soon," Curtis responded.

"Good." I glanced at the monitor of Rio's drone, which was coming in fast on a marina. "DJ, Roman, how we looking?"

"Give us three more minutes and we should be underway." Roman's voice sounded a little shaky. Other than Paris's team, he and DJ had the most complex part of our plan.

"You sure the boy is up to it, LC?" Larry asked.

"He'll make it happen," I said. Roman had proven to be a valuable asset to the family when given a chance.

Rio lowered his drone so we could get a better view of the vessel Roman and DJ were on. Larry squinted, leaning forward in his chair to see the monitor.

"What the hell are they doing? Is that a fucking tugboat? They're stealing a fucking tugboat," Larry said with disbelief.

Chippy laughed. "You gotta use the tools at your disposal."

While the view of the tugboat dominated two screens, Nevada's drone captured the view of what was happening a few miles away. London and Rob sped across the water toward the yacht on one of the pontoons, while Paris, Rob, and C-Note traveled in the same direction on the other, silently blending into the darkness of the sky and the water.

"Grandpa, I don't know if this is a problem or not, but we've got a helicopter landing on the yacht."

"Are they picking up or dropping off?" I asked.

"They appear to be dropping off, but I don't want to get too close. The pilots might see me."

"No, you're right. Back off a little bit."

"Now this is weird," Nevada said.

"What is it?"

"It's probably nothing, but the thermal monitors are picking up a weird heat signature about a half mile from the boat. If we were a little further east, I'd just chalk it up as dolphins or seals, but my gut's telling me different."

"What's your gut telling you, son?"

"From the way the tide's pulling them out?" He looked down at the laptop in front of him, then glanced over at me. "It looks like two bodies, and the heat signature on both are very low."

Chippy gasped.

My heart raced, and I could feel beads of sweat forming on my forehead. "Are you sure, Nevada?"

"Yes, sir."

Chippy stepped closer to the screen. "Nevada, zoom in closer. Jesus Christ, I don't believe this."

"What do you see?" Larry asked, seeing the distressed look on my wife's face.

"He's right. Those are people," Chippy exclaimed.

Nevada got a closer view of the bodies, and sure enough, lying on their backs, motionless, were a woman and a child.

"That's Ruby and Vincent!" Chippy screamed. "Do something, LC!"

"London, I need you and Rob to veer off to the left. There's something in the water I want you to check out," I instructed. "Nevada will direct you."

"Copy that, Daddy. We're on it," London replied, and we watched her boat peel off from Paris's.

While Nevada began giving directions, I reached out and took my sobbing wife's hand. We'd been through a lot of sticky situations in our marriage, but through them all, I couldn't remember her ever being on the verge of losing her shit.

"London, honey, how we doing?" I asked.

"We're searching, Daddy, but it's pretty hard to see anything out here."

A sense of dread came over me.

"Dammit!" Larry shouted at Nevada. "Use that thing and see if you can find Lauryn and Orlando. They've gotta be nearby."

"I'm looking, Uncle Larry, but the only other heat signatures I'm getting are coming from that boat."

"Then we've gotta get on that boat," I said in no uncertain terms. "Curtis, you and Junior, engage!"

Curtis

65

Junior and I were traveling across the water at about seventy miles an hour in one of those 64-foot *Miami Vice* type cigarette speedboats. The engines were so loud we had to use noise cancelling headphones, microphones, and hand signals to communicate with each other. It might have been a lot of fun if my baby sister wasn't on that fucking yacht, probably being held prisoner.

"They should hear us coming soon," Junior shouted from behind the wheel. I had to give it to him. Junior sure as hell knew how to handle this cool-ass boat.

"Hey! Can you explain to me again why we're speeding through the night in the loudest thing on the water if we're trying to catch somebody by surprise? Why aren't we in electric Patton boats like Paris and London and them?"

"Because our job is not to surprise. It's to distract," Junior yelled back. "Hold on, I'm gonna buzz them."

We zoomed past the yacht, and I was sure we had their attention as we circled around it like a bunch of crazy-ass rich teenagers. Junior steered the boat toward the edge of the yacht and steadied it as best he could. As we came up alongside, I fired an AR-15 at them, mowing down at least five of those motherfuckers. The distracted attack caught them off guard, and they took cover. All eyes were now on us.

"We got their attention now! Bring us around again!" I yelled at Junior. "Make a quick ninety degree turn then hit the gas again!"

"I got this. You just be ready! This time they might shoot back!" Junior sped off as fast as he could back toward the yacht.

We came around for another pass, and that's when we saw the tugboat in the distance, closing in fast, then heard the sound of gunshots.

"Yep, these motherfuckers shooting back all right!" I screamed. I got off another round of bullets, suppressing their gunfire. Junior hit the gas before the men began shooting at us again. Their bullets hit the water as we fled, but we escaped without a scratch.

"A'ight, now get us out of the way. It's time to see what Roman and DJ gonna do."

Roman

66

"Come on, DJ man. They waiting on us," I shouted impatiently. DJ was trying his best to hotwire the tugboat we were on, but dude just wasn't qualified. Don't get me wrong. DJ was a real OG, I had to give him that, but he was drug dealer not a thief, and now wasn't the time to act like one. Yeah, I know he'd worked for my pops for a few years and was older than me, but he wasn't a Duncan. It was my brother, nephew, and cousin whose lives were on the line, so it was time for me to take charge.

"Man, move! Let me do this shit."

DJ reluctantly stepped aside, and I ducked under the wheelhouse and started fiddling with the wires.

"See, here's your problem," I said, switching the wires he had been moving around. "This shit ain't gas. It's diesel. You was trying to get a spark from the wrong wire."

I moved the wires, and suddenly there was a loud grumble and that bitch turned on.

"Oh, shit! You did it!" DJ looked amazed as I came from under the steering column.

"Man, come on. You can thank me later. We gotta untie the lines."

We ran to the lines holding the large tug to the dock and released them. By the time I got back to the wheelhouse, DJ was wearing an orange life jacket and navigating the huge tugboat away from the dock. He looked at me through his shades and nodded—his way of saying I'd done good, and he was impressed.

What he didn't know was that this was fun for me. I'd engaged in plenty of criminal activity over the years, and stealing wasn't new to me. I'd stolen jewelry, money, cars, drugs, and trucks.

Still, this was some of the craziest shit I'd ever been a part of. I'd never stolen a fucking tugboat before.

"How the hell do you know how to drive this thing anyway?" I asked DJ as he expertly maneuvered the tug out of the marina. "It's not like driving a car."

"I used to work at the Brooklyn Navy Yard back when I dropped outta high school. Lazy-ass dockmaster taught me how to drive a tug so he could sit on his fat ass all day while I did all the work. I guess it's kinda like riding a bike. You never forget how. You just have to respect the current."

"Roman, you boys on your way?" My father's voice came through the walkie talkies that we'd been issued. I reminded myself that he wasn't singling me out, but checking on me as much as everyone else.

"Yeah, Pop."

"All right. You know what to do. Be careful. We'll be here watching," Pop said.

DJ looked over at me. "Real talk, I see you got heart, Roman. You are definitely a Duncan, for sure."

"Thanks, man," I said. "I can't lie. I ain't never did no shit like this, though."

"Neither have I. Shit ain't never boring working for your family," he said with a laugh just as the yacht came into view. "And with that being said, lemme ask you a question. I probably shoulda asked this beforehand."

"What's that?"

"Can you swim?"

"I mean, yeah." I shrugged. "I ain't no Michael Phelps, but I spent my summers at CYA camp like everyone else."

"Then you might wanna grab one of them life vests over there in the corner, just in case." DJ motioned toward the orange vests hanging on the wall. "We don't want your ass to drown out here."

"You think I might need one for real?" I didn't want to look weak, but DJ seemed to have more experience on the water, so if he thought I needed a life vest, I'd listen.

"For what we're about to do, it's up to you, but you see what I got on." He touched the life vest. "And I ain't got no shame to my game."

I grabbed one of the life vests and slipped it on, making sure it was secure. I'd been reunited with my family not too long ago, and I wanted lots more time with them. I didn't want to chance losing my life underwater.

"Let them know we're headed in."

"The yacht is dead ahead," I said into the walkie talkie.

"I got you in view," Rio replied. "Heads up. I ain't the only one."

"Copy that," I replied.

Shots rang out. Suddenly, the wheelhouse window was blown out.

"Oh, shit! Get down!" DJ shouted. "And hold the fuck on!"

He mashed down on the accelerator, and we both ducked down. Eventually, the shots stopped. We lifted our heads to see what the fuck was going on. That's when I came to the realization that we were moving full speed ahead toward the yacht sitting directly in front of us.

DJ turned and looked at me. "Brace yourself we are coming in hot!"

I closed my eyes and held onto the closest steel pole just before we collided with the massive boat. The tugboat shook and rocked backwards, the sound of crushing metal and splintering wood all around us.

Once DJ and I were able to steady ourselves, we remained tucked low to the ground as we rushed out of the wheelhouse, returning fire. I could hear water coming from everywhere, and in that moment, I was glad I had the vest because it was obvious it wouldn't be long before the tugboat sank.

Lauryn

67

"Get off me," I snarled at Aries as he tightly gripped my arm, yanking me down the stairs. We'd returned to the ship, where Aries was on the helipad, waiting to greet us. "You're hurting me."

"You haven't felt pain yet, you little bitch." Dominique hissed right behind me.

I struggled to get away, but it was pointless. The more I pulled from him, the harder he squeezed. Dominique reminded me she had a gun, slamming it against my head hard, but not quite hard enough to knock me out. My ears were ringing, and I decided to save my energy for when I could win the fight.

We went down two floors, then he forced me down the corridor until we arrived in front of a door. Dominique stepped past and opened it.

"Bring her ass in here," she commanded.

"No!" They dragged me into a large pantry storage room. The shelves of canned vegetables, paper products, and cooking utensils seemed endless. There was a folding chair in the back corner, and that's where they forced me to sit at gunpoint.

"I can't believe this shit." Dominique exhaled, pacing as she rubbed her temples. "A fucking Duncan. She's a fucking Duncan."

"What are we going to do with her?" Aries asked.

"I don't know yet. I'm waiting for Alexander to call me back."

I said a silent prayer that he wouldn't call anytime soon.

Dominique glared at me. "Why the fuck are you here?"

"I was hired to do a job," I answered, sarcastically blowing a bubble and letting it pop in my face. "By you, remember?"

"Don't play dumb, you little bitch." She grabbed a handful of my hair and yanked my head back so that I was looking up at her. "Who sent you? Was it LC Duncan? Is he on to us?"

"Nobody sent me. I was brought here." I blew another bubble.

"If you don't stop blowing those got-damn bubbles."

"I think she was sent here looking for Orlando," Aries suggested. "I told you we would eventually have a problem with his family if we kept him too long."

"You might be right," Dominique replied. "Go get him. And bring along his kid. I know how to get to the bottom of this one piece at a time."

Her words sent a chill through my heart.

"I keep telling you I'm here because you hired—" I was stopped by the sounds of gunshots above us.

"Someone's shooting!" Aries announced as if we didn't hear the same thing he did. "Shit! It's gotta be the Duncans."

Dominique kept her gun aimed at me as she turned to her son. "Go get Orlando Duncan and his kid and bring them to the chopper. Now!"

Aries looked at me once more before he took off out of the room.

"Now, back to what we were talking about." Dominique turned her attention back to me. "Did LC send you? Is that why you're here?"

"If you don't believe me, why don't you just ask Nadja?" I snapped. I'd already sized her up, and although she was taller than I was, she was slender. I knew I could overtake her, or at least try. I just needed to wait for the right moment.

"Who the fuck do you think told me you're a Duncan?" Dominique sneered and put the gun against my temple. "Now, talk."

Suddenly, the helicopter pilot ran in, sweating and out of breath. "Ms. LaRue."

"What the hell is going on?" Dominique asked.

"We're under attack and taking fire." He panted. "It's bad."

I didn't panic. In fact, I felt a surge of hope that my mother had delivered my message and Paris and the family had come to rescue us. I had no way of being certain, though. I still needed to get away somehow.

"Shit. Go get the helicopter ready. We have to get out of here," she ordered him.

"Yes, ma'am." He left.

Dominique stared at me. "I don't know whether to kill you or hold your ass for safekeeping."

"What the fuck does that even mean?" I asked.

"It means today is your lucky day. You're coming with me. Between you, Orlando, and the brat, we are going to have LC Duncan begging on his knees."

Just as she yanked me up out of the chair, there was a loud crash, and the entire boat shifted with such force that it caused both of us to lose our balance. As I fell into the nearby wall, Dominique fell against the metal shelves of canned goods, knocking several pots and pans to the floor as she grabbed at something to hold on to. I steadied myself and spotted the gun as it fell to her feet.

"Shit." She scrambled toward it at the same time I did. Unfortunately, she was closer and snatched it up. "You want to live or die? It's up to you at this point."

I had no choice but to put my arms in the air and allow her to lead me back out. We climbed the same stairs that we'd come down earlier, and when we reached the top, we ducked bullets as we ran to get into the waiting chopper and took off.

London

68

Things were moving fast. Between the roar of the wind and the waves, it was difficult to hear Nevada though the walkie talkie, but Rob and I managed to understand what direction to go in. We'd veered away from the others on Daddy's instruction and bounced across the water.

"Keep going straight about another half mile," Nevada told us.

Rob steered the pontoon while I used a pair of night vision binoculars to look ahead for whoever we were searching for.

"I don't see anything yet."

"Keep going. You're almost there," Nevada said. "I can see you guys in the distance."

Instead of looking in the water, I decided to look up, searching for the green light of his drone. Sure enough, in the far distance, I spotted it. "I see the drone. Right there, Rob. A little to the right."

"I gotcha," Rob yelled. "Wait! I see someone. She looks like she's trying to swim away."

"She's scared," I told Rob. "Slow down."

As we drifted closer to Orlando's family, still trying desperately to swim away from us, I called out to them. "Ruby! Ruby! It's London!"

The swimming slowed down and then finally stopped. She turned around slowly. "London?" She sounded exhausted. "Thank God. I thought they had found us."

"No, it's us!" I screamed with excitement and relief.

Rob pulled Vincent onto the boat first, and I wrapped him into my arms to warm him. His teeth chattered, and his whole body was trembling. We didn't have any blankets, so I slipped my wetsuit jacket over my head and put it around him.

"Mommy?" He cried, reaching for Ruby, who was being lifted into the boat by Rob.

"It's okay, baby," Ruby said to Vincent as she stood there shivering. He took off from me and ran to his mother, who held him tight. "We're okay."

"We got Ruby and Vincent!" I spoke into the walkie-talkie.

"Is Orlando there? Do you see him?" my father asked.

"And Lauryn?" Uncle Larry yelled in the background.

"Not yet, but we're looking," Rob answered, looking into the water just as frantically as I was. My brother was a strong swimmer, so if Ruby and Vincent had made it this far, certainly he should have been nearby as well, and so should Lauryn.

I looked over at Ruby. "Where's Orlando? Was he with you too?"

"No." Ruby shook her head, looking back. "He's still on the boat."

"And Lauryn?"

"She's gone," Ruby replied. "I don't know where she is."

That's when we heard the roar of Junior's boat and heavy gunfire.

"What's that?" Ruby asked.

"That's our family going to rescue you husband."

"London, you and Rob get Ruby and the baby back to shore, then you get back to the others and get your brother and DJ. Their boat is about to sink," my father directed me through the walkie-talkie.

"Yes, Daddy." I steadied myself as Rob turned the pontoon around and we headed back to the marina. "We're headed back now. Two down and two to go."

Paris

69

It sounded like all hell had broken loose on the other side of the yacht as C-Note guided the pontoon boat about sixty feet off its rear, then dropped an anchor so the electric raft would be held in place for our return. I had to give it to Daddy, Nevada, and Uncle Larry. They'd come up with an ingenious plan to get us on the yacht. I wasn't worried about the rescue. I just prayed it wasn't going to be too little too late and we'd find Lauryn or Orlando dead.

"Everybody ready?" I asked when Nevada had given the signal. Both Daryl and C-Note gave me a thumbs up, and we all fell backward into the water, carrying waterproof automatic weapons and enough ammo to liberate a small country. We'd opted to free dive and not to use scuba tanks, just fins and masks because of the close proximity to the boat. We were going to have to move fast, and removing the tanks would slow us down immensely.

Nevada's signal would give us a ten-second lead when the tugboat was going to hit the yacht. This way we could board the boat with most of its occupants stunned or dazed by the collision. The plan, as crazy as it was, worked like a charm.

C-Note an ex-Navy Seal was first to climb onboard, using a grappling hook, which he left for Daryl and me to follow behind. I slipped my hands around the thick cordage, maneuvered my feet against the bottom of the yacht, and scaled my way up. When I climbed over the rail onto the deck, we received no resistance. I could hear all kinds of gunfire on the other side of the ship, which meant Junior and Curtis were doing their to job distract them.

I checked my weapon, made sure Daryl was on board, then slipped in my earpiece and whispered, "We're on the yacht. Do you have eyes on us, Nevada?"

"We see you, Paris." Daddy's voice came through my earpiece.

Glancing up, I saw the drone overhead and gave him a thumbs up.

"Stay low. From what we can see, there are about ten or fifteen gunmen ahead of you, firing at Roman and DJ. We need you to take them down as quickly as you can."

We crouched low as we ran toward the gunfire, mowing them all down before anyone even had a chance to turn around.

"Damn, I hate shooting people in the back!" C-Note said.

"Get over it. Better you shoot them in the back than they shoot you in front. Let's keep it moving." I liked C-Note, but he was such a Boy Scout for a killer.

As we started making our way to another deck, more gunfire came from another direction. Daryl took them out before I could get off a shot. I turned to see five more men approaching, and C-note engaged them.

"C-Note and I will handle them," Daryl said. "You go find your family."

I turned to run off, but movement near the top of the yacht caught my attention. I stopped in my tracks. "Daddy, we got a problem."

"What kind of problem?"

"There's a helicopter taking off from the top deck."

"I can confirm that," Nevada said. "It's the same helicopter that we saw landing before."

"Shoot it down!" Uncle Larry was yelling so loud in the background I almost had to yank out my earpiece. "Open fire and take it down!"

I lifted my gun to take aim, but my father's voice stopped me. "No, Paris. Lower your gun. You can't shoot the helicopter down. We don't know yet if Lauryn or Orlando are on it."

"Got it," I said, lowering my gun. "I'll keep looking on the yacht. Nevada, keep an eye on that helicopter."

I took off toward the staircase, taking out one gunman after another as I made my way through the bowels of the ship. If my brother and cousin were on this ship, I would not stop until I found them.

Orlando

70

I knew the cavalry was coming when I heard the roar of a cigarette speedboat approaching the yacht through the torn-out porthole window. There was only one person I knew crazy enough to drive a half-million-dollar boat like that in the pitch dark. My brother Junior. My only fear was that he might run over my wife and child, who, I prayed, were still swimming ashore.

Once I heard the gunfire on the other side of the boat, any doubts I had that my family had arrived were gone. Aries would be in a panic, and when he arrived, I wanted to be ready. I searched the room for something I could use as a weapon, but the only thing I could find was the screwdriver I'd used to loosen the window. It would have to do. I hid the screwdriver in my shorts and sat on the bed, waiting for Aries or one of his men to arrive. It didn't take long before the locks on the door began to click.

Aries entered the room with one of his security men, who looked scared. Both men looked shocked when their eyes landed on the ripped-out window on the floor and the gaping hole behind me.

"What the hell happened here?"

I turned to the window, then I slowly turned around and stared at him without answering. There was no need to give an explanation. It was obvious what had happened.

Aries searched around the suite. "Where the hell are your wife and son?"

"I told you not to ever discuss them." I squared up with him. Kicking his ass was something I'd been wanting to do for a while now, and the time had finally come.

Sensing that he was about to get fucked up, he reached for the gun in his waistband, but before he could grab it, I punched him so hard that it knocked him backward. I then proceeded to fight for my life. Pulling out the screwdriver, I stabbed the security guard in the neck.

"Aaaaaaaghhhhhhh! You motherfucker!" he screamed. Feeling the damage I'd done to his artery, he pretty much lost all fight.

Aries, however, was still kicking, and he had the gun. He pointed it at me, and from the look in his eyes, I feared he was about to pull the trigger. An image of Ruby and Vincent flashed through my mind. I was not about to make my wife a widow. Adrenaline shot through my body as I lunged at Aries and grabbed his arm. The gun went off, but I'd managed to redirect his aim, and the bullet hit the wall behind me. With a violent twist, I forced his arm into an unnatural angle that caused him to drop the gun. I took off, jumping over the body of the guard, who was slowly bleeding out on the floor. I grabbed the guard's weapon on my way out the door.

"There he is! Get him!" I heard Aries yell as I approached the stairs.

I looked up and saw one of the crew members just as he pulled the trigger. I fired my own weapon, and a bullet tore through his abdomen. I watched him topple down the steps. By the time he hit the bottom, another guy was racing toward me from an upper deck, firing shots. I returned fire. I was determined to make my way up there to jump to freedom, even if I had to shoot my way to the top. I climbed over the body in front of me and made my way up.

"You motherfucker!" Aries yelled as he finally reached the top of the stairs behind me.

I spun around and pulled the trigger, but nothing came out. I was out of bullets.

Aries raised his gun, and I stared into the barrel.

"No!" A woman screamed.

Pow. Thud.

I watched Aries's body fall backward down the stairs and land beside the man I'd shot. Standing beside them was my sister Paris, looking like an avenging warrior goddess.

"Paris?" I jumped down the steps two at a time and threw my arms around her.

"Yeah, O." She grinned. "That was close."

"Damn sure was."

"I'm with O. He's safe." Paris spoke into an earpiece attached to a walkie talkie on her waist. "Yes, Daddy, he's fine. We'll meet Daryl and C-Note back on the raft."

I realized the gunshots had stopped. "How the hell—?"

"I'll explain later," Paris said. "We gotta get outta here. You ready for a swim?"

"You have no idea." I took a step, then froze as a sickening thought hit me. My wife and son had been in that water while all this was going on.

"Paris, wait. Ruby and Vincent. They're—"

"They're fine. London got 'em a little while ago." Paris gave me a reassuring smile. "Now, let's go."

Thank God. I followed Paris up the stairs, and we ran to the rear of the yacht. I looked over the rail and saw C-Note and Daryl. They both jumped in the water.

"We got you!" Daryl yelled up to us.

"Come on, O!" Paris jumped in the water.

I took one final look at the yacht, my prison, then I dove into the water the same way my wife and son had earlier.

Larry

71

The screen displayed the view from Rio's drone, flying above the two pontoon boats that carried LC's kids and their teams away from the yacht. Other than a little tired and careworn, Orlando looked fine.

"Let's go meet them at the shore," LC said.

Chippy wasted no time jumping out of the van.

"I ain't goin' nowhere," I said. "I'm happy your son is safe, but did you forget my little girl is still out there somewhere?"

LC looked like he might sit back down, but then Chippy yelled from outside, "LC, let's go! I want to get there before they do." LC looked torn, but I knew he wanted to leave.

"Don't worry, Grandpa," Nevada said. "I'll stay here with Uncle Larry and man these drones. We'll keep looking for Lauryn."

"I'll keep our radios on," LC said as he climbed out to join his wife.

"Keep your eye on that fucking helicopter, Nevada. Don't lose them," I said when we were alone.

"I'm on it, Uncle Larry."

I assumed no one other than the two of us felt that their celebration was a little premature, until Curtis entered the van with Roman a while later.

"Where's Lauryn?" Curtis asked.

"We haven't gotten her yet. But we will," I said, pulling out my phone to send a text. "That was some hellafied fighting y'all did. Glad you're safe."

"Thanks, Pop." He nudged me with his elbow as he stood by my side, staring at the screen. "Is that where Lauryn is?"

"We don't know for sure," I told him.

"Nevada, see if you can get a little closer to the door so we can see inside." The voice came from the entrance.

I turned around and was completely shocked to see Orlando standing there.

"Shouldn't you be with your wife and son?" I asked.

"They'll be okay. Right now, I gotta make sure my little cousin is too." He looked me in the eye, making a silent promise to see this through with me.

"This is as close as I can get," Nevada said, pulling the drone level with the helicopter door and zooming the camera in. "But I gotta move soon before they spot me."

"It's definitely a woman in there, but there's not enough detail to make out who she is," I said.

"Nevada, can you freeze that picture and put it on the other screen?" Roman asked. "I wanna see something."

"Sure."

Roman leaned forward and studied the screen. "Oh, shit! Curtis, look at this. That's Dominique LaRue, isn't it?"

"Are you sure?" Curtis peered at the shadowy figure on the screen. "Wait a minute! I don't know if that's Dominique LaRue or not, but look at the person next to her."

"I can't see her. The other woman is blocking her," Roman said, "All I see is someone blowing bubblegum. Is that a kid?"

"That's my sister," Curtis said.

"He's right! That's Lauryn!" I yelled with a joyful laugh. We'd finally found my baby. "She's been blowing bubbles since she was little. Do not lose them."

"Any idea where they could be going?" Orlando asked.

"Not exactly, but it looks like they're headed toward Manhattan," Nevada answered.

"Get the call letters off that chopper. You can't go in Manhattan airspace without notifying the FAA where you're going and where you plan on landing," Orlando said. "Maybe you can hack into their database and locate their destination."

Nevada began typing on his laptop, and in what seemed like seconds, he said, "I got it. They've requested to land at the Downtown Manhattan Heliport at Pier Six."

"How far away is it?" LC was now in the van.

"At least forty-five minutes from here by car," Orlando told him. "That chopper will get there in about fifteen, twenty minutes tops."

I looked over at my brother. "You got anyone over there?"

LC gave me a sympathetic look. "All my serious manpower is here. I don't have anyone that can get there that fast."

I took out my phone and dialed. "Dennis, I need you to get to Manhattan in fifteen minutes. I'll send you the address."

"We're over here by the Belt Parkway like you told us," he responded. "We can't get there that fast, but there is somebody in Manhattan that you can call."

"Shit, you're right. I forgot all about them." I ended the call without saying goodbye. "I'll be right back." I stepped out of the van and made a call.

LC may have been well connected, but even he couldn't assist when I needed him most. I had to take matters into my own hand and use the resources I had. Ten minutes later, I stepped back in the van, nudging my way back to my seat in front of the screen.

"I'm starting to lose battery power," Nevada said. "I'm gonna have to turn it around and bring it back or we're going to lose the drone."

"Don't worry about the drone, son. I'll buy another one," LC said.

The drone's battery lasted long enough for us to watch the helicopter approaching the pier in lower Manhattan.

"They're landing," Roman said, pointing to the screen.

Everyone seemed to hold their breath, while I remained calm. The helicopter touched down with ease, landing near a waiting SUV. The pilot hopped out and opened the door. Dominique LaRue stepped out first, gun in hand, which was pointed to the cabin. She reached up and pulled someone out.

"There's Lauryn," LC announced.

Dominique yanked Lauryn at gunpoint toward the car. The driver opened the door, and just as she was about to force her inside, the dark sky lit up with blue and white flashing lights.

"Nevada, don't lose them."

"I only have about two minutes of power left, Grandpa."

"Shit. They get in that car, we might not ever find her again," Curtis yelled, looking at me. "We gotta do something."

I smirked. "Don't worry. I already have. Your sister will be fine."

"What? How?"

They looked around at each other, then pretended not to look at me. I ignored their side glances as I focused on what I was doing.

"Just watch," I told him.

LC looked over at me. "Larry, what did you do?"

"What any father would do. I saved my child," I told him as my eyes remained on the screen.

Roman gasped. "Oh, shit! It's the cops!"

We all watched the screen as thirty officers dressed in black jumpsuits and wearing riot gear swarmed the car. Dominique let Lauryn go and turned to run away, but she was surrounded.

"That's crazy." Nevada chuckled just as the screen went white. "We've lost the drone."

My cell phone rang, and I answered without even looking at the caller ID. "Agent Martinez, I take it the capture went okay." I could feel every eye in the van on me.

"Damn right it went okay. We got her," Agent Martinez replied. I could hear the happiness in her voice.

"Great. And my daughter, is she well?"

"Yes, she is."

"Beautiful. I appreciate all your hard work. Oh, and one more thing. When will my son Curtis be able to pick up the check for the capture of Ms. LaRue? I'm told it's quite a hefty sum." I glanced over at Curtis, who, like everyone else, had his mouth hanging open.

"It is. Tell him to give me a call tomorrow and I'll let him know," she said.

"Very good."

"Hey Larry."

"Yes?"

"Thanks."

"Don't mention it. We still have a bigger fish to fry." I hung up and looked up to six pairs of amazed eyes.

"Dad, you set that up?" Curtis asked incredulously.

I shrugged. "Hey, like Nevada said, this was crazy. Who else could make it happen better than crazy Larry Duncan?"

Epilogue

"It's good to be home," Orlando announced as he and Ruby walked hand in hand into the game room, where most of the family had gathered. His son was cuddled in his grandmother's arms, a sight that brought a smile to his face. His father handed them both a drink and looked to the rest of the family, including Vegas, who were scattered throughout the room, each with a glass in hand.

LC raised his glass. "To family."

"To family," they all replied in unison.

"It's good to have you home, son." LC told him. "And you too, Ruby."

"I think Vincent is happier than all of us," Ruby said, looking over at her son.

Orlando laughed. "Nah, I think Mom got him beat."

"She better get all the love she can, because before you know it, Vincent, Jordan, and Mimi gonna be headed off to that finishing school," Curtis commented, using the cue stick to strike the pool balls while Roman and Nevada, holding sticks of their own, watched.

"True." Nevada nodded. "Now that I think about it, it's a whole new line of little Duncans that will soon be ready to take over the world."

"You mean take over this house," Paris said. "We'd better enjoy this peace and quiet while we can."

"They're absolutely right," Chippy agreed and turned Vincent so that he faced her. "Soon, all of your little cousins will be here for you to play with. We are all going to have so much fun."

"My cousins? Are they babies like the one upstairs with Uncle Junior?" Vincent asked.

"No, buddy," Orlando said. "They're around your age, except Mariah, who's a little older."

"Speaking of which," LC stated. "I guess we need to get to Waycross to pick them up in the next week or so."

"Well, I'm heading that way in a couple of days," Curtis told him. "Once I pick up my check, I gotta get back to take over this bail bond business. I got my own Duncan empire to build like you, Uncle LC."

LC nodded his approval. "I'm proud to hear that, Curtis, and you know I'm here to support you every step of the way."

"I am too, cuz." Roman nudged him. "I'm going back to Waycross with you and help out for a while. I kinda like bounty hunting. I mean, if you cool wit' it."

Curtis put down the cue stick and grinned at his cousin. "You're welcome any time you want. That's what the family business is about."

"Daddy." London walked in with Daryl. "He's gone."

LC frowned. "Are you sure?"

"I'm positive. His suitcases are gone, and his passport and secret stash of cash that he thinks I don't know about. You said you wanted evidence that he's the one who put the hit out on Daryl? I think this is proof."

"Why else would he be in the wind?" Daryl asked. "He was probably happy we were all busy rescuing Orlando and Lauryn. It gave him the chance to run."

Orlando looked over at his father. "What you wanna do, Pop? The man can barely walk. He can't be that hard to catch."

"I think that's a decision Daryl and London have to make. That's their call," LC told him.

Everyone looked at London, who turned to Daryl. "It was you he tried to kill."

Darryl looked around the room, then shrugged. "Real talk, after all that just happened, I think the family just needs to enjoy being together. I ain't too worried about Harris right now. But believe me, he and I will come face to face at some point, and when we do, I'll deal with him accordingly. Let him live. For now."

"Wow, bro." Vegas walked over to him. "That's real big of you."

"I appreciate that, Daryl. It is nice to enjoy the family being drama free for a change," LC told him. "I just wish things would've worked out different between Sasha and Larry. Has anyone spoken to her?"

"I'm not here to kill you, Paris. We have more important things to talk about," he said.

She slowly turned around. "Like what?" she asked, her voice quivering.

"Paris . . ." her mother called out from the other room.

"Mama, not right now. I'm kinda dealing with something," Paris yelled over her shoulder, then focused back on Niles. "What?"

"Nadja has our son."

"What?" Paris flinched, so shocked at his mention of their son that she didn't even comprehend Nadja's involvement until a few seconds later.

"Paris, I don't give a damn about these flowers." Her mother stormed into the room and pulled her around so that they were facing each other. "Nee Nee's on the phone."

"Mama, please—"

Chippy said, "No. Jordan's missing."